The Emergence

Book Two

By J.B. Myron

The following story is a work of fiction. All characters, names, locations and events are fictitious and any resemblance to reality is unintended.

Dedicated to my wife Rachel,

For being my muse and joy.

Chapter 1
Welcome Back

Torrenting sheets of rain pelted the Caldoran swamps. Dense trees were all that broke the storm's opaque sheet, and above them, clouds dominated the night sky. Everything was dark and everything was drenched, including Commander Darius.

The soldier's boots sloshed through the mud and his black cloak clung to his fatigued frame. Rivulets of rain were rushing down his face and his cheeks puffed with each sprinting breath. Alongside him, two Imperial Proctors, wrapped in dark clothing, were also running. Trees zipped by Darius, his vision blurred by the storm. He couldn't hear his pursuers, but he could feel their chaotic magic in the air. Looking down at his chest, Darius clutched a small metal cylinder. He gritted his teeth; *George needs to know.*

A not-so-distant scream and a blast of curling black smoke cut through the trees. The powerful spell left the rain in odd chaotic swirls of ripping speed and misdirection. Magic crackled and a grim looking figure wearing tattered robes exploded from the shifting haze. Black, metallic splotches tainted the man's exposed skin, and wild eyes stared out from his robes. Plumes of smoke were hissing from the strange man's body.

"Smoke-screamer!" Darius yelled.

But the commander's warning wasn't quick enough. A shrilling screech shredded the scene and waves of smoke scattered the downpour. Magic itched Darius' eyes and his heart pounded far too fast as he inhaled the terrible miasma. Only a second whipped by but Darius knew this tactic too well. His eyes found the figure of one of his companions and with his hands spread, he leaped out.

"Get down—!"

With fingers gripping the back of the proctor's cloak, Darius dragged him to the swampy floor. The two splashed into the watery mud, and just in time. With a metallic click, a raging flash of fire ripped through the haze above, blinding Darius and rocking his ears with an incredible boom. He felt the side of his face singe and he heard the bellowing scream of the proctor he couldn't save.

Shuffling, Darius shoved the metal cylinder into the hands of the remaining proctor.

"Get this to the prince," He ordered, "don't stop and don't look back."

The proctor nodded, but as he rolled to his feet to take off, the smoke-screamer came forward to intercept at a blinding speed. A screeching wail followed the blurred enemy and as he came into range, a horrible spear stained a metallic black came shooting forward. Darius erupted with Stromist magic and one of his glowing arms punched forward. With incredible agility, Darius' hand grabbed the enemy weapon just in time; the point was mere inches from the proctor.

"Go!" Darius yelled. The proctor shoved the cylinder under his cloak and took off with his boots pounding against the sucking mud. Now alone, Darius stood aglow, an island of golden ribbons amidst the dark swamp and a darker enemy. Angry and unstable eyes glared down at the commander, and twisted fingers tightened on the other end of the spear.

The two stared at each other for a moment; their eyes were slits of violence and anticipation. Darius could feel the heavy breathing of the enemy vibrate down the spear's length. Adrenaline pulsed under Darius' fingers and sweat formed on his brow. Finally, the enemy burst into action, but in a flash of golden magic, Darius was quicker. The commander yanked the spear towards himself the moment that the smoke-screamer went to move and knocked the enemy forward just enough for Darius to plant a stiff boot into his stomach.

A powerful thud sounded from the impact and tore the smoke-screamer from the spear before launching them straight into a tree. Now, in full control of the weapon, Darius spun the spear around in his fingers until the point was facing the enemy. Without hesitation, the commander charged his stunned foe, magic alight.

Wood splintered as the spear punched into the spot where the smoke-screamer had been. The enemy had shifted out of the way, leaving only a haze of smoke in his place. Darius gritted his teeth, but before he could spin to meet the enemy, his ears burst from a powerful scream. All at once, the haze that surrounded the commander turned into a blackened blanket of smoke and left Darius in a world of pitch.

Rain still pattered Darius and told him where up was, but his eyes were useless. The commander was forced onto the defensive and fell onto his back foot while keeping his spear close and ready. The scream didn't die down, and in moments, sections of the smoke-ridden trap pulsed with life. A diseased fist came thrusting out of the haze, but Darius managed to duck it just in time, only for a sweeping kick to appear and snag his knee.

Darius toppled to the ground, but sucked in a breath before he hit the swamp. Dark waters below sucked him in, but Darius kept the momentum of the fall and rolled off to the side, avoiding a sudden dagger strike. Keeping the roll, Darius tucked his legs and flung himself back to his feet in a single motion. The sea of smoke still conquered his surroundings, but this time, Darius sent a refreshed pulse of magic through his body.

The commander closed one eye and focused his power into his ears. The scream turned sharp but detailed. Another dagger came whiffing out of the smoke, and just as Darius juked the weapon, another came, held by the same crooked hand. Darius ducked it as well as a third strike. His ears perked, he found the bastard; the commander shot out with his spear.

Darius' spear hit squarely and ripped into the once hidden body of the smoke-screamer. The impaled enemy let out a gurgled yell, power waning. All at once, the smoke dissipated to reveal the swampy battlefield and torrenting rain. Thick black blood leaked from the enemy's wound, gushing with each breath—he was still alive.

With a grunt, Darius yanked his weapon free only to punch it back into the smoke-screamer, slamming through the stomach, then the chest, and finally right into the gaping maw of the cultist. A sickly crunch silenced the scene, but then a new scream sounded.

"Shit," Darius said through small panting breaths. He had to admit to himself: he was hoping that was the end of this. But a different smoke-screamer came spinning through the air. This one held twin blades, each sparking and flashing with fury.

With wide eyes, Darius managed to dodge the frenzied strike just in time. The chaotic motions of the new enemy caught a sapling instead and tore it into a blast of splinters. On guard, Darius leveled his spear and the new foe came barreling towards him before a single quip could be thrown.

Commander Darius let loose a quick stab but the inhuman movement of the smoke-screamer slipped by it. The screamer seemed to shimmer and fizzle, her body unable to choose between solid and smoke. A terrible black taint veined across her exposed flesh whenever she materialized and so Darius aimed a steady stab but the hit merely grazed her side, not stopping her assault at all.

Her curbed blades came dancing wildly towards the commander. Darius slipped by one strike and deflected the other on the haft of his spear, only for the unnaturally fast screamer to bring the first sword back in another swing. The blade cut upwards, slacking into Darius' cloak and just missing his side. With a clang, Darius managed to bounce back another strike, but he was reeling on his back feet now as the enemy warrior pushed forward.

A scream of metal and a cut managed to rip into Darius' hidden chain shirt, bursting the rings and bruising the ribs. The Commander let out a groan of pain which was replied to with a screech from his enemy. A sickly plume of smoke belched from her mouth and fogged Darius' face. For a brief moment, Darius felt himself leave his body; an unnatural feeling seized his chest, spasmed his heart, and pricked his nerves.

With a burst of gold, Darius pushed the feeling out of his body and secured his heart. Pins pricked his arms and the rush of Stromism brought Darius' numb fingers back to life and fed fire to his veins. The immense use of magic put a dangerously cold pressure on the commander's head, but he was ready to fight to the end.

Speeding stabs erupted from Darius and with each jab he put space between him and his enemy. The world seemed to slow down and magic-aided senses gave Darius supernatural reflexes. A curling slash missed his chest, another just missed his neck. A glint caught Darius' eye, a third strike was aimed for his belly—it was a stab.

"I got you now!" Darius roared. His body twisted to the side, and the smoke-screamer's face widened with surprise as she slipped right by him. Darius' arms flexed and golden ribbons corded his muscles and before the smoke-screamer could react to the feint, Darius struck back. His spear plowed through her stomach and punched out the other side. Blood bloomed and her scream turned into a gag.

With a flash of magic, Darius lifted his squirming enemy in the air using only the spear and then in a fit of battle-rage, Darius spun her overhead. Her body broke under the pressure and then all at once, Darius slammed her back down and drove her into the swamp below.

Shockwaves ripped the rain away from Commander Darius and his slaughtered nemesis. Through the brief clearing, Darius could see the many twinkling eyes of fresh arrivals staring at him. Yanking his spear free, Darius shoved the butt into the mud below and put the point between him and the unseen enemy.

A line of cultists creeped out from between the trees, walking slow and studiously with their weapons cautiously leveled at the commander.

Drumming his spear up and down, Darius shouted in defiance. If he was surrounded, so be it. "Who wants to take on Darius Feng!?"

***

Emperor Wilhelm's throne room had everything in it but Wilhelm. It was ornate and flushed with golden decorations and crimson walls. Its opulent doors were swung wide open and down the center ran an

8

equally rich carpet that divided the pearly white floor in half. On one side of the divide sat noble councilors, and on the other sat the Tagist clergy. Standing out from this organization was Wilhelm's throne.

It was a comfortable looking chair of twisted metal and plush cushions that the regent, Josephine Heinrich, now sank into. She was costumed in a dark purple dress with an equally dark burgundy cloak to cover her athletic yet exhausted shoulders. Both garments were threaded with silver to form artistic patterns that were rivaled only by the golden circlet of the regent which sat on Josephine's head.

To the regent's right sat an unamused George who was splayed out in his own stiff chair. He was much more casually dressed than his sister, wearing a plain blue shirt and dark pants. All that stood out was his silver circlet, fraying red cape, and completely irritated expression.

A Tagist sage droned on and on, her words a bland hum that assaulted George's ears just enough to annoy him. Every now and again she would stop, fooling George into thinking she was done, only to continue again after a dramatic gulp of water. At this point, the prince wasn't too sure what her point was anymore, and if he was being completely honest, he wasn't sure there was one. Restless beyond belief, George drummed his fingers on the arm of his chair. Each thump caused a wince from Josephine, her own attention waning behind a stiff facade.

"Stop that," the princess hissed under her breath.

The speaking sage abruptly hiccupped on their words and came to a complete stop. "Your majesty?"

"Excuse me," Josephine apologized. "It was merely a cough—please continue."

"Right," The sage resumed. "Now, in regards to the prince's request—"

George's ears perked and a noble courtier in the gallery interrupted. "Which request this time?"

There was a gentle roll of laughs from both sides, putting a frown on George's face, but the sage remained stable and bland. "In his request for formalizing a treaty with the Vagrants of—"

"Ulmi," George cut in.

"Beg pardon?"

The prince sat up. "They aren't Vagrants, they are Ulmi."

"Either way," the sage said. "I agree with Father Sage Clement that formalizing a treaty with them after a decisive victory only shows weakness. We have no reason to concede anything to them for their actions.

George shot a breath through his nostrils; he was all too aware of the secret crimes and *actions* of the Sages themselves. "This isn't about victories or defeats," the prince spoke. "Or about pride. By formalizing a peace treaty with the Ulmi peoples we can define a border and avoid future conflicts."

"The Empire spans all of Jerrovia," an older nobleman disagreed. "It always has and always will. Such a treaty seems to imply that this is not true and that we are open to others taking pieces of *our* land at their fancy."

George wrinkled his brow. "It's not our land— "

The noble shouted. "Your grandfather would be ashamed!"

"Show some respect to the Hero of the North!" A man snapped behind the older noble, summoning a concert of agreement.

"I support the prince's motion." Dame Honora stood up from the crowd and gave George a polite nod. The prince returned it with one of his own.

A sage sneered. "This is nothing more than a popularity contest. This motion goes against the Empire's ideals of order."

"As if the sages know what that means anymore," a wrinkled noblewoman piped up. "It was your secrets that somehow fell into the enemy's hands and cost us a lot of lives!"

"We should not turn so quickly upon our orderly leaders just because the enemy managed to snake our secrets," a different noblewoman defended.

Josephine tapped her fingers in thought, each thump catching the ears of the court. She cleared her throat, emptying the room of discussion. "I agree with my brother," she announced. "Some sort of formalization is required to avoid future conflict."

"The Gavarians would never agree to it," a fresh sage added, although meekly and aware of Josephine's glare.

A young nobleman laughed from the corner of the court. "It's not like we can rightfully ask the Gavarians, can we? I don't know about the rest of you, but I'd say the Duke of Gavaria is awfully quiet."

All eyes fell on the empty seat reserved for the Duke of Gavaria: Fenric. George gritted his teeth; just thinking about the man irritated him. Ever since George was a prisoner, a darkness seemed to find his heart and his mind—his anger was quick. A wisp of smoke flicked off George's fingertips and he watched it dissipate. His heart softened just in time for a new voice to intercede; it was Father Sage Clement. He was an old man that reminded George of a pale, unpleasant turtle on two legs, to say nothing of his personality, which was more like that of a jackass. The old sage always looked at George with a certain hate, and ever since the war, that hate seemed to have grown. Clement stood smug, the usual look of self-righteousness on his face.

"Where is the Duke, Prince George?"

Josephine went to speak but George cut her off. "Fenric chose not to be here. It's not my decision to make for him." His words were stern, but in his heart he felt his anger beat again.

"Hm." Clement idled. "Not your decision? That's a first for you, Prince George."

"Are you attempting to insult the prince?" Josephine answered cooly.

"I'm simply remarking, your Majesty, that the prince otherwise seems to be very intent on making decisions for other people—most notably for you, even." Clement grinned, or at least as close as such a man as he could get to grinning. "Another way to help heal the wounds of the war would be a renewed relationship between the Imperial seat and Barcena's nobility. We all know this, and yet our beloved prince seems very adamant at keeping you from marrying into the province for all our benefit." A grumble of agreeing voices followed from the seats of the sages.

"Amazing," George sneered, "I'm not sure you can muster anything but hypocrisy."

"George," Josephine hissed.

"No," George hissed back before standing up, a dark smoke twirling in his stomach. "You always have a lot to say, Clement, but somehow every word seems to send a chill down my spine."

"George!" Josephine barked.

"No need to apologize for you brother, your majesty." Clement's grin was back, "I understand that the wisdom of the Imperial family at least fell on your shoulders."

The prince shot a finger out, its tip growing red, but before he could say anything, Josephine growled. "Enough! I won't sit here while our court devolves into childhood insults and petty rivalries. For the sake of all our sanity, I'm putting this on recess. We will reconvene on the topic at another date."

George pushed the smoke back down from his gut and bit his cheek. That damnable anger festered in his bones. He swallowed and fell back into his seat, feeling a little light headed for it. His ears remained perked as the conversation continued without him.

"You cannot keep postponing the marriage," Clement argued.

"I am regent." Josephine stood up and the entire room stood up with her. This brought George back to his feet. His eyes were on the back of his sister's head as she took a step forward and challenged Clement with a single lift of her brow. "Am I not?"

Clement looked around before frowning. "You are."

"I am what, Father Sage?"

"You are regent." Clement tipped his head and the room followed the gesture.

Josephine flashed a wolfish smile. "Dismissed."

The standing crowds of sages and nobles all at once began to shuffle towards the exit, with only Father Sage Clement holding his ground to look at the Imperial siblings with a studious glare. Only when the final groups of attendees were passing through the mighty council doors did Clement withdraw his glare and follow suit. As the sage exited the room he let his fingers snag on the edge of the door and pulled it closed behind him.

With a loud bang, the dense door—more suited for a siege than a meeting—closed. The sound caused George to jump and sent a shiver down his spine. Josephine shook her head and walked over to the door. With a heave of her shoulder she tugged it open once again, if only by a crack.

"You can't let the Father Sage goad you like that," Josephine started.

George frowned. "I don't like—" he paused, "is the hallway clear?"

Josephine tucked a slant into her cheek. "Wouldn't it be easier if we just kept the door closed?"

"I like it open," George said.

"I know," Josephine softly conceded. "The hallway is clear."

George continued. "I don't like that he is still walking around as if he isn't a war criminal and a traitor, let alone how he throws his weight around."

Josephine tapped her fingers to her lips, signaling quiet. Walking away from the doors she gestured for George to follow her to the far side of the room. Content with the distance, Josephine replied.

"Until we can gather enough evidence to convict him, we can't be hasty. You should remember what Uncle Caleb advised."

"He advised that you don't marry Gennisberg," George quickly said, "or are we ignoring that?"

"I'm not ignoring that," Josephine quietly corrected. "It's just that the supporters of the motion actually have a good enough point that I can't dispute it without outright saying that Uncle doesn't feel like it's a good idea."

"Good point?" George slapped his sides, exasperated. "What good point?"

"Gennisberg is a powerful count from Barcena, George. We lost a lot of resources in the war and this would help restore what the Imperial Province lost."

"I don't see how, the provinces already give to the Imperial Province," George argued, "we can recuperate the usual way without selling you as a bride."

"I'm not being sold." Josephine frowned. "A marriage with Barcena will increase the resource flow by opening up more private connections between the palace and their nobility. I know you don't know much about politics—" George went to interrupt his sister but Josephine stuck a finger out and continued. "—But! By showing extra care to a province's nobility, the nobles who control the resource flow are more amiable and willing to cut deals and find more stock than they would have otherwise. Besides," Josephine lectured openly, "with Fenric and Gavaria being as silent as they are, we can't rely on their usual tributes to come in, especially when the final report on Fenric returns. The empire can only gain from unity."

George looked down at his feet and knew he had lost the debate. He was outmaneuvered by his sister but still, he could think of one final question to hopefully derail her logic: "What about Williams?"

Josephine flinched and silence grew between the two siblings. Finally, Josephine answered, firm yet somber, "It will be a marriage in name only. Uncle warned us about the man, regardless, so I'll be keeping my distance even under wedlock."

"Does Gennisberg know that?" George pushed. He felt guilty doing this, but he knew he was doing it to protect her.

"George."

Another silence.

Josephine spoke, "I don't like it, of course I don't like it, but this isn't for me, it's for the empire. We'll both be on our guard, as Uncle suggested, but we also need to do our duties."

"So you're going to give in to the proposals?" George probed a bit more bluntly than he had wanted.

"We need Barcena," Josephine responded with a hint of sadness. "With everything that has happened these last few years, we need some semblance of unity to face whatever aftermath is on its way; so I will consider it."

The room fell into a quiet contemplation as George slowly accepted his sister's words. Together they stood there thinking with not a sound between them. George could feel the barrier between himself and Jospehine. She was always the critical one and even now she stood stalwart and unaffected, or did she? George stared at her, he could see her battling something inside, something that meant a lot to her. George brought his hand up to his bearded chin and pinched it thoughtfully.

"Whatever you choose, I'll be there to help," He vowed.

Josephine looked up at him and her battle seemed to fade from her eyes. "I know. I always know that."

Chapter Two
The Most Important Meal of the Day

Evening had just begun and the world was already molding itself to its dusky form. Through the windows of Caleb's tower, George admired streaks of golden clouds carving themselves through hues of pinks and blues. Whatever birds were still in the sky had quickly turned into black silhouettes and gave life to an otherwise still portrait. Inside, George was cocooned at his Uncle's desk, reclined in the comfiest chair he had ever sat in but was graced with the unfortunate company of the most boring papers he had ever read.

Still, the usual scents of the sun-soaked wood that lined the windows or sat by the glass in the form of ancient furniture was giving way to the fresh smell of a clear night. These were the sorts of smells that transported George away from the palace and back to Torskyla or the Nest. Pointedly, though, his thought didn't dare revisit the violence that surrounded them, but rather, the calm, peaceful days in-between marching. Those days were the ones he would sit around fires after a long day and smile with his friends. George smirked, it was funny how looking back trims away the terrible things so you can appreciate the tiny treasures in between.

A polite rap against the door broke George away from his reverie. The door was open, as it had been, and behind its threshold stood Reginald holding a silver plate.

"Oh, come in," George answered.

Reginald tipped his head and made his way over to the messy desk that George called work. With the same judging look of a drillmaster, Reginald studied George's workspace before placing the plate on the only clear portion of his desk. Atop the it laid fresh breakfast pastries, a bowl of blackberries, and a glass of chilled milk.

"Your breakfast, my prince, though I must admit, doesn't it seem a little late for breakfast?" Reginald took a polite step back and folded his elbows square behind his back.

"Anytime is a good time for a little breakfast," George rebutted. Turning from his papers, he looked at his old teacher. The two shared a look long enough for Reginald to crinkle his eyes.

"I have a strange feeling you're about to ask me to be dismissed from your paperwork," the old master said.

"If only it still worked that way, I'd be trading all my work for a game of chess," George answered.

"No grand adventures this time?"

"I think I've had my fill." George's eyes turned dark. "Besides, my last isn't quite over yet."

Reginald shared a sympathetic look before saying, "No, I suppose not." There was a pause before Reginald continued, "You should be hearing back from the Commander soon, and with luck he'll have everything you need to convict the sages and finish this story."

"I hope so." George had a blank stare about him. He scratched his quill idly, scribbling nothing in particular. The tick produced a gleam of knowing in Reginald's eye.

"Don't make your move before you're ready." Reginald read the prince's mind. George focused on his scribble and frowned. His lips curled into a small snarl.

"I just don't like it."

"I'd never ask you to." Reginald stood up straight and took a step back, preparing to leave. "I'll let you enjoy your... breakfast. Take solace in what you can—just send for me if you need anything else."

"Of course, Reginald, thank you." George mustered a smile. The old master smiled back, if only for a moment. Returning to his usual demeanor, Reginald took a few more steps backwards before turning to head for the exit. But before he passed through the threshold, he looked back at his old ward.

"And my prince..."

George looked up from his quill. "Yes?"

"It does the head good to take a break here and there."

George grinned; he knew that tone. "Thank you."

Reginald hardened his stare. "*Here and there.*"

An instinctive gulp. "I know, I know!" George waved his hands and the old man's smile returned as he slipped through the exit.

With a heavy sigh, George leaned back in his chair, eyes refusing to look at the papers he was working on. Instead they flickered over to the dew ridden blackberries. Plopping a few into his mouth, George looked up at the high ceiling. The juices flooded his mouth and sent his mind back on old memories and old friends. From there he thought about when times were simple; his recollections flowed from one scene to another while he mindlessly ate his meal. It wasn't until all the food was gone and the chilled milk was long chugged that George sat idle in his chair with a full belly and regretfully sticky mouth. His hand dug into his pocket and placed his fingers over an old wooden raindrop.

George tumbled the pink trinket around and stared blankly at his Uncles desk. His mind was doing everything in its power to avoid the unfinished paperwork. One by one, George scanned various tomes and books unrelated to his bureaucratic quest and found all sorts of history books and what seemed to be completed journals. The last one caught George's eye the most, as it seemed to be a worn and beaten journal that was probably written long before George himself was even born.

At first, George resisted, but soon his curiosity got the better of him. He carefully pulled the book from its home and placed it on top of his papers. It was obviously an old and dusty book, but its cover still held a vibrant red to it, even if it was otherwise plainly decorated. The book itself was thin and only held his uncle's signature along the spine. George put his fingers over the book and hesitated.

Once again, curiosity won the battle and George lifted the cover as if it were the heavy lid of an ancient treasure chest. Inside wasn't any gold, but rather the simple calligraphy of his uncle, though less refined than how George knew it in the present day.

It was impossible to tell how old Caleb was when he penned it, and George was surprised at the passion in the language. His cool and collected uncle was missing from these pages as George read about the daily exploits and thoughts of a heated youth. To George's relief, the first few pages betrayed that the book was a memoir rather than a personal journal and so George read on without any guilt.

As George continued, he read old romantic poetry, whimsical thoughts, and general wishes of Uncle Caleb, but as George flipped deeper and deeper into the book, the tone changed. Several years, if not longer, separated the last entry of the passionate Caleb and the first entry of a sobered man. Even the penmanship was completely different, and yet it was so clearly Caleb's hand. George narrowed his eyes on one particular entry and a twist formed in the prince's gut at the words:

I'm at a loss of what to do. I have every desire to write in detail about what I mean, but I know better than to do it. I'm sorry that you have to read my displeasure in such a way but bear with my vague words and partial thoughts as I attempt to lift this from my chest: how am I supposed to process such a tragedy? Sophia is dead from the fever and my niece along with her...

George was frozen. "Mom and Josephine?"

Sitting back, George furrowed a brow. "Josephine and Mom? Dead?" Thoughts were suffocating George's head as he tried to process the meaning behind his uncle's words, but nothing made sense. Josephine was alive, and his had mother survived her historic illness and years later gave birth to himself. George chewed his cheek and aggressively flipped through the remaining pages. Nothing, not a single thing to alleviate that question. The rest of the book fell back in step with his Uncle's rambling, except this time the target wasn't so much his personal wishes but rather the elusive history of the empire.

Dissatisfied, George closed the book and shot his attention right at the other untouched manuscripts, hoping for some sort of answer, but all he could find was books on history and the occult. He flipped through stories of old festivals, the conflicts with the Nachtists, the detailed account of his father's marriage, but nothing regarding his mother or sister's apparent demise, not until George stumbled upon an old book styled like the ones kept in the Imperial archives.

Cracking it open, George found the medical report of his own birth. The prince's mind went blank as his eyes scanned the short, methodical sentences.

This was written by one of the Imperial doctors, and held no embellishment. Just as George was always told, the order of events had Josephine nowhere near the incident, and from there the book covered the activities going on in the room that housed the balcony. As the book said, Empress Sophia fell from the balcony while Wilhelm was sparring with Caleb, and when she hit the ground, Reginald was close by and came running to her aid where he—as the book said—removed the baby George from the deceased Sophia.

Concerns swamped George's mind. Firstly, why was George never told Caleb was in the room with Wilhelm. Secondly, why didn't Caleb serve as an eyewitness to dispel the rumors that his father pushed Sophia. And third, why was Caleb keeping all these things to himself. Did he doubt his uncle's sincerity, no, George had doubted enough for a lifetime whilst locked in a shed, but still, a fourth, more paralyzing thought began to creep in: what actually happened the day his mother died, and how did his mother and sister survive the scarlet fever three years prior.

"Prince George?"

George nearly jumped out of his seat at the sudden interruption. An Imperial guard was standing in the threshold and all George could do was gape in surprise at her. She stood blinking and silent, the pause reminding George about the etiquette the guards were put under. Stumbling, George found himself again.

"I'm sorry, what is it?"

"You have visitors in the central courtyard. They refused out of polite courtesy to enter the foyer without your greeting."

Closing the books in front of him, the prince stood up. "Who is it?"

The Imperial guard let George walk past her, making sure not to lead. "The Hero Harris Von Rugosa and his daughter."

***

The central courtyard was the largest of the four palace courtyards and the least private as it sat in front of the main entrance to the palace building. As suggested, the wide flagstoned area sat in front of the main gates to the palace and looking forward from the entrance it gave a clear view of the road that spiraled down past various checkpoints and into the Imperial city below. Being in such a prominent location, the only shade from the afternoon sun were rows of small ornamental trees that lined the western and eastern sides, and under the shadow of a particular tree stood a pair of visitors.

George spotted them right away, and not just because they were the only people not dressed in the Imperial guard's regalia. One was an older man with tight curls gone gray, a frame past its prime, and simple yet expensive clothing. On his hip he wore a symbolic sword, the hilt sealed permanently to the metal scabbard with melted gold. Next to him stood Rosaline in similar clothes with a dark red shirt and pants with a white cloak thrown over her shoulders to denote the colors of Barcena. Her usually wild hair was semi-tamed in a thick braid with errant curls. As George walked out from the massive palace doors, a wide smile broke his face.

At the sight, a brilliant smile of Rosaline's own split her lips but before she could say a word, the old man, Harris Von Rugosa, fell to one knee with one hand on his heart, his head tipped, and the free hand held out palm up in reverence.

"Your Imperial highness, I am honored by your presence. Please forgive my calling and accept my humble request of an audience." The Hero Harris opened one eye to peek at his still standing daughter and growled at her to kneel under his breath.

George held up his hands but before he could wave the situation away, Rosaline ploughed a hug right into the prince's chest. George melted as she squeezed him tight, her embrace popping his back. Harris jumped to his feet.

"Rosaline!"

The prince just stood there dumb and blushing while Rosaline laughed. Finally she let George go and looked at her father. "It's a little late for me to kneel to this lug."

Harris' eyes widened with parental fury but George found his voice at last. "I wouldn't ask her to! Or you, for that matter." A chill wiped from his brow. "Please don't be upset."

"Oh he's fine." Rosaline clung to George's arm.

Harris sighed and shook his head. Something in George told him that Rosaline's father had to be used to her bold nature by now. "I'm grateful for leniency," the traditionalist offered.

George idled for a moment. He stuttered. "Do you want to come inside the palace?"

"Verily." Harris grinned. Rosaline let go of her lover and stood by her father's side as George led them into the main foyer of the palace, as if he were inviting friends into his humble cottage. The truth was the foyer was cavernous and could fit a regular person's entire home inside of it three times over at the least. The decor alone was worth more than some people could make in their entire hard-earned lives, with bejeweled statues and ancient paintings littering every surface. A row of six doors flanked either side of the foyer and a large staircase spanning the width led upwards to a final, massive door. Above it was a painting of George's great great grandmother, the Empress who first designed the foyer into its contemporary theme.

Once inside, George turned to his guests, unsure how to proceed. "You'll have to excuse my manners, Sir Harris, I'm not very good at being a noble."

"Thank the Graces!" Rosaline quickly replied, summoning a frown from her father. George smirked at the quip and Rosaline smirked back, only for the grins to be broken by Harris.

"At last we have arrived," he said to no one in particular. His eyes searched around, as if expecting something more.

"I'm glad you two are here," George agreed. "But, uh, *why* are you here?" He raised his hands. "I'm not complaining of course, I'm just curious."

Harris seemed slightly surprised by the question, but Rosaline quickly answered, "there are a lot of rumors being spread in the south that Count Gennisberg is going to marry Josephine."

"Princess Regent Josephine," Harris corrected.

Rosaline rolled her eyes. "Right, Princess Regent Josephine."

"And so," Harris interjected again, "I decided to make the trip in the hopes to be the very first to congratulate her highness. Excuse my casual tone."

George blinked. "Ah."

"What's wrong?" Rosaline asked.

The prince shook his head. "It's just that those really are just rumors—nothing's been decided as of yet."

"Beg my pardon, Prince George, but then someone should inform Count Gennisberg of this. He was traveling shortly behind me last I heard," Harris said.

Before George could answer, one of the many doors swung wide and through it marched Josephine, her face staring hard and intently at the large door up the stairs as she was no doubt being called to a private meeting of sorts. The group turned to watch as her guards trailed behind her. With a sudden jolt, Harris took steps away from George and Rosaline.

"If you could excuse me, my prince," was all he muttered, as intent at talking with Josephine as Josephine was intent on getting through the foyer. The hero Harris quickly caught up to the procession, but instead of seeing the result, George turned to Rosaline.

"Gennisberg is really on his way?"

Rosaline nodded, eyes studying the man. "Yeah, everyone in Barcena is excited."

"Shit," George swore. He looked away, but before he could delve deeper into his anxiety, Rosaline poked his arm. The prince regarded her and her deep brown eyes for a moment before relaxing his shoulders. "I've missed you," he said.

Rosaline closed her eyes with a crinkling smile, clearly content. "I've missed you, too."

George held his smile for a while longer before the thoughts and questions from earlier clawed their way back. He soaked in the sight of his lover, her calm face contrasting his swirling thoughts. A black smoke tickled his stomach but he knew that at least right now he was safe, he had Rosaline by his side.

"Care to walk the gardens with me?" He found himself asking. Rosaline nodded happily and bowed her head, as if mocking her father from earlier.

"Lead the way, oh glorious prince." As she dipped, a flash caught George's eye, and he noticed the curve of a blue painted ring hidden on a necklace below her collar; the symbol of a Tagist.

Chapter 3
Skin of Glass

The shroud of the gardens covered the pair as they walked along a white stone path. On either side of the pair, spring flowers were already in bloom, leaving large swathes of purples, reds and yellows peeking out of every shade of green. In spite of the color, George's thoughts were drawn to darkness as he stared at Rosaline's collar.

Her fingers were laced with his and a gentle hum was on her lips. Her eyes bounced from tree to tree and her lips tugged back and forth from a thoughtful pout to a fancied grin until finally her eyes snapped to George, throwing the prince into a panic.

"What's wrong?" She stabbed the anxiety.

George sighed. "A lot is wrong."

"A lot, huh?" Rosaline pulled George towards a bench under the great elm tree that dominated the center of the gardens. Together they sat under the speckled light of the tree. Rosaline didn't let go of George's hand and he could feel her fingers tight against his. She had him locked, but he wanted that. Despite his sudden paranoia, he felt secure by her grip.

"You got weird quick, something bothered you recently," Rosaline analyzed. "What weird thought entered that head of yours?"

"I was just surprised," George admitted.

Rosaline blinked. "Surprised?"

He pointed to her chest. Rosaline widened her eyes and tilted her head. "By my...?"

"No!" George blushed crimson. "I guess I didn't know you were a devout Tagist. It caught my attention."

Rosaline held his gaze for a moment and yanked her necklace out from under her shirt. She held the offending piece to the dappled sunlight. "This is what bothered you?" She twisted her lips in thought. "I guess I can understand. I mean, I suppose I never had a chance to tell you, but it's hardly rare for someone to adhere to the Imperial faith." She cocked her head once again. "Is that a problem?"

"No," George said with conviction. "Absolutely not a problem."

"Because I don't agree with the sages," Rosaline defended. "But I can't really toss my religion out the window because the leaders are... traitors..." She felt the word on her tongue. It was George's turn to grip her hand. This stole her gaze and he held firm.

It's alright, really," George said. "I have had a lot on my mind and was just surprised, is all."

"So we are good?" Rosaline squeezed his hand.

"As always." George nodded.

"Good." Rosaline relaxed. "I'd be rather devastated if you didn't trust me."

"Of course I trust you," George said. "You're the most trustworthy person I have ever met."

"More so than Williams?" Rosaline pleaded with big eyes.

George hesitated. "It's a tie?"

Rosaline laughed and playfully hit the prince. "You ass." She clung to his arm. "But thanks; I was worried for a moment."

"A beauty as wondrous as the morning sun," George recited, "as pure as the fresh snow and as unique as the many stars. But her skin is of glass, her beauty merely a symptom of her graceful soul."

A smile formed on Rosaline's face. "And what was that?"

"A bit of poetry." George beamed down at her. "Not bad, huh?"

"It's winning me over, yes," Rosaline teased. "Where did my prince of bluntness read such pretty words?"

"As if I didn't write them myself?" George faked offense. Rosaline bounced a brow and the man gave in. His face softened as it looked at Rosaline's. Her eyes were still and half closed, unoffended and relaxed. Her calmness was befitting the gardens so much so that even the local wildlife mirrored her, with a small yellow winged butterfly flitting about her shoulder. This was the same woman who fought alongside him as a warrior, and the same who treated hundreds as a medic in the middle of battle. Be it in blood and steel or under a tree with butterflies, that look in her eyes never left. She was a rock in a windy world; his rock.

Without realizing it, George had melted into her embrace and the two were twisted. Rosaline yawned gently just as a breeze tickled by. "So tell me," She started, "where did you read it anyway?"

"My uncle's..." George felt it all rush back to him. That temporary reprieve shocked backwards as the smoke licked at his throat. His questions.

Rosaline detached to look up at the prince. "What?" Her eyes settled on his own and she prodded him. "What's wrong?"

"Right before I came down to meet you and your father," George said, "I was in my uncle's study, and I found some hidden books."

Both of them were sitting up now, straight and serious. Slowly George explained what he had read and slowly Rosaline nodded along, intent and listening. The prince spared no details and Rosaline chewed on her knuckle in thought.

"It has me wondering what my next step should be," George said.

Rosaline tugged on her necklace and hummed in thought. "I'm sorry."

"What do you think I should do?" George looked at her, almost like a general to a lieutenant or with how Rosaline sat, maybe lieutenant to a general. "Uncle Caleb isn't here to answer my questions, and I doubt anyone besides him would know."

"How about your dad?" Rosaline asked. "I mean, he would know better than anyone."

George gave her a pitied look. "You know my dad isn't exactly... there."

"Try anyway!" Rosaline lit up. "Tell me how it goes."

"Now?" George cocked a brow.

"I'm not going anywhere." Rosaline slapped her knees. "Well, I mean, I should probably go find my own dad, but otherwise, I'll be around. Go do it! It's weighing on your mind and making you stare at people's chests." She jabbed his side, eking a smile out of him.

"I'd feel bad leaving you."

Rosaline held his cheeks and smiled at him. "Don't worry. I can survive without my prince for at least a little bit. Go confront your dad."

George leaned forward and kissed her forehead. Her smile grew and she leaned into him. "On second thought, give me a few more minutes."

"Deal."

***

After a short walk that barely covered the first floor, let alone the other floors of the seemingly labyrinthine palace, Rosaline found herself alone. She stood in one of the endless hallways, next to a suit of obsolete armor and a massive portrait of someone important; she didn't recognize them. George did show her a few interesting places to visit and even drew her the crudest map she ever saw in case she got bored, but something about studying the ageless decorations of the passageways piqued her curiosity the most. Each item gave her some sort of background to think upon, provoking her to attempt and guess who had placed the object there and why; what was so significant about it?

As she was thinking this, her eyes gradually fell onto an ancient looking piece of tapestry that was all but covered by a stone statue of Emperor Frederick. Even though the statue was small enough to stand on a cherry-wood stool, the tapestry wasn't wide enough to entirely escape being obscured. Taking a step to the side to get a better look, Rosaline realized it was a flag and if she wasn't already staring at it, she might have overlooked it as the usual Imperial flag. It had the plum and wine colors with a falcon soaring down the middle where the colors met, but it was ever so slightly different. The silhouette of the falcon had legs, it was subtle, but the falcon had legs.

Rosaline found herself squinting at the tapestry, a small pain stirring in her head as she did. She couldn't put her finger on it, but staring at the tapestry bothered her. Her eyes widened; that wasn't the only difference. On either side of the falcon, one in the plum, and one in the wine, stood two trees. Rosaline wasn't sure how she didn't notice this before, as they stood out as largely as the falcon did.

A ring formed in her ear and the sound slowly grew louder and louder as Rosaline stared. She couldn't stop though, the more she looked, the more her mind wondered what she was looking at, and yet it didn't want to be known.

The sudden squeak of boots turning the corner yanked her from the flag and Rosaline spun to meet the arrivals. The familiar voice of Williams replaced the ringing. He was walking next to Hector, clearly upset. His usual calm demeanor was furrowed with stress and thoughts, while Hector remained mellow in an attempt to console his friend. Rosaline watched on with wide eyes, as if she was caught in a place she wasn't supposed to be.

"Williams, wait!" Josephine's voice overpowered Williams' and the Regent came bounding up from behind. She was clearly as stressed as the knight. Her dress was wrinkled from her job, matching the crease in her forehead.

As the trio regrouped, whatever Josephine was going to say fell flat, the presence of Rosaline becoming clear. The ex-medic smiled nervously as their gazes collected on her.

"Hello everybody."

"Lady Rosaline." Williams was the first to speak. The worry in his eyes fogged over to some visage of calm. Josephine spoke second, sharper than likely intended.

"I didn't know you were here."

Hector on the other hand had eyes sparkling with joy. "Rosaline! From the bar in Korku?"

"Oh yeah!" Rosaline matched his energy, "George talks so much about you in his letters that I sometimes forget that I only met you that one time. Congratulations on becoming the Imperial Marshal, by the way!"

Hector grinned wide. "My appointment is still probationary. The Stromist masters are still watching my every move and listening to my every breath."

The two paused and looked towards Williams and Josephine. Rosaline regretted her sudden excitement with wince while the two spatting lovers snuck upset glances at each other. Energy drained from Rosalien and she tipped her head, somber like her father. "I apologize for interrupting."

"Interrupting what?" Josephine never took her eyes off Williams. "I don't think there was anything to interrupt, unless someone has something to say?"

Williams closed his eyes. "As if I have much more to say."

"Then I guess Rosaline wasn't interrupting then!" Josephine nearly shouted at the knight, causing him to flinch. A heavy pause fell over the scene before the regent turned from the group. "Carry on! Enjoy! Have fun!" She seethed.

Starting to march away from the others, Josephine turned only to face Rosaline once more. The look in the regent's eyes provoked a flinch from the ex-medic.

"And welcome to the palace, Rosaline." Josephine's voice still sounded ripe with frustration. "Excuse any first impressions!"

With little else, Josephine turned the corner and left the remaining group alone in an awkward silence. Rosaline frowned but was the first to speak.

"How come whenever I see Josephine, she's never in a good mood."

Hector stifled a grin and made a silencing gesture towards Rosaline. The woman bit her tongue and gave the marshal a guilty look.

"It's stressful times," Williams finally said. Rosaline answered with a silent nod and Hector shifted, clearly uncomfortable. The trio remained still, however, just staring at where Josephine once was. That was until Williams broke the seal.

"So what brings you to the capital, Lady Rosaline?"

As sudden as the question, the other's eyes were now on Rosaline. The guest stood up straight and replied, "I was accompanying my father on his own trek to the capital."

"Ah yes," Williams said. "The news he brought with him." It was cryptic but Rosaline knew what he was referring to. "How far out is Gennisberg?"

Rosaline could feel something under Williams' usual chill and she hesitated. "Not far?"

Williams clenched his jaw and Hector braved a comment. "It's not easy for her, either."

The knight looked at his friend and sighed. "I know." Conflict cut whatever was heating his eyes and he stalled. Silence once again took the scene, before a completely bald shaven man and woman came turning the corner, their cheeks flushed from exertion. They wore simple brown tunics marked with the fist of Stromism on the chest. With eyes staring directly at Hector, they tipped their heads.

"The masters are seeking you, Marshal."

"Freedom ends once again," Hector mused with a smile before tipping his head at Rosaline and then Williams. "I'll see you two later."

"I should be moving on myself," Williams added thoughtfully, "I put aside today's errands long enough."

"And I have a lot of aimless pacing to do." Rosaline nodded, summoning a laugh from Hector. With little else all three of the group parted ways, leaving Rosaline alone once again to wander the endless passages of the palace and to study each and every small bit of decoration.

***

Stepping from one bauble to the next, Rosaline treated each decorative piece as an academic study in all its own without really focusing on where she was walking. Her meandering task saw her zig zagging from one wall to the next and back until finally she was completely lost and standing in front of the oldest door she had found yet.

It was made of wood, but had long since lost its lacquer and from the look of the rest of the hall, this was a rather unused part of the palace in recent decades. Not seeing any real reason not to, Rosaline placed her hand on the old copper handle and gave the door a push. After an initial groan—as if the door was waking up after a long slumber—it gave way easily and let the light of the hallway pour into the darker room.

While the inside wasn't completely dark, its only source of light were two rather thin windows, and even still, it looked like vegetation blocked the sun from reaching them correctly. Rosaline took a few steps inside to allow her eyes to adjust to the ancient atmosphere of the room. Her boots clacked against the bare marble flooring and kicked up a layer of filth.

Rosaline could only guess that the room she was in was nestled somewhere near the gardens on the first floor; she never climbed any stairs and vegetation and quiet was all she noticed on the other side of the windows. As for the contents of the room, it looked long abandoned. Whatever rugs once separated the feet of whoever used it and the cold floor were long gone, and most of the furniture was pallid with dust.

Many types of chairs, from plush seats for lounging to hard wooden stools for studying were scattered all about and a single massive desk rested on the far side of the room, sandwiched between two bookshelves. Above the desk was a large portrait of a woman dressed regally. This woman looked a lot like Josephine, but Rosaline figured that made sense, since she in turn looked a lot like her father and this woman was likely an ancestor of Wilhelm.

Still, the portrait piqued Rosaline's curiosity enough to coax her over to it, squinting in the dusky light. In an attempt to get a closer look at it without climbing over the desk, she put her hand on one of the bookcase shelves and applied just a little weight to wrench her a few inches taller. Her hand slipped and slapped the line of books that stood on the shelf, knocking them over one by one. Cringing, Rosaline let herself fall back to the floor.

Turning to the toppled books, Rosaline gingerly stood them back up, until a particular book caught her interest. She paused, unlike all the other thick spined books that were no doubt heavy with words, she was now holding a thin and tall book with thick paper—a drawing book.

Rosaline sank into the desk's chair, eager to crack the sketchpad open. She frowned, remembering how dusky it was in the room and with a kick of her feet, she sent herself and her chair gliding backwards towards the window. A loud, grinding sound cringed down her spine as she scratched the chair loudly against the floor.

"Stupid idea." With regret, she stood back up and picked up her chair, plopped it back down next to the window and gave the floor a once over just in case she left some permanent damage.

She plopped back into the chair and crossed a leg and placed the book on top. She cracked it open, gently so as to not cause any more damage than she had, and poured her eyes over the first drawing.

It was a portrait of sorts, etched in rough charcoal. From the fantastically done lines, Rosaline could make out that it was clearly one of George's ancestors, with a lot of the subject's features matching the prince's. The biggest difference was the wiry and wild hair, something Wilhelm had inherited, but not his children. Content, Rosaline flipped the page.

The next few pages were similar portraits, some of the same man with different styles and experimental strokes added, some of a young woman, and one of an elderly man. Oddly enough, there seemed to be a large gap after that last picture, with the next picture being in ink instead of charcoal, and the strokes much more masterful than the others, leading Rosaline to believe that much time had passed between the portraits and this new picture. From what George had mentioned of his uncle's journal, this must have been a family trait.

The new picture was of the gardens, even Rosaline could recognize it. There were flowery alcoves, cobbled paths and at the center stood the mighty elm tree. She flipped the page, only to find the same picture drawn, with more emphasis on the tree this time. Furrowing a brow, she flipped again to find the same picture, then the same picture again. There were no experimentations being done, just more and more detail being added each time.

She flipped the page again, and this time there was a man standing next to the tree, but he didn't look like any of the people from before. He looked sad, and his face was carved with sigils. She turned the page. There he was again by the tree, except the man from the first portrait was also there, they both looked sad. Confounded, Rosaline sped her way to the final page but before she could get a look at it, her father's voice came calling out.

"Rosaline!"

The ex-medic frowned and closed the book, bringing it back to the shelf but eager to remember where she placed it just in case she had time later. There was something strange about it.

"Rosaline!"

She flinched, frustrated she couldn't delve deeper just yet. Turning from the mystery, she started her walk out.

"I'm in here!"

Chapter 4
Sins of the Father

Wilhelm sat in his room. Not much played on his mind as he concentrated on the chess board in front of him. His eyes were narrowed and yet somehow still misty and distant. All around him were the ornate trappings expected of the Emperor's room: with velvet, silk, and gold laced onto nearly every surface that wasn't polished marble or sparkling granite. This was to speak nothing of the massive curtained bed that dominated the room. In total, the area was big enough to fit a small shop, and had enough stained glass to fit the windows of a church.

Under the speckled light, Wilhelm was in a contest of chess between himself and his servant, Sophia. His face was creased in concentration, fingers trembling over his rook as he looked on. The board itself was a mess, a clear mirror to the mental state of at least one of its players. Sophia herself sat on the other end, a paragon of patience. Her white dress all but screamed the symbolism of the virtue she had practiced in being under the service of Wilhelm. She was quiet as the maddened man stared intensely at the half toppled pieces.

He parted his lips and his voice came out as a defeated squeak. "I don't know what to do."

The stoic visage of Sophia immediately softened. She gave a pitied frown and lifted her hands to weave her fingers into tiny signs. Wilhelm knew her symbols well. She signed, "It's just a game."

The emperor let the rook drop, a seed of lucidity forming in his pupils. "It's more than that—I know it." His heart began to beat faster, his mind itching at a revelation he couldn't grasp. "I know there is more to it all."

A teardrop fell onto the board. "Why can't I be here? Why can't I come back?"

The hand signs of Sophia jumped again. "Wilhelm, it's only a game of chess."

"It's a reflection!" Wilhelm shouted, his arm banging against the board and sending the pieces to the floor. Sophia jumped and guilt immediately cut into Wilhelm's chest. His face twisted from rage back into one of confused sadness. "Where did I go?"

With a genuine frown and shimmering eyes, Sophia held out a hand. Wilhelm reached over the toppled chessboard and placed his own withered fingers on her palm. Sophia gave the emperor a squeeze and looked up at him with large black eyes full of pity, compassion, and maybe a seed of fear. Wilhelm blinked.

He could see his own reflection off her pupils, and on either side of him sat two other women, both their faces veiled and blurred. One had her nails digging into his shoulder while the other sat with her hands in her lap, defeated. Wilhelm knitted his brow, lip trembling. Sophia squeezed his hand again, but this time Wilhelm snapped it away.

A wide white grin split across Wilhelm's face and a maniacal laugh bubbling up from his lungs. "I see you!"

He stood up and pointed at Sophia, his reflection pointing at the strange woman digging her nails into him. "I can see you! I see you! You can't hide! I see you!" He howled a laugh, both dripping with insanity and perhaps now anger.

Sophia rapidly signed. "What are you talking about?"

"Ha!" Wilhelm droned before falling into a fit of sobbing giggles. Tears were streaking down his cheeks as he laughed angrily.

A loud crack sounded and the door to the room was slammed wide open. George was standing in its mouth, eyes worried. "What's going on in here!?"

"Your dad isn't doing well," Sophia signed.

George sped into the room and put his hands on Wilhelm's shoulders, holding him steady. The Emperor could feel his heartbeat readily now that his body wasn't shaking with it. George's eyes bore into Wilhelm's as they met gazes, and Wilhelm could see his son's pupils searching him desperately . Unfortunately, Wilhelm didn't have to search. He could see the reflection in George's eyes just as readily as Sophia's.

This time, much closer, the scary woman from before was staring back at Wilhelm, next to his own reflection. Anger was in her eyes, much more than before. A laugh bubbled up in Wilhelm's throat, a smile taunting the image. Looking at his own reflected shoulder, he could see his son's hands had pushed away the woman's.

"My boy..."

"Yes, Dad."

***

Moments later, George's father started to relax. When the prince took a step back and the emperor found a seat on his bed, Sophia started to sign to Wilhelm, attempting to retain his current calmness. George felt an itch in his chest as he watched the servant interact with his father in almost the same way a doctor might treat a patient no longer capable. It was these moments that made George unjustly hate Sophia as a child, especially when his father would start confusing her for his mother. Even now, George remembered how he disliked it and he still found himself wincing slightly whenever Wilhelm erroneously called her Sophia, not that George was ever told her real name.

Still, George was an adult now, and one who understood to the best of his ability the strange happenings around his family and though Sophia never deserved his ire and therefore didn't need his forgiveness, he found it for her. Just as he came to his conclusion, Sophia turned to him and signed quickly.

"I think the emperor wishes to be alone now."

George whispered back, "I have things I needed to talk to him about."

Sophia frowned and stood up straight. George knew he could tell her to stand aside and that she would. George would be a liar if he said he wasn't that nasty to her when he was little. Regretting the memories, George cast his eyes down from her own and took a step backwards towards the door. "Maybe you can answer my questions instead?"

Sophia gave the prince a suspicious glance and furrowed her brow before following him outside of the room. Before the door could close, Wilhelm let out a final laugh. "I'll see you for dinner!" It was as if he didn't just have an outburst.

It wasn't clear who he meant, but George answered. "See you then."

The door clicked closed and the pair, both prince and servant, were now standing alone in the mighty halls of the palace, or at least alone in the sense of royalty; guards flanked the walls every so often. All too aware of the ears of the soldiers, George decided to walk in silence, prodding Sophia to follow him.

Guarded, Sophia followed George through the many hallways and passages until they found themselves in a less than decorated hallway with less than welcoming stone. The somber atmosphere didn't help to put Sophia at ease, George could see that, but he knew privacy was necessary.

Soon the pair were climbing worn stairs and approaching an all too familiar door at the pinnacle. Swinging it open, George let Sophia step into his uncle's study. George made the decision to leave the door open as he entered, if not for Sophia's peace of mind, than his own.

Now standing in silence, the two stood in the center of the study, surrounded by the many bookshelves as well as Caleb's desk. By their legs sat the couch and short table used by George when he visited his uncle and with an awkward wave of his hand, George motioned for Sophia to have a seat.

Sophia hesitated long enough for George to sit first, miscalculating her feint. His legs buckled and he more fell into the seat than sat, his muscles so confused on whether to stand up or sit down after Sophia's jerk motion that they just gave up. The prince creased his brow and his eyes followed Sophia as she joined him on the far side, her weight more in her knees than the couch, just one leap from standing back up.

"I'm sorry," George started.

A sign. "Oh?"

"For the past, I mean," George continued. He turned to face her and looked Sophia in the eye. "I know it isn't much, but I hope moving forward we can have a better relationship." His own apology stung, especially since it took him this long to even say it, and right before asking a favor.

Sophia squinted at George in a way that held a sharp frustration behind them and in a way that made the prince flinch. He knew what he was asking, and he knew he had no right. He couldn't blame her if she thought he was an ass.

"You asked me here," Sophia signed. "So say whatever you want."

George could hear the sarcasm even if she was forming the words with simple signs. The prince bowed his head in defeat. "I wanted to ask a few questions about my father." He peeked upwards.

Sophia finally let her weight spill onto the cushions as she sat back and signed. "What do you want to know?"

Chapter 5
Many Years Ago...

Young Sophia stared at the marbled floor of the throne room. Her eyes were frozen wide, as if in shock, and a pink rash had taken them over. With a bowed head, she could only see the shifting of guards in her peripherals to the right, and to her left stood a tall man. From her current vantage point, all she could see was the blade strapped to his hip. It was a simple cross hilted sword with burn marks wisped across the steel but more curiously and noticeably, the sword itself was welded shut in its blackened metal scabbard.

Reginald's voice came from above the scabbard and out of view. "Esmachus managed to slip away."

A low thinking hum came from the emperor until finally, Wilhelm spoke. "Is this the only survivor?"

"Of my knowledge, sir," Reginald sounded defeated. Another hum.

"What do you know of Esmachus?" The empress' voice called out. Sophia lifted her head, eyes immediately catching the paired stare of both Wilhelm and his wife, the real Sophia. Her black hair was threaded with gold, and a crown rested neatly on top, giving her a nearly untouchable divinity when paired with her flowing purple robes. Her icy blue stare seemed to bore through the young woman's own shock, capturing young Sophia's attention in its entirety. Forgetting her own ailment, the younger Sophia opened her empty, knife-scarred mouth.

"I'm sorry, empress." Reginald stepped forward. "Her tongue, you see?"

Young Sophia quickly closed her mouth and pitied looks came from both Wilhelm and the Empress. Wilhelm sat forward in his throne. "Do you know your letters?"

A nod.

"We will fetch you ink and paper." Wilhelm sat back.

***

Emperor Frederick's old drawing room was seldom used anymore, but its quiet atmosphere and out of the way location was perfect for the task at hand. Inside, vegetation had just started to overgrow the outside of the thin windows, choking most of the sun from entering the cold room. Despite this, Wilhelm had sat young Sophia beside himself at the desk that, in turn, sat between two mighty bookshelves. Both Wilhelm and his guest peered over the same piece of paper with ink and pen in Sophia's hand. Already on the paper, young Sophia had written a single word.

"Your name is Cassandra?" Wilhelm looked up at the young woman. Cassandra nodded. Wilhelm smiled, lines wrinkling his cheeks.

"We are happy to have you here, Cassandra. I hope you don't mind if I ask you a few more questions? Afterwards, what you want to do will be your own choice."

Cassandra quickly jotted something down on the paper. "I don't mind."

Wilhelm smiled again and turned to face Cassandra completely. "Do you know who Esmachus is?"

Pen scratched paper. "A bad man—a nachtist."

A wince played in Wilhelm's eye, as if hurt by the accusation. Even so, he nodded in agreement. "Why did he kidnap you and the others?"

At this, Cassandra grew pensive and opted to look down at the floor in thought. Her brow knitted as she tried her best to remember through the fear she felt back then, to piece together the cryptic words of Esmachus. She could hear his voice echoing off the wet stone walls, his laughter, his sobbing. Now and then his mumbles made their way to her ears, and as much as she didn't want to remember the contents, she did her best to do so for Wilhelm.

Wilhelm watched as Cassandra carefully wrote her answer, and when she was done, she gently slid the paper over for Wilhelm to read. The emperor's eyes scanned the words, as few as there were and bit his cheek.

"He thought you all were long branching descendants of the Imperial line?" Wilhelm stumbled over his next question before finally asking "Why? Why did he want that?"

Cassandra was quick to answer, cutting the inky response into one of the blank sections of the paper. "He wanted our blood. Now and again he'd take one of us and bring us out into the Imperial woods. He'd always come back alone, angrier than before."

The emperor slumped back into his chair, a disturbed look on his face as he clearly tried to piece the puzzle together. Rubbing his chin, he looked away from Cassandra and towards the window. Suddenly feeling like she caused more questions than answered them, Cassandra flipped the paper over and quickly wrote something new. This piqued Wilhelm's interest as he read the words with an arched brow.

"He wanted to find a 'solution' before the 'Cursed One' came."

***

After that, Cassandra wasn't questioned much anymore. She wasn't sure if she had given the right answers or not, but Wilhelm seemed satisfied with the information she gave and furthermore allowed her to remain in the palace as long as she chose. Eventually it occurred to her that she didn't want to leave since she no longer had anywhere else to go, and found comfort in the safety the palace naturally gave. Additionally, she took well to the Imperial family and found a lot of joy in the company of Reginald, so she elected to be employed by the palace directly and become a personal assistant to the Heinrichs themselves.

One of the duties that came with being a personal assistant to the family, or at least they claimed it was a duty in jest, was spending time with them now and again. In particular, Empress Sophia took a liking to Cassandra and so the new servant girl often found herself being summoned by the empress, not that she minded. If nothing else, Sophia quickly became an idol of Cassandra's, a good example and a paragon to strive for. Almost coincidentally, they even looked alike, as if mother and daughter, save for Sophia's blue eyes contrasted to Cassandra's black.

These exact thoughts were going through Cassandra's mind as Sophia stared at her with a whimsical smile across a chess board. The only sound that interrupted the thinking now and again was a loud bang in the room upstairs where the brothers Wilhelm and Caleb were practicing their 'echo' Stromism (as they always did once or twice a week). But down in the chess parlor, Empress Sophia had once again put Cassandra's pieces in a difficult position. The longer Cassandra stared at her doomed pieces, the more Sophia's smile curled. Finally Cassandra shook her head and signed with her fingers. "There's nothing I can do."

Sophia knitted her brow, as she usually does before a lecture. "Well you have to try something, you can't just accept defeat before the game is even over. Anything is better than nothing."

Cassandra tucked a determined grin into her cheek and leaned forward, eyes almost level with the board as she looked from her piece's perspective. She could hear a humming laugh in Sophia's throat as she did, which, admirably, Cassandra was fishing for. At last, Cassandra figured she found a good enough solution, that might at least prolong her survival. Pinching her rook, she moved it accordingly, soliciting a proud nod from Sophia.

"See? Now wouldn't you have seemed foolish if you gave up before?"

Two hand signs. "Yeah, yeah"

Unexpectedly, there was a gentle knock against the door that closed the pair off from the rest of the palace. They were sitting in a very open parlor with large windows to allow the delights of the garden to be viewed and even felt since the glass was adjustable on metal frames and swivels. To match the very mobile windows, the door to the room was very thin and easily moved, making any knock sound gentle, but in this case, the knock sounded even smaller as if performed by the tiniest hand.

A knowing look found Sophia's face as she looked over at Cassandra, attempting to share the knowledge through a simple nod before turning to the door. "Oh who is it?" The Empress called out in a sing-song voice that would have been mocking to any adult.

The door opened, and there stood one of the palace nurses holding the infant Josephine. Her small palm was held out, clueing who had tapped the door and while the nurse held an amused grin, her eyes were laced with concern. Sophia seemed to have quickly picked up on the concern.

"What's the matter?" She asked with her arms outstretched. The nurse gently placed Josephine into her waiting embrace before furrowing her brows.

"She has a little bit of a sniffle," the Nurse said. "I don't think it's much, but with what's going on in the city, I thought it best to tell you."

Cassandra watched as Sophia gently stroked Josephine's cheeks, looking down at her daughter with worried eyes. "You're probably right, it's likely nothing."

Sophia looked up to meet Cassandra's eyes. "Cassandra." The servant girl gave a slight tilt of her head and Sophia continued, "you don't mind if we finish our game tomorrow, do you? I..."

Cassandra shook her head before Sophia could even finish and frantically signed. "No, no, it's okay. I completely understand, your highness."

A relieved smile cut across the worried empress' face. "Good. Thank you."

***

Loud, angry shouts and grumbles pounded through a thick wooden door. Cassandra sat on the other side, in the hallway. She found herself on a simple bench-style seat with a folded chessboard in her lap and a worried look on her face. Something slammed against the wall, causing the servant girl to flinch in place. She could hear Wilhelm barking something behind the door while Sophia yelled something back.

The door swung open and a short man with a bushy black mustache and sleepy dark eyes came scurrying out. He wore the robes of the sages and Cassandra recognized him as Father Sage Demitri. With the door open, Cassandra could see into Josephine's nursery, the small child wailing between loud hacking coughs. Caleb stood next to the crib with a worried look on his face and his arms crossed. Sophia stood staring daggers at Wilhelm, who in turn was rushing after the doctor.

Wilhelm's hand shot out and grabbed Demitri's shoulder, yanking him backwards. Demitri slapped at Wilhelm's grip before spinning around. Anger foamed at his mouth. "This is most unbecoming!"

Wilhelm's face twisted with rage and his voice caused more than Demitri to cower. "Use your magic!"

"It won't work!' Demitri's voice was more of a squeak now.

"Wilhelm!" Sophia growled from behind the emperor.

The emperor ignored her, standing tall over the sage. "You haven't even tried!"

"Mist-talking can't cure scarlet lung." Demitri straightened out.

"You don't even know if it—"

"Oh I know!" Demitri said. "She has scarlet lung. How many ways do I need to say it? Josephine has scarlet lung. Your child has scarlet lung!"

"Bastard!" Wilhelm pulled back a hand, but Sophia caught it. Caleb's voice came from behind the scene.

"Brother..."

Everything fell silent. Cassandra sat in between the emperor and the doctor. Her back was pressed against the wall and her knees wrenched against her chest, as if every inch away from the scene counted. The chess board was pinched between her legs and stomach, the pieces starting to spill out and clatter to the tiled floor.

Wilhelm shot a look at Cassandra and all the other eyes followed. Cassandra stared back with the wild look of a doe. Furrowing his brow, Wilhelm turned to Demitri, his voice calmer. "Can you at least try."

Demitri rolled his jaw in thought before tugging his robes straight. "Very well."

"See?" Sophia put a hand on Wilhelm's shoulder. "No need to be rash." She hiccuped on the final word, as if stuffing a sneeze down into her lungs. Wilhelm looked over at her curiously and the woman hiccuped again, but this time it came out as a cough. Everyone watched as Sophia buckled forward, her cough turning more and more hoarse. No one looked surprised, but a deep dread was in Wilhelm's eyes.

***

Caleb's little hideaway in the far tower was glittered with colored sunlight. The prismatic glass of the windows broke the light over

Cassandra as she sat on an old couch that dominated the center of the room. What was once a barren spot for the prince to escape had quickly become a proper study. Only a few days ago Caleb had several bookshelves put in as well as a new desk, but even still, Cassandra preferred the old couch.

Her nose was stuffed between the pages of a book about medicinal herbs and anecdotal remedies for everything from cavities to the common cold. As her eyes scanned the words, she could feel Caleb staring at her from his new desk. Eventually the stare became too much and Cassandra lifted her head to give him a dirty look back as if to say, "what?"

"There's nothing in that one, I already checked," Caleb said. Cassandra doubled down on her look and dropped the book on her lap.

She signed. "Maybe you missed something."

"I didn't."

"Maybe you did."

"I didn't!" Caleb didn't quite yell, but his voice turned stern enough for Cassandra to pause. She never really heard Caleb upset before and as much as the whole situation had been weighing on her, and definitely on Wilhelm, she never accounted for how much it weighed on Caleb.

Cassandra could feel her face soften and by some magic, it softened Caleb's in return. The man returned to his usual look of thoughtfulness and closed his eyes. "I'm sorry."

"It's..." Cassandra paused, her sign in the air. She shook the sign from her fingers and picked up the book. With a loud slam, she dropped it on the low table that sat in front of the couch, provoking a jump from Caleb and forcing his eyes wide open. With the prince looking at her again, she continued with her signs. "It's okay, this isn't easy."

Caleb shot a laugh through his nostrils. "We don't have much of a choice but to get through it together."

A knock on the door turned both their heads to it. The prince's look of confidence drained back to a nervousness that didn't suit him. "Come in."

The door creaked open and Reginald came walking in. He wore a macabre visage and a sad frown that put a pit in Cassandra's stomach. Caleb was almost blue as he asked. "What is it?"

"I think it would be best if Wilhelm told you," was all Reginald said before pulling the door wide and beckoning for the pair to exit with him. Caleb slowly stood up and walked over and as he passed Reginald he spoke in a low voice.

"She isn't..? No, she isn't d... no?"

Reginald pursed his lips and closed his eyes. "I think it best, Prince Caleb, if Wilhelm tells you."
This just deepened the pit in Cassandra's stomach. She couldn't keep the adrenaline out of her legs which shook at the knees while she walked over to the door. As she approached, Cassandra noticed she wasn't the only one shaking. Caleb was starting to crack as he put his first few steps in on the stairs downward. His fists clenched and his shoulders hunched. Reginald let Cassandra step by before closing the door behind them all.

With each step, Cassandra could see Caleb shaking more and more, until a golden shimmer appeared around his legs. She reached out to touch his shoulder and Reginald called out from behind. "Master Caleb."

But it was too late, golden magic exploded in waves around

Caleb's legs and with a blast of wind, he turned into a blur, and his Stromism sent him down the stairs with a crack of sound. The force blew Cassandra backwards into Reginald, who in turn was pushed back. The pair found their balance and shared a worried look.

After that, all bets were off, and Cassandra herself sprinted through the winding halls, with Reginald sprinting after her. She was surprised initially at the older man's stamina, but having seen him in action so many years ago, that quickly subsided. What didn't subside was the sickening dread that bubbled in her gut and sent chills to her limbs. Even the pumping heat of her run couldn't banish the cling of death she was feeling as she ran ever closer to her destination. Each guard she passed wore a depressed face, and even the paintings and sculptures seemed to be mourning as they approached.

But as Cassandra cut the corner and fell upon the scene, she felt confusion swell. Wilhelm was laughing. Light from Josephine and Sophia's room spilled out into the hallway—the door was wide open. Wilhelm's shadow was painted on the floor and Josephine giggled in his hands as he held her high. Caleb stood leaning against the doorframe, a pale and horrified look in his eyes that further bothered Cassandra. Demitri was there too, sitting on the bench across from the room with his wrinkled head held in his hands and an indiscernible mutter on his lips.

Cassandra cautioned a step forward; a thick evil was in the air. She could see into the room proper now, and by all means it should have been a happy scene. Sophia was sitting up with a grin on her face, looking at her bouncing baby and husband, but something was wrong. There was no sign that Sophia was ever sick. The color was in her face, and Josephine was energetic and happy. Any smell of disease had left the room, and was replaced with a sinister burning scent, as if someone flooded the area with smoke, if just for an instant. The servant girl's nostrils flared, she recognized that smell.

She froze. Smoke was leaking from under Sophia's eyes. It was just a wisp, just a small flicker and in a moment it was gone again. With horrified eyes Cassandra looked over at Wilhelm, the man full of bliss. A scuff. Cassandra spun around to see Reginald. The old man was standing there with confusion on his face. Behind him Demitri was already missing and Caleb was staring hard at Reginald.

"What happened here?" Reginald asked what everyone was thinking.

"A miracle!" Wilhelm answered with a laugh.

Reginald's face twisted with an anger Cassandra had never seen. "What happened here!?"

***

"What *did* happen there?" George asked. His question pulled Cassandra from her story. The two were still sitting in Caleb's study, though knowing the origin of the area put a bleak color over the entire place that George couldn't help but feel deep inside of him. He very much sat in the same spot Cassandra once did when she had argued with his uncle.

The servant shook her head and signed. "I was never told, but there you have it. Your mother and sister survived the scarlet lung."
"And the day my mother actually did die?" George insisted, unsure if he really wanted to know.

"Up in the sparring room, your uncle and father were practicing their echo Stromism and I was below with your mother playing chess. Your mother won and decided to go check in on the two. I stayed down below to wait for her to return. Moments later, Caleb was coming down to see if I wanted to join him for lunch as apparently your father and mother wanted to discuss something alone." Cassandra turned to look at one of the stained glass windows and squinted in thought.

"And then?"

"And then I heard the scream, same as anyone else near the gardens. She fell—I heard that too—how quickly it ended the scream. Reginald was faster than the rest of us after that but Wilhelm was the second fastest. Reginald stole a sword from a shocked guard and next thing anyone knew, he had cut you from your mother's womb." Cassandra didn't turn to look back at George.
The prince repositioned himself to directly face her, his eyes peering at the back of her head. "How did she fall?" She didn't respond and George frowned before clearing his throat. Cassandra turned back to face him, flinching at the seriousness that saturated George's stare. The prince asked again, "How did she fall?

"I don't know."

"What does my father say?" George asked, his voice firm. Cassandra flinched.

"I-" Cassandra hesitated before signing. "I don't know."

"Soph- Cassandra!"

"I don't know!" Cassandra signed frantically and stood up, her fingers flying into symbols. "I don't know, I don't know and I don't want to think about it!"

George bit his tongue and swore internally. He was too heavy handed; he was being a brat once again. Smoke pumped in his stomach and he could feel the heat of anger, but he didn't know who it was aimed at. His fingertips stained red for a moment and smoke swirled around them as he looked at Cassandra. He opened his mouth, he wanted to ask her, he wanted to say it, but he froze, mouth open. He couldn't ask her to tell him, he already forced so much, but he needed to know. Inside of him a heat and a cold fought, and he closed his eyes.

The world was shut away behind his eyelids as he stood there. His ears were open though, and he could hear Cassandra walking away. He couldn't blame her nor would he stop her. George's mind swirled as she left and as soon as the door shut behind her and her footsteps were on the stone stairs below, he opened his eyes and said quietly to the empty room.

"Did my father kill my mother?"

Chapter 6
Arrivals

Cassandra never said, but to George's surprise, she did wait for him at the bottom of the stairs, though a certain doubt and hesitancy remained in her eyes. She wouldn't say, even if she knew, but an air between the two pressured them both to consider it. It was a heavy silence, and not knowing how to dispel it, they didn't say anything further about Wilhelm. George apologized for his outburst, knowing it was best if it never had happened to begin with, but Cassandra put a halt to his words, showing a level of forgiveness and consideration that George might have taken for granted as a child. After that, she simply said he was definitely Caleb's nephew and then politely excused herself.

George watched her leave for a moment before calling out, "If you need anything, I'll do my best!" Cassandra turned to look at him, already a few steps away. She gave him a soft smile and signed.

"You have enough to do, don't you?" Her footsteps continued and George couldn't help but think that this was at least a step forward in their relationship; If only it wasn't marred by a devious question hanging over his head. The prince looked down at his boots and sucked in a deep breath.

"I hope Rosaline isn't bored..." He chewed his cheek but when he raised his chin, he was face to face with a palace guard. She had a serious look about her face, and a single piece of information: Gennisberg had arrived.

***

Frustration painted over George's earlier somberness until it boiled to a simmering anger. The prince's boots echoed down the halls and a million questions boiling down to two: why was Gennisberg here and who invited him? The thought of Clement or maybe some other unknown traitor only provoked his easy anger and before long he could feel the smoke twisting in his gut again.

George gritted his teeth and looked down at his clenching fist, his knuckles white but his fingers stained red. He could feel a pulse across his hand—the pull of the smokeform. Sucking in a breath, George then slowly released it through his nostrils, only for a stream of smoky wisps to ride out on his breath; this was getting dangerous.

Another breath and George was shoving his hands into his pockets. Inside he rolled his wooden raindrop between his fingers; he just needed to keep breathing. A minute passed and he was standing outside the door of one of the eastern parlors. He closed his eyes and breathed away the last of the churning smoke from his gut. He slipped his fingers free from his bauble and then with a push, he opened the door.

"Prince George!" A wide smile greeted him. Its owner was a tall man with falling curls that complimented his brown complexion and framed dangerously intelligent eyes. He looked every bit the image of a Barcenaean noble: with a red tunic trimmed white and equally white pants tucked into some of the finest leather boots George ever saw, even as an Imperial prince. Already in the room sat Williams with a strained smile. George could only offer the knight a 'what are you doing here' look that was deflected with a glance at the tall man—Count Gennisberg.

The room itself was typical of the palace parlors; lightly decorated in favor of wide windows to showcase the neighboring gardens. Furniture in the room was either colored white or a soft cream, and was constructed of woven wood and thick cushions. Sunlight found its way in easily, filtering through the late spring leaves and casting a mosaic of gold across the group.

George didn't even get a chance to respond to Gennisberg before the man continued. "You know," he said, "I have to say: I'm very impressed with your retainer here. Why, he was so attentive to wait with me while the help went off to fetch you and your sister—" He bit his cheek and deepened his smile. "Pardon me, I meant to say *her highness.*"

Both Williams and George strained a smile at this, but before they could say anything further, someone knocked on the open door. Reginald walked in, standing tall, and took measures to not look at anyone in particular as he announced: "Emperor Wilhelm of the Mortal Empire."

Reginald stepped off to the side and George's father came marching through. The Emperor was drowning in purple robes topped with a crooked crown and a wild nest of golden hair. A surprisingly imperious look was on his face as he took in the contents of the parlor and an air of authority for once seemed to emanate from him.

Gennisberg quickly fell to one knee and put one hand over his heart while he held out the other palm face up. He tipped his head humbly. "My Emperor."

Wilhelm's composure broke as he rolled his eyes. "Graces... Reginald, why is there a beggar in my parlor?"

George and Williams cracked a childish grin and Reginald stifled for a moment.

"My liege," Reginald started, "that is Count Gennisberg."

"Well tell him to get a job," Wilhelm grumbled back before flashing a sorry grin at the confused count.

"Erm." Gennisburg scrambled back to his feet and straightened out his trousers. Both embarrassment and frustration stuck on his face as he attempted a smile. "I beg your pardon, sire, but as your head steward alluded to, I'm Count Gennisberg."

Wilhelm raised a brow but said nothing.

"I'm here to accept Regent Josephine's offer of marriage?"

Wilhelm looked to his son. George stood up.

"Josephine has made no such offer," George corrected. "The idea of an arrangement is still under debate."

It was Gennisberg's turn to look confused, and genuinely for once. "Prince George, I assure you that a decision must have been made, or else why would I be here?"

"That's a good question." Josephine's voice came from the door. She stood with her arms crossed and an annoyed look in her eyes. "I just got done visiting with another newly arrived guest who was spouting the same sort of story."

Gennisberg clenched his jaw and his composure faded for a moment. "I'm not the mad one here. I sincerely received notice that the marriage was accepted—everyone in Barcena is talking about it!"

"You seem awfully concerned," Williams piped up from his seat, gaining everyone's attention. "It was a simple mistake, nothing lost coming all this way... unless..."

Josephine eyed the count, who buckled.

"Regent Josephine." Gennisberg stood up straight as if attempting to project some level of confidence. "I mayhaps already hired a few people and arranged a few things for the wedding."

A silence filled the room. Josephine was staring up at the ceiling, breathing softly. Everyone held their breath, save for Wilhelm, each wondering what was passing through the Regent's mind when finally she cracked a cruel grin. "If any of you ever wonder where my stress comes from, look no further than this room." Her smile faded into a startling scowl. Even though it wasn't directly aimed at him, even George felt the sudden urge to profusely apologize to his sister.

If the parlor wasn't small enough already, someone else rushed in through the door. Except this time it was a face George only knew in passing as one of the stewards of the palace. He was puffing out his cheeks, face red with anxiety and exertion. Reginald collected the man with a stiff hand and pulled him straight before asking, "What is it?"

"For the prince." the steward held out a letter. The paper was curled, as if it had been held in a capsule for some time. The steward elaborated as much as he could, "to be delivered with the utmost urgency, as by the advice of Proctor Johanson and Commander Darius of the 11th."

George's eyes widened and a pang of anxiety hit his chest. Why didn't Darius deliver the message personally? The room fell to silence as George unfurled the paper and scanned its contents.

***

George, Josephine, and Williams marched through the halls with urgent purpose. Wilhelm, Reginald and even Gennisberg trained them, but while the former two were in complete silence, Gennisberg was in an uproar.

"Regent, please, we should at the very least finish discussing the marriage before you run off!"

Josephine didn't pay the count any heed, her eyes flickering to her brother as she said, "that letter explains Fenric's absence."

"I'm hoping the proctor who delivered it can explain Darius'," George replied with a worried furrow of his brow.

"I wish I could say I am surprised that Fenric would go to these lengths," Williams added, "but he is a known traitor as it is."

"But open war against the Empire," Josephine bit her lip, "with open support from Nachtists."

"Regent?" Gennisberg jogged closer to the trio. "The wedding?"

Williams shot daggers at the man. "Don't you think there are more important things right now?"

"Well!" Gennisberg was taken aback. "If that's how the capital trains their knights to talk to the nobility..."

"Shut your mouth, Count." Josephine stopped and turned to Gennisberg. Her eyes were blazing as she lifted her chin high. "Williams is absolutely correct, and if you can't see that, then might I suggest dislodging your inflated head from your ass." She looked to Williams and then George before tilting her head and urging them back down the hall.

As they continued their march, Gennisberg stood in place, mouth agape. When Wilhelm and Reginald walked by he simply pleaded, "Emperor..."

Wilhelm cracked a crooked smile before walking past the count, letting loose just a bellowing laugh.

***

With the procession finally inside the palace meeting room, George slammed the mighty door shut. At the bang, a bounce of dust powdered from various ornamental shields and shelves. As dramatic of a flourish it was, it instantly made George sick in his chest and with a regretful grin, he cracked the door back open. Relief of an open egress settled George back into the moment and he looked around.

The interior of the room was exactly what was expected of a meeting room for a palace. It was large, ornately decorated, and centered with such a massive roundtable, with only the table in the dining room surpassing it. Carved in the wood of the table was a map of the Empire and any surrounding islands known to Imperial sources. This carving was then preserved in a fine and striking varnish that allowed the map to pop, no matter the angle the onlooker was taking.

To light the table, the large bow window that sat on one side of the room was fitted with silver mirrors that bounced the sunlight around the room and eventually cast it straight down overhead and onto the map. In total, it was a simple enough yet still impressive little feature, and one of the reasons George had taken a liking to it as a child.

Williams, Josephine and George all took regular seats while Wilhelm sat in the largest chair by the Northern section of the map, as the map designer intended. This was so no matter where you looked, when you looked up from the Empire, you saw the Emperor. The only one who was missing from earlier was Reginald, who had run off to gather the proctor.

"I bet you're all wondering why I gathered you here." Wilhelm steepled his fingers.

"Dad..." Josephine protested and Wilhelm laughed.

"I'm only joking, Josie." A wide smile crinkled the old man's face. His eyes flickered between his daughter and his son, both sitting in front of him with stern and serious faces. "You know," he started. "Despite the circumstances that put us in this room. I am proud of you both."

Josephine's face softened immediately and George couldn't help but feel something in his throat. That was one of the most lucid things his father had ever said to him and his sister. George stooped in his chair a little, suddenly feeling like his father's son rather than a general. He couldn't figure out what to say, with Cassandra's story fresh in his mind and his childhood questions raging, but his heart spoke for him as he felt the words exit his mouth. "I'm proud of you too, dad."

Wilhelm's eyes flickered downwards, and a sheen washed over them. He looked almost guilty, but strangely peaceful. Josephine sat in silence, her mouth slightly agape as George figured the same questions were roaring through her mind. Williams just looked uncomfortable, but no one could blame him.

It all came to a sudden end when Reginald pushed the door open with the proctor by his side. George sat up straight again, Williams adopted a serious and confident look, and Josephine closed her mouth. Only Wilhelm stared at his children for a while longer before looking towards the beat up proctor.

The man had clearly been in battle, with scratches, burns and bruises all over his arms and face. Bandages and the sheen of poultices covered the larger wounds, and his clothes were the same as the palace servants; his own must have been ruined. He immediately saluted Wilhelm, and then Josephine and then finally George.

"Come in, and report," Josephine ordered.

"Your Highnesses," he started, "the investigation into the loyalty of the Gavarian Duke Fenric Von Jornho has concluded." Despite the clear desperation in the man's eyes, his tone was professional, and he kept to his reporting protocol. George couldn't help but admire the man's courage and attention to detail, even in such a high stakes moment. It was a trait shared by most Imperial proctors.

"What is the conclusion?" Josephine said.

"The conclusion is in several parts. Firstly, Duke Fenric is undeniably guilty of stalling his forces during the second battle of Kors deliberately. My late colleague had secured a confession from one of his sergeants, which was later corroborated by two other officers."

George gripped his chair, a silent rage pulsing into his fingers. Of course he already knew this, but that didn't ease the pain. He was starting to get tired of being so angry. "What else," he felt himself asking.

'Second, Duke Fenric is confirmed to be in league with an extreme Nachtist sect that was originally based in Caldora and the Dwembin Isles."

It was Wilhelm's turn to lean forward, a lucid gleam in his eye as the proctor continued. "This sect has joined forces with Fenric and Nachtists present in Gavaria, for what I can only assume is for the third and final conclusion."

Josephine waved a hand. "Go on."

"Duke Fenric is mobilizing his forces, laced with Nachtist soldiers. His allies from Caldora have already aided him in assassinating and displacing any Gavarian nobility that could oppose his regime. Duke Fenric has the intent to commit and has committed treason against the Mortal Empire of Jerrovia."

The room fell silent. Even with the spring air lacing through the open door, the entire room felt stuffy, as if a barrier of thick air hung suspended around everyone. It was heavy, this weight, as if any word said next, or any action performed would decide the fate of this new and precarious position.

Prince George furrowed his brow and sat up straight. "Proctor."

All eyes fell on George.

"What of Commander Darius?"

A silence.

"I don't know, sire. Commander Darius had given up his chance of escape to ensure I made it back safely. We were ambushed by Nachtist forces."

George bit his lip and looked down. "Thank you, proctor."

"We will have to mobilize," Josephine said. "It's unfortunate but this cannot stand. Fenric's little rebellion cannot gain any more traction than it already has. George—"

"I'll go," the prince agreed. He had sat waiting for this report for too long, and paired with a new concern for Darius, George had little doubts on going. He leaned over the table and stuck a finger towards the province of Caldora. "We can enlist the 10th Vanguard out of Caldora and pull any regulars to augment the front."

"We should also try and get in contact with the 11th." Williams leaned in as well. "If Gavaria is under Fenric's sway, I can't imagine they're going to be safe for much longer."

"Reginald." Josephine looked to the old master.

"Yes, Regent?"

"Send word to the 11th, the 10th, and the Caldoran duke immediately. I'm assigning George as the General in Command. Send Stromist sprinters."

Wilhelm sat back in his chair as his children deliberated. Though his eyes were wide and wild, a content smile buzzed on his lips. George saw it out of the corner of his eye, causing him to stall with his words for a moment before understanding what that smile was—it was pride.

***

"I just got here and you're already leaving?" Rosaline crossed her arms. The ex-medic had been enjoying the spring blossoms that were lining one of the pathways, occasionally reading the tiny plaques with the names of which Emperor or Empress commissioned the planting, when George had appeared with Oathkith on his hip.

"It's Fenric," George explained.

"Then it can't be helped." Rosaline shifted her weight and sighed. "But believe it or not, Reginald already gave me the rundown."

"That man moves quick," George all but swore. "I wanted to tell you myself."

Rosaline shrugged. "Well, you're going to have to let me borrow one of your swords because I didn't bring mine with me." George closed his eyes, wincing. Rosaline pinched the bridge of her nose, she knew that face all too well. "You don't expect me to go with you, do you?"

"I had something else in mind."

Rosaline cocked her head. "You've had enough alone time with Williams."

"No!" George put out his hands. "I mean..." He seemed frustrated.

"I know what you mean," Rosaline teased. "But I told you once, I'm not letting you go. At least not without me."

George knitted his brow but before Rosaline could say another word George pulled her towards him and wrapped an arm around her shoulder. They were close, but a serious look was in George's eyes. "Rosaline, are you sure?"

She nodded, "Of course."

George relaxed a little. He pulled her even closer, his words dropping low. "There is one thing, though. Since I'm leaving, I can't protect Josephine from inside the palace."

"Reginald thought of that as well," Rosaline said with a sly grin, betraying that perhaps her conversation with Reginald wasn't such a quick one.

"What is this conspiracy?" George was befuddled. "I'm supposed to be the General here."

"General or not, Reginald and I hashed it out." Rosaline wagged a finger. "Hector is lingering around in case the worst happens but beyond that, the clever old fox has recruited an old friend of his to act as bodyguard in your absence."

"An old friend?" George questioned. Rosaline nodded and kissed his roughly scarred cheek.

"Yes." She turned towards the palace. "Now let's go find myself a sword."

Chapter 7
Amber Eyes

Even with only George, Rosaline, and Williams gone, the palace suddenly seemed a whole lot emptier—or maybe it was because Ai had left with them, much to the custodians' relief. Josephine wouldn't say it outright, but she would miss hearing the tell-tale hoof-falls of the old horse far out of place, if only for the absurdity of it all. This played on her mind as she walked the halls with Hector. The pair had just gotten started their farewells with the others when Rosaline piqued each of their interests before her departure with stories of a forgotten study in the palace.

The hallways were as they always were: brightly lit by large windows and mirrors, and so tightly decorated with artifacts and art, it was a wonder the entire building didn't sink into its foundations. They were cutting through the halls of the first floor, and being the first of the month, it was ripe with the smell of Tagist incense since the sages had done their monthly cleanse of the palace.

Hector wore a confident and buzzing smile as he walked, which was normal for the man. Not much ever seemed to be on his mind, nor did he ever have much worry to express. His calm and collected demeanor directly contrasted that of Josephine, who for once was wearing her nerves outward, the stress of it all chewing a hole into her lip.

"There's nothing to worry about," Hector said stoically. Josephine silently regarded the man, who seemed to regret his intrusion to her thoughts with a polite smile. The regent waved the unsaid concerns away.

Ignoring the fact that she indeed was worried about her brother and boyfriend, Josephine put on a deadpan look. "Are you afraid of me?"

The question knocked Hector into a half step. "Um, excuse me?"

Josephine focused on the way forward. "Ever since you were little, I've noticed you were awfully quiet and careful around me." "I'm generally really quiet," Hector defended, but it was clear in his face, he was embarrassed, he was caught. Josephin could read it in every expression. She split a small grin.

"I suppose I'll have to tell George when he gets back that his dear friend Hector Gregory is indeed human after all." The princess punctuated her sentence with her best impression of humor.

Hector took a moment, then his eyes lit up. "Ah! A joke!" He laughed, it was genuine, though for some reason, it made Josephine feel as if her joke had fallen flat. Eager to capitalize, or maybe to force the feeling of success, the princess held her head high.

"Comedy runs in the family, after all," Josephine trailed a little at the end. Even just mentioning family put her worries back on her mind, a fact that Hector read just as clearly as the first time. The Stromist marshal cleared his throat. "Never has there been a more formidable pair," He all but announced, "if nothing else, George and Williams are harmonies of each other." He quickly doubled. "To say nothing of the Hero Rosaline!"

"Indeed." His words warmed her fears ever so slightly. Josephine gave Hector a glance, eager to keep the topic off the impending war. "But do I sense some Achian or Kafshe ideology with that mention of harmonies?"

"Are you going to tell on me?" Hector smiled. "I'm a Stromist first, Tagist second, or maybe third."

"Don't let Clement hear you say that," Josephine huffed before looking around the ever decorated hallway. "So where is this room Rosaline was on about?"

Hector pinched his chin, clearly looking for the landmarks Rosaline had described to the pair. The man walked a little faster and overtook Josephine as they cut a corner. "It should be right over—oh!"

The Stromist had preemptively extended his hand as he turned the corner to point out a landmark, but as he actually made the turn, his finger jabbed right into the rugged arm of a stone-colored Achian woman. The Achian was clearly just about to take the turn herself and was now blinking down at Hector's finger.

"Princess Josephine." Hector retreated. "I think you might have summoned the mountain to the halls."

"An Achian?" Josephine said in confused disbelief.

The trespasser was wearing loose pants skinned from some unknown beast, tied tight above the ankle. She wasn't wearing any shoes and in fact now that they were looking, she had left a dusting of dirty footprints across the otherwise immaculate marble floors. Her shirt had no sleeves and was trimmed with old white furs dirtied yellow around the collar, giving her something of a scarf that contrasted tangled black hair.

Folding her arms and flashing amber eyes, she spoke. "I am Kafshe, actually."

"How did you get in here?" Josephine said in an incredulous confusion before sputtering, "*Why* are you here?"

"Opane!" Hector connected the dots. "Princess, this is Opane of the North!"

Josephine's eyes widened. "My brother's keeper?"

A humble smile stretched across the older woman's lips. "Please, Regent, he was very much my own 'keeper' as you put it."

"Either way, excuse my rudeness." Josephine shook her head. "And excuse me if I offended you."

"None taken, I'm clearly out of my element here," Opane offered. "But I am glad to have caught you. Your dragon spirit and George' paramour asked that I accompany you until the Prince returns home."

"Dragon spirit?" Hector gave Josephine a look, who returned it with a raised brow of her own.

Opane chewed her cheek. "The old man who protects the halls here? He cleans and teaches!"

"Reginald, the steward?" Josephine cautioned a guess. Opane's eyes lit up.

"Yes! Reginald. He and..."

"Rosaline?" Hectors turn.

"Rosaline," Opane confirmed. "They both are worried about you with the happenings. As I am already up to date on the ins and outs of the issue, they sought me out to help. I owe much to your family, ironic as it is for a Kafshe to admit to a Heinrich, but I am and so I answered their request. Consider me your escort for the time being."

"I won't say no to help." Josephine blinked, still digesting it all. "Allies in the know are all too few in the capital, but how did you get here so quickly?"

"I was already here," Opane said. "I'm afraid the rumors of your wedding were swirling in Alconia and traveled north and west until I also heard the news. I couldn't believe it, myself, as young George insisted you were already soulbound with the golden haired boy."

Josephine flinched and lowered her voice. "Well, glad you're all caught up regardless. Makes me wonder who has been spreading these rumors, though."

"Assumption is dangerous," Hector chimed in his stoic way, "but I have a feeling it is Clement."

A groan escaped Josephine at just the name of that headache of a man. "Opane," she changed the subject, "we were about to go look into a mysterious room, shall you be joining us?"

The kafshe nodded. "As far as I'm concerned, I'm going to stick with you until all is safe." Opane lingered a gaze on Josephine, as if looking inside her. "Though I see you are well balanced already." Josephine cocked a brow at the comment and Opane shook her head. "Lead the way, please."

Together the three continued onward down the opulent hall, all but following the tracks left behind by Opane earlier. It was a relative silence, up until Hector spoke.

"I'm sorry, but you had me curious," He addressed Opane. "You called Reginald our dragon spirit?"

"Ah," Opane flashed a guilty grin. "Think nothing of it. Ever since the dragons died out, there were stories of a dragonchild who was favored by the last spirit of the last dragon. Your Reginald has spirits about him that just made me think that perhaps he was said child—not to mention his rather warm Altar of Harmony."

Josephine shot a breath through her nose, now that Opane mentioned the story of the Dragonchild, it all made sense. Growing up in the palace she was more than aware of the stories, and putting on her best Reginald voice, she did her best to relay a summary. "An old Alconian legend, the Dragonchild was a folk hero from the eastern mountains. Supposedly, he was raised by Jerrovia's last dragon, only to get stuck in a tragic mess of fate." Her eyes flickered to Opane. "Our Reginald, yes? He'd have to be quite old though."

Opane smiled, perhaps impressed by the regent's knowledge. "I suppose so. Thank you for indulging my creative curiosity, at the very least. I am a fan of stories, and retain many of my own from the People of the Stone."

"Care to tell me one?" Josephine was definitely welcoming the distraction.

"I could, or perhaps Hector has something to show both of us." Opane had stopped walking, her hand pointing at the Stromist Marshal who was about to press a hand against the face of the study door.

"Also good," Josephine admitted.

Hector looked over his shoulder. "Then here we go, my regent." The man threw the door open.

Despite Rosaline's testimony putting her in the study only hours earlier, the old mildew smell was still rank, and spun around the room with the wafting air let in from the hallway. The thick air stung Josephine's eyes briefly as she adjusted to the mote filled air and she watched the light attempt to filter in through the vine-covered windows.

"Graces..." Josephine said, "I'll have to talk to the custodians about this one."

"Just don't be too rough with them," Hector concluded, "I bet they see so many doors a day that it is hard to tell them apart."

Opane walked in past the two and folded her arms. "Quite a peculiar space." Her eyes trailed up, and Josephine followed the amber gaze until it rested on the face of the woman in the painting.

"Ah, my Great Grandmother, The Golden Empress," Josephine tucked a slant into her cheek. "An untouchable woman. Some say we have very similar faces, but I never could see it."

The other two bit their tongues.

"I suppose it makes sense her portrait is here," Hector said, "Rosaline did mention she found writings here by your grandfather Emperor Frederick. Perhaps he wanted to show respect to his mother."

"The Golden Empress," Opane aired to no one in particular, "to imagine the Bloody Emperor was her son."

Gliding her fingers across the old spines of the books shelved on the dusty old furniture, Josephine gave a thoughtful hum. "A controversial man, to be sure."

Hector caught his words, but the look on even the Marshal's face betrayed his true feelings about the man. Opane's distaste wasn't as well hidden, being ever present in her reflective eyes.

Josephine gave a grim, if apologetic smile. "He was a madman."

Opane relaxed. "Perhaps that is why his room was abandoned, no?"

"I'm not sure."

The Kafshe thumbed a book from the shelf and cracked it open. Josephine looked over; the pages were yellow and dusty. As Opane flipped through the pages at random she asked, as if she was testing the princess, "do you know what drove him to ignite his war?"

Finding a book of her own to peruse—a small book with a rough green cover—Josephine thought about the question. "I never met him, so it's hard to say for sure." She opened the book, finding maps of the Dwembin Isles and its major settlements.

"Surely you must at least have a guess?" Opane closed her book with a clap. "No one just starts a war that ignites the entire empire for no good reason." The Kafshe's eyes dug into Josephine. The princess hesitated, Opane wasn't testing her, this was about the Dweller's war. Could both Emperor Frederick's Northern war and the recent Northern war have been connected? It made sense.

"Hm." Josephine chewed her cheek. "I have no doubts the reason Frederick publicly gave was true, though. He wanted to unite the entire mortal empire and finally secure the allegiance of the Ulmi and outliers in the Isles."

Opane put the book back. "But he never went after the Achians, or the Paleskins, just the North."

Gently putting the book of maps onto the desk nearby, Josephine sank into the dusty chair. A plume of dirty air puffed upwards which caused her eyes to water ever so slightly and her nose to wrinkle. The thick atmosphere of the study was definitely more apparent in the embrace of its ancient furniture. "I'm not sure."

Hector was frozen, eyes flickering as if calculating. "I have a thought."

"Oh?"

"If Wilhelm's recent Gavarian war was just a symptom of a greater plan, and Frederick's Great Northern War was partially responsible for setting the stage for it, what if it too was just another peg in the plan?"

Josephine's face softened into contemplation. "I was just thinking that, but could the plot really be that old?"

"If it's the Dweller, it could be," Hector suggested. "She's been banished into the void since time immemorial—she has nothing but time."

"The old stories say she was banished by the Graces for her chaotic behavior and sinister ways of granting power; an enemy of order," Josephine recounted, "So why then, would the Graces only recently work in conjunction with her? Why send their magic to aid her agents in the north? I suppose it could be as George hinted at, that perhaps both parties are trapped in the void. But then how would she have been responsible for my Grandfather's decision of conquest. Or even, why do both parties want my brother dead? Or how does any of this release anything from the Void? We are missing a piece."

Without standing up Josephine grabbed an old book on the bottom shelf that was clearly a sketchbook, and placed it on the regal desk that sat by the shelves. She flipped through the book until the first blank page, now mottled with age, and then roughly opened one of the desk drawers, the old wood protesting with a sharp creak. She rummaged through the drawer, doing her best to ignore the disgustingly moldy smell she was summoning. With equally wrinkled noses, both Opane and Hector peered over her shoulder, steeped in curiosity.

Snatching an old piece of charcoal, Josephine let out an "a-ha!" and then pushed its point against the paper. "Here's what we do know," She said smartly, "the Dweller used dreams to provoke the

Ulmi peoples and Titanspoke-worshiping giants into a war with Gavaria, and used the paranoia rooted from my grandfather's old wars of annihilation and conquest to fan the flames. During this, the agents of the Graces, our own sages, pushed to get my brother up north..." She fell silent as she started to scribble the rest of the story down. Running out of room, she flipped the page, only to be met with a wonderfully illustrated drawing of the old elm tree out in the gardens, this gave Josephine pause.

"Oh, yeah, your grandfather loved sketching that tree," Hector commented, "Rosaline did say found plenty of tree pictures of it in his sketchbooks." While the Marshal was talking, Josephine was wincing in pain, her eyes glued to the page. Golden runes fluttered around the tree, dancing on the paper and conjuring an extreme and piercing sound into her ears. The deafening ringing rattled her brain with pain.

"L-letters," Josephine managed, tears forming in her eyes from the strangling pain. "So many letters."

Hector panicked. "What? I don't see anything? Princess!?"

Opane put a hand on the princess. "Are you alright?"

Josephine's brow knit, the screech ripping her mind's eye into a flurry of red. The words hurt, the letters hurt, yet they danced all the same. The sound was getting louder, and louder, and just as it seemed it couldn't get any louder, Hector suddenly slammed the book closed. Josephine let out a breath she didn't know she was holding and slumped forward in her chair.

"What happened?" The man was worried. "Your nose!"

Droplets of red splattered onto the desk's surface. Josephine could hear the man, but it was coming in muffled, her head pounding with whiplash. She could feel the warm drips coming from her nostril, and a wetness under her eyes. Her heart was pounding, and her fingers were numb. Closing her eyes, Josephine sucked in a huge gulp of air and did her best to sit back upright. She looked over at the other two, who looked back with worried expressions.

"Regent?" Opane asked slowly.

"I can't remember what the words said." Josephine muttered, in disbelief.

"What words?"

"There were words on the page."

"No," Opane shook her head, amber eyes wide, "there weren't."

Chapter 8
Uncle Caleb

Caleb's cabin was a salty wooden box lit gold with candles and decorated with loose papers and bookmarked tomes of many colors and persuasions. The sound of the open ocean lapped outside his small, yet illuminating window, and the deep scent of tea and ocean air swirled all around his abode. He himself sat in a rickety chair that creaked with the planks and the sway of the ship. In front of him, on a desk whitened by sea wind, was a familiar journal, and next to that was a book he had secured from a hidden vault in Alconia. He wasn't alone, as a Stenling woman stood leaning against the wall.

Like all Stenlings, she had brilliant red hair that contrasted a copperish skin-tone, and also like all Stenlings, she had a sixth digit on each of her hands—it perhaps nature's way of showcasing their natural talent for craftsmanship—as well as strange natural markings that tattooed her face and exposed skin. She was dressed similarly to Caleb, with both of them wrapped in thick grey cloaks, stiff with wax to fight off the soaking sea winds, and dense pants and boots of similar stormy colors to match.

Nothing about Caleb other than his signet ring and high quality boots marked him as a noble. And as he intently stared down at the pages of his manuscripts, it would be more likely someone might guess he was a frustrated scholar rather than a prince.

"Victor Heinrich fought the Vagrants, not to conquer them and build an empire, but because the empire already existed, and the Vagrants had rebelled in a civil war. IAO was his key to victory." Caleb bit his lip.

Asharah, the Stenling, snorted. "I know, Caleb, you've been spouting the same story all trip. I didn't get you those books for you to turn into a parrot."

"I'm just trying to piece it together. Why was IAO such a key figure in this?"

"Caleb... really? They guy was an absolute legend, he invented Stromism."

The prince frowned, not content with the answer. "I know, but something doesn't sit right. Why did it need to go that far to win against the Vagrants, how were they so powerful."

Asharah winced. "Maybe you're giving the ancient Imperial army too much credit. I mean, even the modern army struggled in the war against them."

Shooting a hot breath through his nose, Caleb scoffed. "They had help."

"Who is to say they didn't have help back then?" Asharah wagged a finger.

"You don't think..." Caleb cocked his head to the side. "The Graces helped them out back then as well, do you?" Before Asharah could answer, Caleb's frown deepened. "No, that makes no sense: why would the Graces, who benefit from the Empire, support the Vagrants, who threatened to disrupt their priesthood and grasp of control over Jerrovia if they took over?"

"Why'd they do it now?" Asharah countered.

At that question, there was a knock at the cabin door. Asharah pushed off from the wall to stand up straight. Caleb fixed his posture. "Yes?"

Without answering, the door swung open, letting in a dreary draft laced with salt. Stepping in was a tall woman with silvering brown hair, the same grey cloak as Caleb, and even fancier boots than the prince himself. On her hip she wore a long and slender blade enclosed in a black scabbard with gold etching along the side that read 'serpent'. She was removing her rough leather gloves and flexing her frozen fingers as she walked in. "I'm afraid, dear cousin, that the sun is starting to leave us for the day." Her voice was smooth and dappled with the lilt of nobility.

Caleb immediately put on a smile and relaxed. "Catherine. We were just discussing this and that, you know how it is: theories and conjecture that would make Clement's face red."

Catherine rolled her eyes. "I didn't snag you the best ship in Embla so you could pretend it was your study. The others are wondering if the Prince Regent still exists, and I think it would do the sailors good to see you again. I don't like their grumbling."

Caleb opened his mouth to say "I know," but Catherine cut him off with a pointed finger.

"Now I did warn you that sailors aren't exactly fond of wild goose chases."

Asharah smirked at this. "And yet, we have a crew and a boat."

Catherine gave the pair a snake's smile. "Well, I couldn't let Caleb have all the fun." She stood up perfectly straight and nodded towards the door. "Now come."

Stepping out from the cabin and into the ocean air was a slap in the face. Going from the stuffy salt-laden room to biting gusts of afternoon wind definitely woke the Prince Regent up. Caleb pulled his cloak tighter against himself as he made his way across the ship's deck, his footfalls deafened by the sound of rippling waves. All around him was the color grey, from the cloaks of the sailors, to the sky and even the water itself. It was a storm without the storm, but that didn't stop a sour mood from emanating from the crew.

As Caleb walked the deck, the sailors turned to look at him. Most were from Franla or Embla, with chestnut or black hair cut short and salted tan faces. A couple Stenlings also manned the ropes, giving Asharah a nod or two as she strolled with the Prince. Everyone gave Catherine her captain's due and offered her quick respectful salutes as she led the others. Caleb couldn't help but grin at the authoritative air about her, reminding him a bit of her sister Isabella, if only a lot more benevolent.

Despite his amusement, he couldn't help but feel a sudden dread in his gut. Tucking a frown in his cheek, he looked out to the foaming waters. Something in the air didn't feel right.

"Is everything okay?" Catherine stuffed her elbow into his side.

"The air feels like its shifting." Caleb frowned.

Catherine looked up to the sky and squinted. "I don't feel it."

"Maybe you're overtired," Asharah suggested from Caleb's other side.

"You were up all night." Catherine rubbed her chin and gave the prince a sidelong glance.

"What are you suggesting—a nap?" Caleb gave them both a look.

Thud! Caleb walked right into one of the sailors. The sailor let out a disgruntled yelp, but before he could fall onto the wooden floor, Caleb grabbed the man. Yanking him back to his feet, Caleb let out a quick apology while Catherine pinched the bridge of her nose.

"I'm sorry about that." Caleb brushed a fiber off the gruff sailor's shoulder. The man simply stared at the prince with deep set eyes, neither smiling or frowning. Eventually he let out a grunt and walked off. Caleb furrowed his brow and the feeling in his gut sickened until Asharah's hand gripped his shoulder.

"Maybe a nap would be good," she said.

"That or you could keep walking flat into all of my sailors," Catherine quipped. Caleb cracked a smirk.

"I prefer the nap."

Catherine stabbed a thumb behind her. "Then you know where to go. Consider this walk around to show that you're still alive, a failure."

"I'll get it next time, boss," Caleb saluted, making Catherine pale.

"Caleb! You're gonna make the others think this whole trip was my idea. It's bad-hat to have the regent saluting a countess."

Caleb stretched and let out a long sarcastic yawn. "Words to sleep to."

"Asharah, can you lead the esteemed prince to his cabin and then give him a smack for me?"

Asharah perked a brow. "By all means."

Caleb weighed his head back and forth before giving it a shake. "I'll make it there okay on my own. I have a thought or two I want to work on while I walk."

"All few steps?" Catherine looked over the prince's shoulder to the immediate cabin they only left moments ago.

"A think is a think," Caleb defended. "I'll see you two at dinner, okay?"

Catherine gave a shrug and Asharah mirrored the sentiment. Suddenly feeling the weight of his tiredness, Caleb offered them both a small smile before turning around. Almost immediately he was struck with that heavy feeling from before; a feeling he couldn't quite place. He chewed on his knuckle, definitely not a fun feeling to sleep with.

Either way, it only took a few determined steps filled with nebulous thoughts to put himself back at the entrance to his cabin. Ignoring the confused looks of the sailors he just double passed, he slipped in.

Caleb closed his cabin door and pressed his back against the wood. A swirl of salty wind gusted through the room, running a chill down his back. He let out a sigh and slid down the door until he was sitting. He hadn't truly noticed it before, but he was exhausted. His eyes felt like they were pulsing from staring at words all day and his mind felt bloated and burnt out.

The prince regent let his shoulders drop, having just realized he was clenching them. A lot of weight was on him, as it had been for the past few decades, and now perhaps the only solution he could think of was dependent on finding an island that might not even exist. He closed his eyes. Between the stress of the journey, the anxiety of what could be happening back home and the guilt of leaving his niece and nephew on their own, he didn't even have the energy to go find his cot.

"Remember what's at stake, here," he whispered to himself. "For your brother, for Sophia, for the Empire." He let his head droop. "Just last a while longer..."

***

Caleb jolted from his sleep as the door against his back rattled under his weight. Someone on the other side was trying to push it open. Something felt wrong; Caleb slipped back up the door, keeping his weight against it. The door rattled again, and the prince could feel the caution of whoever was shoving the door was putting into each attempt, as if trying to open the door in silence. The prince frowned and snaked his fingers around the knob of the door.

Another shove came, but Caleb whipped the door open at the same time and a sailor came tumbling through. The thug nearly fell face first onto the ground, yelping in surprise. He held a long thin blade in hand. Caleb didn't need any more hints and before the sailor could figure out what was going on, the prince slammed his elbow into the back of the man's head, sending him to the floor with a crack. Caleb's eyes widened, *what about the others?*

Giving the unconscious assailant one last glance, the prince slipped out onto the deck of the ship. Outside, he was immediately met with the swallowing night sky over an endless ocean. The waves were still high and rippling, with the crash of the water filling what would otherwise be a deadly silent night except for one small detail.

Caleb looked down at his feet; irregular vibrations were seeping up through the planks. Underneath the oppressive sound of the ocean, he could hear metal clanging. "Shit," he hissed between his teeth and broke out into a sprint. His boots slammed against the deck and he made his way to the bulwark door that led below. Outside, no one was manning the sails or wheels, the ship clearly stuck in a circle. Caleb's stomach sank and he clenched his jaw.

Wrapping his fingers around the damp wooden handle of the deckhatch, Caleb yanked it open to be met with the orange glow of down below. Ignoring the ladder altogether, he jumped in. Caleb landed with magic ribbons shimmering around his legs, and his eyes dilating to adjust to the different lighting. Shadows from the room over spilled in, and along with it came the clang of weapons and grunts of fighting. In his current room a blue mist hazed around knee deep off the floor and the bodies of the dead were stuck in time with splurts of blood frozen in air by the magic. Caleb let out a disturbed grunt and pushed through with his magic.

Caleb slipped into the next room but quickly froze. Asharah was wrapped in a wrestling match with one of the larger sailors that worked the ropes, and next to her a few Stenlings were in similar combat with other sailors. Off to the side of the room, Catherine had her sword, the serpent, drawn. Across her way, a sailor stood with a serious look on his face. In his right hand he held a blade made of a crystalline blue that had wisps of mist steaming off of its edge. With every breath, that same mist parted his lips.

Not waiting a single moment longer, Caleb rushed into the room and slammed into the back of the enemy who had Asharah in a hold. The man went flying to the floor and in the corner of his eye, Caleb saw Catherine engage the mist-talker.

Her blade thrust forward, using its length to its advantage, but the mist-talker was quick to slap it away and come swinging in with his own blade. Catherine managed to catch it along the edge of her own. Her eyes widened as the enemy blade grew with each chanting breath, her shoulder struggling.

"Caleb!" Asharah shouted and Caleb was forced to look away. A few other sailors were closing in with swords and knives.

"Why are you doing this?" Caleb growled at the closest sailor, a woman holding a curved blade. He asked, though he knew.

The hate in the woman's eyes and the presence of the mist said everything.

"Shut your mouth, traitor," the woman hissed before slicing at the prince. Caleb juked to the side, his body shimmering with magic. He pushed in close and struck out with a hooked fist. The sailor pulled back in time for his fist to swing past her, but before she could regroup, a blurry image of that same fist came out of thin air and slammed into her jaw. She twisted in pain, and Caleb's other hand came cutting in, his fist ramming into her stomach, only for another mirroring image of his attack to slam in right after with the same force. The sailor buckled from the double blow. Caleb grabbed her sword hand and fit his boot on her knee, and then in one fluid motion he wrenched the weapon free while kicking her to the floor.

Caleb jumped back into a guarding stance, this time with a weapon, but the woman was unconscious. To his right, Asharah had just slammed her head into one of her enemies and stolen their blade and to his left, Catherine had slipped out from under her clash and put distance between herself and the mist-talker.

"Catherine!" Caleb made his presence known but the countess simply grinned.

"Happy to see your echo Stromism is as strong as ever." Catherine dodged a swipe. "Must be all that..." Another swipe and Catherine scowled. She put a false step forward, feigning the mist-talker into a lunge. She lunged forward as well, twisting her body so only her shoulder faced the man. The mist-talker's blade nicked by her neck, but with a shake of Catherine's elbow, the serpent stabbed deep into the man's chest, ripping through and punching out the other side.

The mist-talker gasped wordlessly and Catherine slipped her blade back out, flicking the blood free while her assailant crumpled to the floor. A final breath exited the mist-talker's mouth and his sword dissolved into a plume of blue fog. From Caleb's right, the sound of a knife sliding out from between bone and flesh caught his attention. Turning, he saw Asharah had finished off her assailants. Red ran liquid up to her elbow as she gave the prince an exhausted nod.

"I forget what I was saying," Catherine said. Though she put on an act, there was a shake in her voice and Caleb knew the reason; killing never got easier. "Training with your niece, or something. Bah, it was witty." She complained, she projected.

Caleb shook his head and pushed through the adrenaline of his own. "What happened here?"

Asharah cut in, "We can talk later, we need to secure the ship!"

A nod from Caleb and the regent was focused once more. "Collect the survivors and order them to the top deck, but be careful." He then looked to Catherine, but the countess was already rushing to the ladder. With little else, Caleb rushed behind her.

The pair climbed up the ladder as fast as they could, nearly ripping it from its mounts. When they finally exploded onto the deck above, they were assaulted by a crisp burst of air, reminding them how stuffy it was down below. The metal tinge of blood left their nostrils as it found the salty brine of the ocean instead. Catherine looked this way and that before turning to Caleb.

"Where is everyone?"

"Everyone that's left was probably downstairs." Caleb nudged her shoulder and ran over to the captain's wheel. The spoked circle was stuck in a heavy right turn with a bloodied man laying by it. Feeling guilty, Caleb stepped over him and grabbed the wheel. Immediately he felt the weight of the ocean under the spokes and his knuckles whitened. He strained and grit his teeth, shoulders heaving as he put his weight in straightening the wheel. Finally he found purchase and cranked the wheel straight again.

"Catherine!" He yelled over the sound of the sails filling with air. She ran over and took the wheel from him.

"Find the falcon," Catherine instructed, jutting her chin over to the mounted opticals on the back rail of the ship. The prince expertly brought the lenses to bear and gazed up at the sky, quickly locating the constellation. One or two minutes passed between him and Catherine, and the ship was once again heading due east.

The deck hatch opened and out crawled Asharah with two Stenlings and one sailor from Franla. Catherine's eyes widened and Caleb felt her anxiety as she spoke. "Asharah, tell me there are more coming up."

Asharah looked at her feet, an exhausted pain on her face. "This is all."

Caleb furrowed his brow and fell back against the rail. He ran his hand through his hair and let out a long breath. A moment of silence fell over everyone, with only the whipping sails and rolling water sounding across the deck. This was assassination at its finest; nearly a whole crew of agents. Frustration was welling in the prince regents chest, frustration two decades deep. Caleb had to find the end of this path, he just had to. Too much and too long—Caleb was running out of time and space. Even still, Caleb wasn't a Frederick, he never would be, and so another moment passed and finally Caleb wrenched himself from his woe. He mustered his most confident voice and said, "I don't blame any of you if you want to turn around and head back home."

Silence reigned again and everyone felt it.

A Stenling man, one eye closed and bleeding, stepped forward. "Balls to that, Regent! I won't give those bastards the satisfaction!"

The tired crew all cracked sleepy grins, Caleb included.

"To the east then." He gave Catherine a glance. "Is this enough of a crew?"

"To sail? Yes, to stop sailing? Maybe."

Caleb let more of his weight fall onto the rail. "Let's go find our rock, then..."

Chapter 9
George the General

The last time George found himself marching north through Caldora, he was a runaway hiding behind the real soldiers. This time he was a general leading them. What took weeks back then seemed to take only moments as George marched past the Imperial Forests and through the ancient hills. His mind wasn't stuck on fantasy as it was back then, but rather the wellbeing of not only his friend and mentor Darius, but Gavaria and the 11th.

He even looked different this time around; Five years of age broadened his shoulders—now wrapped in Franklin's tattered red cape—and his face wore the sober look of someone who knew the price of battle. His helmet bore small falcon wings on either side plated in the same gold that decorated his fitted armor. Oathkith was on his hip and Rook was on his back. With his feet firmly planted in the ground of one of the northern hills, the border of Gavaria laid ahead of him.

Williams and Rosaline, his two Lieutenants, stood by his side, looking out over the rolling hills that lead into the northern province. A gentle white fog hung in the dips and valleys of the hills, vestigial of the spring rains that had been showering the region. Behind the pair, the sounds of an army composed of both the 10th vanguard and Caldoran regulars breaking camp were clanking and hammering away.

"No response from the 11th still," Williams said grimly, the words weighing on George's thoughts. The prince furrowed his brow, but before he could say anything, a scratchy voice called out.

"Prince George!"

Both the General and his Lieutenants' eyes snapped forward to one of the hills that laid ahead. A blanket of fog cloaked it in its entirety, all save for a dark figure that stood at the crest. He was a tall man, with snapping black robes. His right arm was bare but his left was completely hidden in his outfit. The man had long shaggy grey hair and a clean shaven face. A massive scar ran along the right side his jaw, or so it seemed at first. In reality, a dark, insidious metal had scabbed over his face, with loose speckles marking other parts. He had the taint often seen on those who have used or been sickened by smoke screaming, but his eyes still seemed sane, or as sane as a smoke-screamer could be—he was a recusant.

George reached for Oathkith and the other two grabbed for their swords as well, but the man held up both hands, revealing his left arm to be little more than lumps of that tainted metal.

"Hold your weapons," he goaded with an irritating smile. "George Heinrich..." He said George's name as if feeling it out. "I have a bit of a deal to make with you." The whole situation turned George's stomach.

"Who are you?" George shouted back.

"An old friend of your dad's!" The man called back, "Esmachus of Dwembin!"

Williams turned to George and whispered. "Do you know that name?"

"He's from Frederick's war," Rosaline whispered back.

George gritted his teeth as Cassandra's story seeped back to the front of his mind. He yelled out, "You're one of the Nachtists!"

Esmachus let out a bellowing laugh. "More on point, I'm *the* Nachtist, *the* Nachtist who has a proposition for you."

"We shouldn't listen to him," Rosaline's grip tightened around her sword.

Williams shifted. "He's already said enough."

George gave them a nod. "Agreed."

"Would you believe me if I said I found a way to avoid any and all further bloodshed?" Esmachus called out to the scheming trio. George hesitated, but it was long enough for Esmachus to continue. "War and battle is senseless. I have a feeling you learned the same when you were last in Gavaria, and I agree. I found a way to avoid it, if you would just listen!"

"No, George," Williams grimaced. George let out a frustrated growl.

"Speak quickly!"

"You're not stupid, George," Esmachus called out. "I'm sure you know what I want. Turn yourself over, and we can avoid any and all bloodshed, now and forever." George frowned and a low growl started from Williams. Before the knight could speak, Esmachus continued, "and Commander Darius can walk free."

Both George and Williams were struck with sudden anxiety, their faces wide with surprise. George roared across the hills, "hand him over!"

"He's playing with you two," Rosaline warned. "Don't fall for his trap."

"You know what I want!" Esmachus called back. Williams slipped away as George took a step forward.

"I already died in a shed along with my doubt!" George yelled. "If you wanted me to hand myself over so simply, you should have come then!"

"Don't be so stubborn!" Esmachus stood tall. "Haven't you thought that maybe I am doing this for the *good* of Jerrovia!?"

George let out a cruel laugh and a burning fire entered his stomach. He pushed forward another step and sucked in a breath. He could see Franklin in the fog, alongside Jonsberg and Lawrence. "For the good of Jerrovia?" George said, "is that why you conceived a war and saw thousands dead? For the greater good? Is that why we are all suffering because of you and your ilk? For some greatness?" George felt the smoke and his voice turned harsh. "You picked violence—a last resort. Is the life of others your currency for peace?"

Esmachus hissed. "George..."

"Is it!?" The general yelled across the hills. He was staring down the man who orchestrated it all; he was the Dweller's primary agent upon this land. The killer, the madman, the murderer and bringer of swords—a life is worthless to such a person. All those eyes that stare at George at night, all those scars in his heart; the smoke curled. "Tell me!" George yelled. "You bastard—tell me these lives are your currency!"

The words ripped across the fog and Esmachus bellowed in return "Yes!" His words were a roar thick with saliva and pain. "And I will spend it!"

"Enough out of you!" Rosaline barked back, taking a step in front of George. The general had never seen her so upset, but he could tell the Nachtist had found her sore spots. "Your words are empty. If you had once cared, that's long since faded into madness!" Rosaline knew what she was saying, more so than George. He watched her eyes. Her words weren't out of pure frustration, they were calculated; it worked.

Esmachus' face twisted for a moment, as if caught off guard. He opened his mouth and shouted, but his words were drowned out by the sudden clank of boots and weapons behind George. Williams was spearheading a group of soldiers. Esmachus swore in the distance before calling out.

"You're dooming everyone, George! Know that!"

George scrunched his nose, but before he could say much else, Esmachus burst into an inky smoke and the wind carried any trace of him far away. The soldiers still continued their charge to the hill just in case, with Williams giving George a look over his shoulder. George met it with one of iron will. It was true that George lost his hesitancy in the north; he lost his doubt and his self loathing. It was replaced with his anger as well as his tenacity. The prince knew Esmachus picked violence and he knew the man did not seek parley; he never did. There was only one choice and that was to get to Jornho and stabilize the area before it all slipped into complete destruction, and regrettably, it had to be by the sword. Beyond that, his attention turned to Rosaline, as her eyes held the glint of something he needed to know.

"I hope he never shows his face again," the Lieutenant was saying. She turned to George. "If he does, promise me you'll never talk to him alone."

Her voice pushed his smoke back down and forced the curl of a grin on the prince's face. Something about her simplified the world. "What do you know about Esmachus?"

"Promise first." The heroine furrowed her brow.

"I promise."

"Promise me again?"

"I promise, I swear," George said lightly. "Tell me about this man, please."

Red flecked brown eyes studied the man's face for a moment. "Esmachus was one of the lesser known heroes of Frederick's war of Annihilation. He fought alongside my father and even your own. That said, he went missing about halfway through the war." The lieutenant chewed her cheek for a moment. "Something about a big defeat and massacre. My father never told me the specifics but it was enough to break Esmachus and he slipped away in the middle of the night. He was sick of the conflict and cyclical nature of war."

"Ironic," George couldn't help but add. Rosaline nodded.

"He was crazy. He *is* crazy. He reappeared once before to my father as the war ended and they ended up in a fight. He couldn't beat my father in a game of swords and he fled, only to ambush him again and again. By the fourth battle, Esmachus disappeared for good, but my father was and is forever looking over his shoulder. He never beat my father with swords, but he scarred his heart." Resaline twisted her lips, her eyes pained at the thought of her father's paranoia, the fuel of her own intense upbringing. "They once were friends, but by the end, Esmachus hated my father as he was a symbol of heroics, the false glory of war. Maybe he saw my father as conflict itself and thought that if he could end him, he could end it all."

"And now Esmachus spearheads his own war," George pondered. "When ending conflict is more precious than life itself, that's madness, isn't it? A war to end war."

"A means to an end, he must suppose." Rosaline sighed. "But to what end, I don't know."

George looked out over the hills. "If that man was to win, I can't imagine an end in which peace reigns."

Rosaline didn't respond. She had a look on her face, one that George knew meant she was lost in her thoughts. Her eyes fell to her weapon and George could feel her frustration. A pacifist with a blade is hardly a calm sight. He draped an arm over her shoulder and pulled her gently against him.

"Leiutenant," he said in his best military voice, "double the nightly patrols and increase the scouts' distance as far as safe. Let's keep distractions far away from our camp."

Rosaline cocked a brow and looked up at her paramour. "I'll let the Commanders know." A small jesting smile. "Mister General Sir."

***

Entering Gavaria proper was exactly what George expected; tall trees and ambushes. The smoke-screamers luckily didn't have enough of a grasp on the region to build a proper field army. This revelation gave George confirmation that the proctors and Commander Darius did manage to get the news of their encampment to the capital earlier than Fenric or Esmachus were hoping. What that meant, however, was that there was no proper army to fight, and instead of pitched battles, the marching 10th vanguard and Caldoran regulars were plagued with the paranoia of smoke-screamer strikes and ambushes behind every bend or hidden in every shadow. The increase in surveillance from George's orders helped, but only to a degree when it came to the slippery Nachtists.

It had only been a handful of days of marching into Gavaria, but between the sudden raids and the incessant spring rain, things were looking more muddy and sleepless than any good general would hope for. One such day was haunting the army as they had just finished digging in for the evening. The soldiers were mottled with mud and sweat, with a select few still sporting old rusty stains of blood from that morning's raid. It was impressive how many Nachtists that Fenric and Esmachus managed to garrison in Gavaria under the Empire's noses, but then again George suspected it was in no short blame of the Sage's growing neglect of their supposed duties. Regardless, the cowardly tactics of the enemy had the military on edge, George included.

He stood with his hands red from setting the palisade for the night and now stared out at the conifer forests of Gavaria. Spring lightning bugs blinked in between the boughs and misting rain, giving the trees menacing eyes all of their own. Williams was beside him and handed him a hot tin cup of pine tea, a poor-man's classic from their days at 'The Nest'. The warm metal brought some life back into George's fingers as he held the steaming beverage under his nose and he took in the evergreen scent.

"You know," Williams started as stared down into his own cup. "Typically, the general doesn't waste their energy setting up the earthworks."

"I needed to clear my head," George said. He took a hasty sip of his tea, regretting it as it burned his tongue and steamed down his throat. He coughed the pain clear and grimaced. "It doesn't hurt morale, either."

"I suppose it doesn't," Williams agreed. The knight blew on his tea for a moment before taking a tiny lap of it. "So what fills your head now?"

George looked at his friend and frowned. "I'm worried about Darius, about how we are going to take Jornho, about the regulars and vanguard of Gavaria."

Williams froze, catching George's attention. The pair looked forward, someone was moving through the trees.

"Esmachus?" Williams whispered. George clenched his jaw and reached out with his Stromism, feeling the vibrations in the air. He took a deep breath and opened his altar of creation to the presence of others. He shook his head.

"There's more than one." He squinted. "Something isn't right." He whipped around and Williams followed suit. There across the tents, those on patrol by the western flank of the earthworks were talking to three soldiers who had just emerged from the trees dressed in the filigree of the 11th. There was a short exchange and then one of George's soldiers broke off towards the prince, likely to tell him the news.

"George?" Williams wrapped his fingers around the hilt of his blade.

"I don't know..." George reached out further with his Stromism and stepped closer to the growing scene. Soldiers were starting to crowd with gossip.

"The 11th is alive...?" One soldier asked blatantly to another.

"Reinforcements?" Another questioned.

George felt something tug inside him and the world of the smoke and the mist became clearer. His eyes clouded over and he could feel the altars of the newcomers—black and chaotic. "No!" George yelled. "Smoke-screamers!"

Before anyone could react, the closest smoke-screamer in disguise exploded into a ball of fire. The blast ripped across the earthworks, igniting three of George's soldiers and causing a boom of chaos. George tore Oathkith free and alongside Williams, charged to the fore of the blackened scene, but before they could get there, archers from the camp had already loosed their arrows. The projectiles knocked the remaining two Nachtists to the floor, faces split.

In silence George and Williams stared down at the gory mark of the explosion and did their best to ignore the charcoaled smell. It wasn't much of an attack beyond that initial surprise. Looking up, George caught the tired stare of one of his soldiers who survived the blast. The prince frowned, or maybe it was a grand attack after all, just of a different kind.

***

A few more days passed and the spring rains finally gave way to a small spell of comfortable warmth and dryness. Without the sky locked in a grey gloom, or the wind howling with the threat of early season storms, the world became a little brighter, or as much as it could with all things considered. The morale of the soldiers still weren't the best as George marched them north, and he could feel it with every step. To his credit, the mumblings were at least loyal to him and the cause, if not shocked and frustrated with the tactics of the enemy. Even still, George wasn't sure how long that would stay true under the pressuring circumstances.

One comfort was that they had finally set themselves onto one of the more well kept parts of the Imperial road that cut north through Gavaria, giving them a clear indicator that they were close to their destination. The second indicator came only two days later, when George was trapped in his thoughts and staring down at the pavestones as he marched alongside his soldiers. He found a strange calm and solace in his steps. George tried his best to avoid stepping on any crack or seam, perhaps a childhood game to remind him of his humanity that he had felt slipping these last few weeks.

But even with an innocent trick, his thoughts were grim as he imagined the walls of Jornho and the conflict to come. Solutions and questions alike flooded his thoughts and before he could get too deep into them, everything seemed to manifest as he looked up from his feet. There, just over one final hill, he could see the tops of the Jornho walls; it was a sight he hadn't seen since he escorted Josephine on the very same road he now marched. He stepped on a crack and looked to one of his standard-bearers that paraded by him. The man wore a helmet of falcon feathers and held the flag of the Empire aloft. George's gaze caught the man's attention and he looked back at the prince.

"Sound a stop atop the hill just ahead, we set up there."

"Yes sir!"

George looked to his other side, at Williams and Rosaline. "Let's hope for a quick siege."

"You don't suppose they'll just give up?" Rosaline half-joked. Her fingers nervously toyed with her Tagist necklace.

"That would be a sight," Williams added.

George watched Rosaline fidget for a moment, his eyes stuck on the dapple of her blue ring. Wrenching his eyes back to the walls he forced a boyish smile. "Maybe Fenric will forget to close the doors."

He joked, but something was gnawing at his chest, as if something awful was staring him down, but from the inside.

Chapter 10
The Siege of Jornho

The Nachtists that hid behind Jornho's stout walls didn't dare sally out to attack George and his army. They knew very well that they wouldn't win a direct conflict and instead were going to rely on attrition; to keep George and his men waiting and harassing them with ambushes to both their encampment and supply lines. The wrinkled old Duke Peter of Caldora, a lanky and sun-dusted man, spouted that exact scenario as soon as George finished setting up the map-pieces for the battle table. Together they stood with Rosaline, Williams and several other commanders in a spacious white tent set in the eye of the siege camp. The smell of sawn wood and salted meals permeated through the bleached canvas and mixed with a fresh forest scent every time the wind decided to billow against the structure.

No one was going to disagree with Duke Peter, because he was right, and everyone already came to the same conclusion. George cleared his throat and looked down at the pieces before him. They mirrored the walls and towers of Jornho as well as where his siege camp was. Settled atop the closest hill by the road, his army was only a short sprint to the gates of the city. "I know I'm speaking the obvious," George said, nodding at Peter, "but time isn't on our side, so we are going to need to find a way to make this a quick siege."

"An oxymoron!" Duke Peter blurted before realizing his mistake and shaking his head. "Sorry, my prince."

George waved a hand. "We are all on edge after our march."

"A good point," Williams added. "Morale isn't the best."

Rosaline chewed her cheek. "Even so, the longer we wait, the worse it'll get."

Commander Maelinn of the 10th nodded her head. Even while giving an affirmative, her eyes were narrow with a fierce and energetic green that matched the heat of her scarlet hair. "But if you plan on rushing those gates, I can only see that morale spoiling even more. I'm sure our best Stromists could leap it, but not enough to survive an assault."

"No." George rubbed his chin. "Nothing so rash and wasteful."

"Then what, sir?" Maelinn asked.

The prince looked down at his hand that laid flat on the table. The growing frustration in his gut was evident on the tip of his fingers where tiny flashes of red were pulsing up and down. A large part of him wished he could control the smokeform just a little more, just enough to use it here.

"My prince?" Duke Peter asked, his dark eyes looking down a long nose. George rolled his jaw and looked back up to meet the man's gaze. He sighed.

"For now, let's have the scouts do another look around the perimeter. If there is any weakness at all, I want to know about it before we settle on a plan."

"Just remember," Duke Peter leaned over the table, catching everyone's eyes. "Time really isn't on our side."

"We know," Rosaline said with a stoic glance. "But hopefully prudence is."

That received a round of agreeing grunts.

***

George sat in his tent. It was a smaller tent that boasted the same bleach white canvas as all the others. The choice of tent was Williams' idea, as the knight figured an inconspicuous tent would aid in the case of infiltration attempts from the Nachtists. Due to the smaller size, there wasn't much room for things to be stored, but George traveled light anyway and the more he looked around the tent, the more he realized he was picking up Commander Darius' habits. It was an extremely clean area, with all his belongings organized in one single corner, his cot in another, and a simple table barely big enough for one person sandwiched between two chairs, one of which he now sat on.

It was evening, and he had just come in from his round around the camp. Ladders were being fashioned from the nearby wood, and some engineers were already putting wheels on a battering ram. He didn't waste time ordering the construction of catapults, just in case the Nachtists were truly teamed up with the Tagists and Mist-talkers were stationed along the walls.

George stabbed his fork into the steaming potato in front of him and kept it there, watching the steam swirl about. The wispy vapor reminded George of something he could call existing between the hectic smoke and calm mist. He sighed, wondering how to capture that same balance inside himself during the smokeform. Surely, if a potato could manage it.

"General." A familiar voice called out from behind his tent flap.

"Come in."

Maelinn pushed the canvas aside and walked in. She gave a tall salute. "I've returned with the scouting report."

George let go of his fork and turned to Maelinn "Good news?"

The Commander folded her arms behind her back. "Both, sir."

The prince stood up to meet the commander with respect. He gave her a nod. "Bad first."

Maelinn deflated a little, but kept her fierce demeanor. "The scouts were able to track down some of the farmers who used to live in the area and collect testimonials from them." She paused, and George raised a brow before nodding for her to continue. "Well," she said, "before the Nachtist revolt, a lot of the higher ranking individuals of the country were subdued or absorbed into Fenric's inner ring, including General Tobias."

George couldn't help but feel a sharp pain at the name. "Tobias?"

"I don't want to believe it either, sir," Maelinn cast her eyes downward. "But the testimonial continued, saying that perhaps it wasn't so consensual. The Nachtists had used an evil magic to taint a lot of the naysayers and in doing so scattered the leadership of the Gavarian army and the Gavarian regulars. With the province in disarray and those not conforming to Esmachus and ultimately Fenric being subdued, well, we have seen the result. Rotted from within and scattered."

A pit fell in George's stomach, there may not be any local reinforcements after all. Maelinn seemed to notice the shift in mood, piping up again. "But General, the good news."

George met her eye and nodded.

Maelinn cocked her head to the tent flap, "Commander Darius of the 11th, sir."

The canvas ripped open and in walked Commander Darius. His curly hair was a mess and he was unshaven. His armor was dented and scratched, and he wore the face of a guerilla. On that face, he split a wide, white grin. "The good news, Georgie boy," he started, "is that as scattered as we may be, we know when to make a dramatic entrance. I bring with me some vestigial of the 11th and regulars."

"Darius! I thought you were a prisoner," George couldn't help but move forward, Darius mimicked the action and the two gave each other a brief hug and slap on the back. Darius let out a snorting laugh.

"You know I swore I'd never do that whole prisoner thing ever again. Speaking of, I bring even better news."

George pulled away, all his anxiety melting. "What's that?"

"My escape from the dungeons of Jornho showed me a path into the city, not big enough for an army, but a select few could slip behind the defenses." Darius folded his arms behind his back, turning fully into his Commander role.

"And open the gate." George finished the thought.

"Exactly," Darius agreed.

Maelinn stepped forward. "I volunteer, sir."

"Noted, but not so fast," George said. "We'll need a few days to integrate what forces Darius is bringing along and to put the plan past the war table."

"Understood, sir."

George nodded his thanks and then looked at Darius, holding out a hand. "Welcome back, Commander."

Darius gripped George's hand. "Good to be back, General."

***

"So that's it then?" Duke Peter stood at the edge of the camp. A rustling night breeze tousled what hair he had left. He stared at a dark clad George with squinting doubt.

George stood next to Williams, Rosaline, Maelinn, and Darius. He gave a sigh. "Yes, that's it."

Duke Peter shook his head. "I hope you understand how unconventional it is for the *general* to attend a covert mission. Don't get me wrong, I admire your willingness... but..."

"There has to be a million better choices than sending the general, a commander, and two lieutenants," Maelinn threw in.

The prince looked to his companions then back at Peter and Maelinn. "As I said before, Rosaline and Williams will cover me while Darius leads the way. We all have experience doing this sort of thing and this is a delicate situation, where time is of the essence." He crossed his arms. "This is the fastest and most secure way to get that gate open. I understand your concern, but I need you to trust me in this and stand by Baldra of the Gavarian regulars and to be ready for when that gate opens." George pointed at Maelinn. "I need you and the 10th ready as well."

Duke Peter dipped his head. "I'll trust your judgment, prince."

"Of course, sir," Maelinn saluted.

"Thank you." George turned to his companions and waved them forward. "Let's move while it's still dark."

With little else, the four split away from Peter and Maelinn before making their way down the darkest side of the hill. Their steps were careful and calculated, already making sure not to let their boots swish through the grass too noisily. At least nature was on their side as the spring calls of frogs and insects filled the night air with a chorus to cover them and even the moon seemed dim, caught in a silvered crescent.

Darius took the front while Williams winged George's right and Rosaline his left. They stood tight together with each focusing on their own directions to maximize any detection of threats. They moved at a quickened pace while in the grassy and shrubby open of the hills. Unfortunately for George, Jornho routinely harvested any timber that grew too close to the walls of the city, leaving the cloak of the night as his group's primary source of comfort.

This feeling of comfort faded the closer they got to the walls of the city. The walls were squat, but thick and held plenty of room for patrols along the parapets. While it was too dark to see any prying eyes up on the walls, George was sure Nachtist guards were there, waiting precisely for what George was planning.

"This way." Darius whispered, pulling the group away from the distant walls and sending them parallel to it. They plotted along, with the grass growing taller as they pushed further from the roads and gate, until the vegetation was up to George's waist. Darius was snapping his head back and forth, as if looking for something, before suddenly disappearing under the grass.

"There's a slope." His voice called up. Williams was next to disappear, and then Rosaline. George squinted and moved forward until suddenly he felt nothing underneath one of his feet. He lurched forward and fell through the air. Williams' hand caught his arm and set him straight in the small gully the group had disappeared into. Darius was frowning at him.

"What did you tell Duke Peter, again, that you were an expert?"

"I didn't say 'expert' exactly." George quipped back.

"It's amazing we ever escaped Galmun Blue-Breath's camp," Rosaline said with a small grin. George offered a sly wink.

"Regardless," Darius whispered. He thrusted his finger through the dark and back at the steep slope they came down from. "Look."

There, abutting the slope was a fresh opening, with brittle stone laying at their feet along with loose soil and bits of rusted iron. A cold and hollow air seemed to radiate about the mouth of the man-made cave, and along with the chill was an ancient smell. George furrowed his brow, but Darius clapped a hand on his shoulder before ducking in. Rosaline followed, then George, while Williams took the rear.

The group was swallowed by the darkness and each step gave a soft tap of boot on stone steps. Before they could go much further down, Darius cracked a firestarter against a short torch and lit it. The orange glow of the small flame illuminated the immediate area and put the group in a small cage of light, surrounded by stone walls with ancient steps below them.

"It goes a bit deeper," Darius said, "so watch your step until it levels out."

"This is pretty extravagant for a sallyport," Rosaline commented as she brushed her fingers on the walls, tracing patterned carvings of shapes and flowers.

"I don't think it's a sallyport," George commented as his Uncle's lectures slowly seeped back to the fore of his mind.

"Ruins." Williams answered, getting a grunt from Darius.

"I was surprised too, so far from Caldora and the Imperial Forest, but I wasn't about to look a gift horse in the mouth."

The prince nodded, and kept his eyes on the walls as he walked. Eventually the stairs flattened to a tall hallway and along with it, the simple patterns on the walls grew complicated. The flowers turned to rolling hills and the more geometric shapes turned into engravings so old, it was hard to gather much detail, but the unique shapes in between the rest were undeniable: bulls walking upright along with frogmen. Idyllic landscapes and old wooden halls showed where those bullmen gathered while the frogs were sitting in circles by swamps, as if having lectures, but most confusing of all, there were also creatures with four arms and feathered elbows watching them from the nebulous skies.

Squinting, a sharp headache started to form in George's skull as he stared. A small screeching whistle was in the back of his head, making it all the worse until finally he wrenched his eyes from the mural. It didn't solve the problem, though, as his eyes caught a different picture.

The ringing was immense as he caught a fuzzy glimpse of the new mural. A featureless man was hammering away at a massive anvil, crafting human-looking figures which then leapt down from the great smithy and marched towards a land between many hills . In that valley, the figures were handing nondescript objects to a smaller race of otherwise identical heritage. They were of many different faces and features. George's head was throbbing and he could feel a warm trickle under his nose when suddenly Darius pulled the torch away from the wall, having walked too far ahead.

Williams put his hand on George's back. "You stopped?"

George wiped the back of his glove against his nose and nodded along. "Just got caught in the pictures is all."

"Keep up," Darius whispered behind him.

The walk through the ruins took another twenty minutes before the ancient styling of the hall had turned into a soddy and soiled catacomb of a more recent era, with a broken wall separating the two worlds from each other. Now the group was cutting through a maze of sarcophaguses that very likely held Fenric's ancestors inside them. The dusty smell of the ancient halls were replaced by the sharp metallic musk of soil and stone as it seemed that the Gavarian tradition of burying the deceased in the soil of their birthplace was strong even when sarcophaguses were involved. Rosaline walked with a furrowed brow, her eyes lingering on the symbols of the Tagists.

"Through here and up a set of stairs and then we will be in the temple by the castle," Darius explained in a hushed voice. "From there we can follow the wall set behind the temple to the gates. The temple has been cleared of sages ever since the Nachtists took over, but keep your wits about you regardless."

"How did you even find this place?" Rosaline couldn't help but ask.

Darius paused. "After I escaped the castle, I needed to lay low. A Tagist temple seemed like a spot a Nachtist would forget to check—the rest was luck."

Williams nodded. "Let's hope that the same luck is still with us."

"It is," George said with optimism. "Now let's move."

Rosaline was caught again on a faithful image before turning to George. "Right behind you."

Chapter 11
The Battle of Jornho

George and the others made their way upstairs and into the temple proper. The egress from the catacombs put them in a room behind the altar. The place looked like it would smell of incense, but the subtle lack of that usual musk which George had come to associate with Tagist temples was gone. All that was left were various bits and artifacts crowded on top of each other without much order or care. Nothing of silver or gold was left in this impromptu storage area either, further cementing the fate of the sages who preached here. As awful as it made him feel to admit it, George was relieved to find out the place was sacked as it meant that the sages weren't working with the Nachtists.

Rosaline opened a tin pot and gave a sniff. She made a disgusted face and quickly put the lid back. "I don't think there is anything of use in this room." She idled and spoke under her breath, "Guess there is no sanctity anymore." The tone wasn't hateful, but almost sad.

George was pulled from his thoughts and nodded. "Let's move out."

They made a sharp turn out of the storage area and spilled out into the sermon room. Immediately George's eyes adjusted with recognition. He stood by the raised platform where the sages would preach, and looking up, he could see the balcony he once stood behind alongside Fenric. He could see the very rails he looked down from, and now he was looking up. He knew something was wrong back then, if only he had known more. Shaking his head, he gave Darius a hand signal and the Commander took the lead once again.

The night air of the city was warmer than the dusk of the catacombs and certainly warmer than the ancient hallway. It was well welcomed to be greeted by the loud and incessant croaking of nighttime frogs and the chorus of crickets. Being in the upper district of Jornho meant that the buildings were stone, and since they were stone, they were raised higher than their stout wooden neighbors in the lower district, casting a mosaic of long moon-lined shadows across the streets.

George furrowed his brow and instinctively drew Oathkith, and his companions unsheathed their own swords in response. This wasn't his first time on the night streets of Jornho, but this time, something was pointedly different.

"It's quiet," Williams whispered. "Beside the frogs, I mean."

George nodded. "Fenric likely ordered a curfew. It's easier to track infiltrators that way."

"Infiltrators like us," Darius added. He nudged his chin to an alleyway. "I suggest we keep moving."

The group slipped in between the buildings, working their way towards the walls. There was hardly any sound in the city that would suggest it was inhabited, giving the entire place an abandoned or even ghost-like atmosphere. If not for the sounds of mid-spring's nature, or the night breezes howling through the alleys, George was sure their footfalls would be like thunder. A certain anxiety filled George, though, since no sound meant that he couldn't hear the enemy either. With that in mind, he started channeling his Stromist energy.

It took a moment, but before long George could feel the tug of the altars surrounding him. Darius' cleanly balanced Stromist aura hummed alongside Rosaline's, which rang in front of him and was surprisingly strong for a non-Stromist, while Williams' modest altar blipped behind. Further out, George could feel a dark and chaotic smoke. It was impossible to count how many tainted alters he felt, but he at least knew how far away they were. He clenched his jaw, eager to retain his concentration.

George's eyes widened as the group met the end of the alley way. Darius was just about to poke his head out onto the street with the closest wall tower straight ahead when George grabbed his shoulder and yanked him back. Everyone froze, and a patrol of Nachtists walked right past their nook. They were deadly silent and extremely focused. It was almost inhuman, but then again, these were desperate people who had been waiting for this moment for longer than George had been alive.

Darius gave George a look and the prince refocused on the altars around him before giving Darius a nod and taking the lead. Sucking in a breath, as if a loud exhale would give them away, George slipped across the street. The few seconds he spent running from the alley to the wall on the other side of the road were heavy, exposing minutes. Even after finding the wall, George couldn't help but feel panic when he couldn't see the way into the tower right away. Luckily a second look revealed an alcove in the shadows of the structure which led to stiff double doors banded with iron.

The prince put his hand on them, and reached out beyond them, he felt a single presence beyond the threshold. It wasn't moving, perhaps sleeping? George rolled his jaw and looked over his shoulder to his companions and held up one finger. They nodded and George gently pushed in on the door with his sword hand, tension rising into his throat.

Cold air slipped by George as soon as he opened the door. The night breeze swirled into the warmer room, sending the candles inside into a flickering fit. Cots lined the walls, and on one of them, a woman with speckled metal all over her face was sitting and reading by a candle. She was staring up at the group with wide eyes, who in turn stared back with equally shocked expressions.

Without breaking the gaze, she slowly reached over towards a rusty axe in the cot next to hers. The Imperials quickly sprung into action, but before George could grab the reading woman, she let out a horrific screech and a torrent of smoke erupted from her lungs and nearly blew the prince back.

"Hold your breath!" Darius commanded. George bit his lips closed and his eyes watered. The smoke-screamer didn't relent though, and after her initial screech, her legs were engulfed in the smoke. She shimmered with unnatural speed as she evaded the prince and shot through the double doors. George sent his own magic to his feet, but Darius grabbed his shoulder and pulled him towards the stairs upward. "We just have to move, George, fast."

"Right," George growled with frustration, they didn't have as much time now. Together, the group sped up the old stone steps and sure enough, by the time they reached the top of the tower, a bell was ringing across the city.

Bursting out onto the walls, George immediately was met with a smoke-screamer. The prince didn't hesitate, and he stabbed Oathkith right through the man's gut, the blade shrieking through the man's hauberk, and out again as George brought the sword back around for a swift cut across the throat. The man went gurgling to the floor. Violence once more, a life wasted.

A quick look into the city saw it swarming with activity and the quiet night of crickets and frogs had swiftly turned into a clunking machine of war. Even on the other side of the parapets, looking out into the black and purple hills, George could see the torches of his army waiting.

Rosaline pushed past George and brought up her sword to catch a falling axe. Behind the prince, Williams and Darius were holding back reinforcements coming up the tower. George rushed forward to help Rosaline with her enemy, but as the prince closed in, the smoke-screamer burst into a plume of smoke for but a moment before reappearing to his side. George juked under to avoid the enemy's axe. As he ducked, Rosaline lunged over him, catching the smoke-screamer by surprise and sending the tip of her blade into his neck; a quiet prayer or apology was on her lips. George kept his momentum and kept rushing forwards. His eyes were now dead set on the gatehouse in the distance, to say nothing of the enemy guards in the way.

"Come on!" George called over his shoulder. Williams and Darius broke from their engagement and sprinted behind the prince, while Rosaline ran beside him. The four turned into a sprinting whirl of blades. Ducking under interceptors, spinning past plumes of smoke, and skidding by spears and axes. A few arrows barely missed them as they made their approach, until finally, up ahead, three smoke-screamers stood shoulder to shoulder by the entrance to the gate house.

They immediately screamed out a cloud of smoke, using the magic to make their movements faster than normal as the group of

Imperials collided. George could feel the control over his movement lessen as he entered the cloud, breath held. The chaotic wisps made him feel weightless, barely in control of the force behind his muscles and direction. His enemy's spear didn't have that issue and came thrusting towards his face. He felt his heart drop and adrenaline snap through his body, and with a sudden rush of his Stromism, he only barely managed to regain enough control over himself to move to the side. The blade of the spear bounced off the cheek guard of his helmet, and as George pushed past the range of the spear, he sent his head bucking forward with magic and slammed it into the surprised smoke-screamer's face. With a crack, the enemy was blasted into the floor.

To his left, Darius cut down the other two smoke-screamers with a single golden-ribboned strike, saving Williams and Rosaline who were completely out of control in the smoke. Pulling the two regulars in by the neck of their breastplates, George stormed the gate house.

Inside, a myriad of gears lined the walls, forming a contraption controlled by a single capstan with four big spokes. It was clear just by the size of the wooden contraption that it normally would take four well built individuals to turn the thing, but George couldn't spare to leave the entrances to the gatehouses unguarded. The prince-turned-general looked to Darius. "Help me turn." Looking at the other two. "Secure the doors."

"Right."

Rosaline and Williams split up, one on each of the gate house's doors. Already on Williams' side—where they had come in from—the door was ajar with enemies attempting to rush in. George slammed his weight onto the capstan and pushed all his magic into his arms. The sound of metal striking metal filled the air alongside grunts and yells as he pushed off his feet, forcing the capstan to budge. Darius' face strained purple on the other side and soon the wheel was moving with force. The gears all around them clanked and groaned, and the shriek of the gate below rising vibrated the whole structure.

Before the pair could finish, a smoke-screamer slipped by Willaims and came barreling towards George like a wraith. George caught a glimpse of the assault from the corner of his eye and quickly flipped around. The capstan jolted backwards without George's push and Darius' eyes seemed to bulge as he attempted to keep it level.

The smoke-screamer rushed right into George, but the prince was quick, grabbing his enemy's arm and slamming them into the capstan. Pinned between himself and the mechanism, the smoke-screamer ripped out a dagger, but George narrowed his eyes and a bolt of magic rushed down his arms.

"George!" Darius strained.

George yelled, "I got it!" All together, the prince shoved his full body weight into the smoke-screamer, and with a boney crack, the dagger fell to the floor and the capstan was knocked back into rotation. A loud clunk sounded as the gate locked in place, and a second later, an immense roar shook from the hills—the battle had begun. With a kick, George broke the release mechanism, fusing the gears in place, before turning.

"Rosaline! On me!" George shouted.

The medic obediently slapped away an enemy spear before retreating to the prince. George hooked an arm around her waist as golden ribbons of magic swirling around his body. Rosaline cocked a brow, but before she got an answer, George blasted off into a sprint, right through the door she was protecting. The enemies on the other side were knocked off the wall by the force and without stopping, George leapt after them. Wind whipped at the pair's faces before they landed with a ground shaking boom. A second later and Darius was landing behind them with Williams in his grasp.

They were still on the city side of the walls, in front of the gatehouse. Through the now opened maw, they could see the Imperials on their way from the hills and in the opposite direction, they could see the Nachtist army forming. The group was in between both, but their presence kept the enemy from closing in completely on the threshold. Rosaline put her back to George's and Darius and Williams winged them, swords ready.

"George!" Esmachus broke from the Nachtist ranks. He leveled a blackened blade at the prince. "We could have avoided all of this, but know now that I'll take your life as compensation for the wait!"

Darius spat on the ground and Rosaline glared. Williams looked at George and George answered, "you'll never get close enough to try."

The ground shook and a mixture of fear and determination blinked in the eyes of the enemy. George's army stampeded past him and the enemy screamed up a wall of smoke, but instead of rushing right into it, the front line stopped and used their running momentum from earlier to launch a rain of javelins. Unlike with the mist, the javelins sank right through the smoke, spinning and spiraling wildly and quickly. Gurgles, thwacks, and yelps marked their targets and in moments, the two armies clashed. The force and trained precision of the Imperials pushed the Nachtists back, bowing their line inwards—they did not expect a direct fight and didn't have the numbers to deal with one.

"George!" Maelinn yelled over the fight. George looked up just in time to catch Rook. He slung it around his arm and focused back on the bending enemy line. He pointed his sword forward and rallied his troops.

"Center push!" He yelled before rushing forward. Darius split off to join the 11th, but Rosaline and Williams stayed by George's side as the newly invigorated Imperial line continued their crash into the Nachtists. Darius was right, they were dangerous to fight alone, but in a large group, they didn't have a chance to use their mobility. Before long, George's line managed to split the enemy down the middle and opened up the way to the castle. George looked to Williams who gave a nod, and together with a small contingent of elites, they split off from the battle while the rest of the Imperials mopped up the broken Nachtists, though Esmachus was nowhere in sight.

Night's brisk wind whipped all around George and his soldiers as they rushed through the streets and threaded their way to the castle. While George was glad that the battle turned in their favor so quickly, he still felt an ounce of anxiety in his chest. With every step he took towards the castle, he knew he was closer to Franklin's murderer, Tobias' tormenter, Darius' captor, Osbert's traitor. His anxiety quickly turned to a slow burning rage, a rage that warmed his fingertips against the spring night. He looked down and once again, tiny strings of smoke were spiraling into his gauntlets; the smokeform was calling. Breaking his eyes away and looking forward across the dusky streets and silhouetting castle in the distance, he did his best to expel that growing feeling.

"This is it," Rosaline said between sprinting pants.

"I know," George said, his lips forming a grim line. He looked up at the top of the castle, to the tallest bastion that looked over the city. He could feel Fenric staring down at him with eyes as cold as the moon. "I know."

Chapter 12
Fenric Kinslayer

It was dark inside the castle, dark and quiet. An eerie aura permeated every facet, from the dust covered chairs, to the expressionless portraits. As George and his group walked over a faded red carpet, he couldn't help but get the feeling that no one had lived in this castle for quite some time. No servants scurried about, no candles were lit and the only light was what weak offering the moon could push through the small windows. The castle was hollow and cold, the castle was dead.

Even so, George and his contingent of soldiers had their weapons drawn and ready, eyes scanning every hidden corner or opaque shadow, but when nothing jumped out at them, they beelined to the first set of stairs that lead to the highest bastion. Their footsteps were thunder in the otherwise deathly silent stairwell. Even the battle of outside was muted behind the soulless stones of the castle. George led the charge up, his heart pounding in rhyme with each crashing footfall.

Doors and windows whipped by, and with each one, George started to shake more and more with anticipation; his sword hand squeezed Oathkith. Without warning, one of the doors swung open and a pair of arms reached out, pulling George through the door frame. George's heart leaped and he went to crack his pommel over his assailant when he froze. Shaking blue eyes stared up at him, reddened with tears. George's soldiers hurried in after their prince, but also came to a stand still at the sight.

There in the dusty, sad room stood Hilda, Fenric's mother. Her fingers shook as they gripped George's arms, the prince's sword still raised to strike. Williams and Rosaline pushed through the soldiers to stand next to George. "Duchess Hilda?" The prince managed.

"A monster's mother," was what a voice in George's mind couldn't help but think—the voice was dark and lined with smoke. Hilda let go of George and sobbed pleadingly. "Please, my prince, spare him."

George gaped down at her while some soldiers started to wing the hysterical woman. "Please, my prince." She held her hands together to beg. "He has regret in his eyes."

George took a step back, a sudden cold stone knocking his anger aside. Hilda caught his eye, staring deep in them. She was ragged, tired, and looked as if she was starving herself. George's fingers shook and she let out another sob but all George could do was stare.

He started to turn, but she threw herself at him. The soldiers quickly intercepted, knocking her to the floor, but she wriggled and squirmed with one hand reaching out to grab George's ankle. She stared up at him, eyes shimmering. "Don't kill my son."

George felt a pressure behind his own eyes and he cleared his throat. "Secure her." A soldier ripped her hand from George's boot and she let out a sharp yelling sob. "Don't kill my son!"

George bit the inside of his cheek, a gross feeling rattling inside of him, but ultimately he tore himself from the scene and took one step through the threshold to the stairwell. "Williams."

The knight looked up from the scramble on the ground. "Yes?"

"Make sure no one goes up these stairs." A pause. "I'll be right back."

"Are you sure? I can-"

"This is my responsibility. Just watch my back." George looked back at his friend, an unsure look in his eye as he tried to give a reassuring smile. "I'll be right back."

Williams gaped for a moment. "I know you will. I'll be here."

Rosaline was shaking her head. "You're not leaving here like this, not without me."

"Please," George turned to his lover. His eyes were set in a sober seriousness and the tone of his voice flinched Rosaline. The heroine of the north stared at the prince for a moment before closing her eyes.

"Don't leave me with regret," her voice was a plea.

"I won't. I'll be gone for only a moment."

Stepping out, George started to climb the stairs again, but this time with a fraction of the speed or energy. Instead of running, he walked. Instead of anticipation, he rolled his sword in his palm with concern. "A boy's mother," was what George's mind couldn't help but think. He looked down the length of his blade, a boy who did so much and caused so much. "A wretch," a dark smoky thought whispered.

"A son," George said out loud, countering the thought. His voice echoed and the words stayed with him until he was face to face with the final door: a simple wooden frame with a simple wooden panel—the final threshold between him and Fenric. He looked back down at Oathkith and he could feel his father's hate for war radiate from it. Turning his head, he stared at Rook. Franklin's shield was scratched and marred, but the words were still etched in the back as clear as the day Williams gave it to George. Somewhere in the shield, George swore he could feel Franklin's disdain for it as well. With nothing else to distract him, the prince pushed the door open.

Exiting onto the rooftop of the bastion, George was faced with the endless night sky above and a howling battlefield below. The parapets of the tower marked the edges of his stone arena, while his opponent stood on the far side with a sword drawn. Fenric only wore a breastplate, leaving his limbs free. His arms were bare, but his legs were covered in dark cloth. A sad black cloak was pulled over his shoulders, similar to one that a mourner would wear during a month of grieving. His eyes were stained pink under the moonlight and his tarnished golden hair was a mess. The duke rolled the sword in his hand.

"George." Fenric's voice was hoarse, but determined.

A stiff wind blew between them, a thin wall that sheathed the fighters from each other. George couldn't help but shiver, the wind was colder up here. He went to call out, to yell with the smoke, but instead, George's voice came out soft, if confused, "Fenric."

Neither of them moved. Something about the situation felt surreal and the whole thing furrowed George's brow. He wanted to yell for Fenric to give himself up, he wanted to scream at him for his actions, he wanted to feel that same rage he felt in the war room of Korku, but all he could manage was a genuine question, steeped in curiosity and sadness. Hilda's eyes flashed across George's mind. "Why did you do it?"

Fenric stayed still. "All that matters is that I did it."

George twisted a frown and found his footing. "Throw down your blade. There has been enough death over this already."

"I'm sure you offered this same deal to the others who wetted your blade tonight." Fenric spoke coolly.

George shook his head, his eyes never leaving his childhood nemesis. "I am not here to debate: drop your sword."

"I won't." There was no emotion in the Gavarian's tone.

"Fenri—"

"Kill me," Fenric demanded. He pointed his blade at George. "There is no other way to get to me. I won't go quietly."

"I don't want to kill you," George admitted to his own surprise. "Really?" The dark thought was back.

A snort. "No? What about our time in the war room? You snapped my sword—where did all that anger go? Don't you hate me?"

"I do," George said. "I hate everything you've done." Even still, now being face to face, with a life in his hands, how far did his hate go? "As far as it needs to go," George's dark thoughts answered. A wisp of smoke stained the prince's cheek red for a single moment.

"Then kill me." Fenric yelled. His emotion came back to his voice and his yell was deep and passionate. George frowned, his face furrowed and hesitant. An otherworldly black plume of smoke blasted from Fenric's mouth. "Fight me!"

George held up his sword and shield but before he could respond, Fenric rushed him down at a breakneck speed. Fenric's blade slammed across Rook, with George having just managed to get it between them. The prince's shield arm recoiled, slamming back into his own chest and knocking George backward. Fenric let out a horrific scream and smoke billowed all around him. In a blink of an eye, Fenric exploded into a sheet of black smoke, only to reappear behind George. George pushed his own magic to the limit just in time to avoid Fenric's strike, but then quickly came his next.

Fenric's sword slammed into George's helmet and knocked it clean off. A painful ring barraged the prince's ears, but his eyes snapped to a starlit flash of steel. Another swing, this time Rook caught it, but again the force knocked George back. Fenric's boot came up and kicked George completely over.

The prince fell backwards onto his behind, skidding slightly on the ground. He looked up to see Fenric walking towards him, flickering between a physical form and pure chaotic smoke. "Why aren't you fighting me, George?" His voice creeped along the ground. "I'll kill you if you don't and then what was this all for?"

Gritting his teeth, George sent all his magic down to his feet and his legs shimmered with gold. He kicked off the ground, launching himself backwards and straight back into a fighting stance. He put up his sword and shield and then with another kick, launched at Fenric. Fenric slipped to the side, but George anticipated and swung out with his shield. Fenric poofed into a cloud of smoke and the shield slipped through before he rematerialized, black metal now speckling his face. Fenric lunged with his blade.

Using his blinding speed, George avoided the sword and swung with his own. Fenric caught it along the length of his blade and then sent out a riposte, which George parried, and before long the two were exchanging blow after blow, with neither of them getting the upper hand. George pushed more of his magic through his body and his muscles strained and his veins popped to keep up with Fenric. The duke wore angry eyes on an otherwise emotionless face.

"You won't beat me without your smokeform," Fenric goaded as he ducked a blow. "Why aren't you using your smokeform?"

Oathkith swung for Fenric's neck and the duke pulled back just in time for it to miss. Frustration filled George's eyes and smoke hissed into his reddening fingertips. Fenric cracked a smile. "You can't control it, can you? You're afraid to use it."

"I don't want to kill you," George said through his teeth. "I'm capturing you alive."

"That's not an option," Fenric took another step back. "I have made my covenant with the Dweller and with Esmachus. I'm evil." The word cracked, as if it hurt to say. Fenric held up his sword and smoke spiraled around his arm. "I'm responsible for Franklin's death and I murdered my own father in his sleep." A pause. "I even slaughtered old Jonsberg."

George's eyes widened and Fenric's eyes faded to a strange remorse. The duke bent his knees and he cracked an insane grin. "Heart attack in his sleep, or smoke in the lungs, who can tell? I destroyed Gavaria. Just like your father destroyed the Empire."

A cold wave hit George and his jaw tightened. Fenric pushed. "He and I both know the Dweller. He's about as innocent as I am. Using the Dweller to revive your mother and sister..."

"Shut up!" George roared.

"Then kill me! Fight me!" Fenric roared back. A burst of tears exploded from his eyes and ran hot down his cheeks. "Unleash your anger, damn you! I deserve every ounce of it!"

"I will not!" George screamed, but the red on his skin was growing, creeping up his neck and around his eyes and ears. White shocks formed around his hair.

"Then I'll slaughter you," Fenric bellowed the words across the stones, "the same as your father slaughtered your mother!"

Time froze. George knew it was true, but there he stood with the smoke hissing into his body as Fenric stared on, covered in a smoke of his own. It was a battle, but George's mind had lost to the dark thoughts.

"It was all because of you," Fenric said with a gross calmness. "The Dweller wanted you dead, and what better time than when you were unborn… but you didn't die… your mother did, alone, by your father. Your father killed your mother, because of you!"

George's eyes dilated and his hair turned a stark white. His look of shock dissolved into one of pure battle fury; his face was a bloody red and his body hissed as it soaked in the smoke. Fenric's sword arm hissed as well, and black metal creeped up his skin. Fenric screamed and a torrent of smoke funneled into the air, only to ignite in a cone of fire. The orange heat evaporated the duke's tears and his voice bellowed, "Fight me!"

This time, George let out a shaking howl, creating an unsettling rumble across the stone tower. He pushed off with his feet, cracking the floor below. Oathkith and Fenric's sword slammed into each other with so much force, the two opponents were forced to bounce off each other. Fenric skidded across the stone while George used the momentum to kick off a parapet and launch back at Fenric. Oathkith itself was turning red in George's hand as he came down with a swing. Smoke screamed from Fenric's mouth, his arm turning into thick metal and took a direct hit from the blade. A fiery crack erupted on his arm and spat out hissing black steam as Oathkith lodged into it.

Using his other hand, Fenric slammed his fist into George's gut, shattering the prince's breastplate. Black blood dripped from Fenric's knuckle, dissolving into smoke as it hit the ground. Ignoring a sharp pain across his ribs, George let out a roar and slammed his head into Fenric's face, knocking the duke back.

Bursting into smoke once again, Fenric appeared behind George, but this time George spun around with incredible agility. The duke tried to deflect the attack with his sword, but Oathkith sliced right through it, cutting Fenric's weapon in half. Fenric's eyes widened and Rook slammed across his face with a resounding crack. He went flying, slamming into one of the parapets. With black blood dripping down his chin, Fenric blinked into a cloud of smoke just in time to avoid a charge from George.

Stone splintered through the air as Oathkith exploded into the parapet. The duke jumped back to put space between him and George before letting out another scream. Floating black swords appeared in the space around Fenric, accompanied by a lingered shroud of smoke.

Each one swung and stabbed at George simultaneously but all they managed to do was slow his approach, the prince parrying each and every hit with sword and shield alike. Fenric took another step back and grimaced. His eyes blurred with smoke and with a final shout, he sent that same black metal back down his sword arm, turning his hand into a gnarled spear head. Alongside his blades, he rushed George.

All George could feel was blinding anger. The world was red and he couldn't make any sense of it. All he felt was chaotic energy ripping at his mind and sending untold power through his body. His bones were shrieking in pain and his blood was boiling but all he could feel was rage. He saw Fenric dive at him, it seemed like slow motion as Fenric sped at him with his endless weapons. George put Rook in front of him and threw Oathkith into a medium guard. He let out a battle-cry and charged in return.

The two slammed into each other. George managed to juke between the swords, avoiding them. Fenric's spear hand collided with Rook, forcing the duke's eyes wide with sudden fear. George stared him down, almost nose to nose, but the smokeform couldn't make out what he saw, only the red of battle. Rook pushed forward with incredible strength, peeling Fenric back just enough that when Oathkith came around the side, it sliced through the duke's arm with a ripping metal shriek before slamming into his chest. Rook came back around and smashed into his chin, and then Oathkith stabbed into Fenric's leg. The duke let out a scream of pain, but it was a gurgled smear to George. The smokeform yanked Oathkith downward, forcing the duke into a kneel. Fenric looked up at George, a teary look of acceptance on his face, but it was covered in red, stuck behind the smokeform's battle lust. George's shield arm flexed and with a final blow, he cracked Franklin's shield across Fenric's metallic jaw.

With an immense force, the duke was sent into the air, a frightful yell emptying his smoke filled lungs as he was knocked clean off the tower. Fenric's face disappeared from George's view, sinking into the night sky as his body plummeted out of view. The battle rage in George suddenly froze, registering what just happened, but by time the red faded from his vision, Fenric's scream had stopped and there stood George, alone, bleeding profusely and in pain on top of the tower.

The dark thoughts still swirled as George attempted to regain control. He did it, he killed Fenric. No, he killed a traitor. No, he killed a son. No, he killed a murderer. No, no. George's mind was gripped as the smoke pulsed through him. The headache forced him to his knees.

"The cursed prince," Esmachus' voice hissed. "A strange child. Who is he, really, and who can he trust?"

George looked up. The Nachtist was standing on a parapet. They simply stared at each other for a moment, the general huffing and puffing.

"Certainly not himself," Esmachus mused.

"Quiet," George growled. He rose only to buckle under the sudden pain of his wounds. Oathkith bit the ground and kept him on his knees. "I'll slaughter you." His voice was dark; he didn't mean that, did he? He's already killed so many.

"Hm," Esmachus hummed. "I gave you a choice once, out of mercy." He stepped down from the parapet and a thin knife appeared in his hand. George stared on, his body too numb to move.

"Hey!" Rosaline shouted. She came barreling through the door with Williams hot on her heels. Esmachus spun to her, eyes wide. The Nachtist swore under his breath and then smiled at George.

"Seems we will have to talk another time." The man's eyes stuck on Rosaline for a moment. "But really, beware Tagists in your midst. They are unpredictable, as you Uncle and his crew must have learned." He spat, "Especially those of Harris."

The Imperials jerked forward, but before they could take another step towards Esmachus, he exploded into a gust of smoke, which the tense night wind quickly stole away.

Chapter 13

Josephine the Regent

A dense gloom choked the night sky over the Imperial Gardens. Wind whipped through the branches of the great elm that stood center and a sharp rain cut into the gust, stinging Josephine through her night clothes. She stood alone, not remembering when she had stepped out into the gardens and much less when the storm began. The lily-white mantle she had around her shoulders was threatening to rip off into the whirlwind surrounding her, a whirlwind which sent a deep, drenching chill into her bones. Josephine held herself and took a step towards the tree.

Standing under the boughs of the elm was a figure wrapped in dark purple robes and glinting armor. He faced the tree, and so all Josephine saw of the man was a long grey mane and a crooked crown. She squinted through the wind, cautiously taking another step. That was her father's crown, but everything else was different.

"Dad?" Something felt weird. Unreal.

"No." The figure's voice was deep and powerful, cut with aged wisdom and mountains of stress and paranoia. He turned, to reveal a face Josephine only knew from paintings. She gasped; his face was wrinkled, unsmiling and deeply cynical. A broken sword hung loosely in his grasp.

Josephine held a hand up, as if attempting to put something between him and her. She took a step back, letting the storm provide more of a buffer. Branches creaked overhead as if the elm itself protested the meeting. Finally Josephine responded, incredulous.

"Grandfather?"

Emperor Frederick's face didn't change, nor did he take any steps forward. "What veil is so thin that we could speak, Josephine?"

"A dream?" Josephine surmised. Emperor Frederick let out a thoughtful groan.

"Be careful with dreams," he warned, "for it was a simple dream that led me down my own path, the very same path that damned me."

Josephine didn't respond. Instead she spun around, as if to confirm her suspicions. The world was blurry, and except for the storm that dressed the area, it was quiet with not another soul in sight. She brought her attention back to the elm tree, only to startle backwards, nearly tripping, when she found herself face to face with her grandfather. Wearing a grimace, she asked. "Why am I seeing you? When did I fall asleep?"

"My dream..." Frederick continued while not paying any mind to Josephine. "I saw a great danger coming in from the north. The Vagrants were going to attack the Empire. A dark force was riding behind them, using their hordes to destabilize the Imperial lands in preparation for an invasion. An angel, a Grace—or so I thought—warned me in my dream of this, she encouraged me to put a stop to it, to save Jerrovia before it could come to pass. So I set out to destroy the Vagrants before they could destroy us." He paused. Josephine was staring at him with wide eyes.

"The Dweller?" She murmured.

Two arms appeared from behind Josephine and gently wrapped over her shoulders, casually clasping in front of her. A woman's voice teased in her ear. "Josephine, don't you see the pain in your grandfather's eyes? His choices brought him so much turmoil, and led to all the turmoil of today."

"Who?" Josephine turned to look, only to freeze in fear. A deep, primal fright curled in her stomach as she looked into the blurry face of the woman behind her. Only two smoky grey eyes peered from the disturbed visage. Josephine protested. "N-no..."

"All around the world, people are in pain," the voice continued, echoing in Josephine's ear. "Just let me out, and I can take it all away. I can bring true peace. I don't need much from you, Josephine."

"L-leave me." Josephine stuttered, frozen in place.

A pale blue hand reached for the Regent's chin, gripping it caringly before turning her to face the Dweller in earnest. A blurry smile formed over the creature's face. "Save them all from their choices, from their pain, from their turmoil." The world faded away behind the Dweller. Gennisberg's face appeared in the darkness behind the devil, then Clement's, then a golden dagger and finally, a mysterious man covered in strange runes. He was walking past the pair now, out of view and Josephine could hear her father's voice behind her. The Dweller squeezed her chin. "The ritual has already begun, just let it be, and let me hold you all as a mother would."

***

Josephine woke up with a start. A gentle hand gripped her shoulder and guided her back flat against the bed she was laying on. Her heart was pounding, and her eyes were panicked and wide, only to calm as she took in her surroundings. She was laying in the infirmary bed that was installed in one of the impromptu medical rooms for her around the palace. It was a plain room with plenty of light leaking in through numerous windows. To her left sat Opane, her fingers laced over her knee and to Josephine's right stood Reginald. Josephine sucked in a breath and let out a shuddering exhale, looking for her confidence.

"You seemed like you were having an awfully bad dream," Opane mentioned. This earned her a cautionary look from Reginald, one not unlike that from a mother hen or perhaps Barcenian tiger. Josephine furrowed her brow and looked to Reginald.

"How long was I asleep?"

Reginald stood up straight and offered her a slight bow of his head. "Only through breakfast."

Rubbing her temples, Josephine replied, "that's not too bad."

"Ah" Opane chewed her cheek. Josephine looked up at her. "What?"

The door to the medical room swung open. "Josephine!" A strong, sophisticated voice called out in a trill. A tall woman who looked very much like Josephine, with long golden hair and bright blue eyes, walked in. She wore an elegant dress and sparkling jewelry. Her smile was similar to a snake's and contrary to her bright eyes, they held a certain cat-like quality to them. Despite being the same age as her sister Catherine, she had a touch more gentle youth in her cheeks.

"Cousin Isabella," Josephine said with more shock than authority. She went to stand up, but before she could speak further, Isabella cut her off.

"I see you're still having your fits, dear cousin," Isabella started. "And I was so hoping to enjoy breakfast with you after all this time." She put her hands on her hips and gave Josephine a sly grin. "Let us hope such a disaster doesn't strike during your ceremony. How irresistibly terrible would that be?"

Josephine squinted, plotting to her feet. "As devious as ever I see—wait, what ceremony?"

"My goodness, Reginald, did she bump her head when she fell asleep?" Isabella gave a chiming laugh. Reginald closed his eyes and dipped his head, either out of polite wariness or annoyance. Josephine gave her a sidelonged look, coupled with one from Opane. The Duchess returned Opane's look with a flashing glare that made the Kafshe bristle. Flickering her eyes back to Josephine, Isabella pursed her lips, all amusement draining. "Your wedding, dear. You know I wouldn't miss it for the world."

"I'm not getting married," Josephine groaned; this was getting out of control.

"I beg to differ." Isabella clenched her jaw. "I didn't coach in all the way from Franla for you to get cold feet. Money is no object, dear, but I utterly hate wasting good resources and I've already gone ahead and booked your band and entertainment."

"You what!?" Josephine's eyes widened, voice breaking in surprise.

"And!" Isabella stepped forward. "I went ahead and hired you some decorators, because that garden of yours is far too plain for an Imperial wedding. Leave it to the main branch of the family to be so dull." Josephine gaped but Isabella cut her off with a wink of her eye. "No need to thank me, cousin. I have long wondered if you would ever marry, what with that stony expression of yours scaring everyone off." She bobbed her head from side to side. "And I always held little hope for your brother..." She leaned in and whispered loudly. "Being so... intellectually challenged."

Opane blinked. "You can't mean George?"

"Excuse me?" Isabella turned to Opane with such a powerful gaze, Josephine could see even the wise Opane suddenly question what she had told the duchess. Opane furrowed her brow, clearly thinking of how to approach the woman and Isabella's stare melted into a pitying smile. Josephine piped up, catching her cousin's attention.

"There is no wedding," She said, finding her voice and standing firm. "It was a rumor."

"A rumor?" Isabella's face dropped into an unamused pool of disgust. "Who would ever make such a virulent rumor as to catch my attention?"

"Perhaps the Father Sage?" Opane offered.

Josephine raised a brow. She thought the same, but she also wasn't sure enough about it to be declaring it to someone like Isabella. Either way, Josephine felt that Opane was probably right. Clearing her throat, the Regent spoke steadily. "I have reason to believe that Father Sage Clement aided in the rumor. My marriage to Count Gennisberg has been pushed by the Sages for some time now and a rumor would only add pressure to it."

"I see..." Isabella couched her chin between her thumb and finger. "Well! Would you at least come see my arrangements before you so frivolously dismiss them?"

"I think... I might first have to confront Clement about a few things," Josephine replied. Isabella gave a deep frown.

"So it may seem..." She perked up suddenly, eyes wrinkling with a brand new smile. "Either way, I'll be around longer yet, dear. You tell your favorite cousin how the talk with Clement went and we can work around it." Her voice dropped to one of a threat. "I won't have my name attached to gullibility."

Josephine twisted a frown and went to walk around her cousin with Opane following. The regent quickly said, "there will be no wedding," as she passed Isabella.

"There will be something," Isabella promised, before crossing her arms. Wise Reginald chewed his cheek and let the procession pass him unquestioned.

***

Josephine stomped down the halls of the palace with a determined look blanketing her face and a curious thought wrenching around her head. This rumor had gone too far now, to have gotten the notice and involvement of her cousin Isabella. If Clement was indeed behind the rumors, he would have Void and fury to pay. A piece of her was in shock that she ever even considered marriage, and another piece of her wished she could tell Williams the same. Her face softened and worry seeped into her eyes; hopefully he was healthy and unharmed.

"Josephine." Opane spoke. Twice in one day now, Opane was clearly caught off guard as Josephine turned to her with a sharp look in her eye. Opane grimaced. "Did I offend you just now?"

Letting out a long sigh, Josephine shook her head. "You're fine, there is just a lot on my mind."

"That would make sense, no?" Opane fell into step beside the regent. Silence reigned for a moment before the Kafshe spoke up again, this time with a slow and deliberate tone. "May I ask you a question?"

"Hm?"

Amber eyes peered at Josephine. "What was your dream about?"

Josephine stopped walking for a moment. The pair stood staring at each other before Josephine crossed her arms and continued her pace. "Nonsense. It's always nonsense."

"I only ask because you were mumbling," Opane said in a neutral tone. "You mentioned your grandfather."

"We've been spending too much time in his study," Josephine countered. "It's rotting my brain."

"If my loyalty is in question, I will not object." Opane kept up pace with the regent. " But I will say that your brother told me all about his own dreams. I may not know much, but perhaps I can help, should they be similar."

Josephine rolled her jaw in thought for a moment before looking around. The hallway was empty, or rather as empty as it ever could be, with the closest guard being a handful of doors down. Looking back to Opane, Josephine whispered. "The Dweller is getting closer to her goals. I'm not sure if George's victory slowed her down as much as we had initially hoped. Let's just find Clement and push our lead. We've sat idle for long enough."

"Ah, and I thought you were waiting for evidence?" Opane knit her brow.

"We'll get it." Josephine assured before pursing her lips into a thin line. The regent paused, and she could feel something thicken the air, as if a sudden pressure was added to the hallway; *Clement*. Turning to face forward again, she confirmed her instincts as Clement turned the far corner. A surprise look stretched his face when he locked eyes with Josephine. The regent couldn't help but send a deadly glare his way, breaking the man's step. He definitely had the look of a guilty person.

"Regent Josephine and um, yes hello," Clement greeted the two with a nod of his head, intent on walking by. Before he could get by, Josephine cleared her throat.

"Father Sage Clement, I was just looking for you."

The old man stopped mid stride and stood up straight. He turned to Josephine and straightened his bright blue robe. "And what may I help the Regent with? Has your brother caused you more trouble to be cleaned up?"

"Actually, it was regarding my wedding," Josephine said, a drop of poison in her voice.

Clement raised his brow. "Indeed?"

Josephine nodded. "And how it's not going to happen."

"And yet, all these people are here for it..."

"About that." Josephine folded her arms square behind her back, not unlike her teacher Reginald. "I was made to believe that people were flocking to the palace due to a rather potent rumor."

"A rumor?" Clement cocked his head to the side.

"Clement, cut the shit," Josephine hissed. "You dispel this rumor and send these people home. I'm not marrying Gennisberg, I've made my decision."

"You say that as if this rumor was my doing." Clement frowned, his fingers curling into fists.

Josephine gritted her teeth. "Dispel it, and then send Gennisberg home."

"Regent, I think you should think this through-"

"I've thought of it plenty." Josephine looked past Clement for a moment then at Opane. Silent support radiated from the Kafshe. After a brief pause, she looked back down at Clement, resolute on her next move. "Get it done."

Clement barely managed to spit "Yes, your Highness," before Josephine pushed by him with Opane hurrying after her, the court drama throwing her usual wild grace for a loop.

***

Emperor Frederick's study, having been a heavily frequented area by the Regent as of late, was no longer layered in dust, and the vines outside the windows were trimmed back to let in a late morning glow. A fresh citrus scent saturated the room, mixing with the old odor of mildew and yellowed pages. The door swung open and Josephine came marching in with Opane trailing behind. As soon as the Kafshe breached the threshold, Josephine slammed the door closed behind her.

Opane's eyes studied Josephine. "So what's your plan?"

Biting her thumb, the regent looked to the window. "We are going to visit the Imperial Cathedral." She turned to Opane. "And break into the record vaults."

The Kafshe raised a single brow for a moment before settling into one of the newly upholstered chairs. She sank into the cushion and looked up at Josephine. "Grant me patience, Josephine, but can't you demand the records as regent?"

"As if they would keep anything sensitive in the vaults if they knew I was coming, and there is the very real chance that what I want isn't even there but elsewhere... Clement's office perhaps." Josephine returned to biting her thumbnail.

"Do you really think Clement would leave any evidence in the Cathedral?" Opane asked.

Before Josephine could answer Opane, there was a soft sound, much like the rustling of clothes that sounded from behind the door to the study. Josephine's eyes snapped to the location it came from. Keeping focus on the door, Josephine walked over with a certain suspicion on her mind. With Opane watching over her shoulder, Josephine wrapped her fingers around the door knob. A shimmer of gold spiraled up her arm and in one swift movement, she swung the door open, reached into the hallway and grabbed a handful of shirt. Ripping the spy into the room, Josephine slammed the door shut once more. Cassandra went tumbling to the floor, a painful cringe in her face as she signed frantically.

"Cassandra!?" Josephine dove to help the woman to her feet, "I'm so sorry! I thought you were... well nevermind, what are you doing here?"

The servant blew a puff of her hair from her face and signed. "This room meant a lot to me way back when, I was just curious to see it again, but then I heard voices."

Opane was squinting, confused. "What are her fingers doing?"

The regent turned to the kafshe. "It's how she speaks."

"Oh..." Opane doubled her focus on Cassandra's fingers, as if intent on cracking a code.

"How much did you hear?" Josephine jumped right to it.

A single quick sign. "Enough." Then a hasty follow-up. "But don't worry, it's not like I can breathe a word about it."

Opane was rubbing her chin in thought. "Josephine."

"Hm?"

"Would not three be better than two?"

"I couldn't ask her to do that," Josephine said.

"Why not?" Cassandra signed. Josephine bit her thumb.

"I don't know, I just always thought that between you, myself, and my brother that..."

Cassandra shot a breath through her nose. "Not you too." A silent groan. "You were an ass as a teen and George was an ass for twice as long but..." Josephine watched her fingers in silence, unused to being insulted so directly but unable to find irritation at it, only a slight shame. Cassandra continued. "Despite all that, I helped take care of both of you as well as your father and your mother." The word stung. "But this isn't about how children treated me or how I feel about all of that, the reason I stuck around behind that door after hearing you talk is that maybe I too want to go into the Cathedral."

"You want to sneak in as well?" Josephine pondered.

Opane gave a sage nod, not quite understanding the back and forth. "I'm sure her silent words will come in handy."

"Yes," Cassandra signed to both. She hesitated for a moment. "I want to see if Father Sage Demitri left anything behind before he disappeared."

Chapter 14
Ancient Truths

In the upper reaches of the Imperial city, just outside the gates that lead up to the palace's front courtyard, sat the Imperial Tagist Cathedral. It was a tall building made of brightly stained glass and old dense rock, giving it a surreal look that was both contemporary and extremely ancient. A spire topped with a copper dome capped the building, and a bell hidden inside kept track of time for the denizens of the city. The vibrations from the bell striking noon were still in Josephine's chest as she looked up at the gleaming copper roof. She sucked in a breath, as if centering herself before dropping her vision to the mighty double doors of the building, already wide open. As customary, the Cathedral kept the front door open at all times, so that anyone could wander into the vestibule of the building and access the main pews through the smaller, more easily handled doors inside.

Of course that didn't mean the Cathedral didn't screen their guests somehow, and the moment Josephine stepped into the shade of the daylit vestibule, a sage dressed in simple blue robes with hair braided into a crown froze in shock. Her eyes jumped from Josephine to Cassandra, to Opane, and then to the five Palace Guards that now stood around the exposed double doors.

"Regent Josephine..." She said with tentative surprise. "I wasn't told you would be visiting."

"And yet here I am," Josephine said with a heavy air of authority. As if taking a page from Isabella's book, Josephine had adorned her rich burgundy dress with shimmering jewelry and topped it off with her regent's circlet, giving her a halo of dominance. There was a pause and Josephine narrowed her eyes, intent on keeping her momentum as she asked, "Are you going to open the door?"

The sage paled and leapt to the door before yanking it open. "Apologies, regent."

With the door open, Josephine walked through with Cassandra and Opane right behind her. Cassandra wore her usual dress of silken whites and silver baubles while Opane walked in covered by her usual furs, a sight that forced the sage to linger a moment as the Kafshe and her shared an uncomfortable glance.

The group moved from the simple vestibule lit only by the sunlight that spilled through the double doors and into the intricately illuminated nave of the cathedral. Row upon rows of pews filled the area with pillars on either side and the high, vaulted ceiling of the cathedral was quilted with hundreds of colored windows, bathing the area in rainbows. A few of the pillars had ingenious curved mirrors on them, directing a portion of the light to the pulpit, where the Father Sage would stand to perform the sermons.

Josephine pursed her lips. The sage from earlier rushed from behind her and stood diligently at her side.

"Is something wrong, your highness?"

The regent shot her a look. "I wish to use the private prayer room."

"Ah..." The sage frowned. "It is in use, currently."

"Show me the way, I'll wait."

With a reluctant nod, the sage dipped past the pillars and through one of the auxiliary doors. The group spilled into a side hallway with old murals and gilded molding until they came to an equally exquisite door that had a heavy look to it. The sage idled by it, staring at Josephine and her two followers. Cassandra cocked a brow at the sage and Josephine sighed.

"Is something on your mind...er?"

"Sage Maria," Maria answered quickly. "And no, sire, all is well."

Another awkward pause as the sage continued to stare. Opane knit her brow and shot a pitying look at Maria. "I wonder if your door is lonely without its guardian?"

"Oh yes!" Maria gave the group a suspicious look before frowning and bowing her head. "Excuse me, sire." She began a hurried walk away and once she turned the corner, Josephine let out a long sigh, deflating from her proud stance from earlier.

"I doubt we will be alone long before a different sage comes by to be our official escort," Josephine said, but before she could say anything further, the door to the prayer room opened with a heavy shrug. The group stiffened for a moment, and then all at once gave an incredulous look save for a confused Opane. Hector and an older man with a white beard that reached his belly shared the look from the doorway.

The Stromists acted first, each putting their hands to their hearts and bowing their heads. "Regent Josephine."

Josephine furrowed a brow. "Odd seeing the marshal and one of the masters coming out of a Tagist prayer room."

The master let out a long exhale. "To soothe the Tagist more than our own souls, I assure you."

"Father Sage Clement has been getting vocal about the masters supposedly slacking in recognizing Tagism as an equal religion," Hector explained. The Master scoffed.

"The Tagists simply just don't understand the mind of a Stromist diligent and simply lump us with Stromism practitioners. Once again, Clement has accused me of ancestor worship and defiling the minds of young Stromists with my lessons of personal balance."

Hector flinched. "As you can see, a few soft spots have been prodded recently."

Josephine tapped her chin. "I see..." She turned to the master. "Could I borrow the marshal from you?"

"It is your right," the Master tipped his head. "Shall I be dismissed, then?"

"Of course, thank you, Master."

The Stromist master gave another deep bow of his head before wandering off, leaving Hector alone with the trio. Hector cocked a brow. "What exactly are we up to, Regent?"

"I need you to cover this door, tell any sage who comes by that I'm busy praying and I instructed you to guard the door. They shouldn't raise too much of a brow from me using the new marshal for guard duty."

"No, but they might be a bit annoyed you're using a Stromist instead of one of them," Hector advised.

"I'm sure you know how to deal with an annoyed Tagist by now, Hector, please do this for me."

Hector bit his lip. "Of course I will, anything for the Regent." He bowed his head. "And a friend."

Josephine smiled. "Thank you."

***

With their alibi secured, the trio made their way deeper into the cathedral. The many branches of the building were an intricate maze of ostentatious decor that reminded Josephine of the palace, if only more tailored to the theology of the Graces. Since depictions of the Graces were frowned upon by the Tagists, in their place among the paintings were halos of light or at most a nondescript hand reaching down to help some poor Imperial back to their feet. It all came from the idea that the Graces were housed in the sky, among the blue, among the sun. Josephine dragged her fingertips across the bumpy paint. But now, with George's report regarding Galmun's question about where they truly live, she had her doubts. If they indeed were stuck in the void like the Dweller, it only made sense they would ally themselves... but why now, why not before, and how do they intend to escape?

"Are you religious?" Opane whispered. Josephine shot her a look, initially startled by the sudden inquiry. She replied.

"I'm not sure."

"Then I'll bother you no longer on it," Opane answered.

The trio walked in complete silence while Josephine confidently led them through the cathedral. In truth, she only partially knew where she was going, relying on an old memory of the day she chased a six year old George through the passages, all to Reginald's disappointment. As they continued past the intricate paintings, statues, and murals they eventually came to a tight turn that was right past a set of doors. If Josephine's memory served, down that turn was the staircase that led into the depths of the cathedral cellars and vaults.

She quickened her pace, eager to get off the first floor, with Opane right behind and Cassandra trailing after them. They cut past the doors and just as Josephine and Opane turned the corner, there was a loud creaking. One of the doors had opened and while Josephine couldn't see what was happening she heard a surprised gasp of an unknown voice.

"Oh hello! What- what are you doing here?"

Josephine peeked back past the corner to see the back of a sage and a frantically signing Cassandra. A blush hit Josephine's face as she realized what Cassandra was signing.

"I really really need to use the bathroom, can you show me the way?"

The sage seemed at a loss of what to do, then as Cassandra clearly caught a glimpse of Josephine watching, her sign changed. "I'll take care of this one, keep going."

Josephine signed back. "Thank you." The regent slipped back down the empty hallway.

"Will she be okay?" Opane whispered.

"I think so," Josephine answered. "If not, I can raise fire and brimstone about it after we get what we came here for. Besides, her alibi is that she needed to use the toilet, who is going to argue with that?"

Opane nodded with determination. "Her visit to the toilet will not be in vain, then." Josephine gave Opane a look, unsure for a moment if this Kafshe was that straight-laced or was simply finding humor in a monotonous way.

Now whittled down to two, the pair quickly located the thick metal door that blocked access to the lower levels. The hinges were located on the other side of the door and a massive iron lock kept the threshold closed. Josephine was the first to spot it and the first to swear under her breath. She put a hand on the door and swore again. "I don't know what part of me expected the door to be unlocked."

"Probably the part related to George" Opane answered deftly. Now Josephine was confident this Kafshe was finding humor in this. Opane lifted the lock into the palm of one of her hands. "Pretty dense metal..."

Gnawing on her knuckle in thought, Josephine said. "If you check the area to make sure no one would be alerted by sound, maybe I can snap it with my Stromism."

"Or..." Opane looked over at Josephine with a look that might have been subdued pride. The hand holding the lock suddenly crackled with frost, and a few frozen seconds later, the metal lock crumbled to the floor onto the stone floor. Opane shook frozen metal sand from her palm, unharmed, and gently nudged the door open. A stale, cold wind sighed through the now open threshold. Opane's smile curled even more. "After you, Regent."

"I guess the stories about your magic are true after all, huh?" Josephine offered with a straight face before pushing into the dark stairwell. Opane simply grinned at that. Josephine stopped in front of her, and as Opane closed the door behind them, they were veiled in complete darkness. Josephine looked behind her, Opane's amber eyes reflecting through the black. "If you don't mind putting some of your Kafshe magic to more use, I can't see the steps."

"Of course."

With a snap, a winter blue glow flickered from Opane's hand, revealing a spiraling staircase so long that they couldn't see the bottom. Murals still painted the walls and were engraved even on the steps.

"Grandeur even in the dark..." Josephine muttered to herself. A piece of her wondered if the Tagists were always this haughty, and another piece of her figured she was about to find out. As they reached the bottom step, the light from Opane spilled over a cavernous room of bookshelves and glass cabinets. Scrolls, books, notes, and grimoires alike were neatly organized amid both, and artifacts of both dubious and recognizable acclaim were stashed in between furniture.

"Do you know what you're looking for?" Opane asked before plucking a candle from a wall mount along with its striker.

"Something I'm not supposed to know," Josephine answered.

"Maybe not then..." Opane lit the candle and handed it over to the Regent.

"If we can't find anything down here, the only other option is Clement's office and that's all the way up top. Split up, we can cover more that way."

Opane eyed the candle she just handed to Josephine. "...You don't say?"

Josephine ignored the sarcasm and beelined right to one of the shelves. She was immediately met with well kept tomes and even newly bound spines, each designated with a title and author, save for some that were merely titled, and clearly many years after they were written. As the regent thumbed through a book describing the life of an ancient Mother Sage, it dawned on Josephine how much of a wild goose chase she was on. She didn't know where to start, and there were enough books to satiate her uncle for a lifetime.

"The Mysterious Ways of the Achians," Opane read out loud from another corner. "You know, I doubt they would be considered so mysterious if the Tagists just asked."

Josephine huffed at the distraction. "Aren't you Kafshe? I hear the Achians don't even talk to their own kind once they leave the mountains."

"My parents willingly gave me to the Paleskins." Opane idly flipped through the old book. "Or at least my mother did, my father was against it but either way, they were shamed out of the clan. I know this because I asked, granted maybe I wouldn't have if I was a kidnappee like most. Either way, there's always someone to learn from, boundaries be damned."

"That's insightful." Josephine narrowed her eyes on a book with yellowed pages.

"I try my best."

Josephine opened the book, finding a lineage of mother and father sages. Her eyes widened and she started to flip through it. "You mentioned most are kidnapped?."

Opane paused and slowly slid her book back into its spot. "How much do you know about the nature spirits?"

"Humm..." Josephine said, her eyes hungrily scanning the pages of her book. The lineages seemed to end around two-hundred years ago, making it an old book indeed, and with each page, she got further away from the present.

"Well." Opane continued. "Achians are prized among the shamans, especially ones who are sensitive to the ebb and flow of the nature spirits. Some Achian parents consider a life with the—as you call them—"paleskins" better than life on the peaks, other times, the shamans steal them in the night to keep the ways of the spirits moving in the lowlands." By now she was just in a tangent, "You see, the spirits are born from the natural mixing of ambient smoke and mist—"

"This book only goes back six-hundred and two years," Josephine interrupted. Opane sputtered and put a hand on her hip.

"What?"

"Why is that?" Josephine slapped the book closed and looked up at Opane. "My uncle's book on IAO went back seven-hundred years, but was written four-hundred years ago and depicted the empire already formed and fighting the Ulmi in a civil war, while Tagist history tells that Victor Heinrich and IAO carved the empire out seven-hundred years ago together and settled it into order using the blessings of the Graces and Tagist doctrine. Shouldn't there be ninety-eight more years of Mother and Father Sages leading to the founding of the empire? Why does it start abruptly a century after the supposed founding in Tagist history, and the supposed end of the first Vagrant war in my Uncle's book?" Opane opened her mouth but before she could speak, Josephine continued her rant. "This is putting a hole in how important the Tagists were during the formation of the empire, and if the empire was already formed prior to IAO, then even more so. How did the Tagists enter politics, and what did they have to gain by inciting the Ulmi and Giants against my father?"

Opane frowned. "I don't suppose they would have kindly written out all the answers and stuffed them down here..."

Josephine shot a breath through her nostrils. "I don't know why I would have thought that either. We need to go to Clement's office. If there is any hard evidence, that's where it would be." A worried look etched on Josephine's face.

Opane raised a brow. "What's wrong?"

"There is a reason I was hoping my answers would be down here, as his office is at the pinnacle of the central tower and I don't know if he is even out of it, right now."

Opane looked down and pursed her lips in thought. "Whatever you decide, I'm here to keep you safe and I'll back you up."

Letting out a long sigh, the regent started back towards the steps. "Well, then let's get a move on."

***

Back in the hall, the two had their tongues between their teeth and care in every step. Now knowing the stakes of how far they needed to go to consider their infiltration a success, they were doing their absolute best to remain undetected. Time was also of a factor as Josephine knew that Hector and Cassandra couldn't bat away all the inquiries they must have been getting forever. From what Josephine remembered of the layout of the cathedral and how it looked outside, there must have been a central stairwell somewhere in the altar room, which would be an issue if the altar was being attended by any sages. Eventually, Josephine and Opane came to the conclusion that there was only one way that Josephine could get through such a congested area and up the stairwell undetected, and Opane was less than thrilled with the plan.

Together they slipped through the quiet halls in complete silence until they got to a T-intersection where the inward direction was a sharp right from where they were and was marked by a decorative archway. It didn't take an architect to know that something important was through that archway, and in the case of their impromptu mission, that would be the large altar room along with the central stairwell that nestled somewhere inside.

Josephine peeked around the corner, looking into the room in question. There were indeed plenty of sages, four in fact, doddering over relics and artifacts as well as discussing this and that over an open book of parables. Squinting, Josephine could make out the edge of a doorway rather close to the opening of the room and with luck, though that was her way upward.

She turned to look at Opane. The Kafshe had her eyes closed, as if mentally preparing herself. Josephine steeled her gaze. "Ready?"

Opane peeked out with one amber eye. "This goes against all I've done to break stereotypes, you know? Do you think they'll even buy it?"

Arching a brow, Josephine answered dryly. "It's a bunch of uptight Tagist sages."

"Ah, stereotypes." Opane craned her neck back and forth before stepping out of her hiding spot. "Don't tell anyone else I did this."

Josephine watched as Opane strode through the hallway with an uncharacteristic chest-puffed pride and right into the altar room. The way she walked and the air she put about her forced the sages to do a double take before registering the errant Kafshe in their sacred room. Everyone but a sage still engrossed in the book of parables were gaping, looking for words. Opane put her hands on the shoulders of the reading sage and leaned over him so she was against his ear.

"Yabbadai!" Opane bellowed, causing the reading man to flinch and turning the silent shock into a sudden uproar.

Accusations went flying as hands meant to restrain the intruder shot out, but Opane simply dove and weaved between the sages and the artifacts. All eyes were on her, giving Josephine the blindspot she was looking for. With all backs turned and set on capturing Opane, while the Kafshe yelled in the language of the wild, Josephine slipped through the hallways and through the doorway to the stairwell.

The regent was met with a darker set of stone stairs and a cool, dry breeze spilling in from somewhere above. She was in the heart of the cathedral now, and there was no turning back. Attempting to muster the same confidence as Opane while simultaneously tightening every muscle in the hopes of softer and quieter footfalls, Josephine started up the stairs.

Every step had her mind repeating a solemn wish that no one enter the stairwell, and every time she passed a door, her heart pounded a little heavier, envisioning what would happen if it were to suddenly open. Now and again she would hear voices, which made her stomach tighten, and when she heard a door close in the distance, she nearly bolted into a run before realizing that it wasn't a door connected to the stairwell. Settling back to her silent rhythm, Josephine looked upward, eager to get this over with.

***

Serendipity was on Josephine's side as her fingers tightened around the doorknob of Clement's office. It was locked but the frame of the threshold was so old that it didn't take more than a simple push laced with Stromism to swing the door inward. Josephine walked in with the door, closing it behind her. Immediately she was met with the light of Clement's office, a sharp contrast to the stairwell that brought her here. The room was very much a circle with rectangle windows in every perspective, drowning the office in the midday sun.

Neatly organized shelves were bolted in between the windows and any bare wall was covered with the blue flag of the Tagists. The furniture was made of strong oak, booted with gold on slick stone floors. Even Clement's desk was lined with gold, glinting the light from the windows and inviting Josephine over.

She obliged with a sense of urgency in her step and pushed Clement's upholstered sitting chair out of the way, leaving his many drawered work-desk at her mercy. The desktop itself was clean of papers and only had weights and inkjets, so Josephine skipped right to the large center drawer. It was locked, but considering the frozen lock on the first floor and the busted doorframe on the top floor, Josephine couldn't find any reason not to force this one open just the same.

Sucking in a breath she held up two fingers and focused heavily on her fingertips. A streak of golden magic laced around them. She placed the tips against the circular metal lock and with a sharp exhale, she stabbed her fingers forward. With a soft pop and a wooden crack, the lock was pushed into the drawer and the metal mechanism snapped, giving the drawer a sudden slack.

Pulling it open, Josephine was met with disappointment. Inside was nothing more than simple notes and memorandums. She flicked through a bunch of them, finding nothing but things that should have been filed away elsewhere. Gritting her teeth, Josephine looked to the next drawer and repeated her lockbreaking scheme.

Drawer after drawer, the regent broke their locks and scoured their contents, finding nothing but the mundane. Her heart was starting to sink into anxiety, worried that she did all this for nothing. All she really gleaned from her highly controversial trip into the cathedral was a few missing years with no further information. Josephine furrowed her brow and with a rush of frustration, slammed the drawer she was looking in shut.

The drawer cracked from the force, slamming into the wood behind it with a resoundingly dull thud. Josephine froze. She reached out and pulled the drawer back open and slammed it shut again, another dull thud. Flickering her eyes over to the central drawer, she ripped it open and gave that one a heavy crash back into its place—a sharp thunk, wood against wood.

Excitement flittered in Josephine's stomach as she returned to the cracked drawer and yanked it off its tracks, sending it clattering to the floor. There, set behind where the drawer was, was a now revealed compartment door. Josephine swallowed and pushed it aside, reaching her hand into the dark recesses of the desk. Something leathery found her fingertips and she pulled it out.

Josephine looked down at the wrinkled book she held in her hands. Despite its immense weight, she felt like it was floating on her fingers, not daring to grasp it in the fear it would disintegrate. It was a hearty book and older than any she had ever seen. There was no title, no author, just a blue thumbprint pressed against the center of the black leather cover. She sucked in a breath, as if the heat from her lungs would melt the old manuscript, and peeled it open.

She was met with a dark and strong handwriting, penned on yellow vellum pages. It looked as if the script was routinely reinked, and Josephine only had to read a few lines in order to realize why.

This book was older than seven-hundred years. She didn't know how much older, but her eyes were glued to the text as she realized she was reading the words of the very first sage: a strange woman from the Arctic Mountains.

Narrowing her eyes, Josephine continued reading. The book spoke of the Heinrich Empire in the south, ruled by Victor Heinrich and his provincial lords. It spoke about how every year, Victor would enact a great ritual with the lords at the palace, a magical scheme to keep the Graces at bay, to keep them imprisoned in the void, and how in an attempt to put a stop to it, the sage gathered the people of the north to overthrow the Heinrich dynasty and put forth their own.

Josephine flipped through the pages, getting deeper into the story. She found pages upon pages describing the war, how the sage taught the northern people and the giants the power of the Graces through mist-talking, and how the empire was crumbling under the weight of such a magic. Next, the pages lamented the coming of IAO, and how such a mysterious man brought with him a new magic rumored long dead and with it secured the Empire once again.

The handwriting ended there, only to be picked up by a fresh hand. This told the tale of the second sage, and how when faced with annihilation, he decided to betray the northern peoples to the Heinrichs and claim allegiance with the empire. From there, more sages wrote in, each describing their attempts to assimilate into the empire and gain the trust of the political structures and to intercept and quietly overthrow an existing church called the Iacine. Josephine frowned; but why, it couldn't be simply for survival, and why keep such a book?

Newer texts talked about censorship, secret plans to wipe clean the slate, and eventually make the sages historically always a part of the structure. This theme continued, a theme of taking over from within, laying in wait, but laying in wait for what? Josephine flipped further into the book, passing endless stories of countless Mother and Father Sages until she was hit with a handwriting she recognized, one she had seen before.

In Clement's hand, she read about how the time had finally arrived. The Graces were closer than ever, their visions stronger than before, and how the seeds of the north would once again come to the Sage's aid. Josephine closed her eyes, letting it all sink in.

"An instruction manual, really," Clement's voice caused a cold shock to seize Josephine. She opened her eyes to find the Father Sage standing at the doorway. "Passed down from one Father or Mother to the next, so we never quite forget the truth, never quite forget the sins of the Heinrich." He took a step forward.

Josephine snapped the book shut and took on a fighting stance. "Don't you come any closer."

Clement stopped and crossed his arms. "Very well."

"Why were my ancestors keeping the Graces locked away?"

"I'd like to know that myself," Clement hissed. "By all means, the Graces have only shown mercy and passion to their flock, and yet it would seem that the Heinrich dynasty alone managed to keep them from their true home among us. From what I can gather, it's simply because the Heinrich don't want any competition. Just look at your grandfather for proof, so eager to destroy anything not under his control."

"The Dweller is locked away." Josephine rounded to the side so the desk was no longer in between them.

Clement gave a shallow nod. "She is, but she is not the same as the Graces. She's corrupted, sick... evil if you will."

Josephine pointed the book at Clement. "Letting the Graces out would let her out."

Clement opened his hands, as if showing that he had nothing to hide. "With the Graces by our side, we would have nothing to fear from the Dweller."

Squinting, Josephine shook her head. "Your actions against the empire and her people are inexcusable."

"And so what do you plan to do, *Regent?*" A deep scowl carved into Clement's face.

Josephine tucked the book under her arm and stood up perfectly straight. "I *plan* to throw you into a cell and get to the bottom of this properly. Consider yourself under arrest."

"I don't think-" Clement started.

"Kneel!" Josephine shouted, her fists glimmering with Stromism.

Surprised, Clement knelt down. He found his poison and spat. "A Heinrich through and through."

Josephine's mind swirled with the new information, a conflicted feeling growing in her gut. She forced herself through it with anger. "Close your mouth! Put your hands out front."

Clement hesitated.

"Do it!"

The father sage did as he was told, and before long, others were running up the stairs to check in on all the shouting, Hector, Cassandra, Opane and the Stromist master included.

Chapter 15

The Runic Man

A line of city guards blockaded the way to the cathedral and directed traffic away from the road that wound up towards the palace. A crowd of citizens were mumbling just outside their perimeter, gossiping and whispering as palace guards did their best to drag Clement up the road with their bodies acting as shields to keep him from view. Quietly escaping the chatter and clamor, Josephine was already well ahead of the arresting party with her three friends at her heels.

"Is that the missing piece of all this?" Opane nudged her chin towards the ancient book that Josephine was holding tight to her chest. Josephine offered her a glance.

"It'll see Clement guilty."

Cassandra signed, her mind clearly racing as fast as Josephine's—as fast as everyone's. "Are you... going to reveal the whole thing?"

That question was nagging Josephine before Cassandra even asked it. A lot of things were nagging Josephine. She knitted her brow. She had the facts in her arms, as biasedly written they were, but she didn't have the motivations. Shaking her head, she knew that wasn't true, she knew the Tagist's motivations, it was her own family's that she didn't know.

Hector watched the exchange, and when Josephine started shaking her head, he relaxed his shoulders. "I think that's wise, Regent. There is no need to expose everything all at once and shock everyone's systems. I imagine some might think it a hoax or fabrication."

"Clement's involvement in the war is now unmistakable, even if the rest of it is seen as false," Opane reminded. Josephine exhaled.

"I'll reveal enough to see him guilty, the rest, I'll hold onto for a while longer." She pursed her lips. "I don't have the full story." Josephine looked down at the book in her hands. What sort of secrets did Victor Heinrich know, what was this ritual, and how did it work? The more Josephine thought about it, the more her head hurt, as if something was whining in her ear, a sharp, screeching sound whipping her into a headache. It reminded her of something, but she couldn't remember. A piece of her swore she felt this sort of headache and heard this sound before.

"What in the..." Hector's voice brought Josephine's attention back to the fore. She looked up towards the palace. There was a mass of people all in colorful clothing globbed up by the front courtyard. Palace guards were weaving between them all, and standing on an overturned box was Isabella Heinrich in a stark yellow dress.

A groan found its way to Josephine's throat and she quickened her steps until she was in earshot of Isabella, an errant man dressed in frills nearly bumping into her as she entered the scene. Josephine threw her voice over the clamoring of the strange crowd, "What's going on!?"

Isabella immediately turned to Josephine with a big smile on her face. She leapt from her pedestal to stand right in front of her younger cousin "Well, dear," she started. "I was very much upset when I heard there would be no wedding, and I was also very much distressed in having already paid for all these bits of entertainment, you see…"

Josephine squinted. "Uh… huh…"

"So I decided to use them regardless of your dreadful marital status. We can mark it as a little ball, settled and paid for by your favorite cousin." Isabella gave a wink while maintaining her wide smile. A gruff man came in from the side with a frightened look on his face.

"Duchess…" He started before anyone else could respond to Isabella's presumptuous plans. "The working lads dropped one of the wine barrels, we are going to be short of the quota you sent."

Isabella's smile faded as she turned to the man. Fear radiated from the poor fellow and Isabella started a slow and deliberate speech. "If I drop a coin, I can find ten more of it in my pocket. Similarly, if I lost a steward because he couldn't solve a simple problem without my input, I could have ten more of him by the end of the day." She narrowed her eyes. "Fix it, I'm busy." Isabella flickered her eyes back to Josephine, as if implying her company. The man paled.

"My apologies."

"Shh!" Isabella turned from the man and smiled at Josephine, the duchess' face brightening as if she didn't just threaten a man's livelihood. "Don't you think this will be just wonderful? A little dancing would do you some good—your cheeks are absolutely pale and don't get me started on those bags under your eyes. My goodness, you'd think there was no blood flowing through your body."

Josephine closed her eyes and gave a slight shake of her head. "I don't think I know a brighter personality than your own, cousin." She opened her eyes just in time to see Isabella's smile shrink.

"As long as you don't forget it, dear." There was a stern tone in the Duchesses voice.

Deep inside, Josephine couldn't help but feel done with the day already, and even if it pained her, she knew the quickest way to end it wasn't to antagonize Isabella or even play her game. Sucking in the deepest breath and remembering Reginald's oldest lessons of etiquette, the regent forced a small smile. "I'm sorry, I've just had a long day." She looked over the crowd of people which Isabella had invited against her will. Forcing her smile to stay on her face, she added. "I'm grateful for your generosity."

"That's better," Isabella said with little cover. Josephine's eyes stayed on the crowd. A strange feeling buzzed in her head as she stared at the people there. Heads bobbing, Colorful shirts threading. People hauling this and that. It all seemed peripheral, and the more her eyes searched between the people, the more desperate she suddenly felt. Her heart rate was increasing, and that whining screech she heard in her grandfather's study was growing in her ears.

The sound grew, piercing her thoughts until finally her eyes fell on the face of a man with a lute strapped to his back. Josephine's eyes widened. He was covered in costume, concealing his skin save for his face. A somber visage peeked out from long black hair and a straight, equally dark beard, but what caught Josephine's eyes was the color of his skin, the sheen of gold and carved with strange runes. Her eyes started to water, as if she was staring at the sun, and a pain started to ripple in her head.

Hector's voice sounded next to Josephine, but it was distorted. "Princess, are you okay?"

"That's...him from," Josephine barely managed. Her head was becoming dangerously light and heavy all at the same time. The world was blurring and she could feel the tug of her narcolepsy deep in her chest. "My dream." A cold blackness washed over the back of her head and with a dizzying feeling, her vision blurred upwards.

***

Josephine woke up with a start. Her head was throbbing with the scars of nightmares she couldn't remember, and her body had a certain stiffness to it. Her cold blue eyes scanned the darkness all around her; it was clearly the middle of the night. She was laying in her bed: a monstrous thing stuffed thick with feathers and large enough to accommodate five more of her. Violet curtains draped around the vessel, blurring the light of the moon that leaked beyond the silky veil.

Tearing the covers off of her, she slipped out of bed. Her bare feet clapped against the cold marble floor, and if she wasn't already a royal used to certain customs, she might have been surprised that her clothes from earlier had been replaced with a comfortable verdant nightgown. She launched herself forward, through her curtains and into the greater cavity of her lifeless room. Her movements were propelled by a lingering emotion brought back to the waking world from her faded dreams.

The palace was dark except for the silver rays of moonlight gleaming through the windows, and as she approached the door to the hallways, her hand instinctively went for the candle holder.

Josephine watched her fingers hover over the utility, but her brow furrowed in thought. Something deep within her told her she wouldn't be needing it. Whatever it was she had dreamed, some foggy answer was given to her, and she knew where she had to go.

Her door opened silently and the chill of the enclosed hallways washed over Josephine's frame. A shiver formed up her spine, and while she was indeed feeling the cold of a spring night, an unsettled feeling crept along with it, injecting anxiety into her heart. She continued onward into the halls, the only sounds accompanying her being that of her own footsteps.

Eventually, Josephine found her way down a flight of stairs to the ground level. She had taken to walking with her arms crossed and guarded. Occasionally she'd pass a silent guard, the orange glow of their lanterns stealing whatever night vision she had adapted in between their posts. None of them asked where she was going, or what she was doing, but she could feel their curious stares.

Josephine quickened her pace, only slowing for a brief moment as she passed the red door. It caught her eye and for some unknown reason she brushed her fingers across its surface as she passed it. A sharp turn after that door and she was pushing open a completely different door flanked by guards, and thus stealing her night vision once again, to reveal a midnight darkened parlor room that oversaw the gardens outside.

Immediately she was hit with a stronger bite of the cold night, with only glass panes and a thin wooden door separating her from the outside breeze. Her heart was in her throat, but she decided to stand still in the center of the old room. Something about that room disturbed her, and why she felt the urge to go here disturbed her more. Bit by bit, as she stood uncomfortable, her vision readjusted to the darkness and as it all came into focus—a slight movement through the window caught her eye.

Squinting, she could make out two figures over by the old elm tree, but not much else. Josephine took a step towards the thin door and pushed it aside before throwing herself out into the dark and frigid gardens. The cobble path underfoot froze her naked feet and the wind bit through her gown. She never felt so vulnerable, and with each step that feeling grew. It was as if some unseen force was staring right at her, waiting for something. She mechanically jogged up the path towards the tree, only to stop as a secret scene opened before her.

There under the tree was her father in his own nightgown, a stark white to contrast the black of the night. His hair was being tousled by the breeze and kneeling by his outstretched arm was another figure. The second was a man clothed in black, with a hood hiding his face. Something glinted in his hand, something the figure was pressing against her father's arm. Josephine's eyes widened. A golden dagger.

"Stop!" Josephine felt herself yell and the world seemed to swirl into a surreal mess in her head. She pumped her legs and ran up the rest of the way towards the two. The man in the hood jerked away from Wilhelm and stared at her with wide eyes on a rune covered face. Josephine's head suddenly burned with that terrible whistle. *It was him!*

Wilhelm simply smiled a clueless smile as his daughter approached, but before Josephine could even get under the canopy of the elm tree. The runic man's body erupted in a golden light. The powerful wave of brightness knocked Josephine back, stunned and surprised. Already the palace guards that had been watching

Josephine were funneling out from the parlor behind her, but as she laid propped up on her hands, staring from her back in shock, she watched the hooded man bound up the palace walls, legs covered in sharp golden ribbons of magic.

"Father," Josephine managed, "who was that?"

Wilhelm tilted his head, eyes cloudy. "Who was who?"

Chapter 16
The Heinrichs

"What were you doing?" Josephine had her arms crossed. A thick quilted coat that fell below her knees now covered her from whatever chill the night offered, not that she needed it. A fire roared in the hearth of the sitting room she and her father were now stuffed in, blanketing the room in a dense orange heat. Wilhelm sat on a plush couch, still in his nightgown and a guilty look on his face that made Josephine feel as if she was scolding a child.

"Josie, I don't know what you mean." Wilhelm was as earnest as ever, if not completely clueless.

"You were outside with a strange man."

"No I wasn't."

"Dad." Josephine frowned. "You were outside..."

Wilhelm smiled and nodded. "For some fresh air."

"...With a strange man."

"What?"

"He had a knife to your arm," Josephine pleaded. "What was he doing?"

Wilhelm looked down at his arm and for the first time in Josephine's life, she noticed a collection of slashing scars on his inner forearm. Josephine grabbed her father's arm and examined it. There were at least three scars she could make out, each a different level of healed and faded, each scored at a different time.

"These aren't from the war," she said more than asked.

Wilhelm looked down at his arm. "Nope!"

Josephine let go of her dad's arm and sighed. "What's going on?"

Wilhelm put a finger to his lips. "A secret."

"Can't you tell me?" Josephine stood up straight. "I'm the regent."

Wilhelm shuffled in his seat.

Sucking in a breath, Josephine pinched the bridge of her nose. What would George say? He always had a better relationship with their father. Thinking it over, she looked back at her dad. "I'm your daughter."

Wilhelm's face softened, steeped with even more guilt. He looked back down at his arm and sighed. "I have so much pain in my chest, Josie." His eyes started to water.

Josephine sat next to Wilhelm and put a tense hand on his shoulder, it was an awkward touch but she was trying her best. "Why? Why dad? What's going on?"

"It's the least I could do to make up for my mistakes..."

"What is?"

Wilhlem held out his arm. "The ritual."

The world froze as Wilhelm's words bounced around in Josephine's ears, and that dense ringing joined her thoughts. It hurt her head to even think about, then she remembered—the ritual, Victor's ritual. She could see the accusing eyes of Clement in the back of her memory as he condemned Josephine's family. "What ritual, what does it do?"

"I don't know."

"What does the ritual do, Dad?"

A cloudy look misted over Wilhelm's eyes once again. "What ritual?"

"Damnit." Josephine stood up, defeated and agitated.

There was a knock at the door and Josephine called out. "Come in."

Hector peeled the door open and stepped in at attention. "I gathered the intel from the city watch, it seems our friend made a hasty escape in the direction of the Imperial Woods. I already authorized a chase with two Stromist squads, though I'll admit, he managed to outpace even the palace guards. He's really fast—this might turn into a tracking situation."

As Hector spoke, the cogs in Josephine's head turned. Her father told her all he could, but he was such a mess in so many ways, that the truth was never going to come from him. But this runic figure, he would know, he would know what the ritual was. He would know why it exists, what it does, and why her family seems to be the target of not only it, but hundreds of years of secrecy and war surrounding it. At this point, who could she even trust to deliver that level of information, that level of intimacy to her own self, family, and ideals. She frowned, having already made up her mind before she even left the gardens earlier that night. "I'll be joining the chase."

Hector's eyes widened. "Regent Josephine, I don't know..."

"Are you talking back to me?" Josephine snapped with more frustration than she intended.

Hector shook his head quickly. Despite his new position, Josephine could still see the young, smiling friend he was to George, and the stupid antics they always got into. She cracked a grin that winced with the seriousness of the situation. "Then I'll be going."

"At least let me join you."

Josephine chewed on her cheek for a moment before looking down at Wilhelm. "Actually, I need you here, to look after..." So many different titles flashed through her head, but only one felt right at the moment. "...after my father."

***

The sky above was bloated with grey clouds threatening to open up into a late spring rain. It was bad enough that the dreary atmosphere reminded Josephine of the sort you'd expect at a funeral, but if the sky decided to open up, she wasn't sure she would be able to find whatever tracks her runic prey had left. She wasn't alone in the hunt, though, Opane stood next to her, adamant that she had to come with, if not for Josephine's sake as her bodyguard, than for her promise to Rosaline. Together they stared out over the city from the palace hill and their visions drifted over the buildings until they met the docks and the expansive Imperial Sea which sat as gloomy as the sky above. While they stood there, waiting for an Imperial carriage to come around, Josephine couldn't help but wonder what was going to happen if she caught up to her mysterious target. She paused. No, *when* she caught up.

"Your face of determination looks identical to your sibling's," Opane commented.

Josephine shot a breath through her nose. "A lot is at stake here."

Opane thought in silence for a moment. Finally she asked. "What exactly is at stake? What happens if you don't catch this man?"

"Then I'm left in the dark, and whatever secrets this world is churning on will stay hidden, to the ill of everyone involved," Josephine answered. "Whatever is being hidden, it caused the war you and my brother fought in, it killed Franklin, it destroyed Fenric and Gavaria, it put Tagist liars in charge, put my family in the dark, and caused countless conflicts throughout history. It's about time we bring it back to the light."

Another pause. "Are you afraid at all about what you might find?"

Josephine stood tall, but her voice betrayed her anxiety. "Of course."

The grind of wheels and the clop of horses broke the conversation as Josephine's carriage came into view surrounded by mounted Imperial guards and two lightly dressed scouts. The guard with a captain's elm pounded into his breastplate spoke first. "Your majesty. If it pleases you, we will send scouts out ahead of us to interact with the Stromist trackers the Marshal issued and follow the trail."

Dipping her head, Josephine said, "of course, but let's not use that as an excuse to slow our pace." She looked at the man. "This is no slight matter."

"Hold it!" All heads turned to see Gennisberg huffing through the courtyard. It seemed more of a show than truth, as his chest wasn't heaving too much and a big smile was planted on his face. Collectively both Josephine and Opane's faces fell into scowls and before Josephine could address the count, he started talking.

"Excuse my interruption, Highness, but I must *insist* I come along. The whole ordeal seems like such a dangerous one, and I'd be right mad to not see myself aiding—"

"Do you have that little faith in the Imperial guards?" Josephine crossed her arms, not even bothering to acknowledge her interruption. "Or perhaps you think of me as delicate?"

"Absolutely not!" Gennisberg perked up, a sudden panic in his eyes. "I was simply saying—"

"Good day, Count Gennisberg," Josephine dismissed the man.

"But-!"

"This conversation has met its end." Opane stepped in between the two and the captain who was speaking with Josephine earlier put a rough hand on Count Gennisberg's shoulder.

"Time to leave, Count Gennisberg."

The count pursed his lips and gave Josephine a long look, who returned it with a steely gaze. A moment passed and Gennisberg silently turned from them and started a defeated walk back to the palace. Josephine squinted at the back of his head; she never trusted him, and now seeing his sponsors arrested for treason, something about him walking around freely didn't sit right with her. Perhaps this is the feeling George was describing the other day.

"My lady." The coachman looked over from his bench at the front of the carriage. "We can depart at your word."

Peeling her eyes off of Gennisberg and back to the scene at hand, she gave a nod.

***

Beyond the city and its salty harbor, and past the farms and fields that fed the capital was the Imperial Forest, a dense sea of trees and shadows. Normally all travel through the forest clipped the northeast corner of the forest, giving travelers a short glimpse of the wilds before spilling into the hillocks where the Achian mountains meet Caldora, but after meeting with the first Stromist scout, Josephine's group was told they needed to head straight west, right into the thick of the infamous woodland.

It wasn't long before the party found themselves on seldom used roads, with the only partakers being the soldiers who occupied the small outposts here and there, as well as the myriad of people who went into the woods to escape whatever lives they lived. As such, the usually paved stones of the Imperial roads eventually gave way to simple dirt paths and before long, even those gave way to some wild cousin, where the roads were scarred and gnarled with roots, thinning the way and forcing Josephine to abandon her carriage and the horses.

Now on foot, Josephine walked in the center of a ring of guards with Opane on her right. More than once the captain had suggested turning away and simply allowing the scouts to handle the chase, but Josephine was adamant; this was something she had to do, if not as a curious victim, than as a Heinrich left in the dark.

Her thoughts festered in her head while her ears were swallowed by the sounds of the immense forest. The trees were massive and oppressive, with thick branches and an endless ocean of leaves that left the road below in a constant shade. Only a rare speckle of golden sunlight ever glittered down whenever a high breeze rustled through. Birds of all sorts chirped, sang, and screamed along with whatever other beasts called the thickets home. Opane kept her lips pursed and her eyes wide and alert, she seemed more at home here than Josephine, who could only think about stories of the monsters and creatures that called this place home.

At a certain point, the stories found their way into the fore of Josephine's own mind and before long she had strapped a sword to her hip and found her thoughts quieting so she could focus on her surroundings. Subconsciously, her hand found its way to the handle, giving it a squeeze.

"Who goes there?" The captain shouted, pulling Josephine's eyes into the distance, where the road turned behind some trees. There at the edge stood a lone figure.

The figure was short, with pale white and pink skin, large black eyes, an upturned batlike nose and a braided beard of coarse hair bobbing off the chin of an otherwise bald head. He was dressed in thick furs, giving him the appearance of a lion's mane around his neck and on his hip was a curved blade. A paleskin.

"Lor Kabblest." The paleskin answered. "We have found one of yours."

Josephine never heard a paleskin speak before. The voice was alien, somehow sounding like a raspy whisper and a loud and confident proclamation at the same time, almost like a tunneling wind. She imagined that it is exactly how the ghost of a sinister warrior might sound. It would seem Josephine wasn't the only one taken aback by the voice, as everyone suddenly seemed much more on edge.

"What are you saying?" The captain demanded.

"No harm," Lor replied. "I will bring you to your comrade."

Josephine started to walk but then noticed no one else was. The captain looked back at her. "Stay here your majesty, I'll go first to ensure safety."

Josephine frowned but before she could argue, Opane leaned over to speak into her ear. "Your troops will feel more at ease this way. I do not think this man has ill intent, myself, but let them check."

The regent gave a nod of her head, sending the captain away with two other guards and leaving Josephine and the others standing still in the strange forest. Each minute in waiting felt like an hour, with nothing to occupy the mind but vain attempts at deciphering the cacophony of forest sounds and picking apart anxious thoughts. Before long, Josephine took to playing with a toggle on her sword belt and staring into the darkness between the trees. Just as her mind started to sink into questions about the runic man they were chasing and the strange ritual and history of her family, the captain's voice pulled her back.

Looking over, the man was standing with three more paleskins and beckoning them all clear.

***

Josephine didn't know what she expected the paleskin settlement to be like, but when faced with it she found it both unique and oddly usual. It was usual in the sense that she could accurately point out the location of each activity, be it a place to tan hides, process plants, or even smith metal, but at the same time, the buildings were like that of which she had never seen before. Under the tall canopies of the trees and in a meadow laden clearing, the paleskins had constructed small domes with thick wooden frames and woven walls plastered with clay. The domes's entryways were separated from the outside world with marvelously stitched and decorated rugs of many colors. The fine stitchings etched stories of deeds and adventures of various paleskins and Kafshe, with a few rare images of humans spattering in between.

Before she could look deeper into the meaning of the closest rug, Josephine's attention was grabbed by the shaman of the village, a serious looking paleskin covered in tattoos and stripped nearly naked if not just for a long loin cloth and various bands of jewelry. He stood with the captain of Josephine's guard as well as Lor by a blackened pit that housed a crackling fire— a pit which marked the exact center of the clearing.

As soon as Josephine made her way to the shaman, he started speaking a dense language that Josephine very clearly didn't know, but thankfully, Lor started speaking soon after, supposedly translating. Opane idled by the Princess, ears supposedly sharp for any trickery in translation.

"Good day, good sky, and good ground, Imperial," Lor started, "it is unusual to see your kind this deep into the great woods, let alone twice in one day."

Josephine looked to Lor. "Twice?"

Lor spoke to the shaman in their Kafshe language before beginning to translate again. "Yes. One of your ribbon warriors had injured himself in our territory. We casted his ankle and request you take him back with you."

"Can I see him?"

Lor nodded. "Of course."

Josephine motioned for him to lead the way and the group started their trek through the swishing meadow grass towards one of the strange paleskin buildings. As they walked, Lor spoke.

"Our healer lives down this way, your warrior is probably still resting."

"How'd you come to find him?" Josephine wondered out loud.

Lor stopped for a moment and looked at Josephine. His dark glassy eyes scoured her face for a moment. "Same way we found you. The shaman felt your alters. Your warrior was expending a lot of power chasing something."

Opane raised a brow. "I should have guessed it myself, shamans have a greater ability to sense altars, far beyond my own." She looked at Josephine. "I would advise asking the shaman to search for the runic man's altar."

It was Lor's turn to perk a brow. "I can ask for you." He stopped by the entrance to the building and pulled aside the thick blue fabric blocking the way. Josephine ducked through first.

Her eyes took a moment to adjust to the dim interior, where only a small circular window by the stove let in any amount of light. The thresh floors were freshly laid and across the room an Imperial soldier was propped up on a bed with a sober look about his visage as soon as he spied the regent. Before Josephine could take another step forward, another person entered her vision from off to the side, freezing Josephine in place.

A man with old wrinkled eyes and dull robes stared at Josephine with a sense of both fear and wonder. It was a human man who wore the blue of the Tagist sages. Josephine stuttered on her words for a moment before saying, "a Tagist?"

"What luck, right?" The soldier called from his reclined position. Josephine acknowledged him with a tilt of her head, but didn't take her eyes off the sage.

"Perhaps it would be best if we discussed the topic in private, Princess Josephine?" The sage offered with a quiet voice laced in exhaustion.

Josephine spoke slowly. "Opane."

"Yes?"

"Can you gather the soldier's report, I'll be right outside."

"I'd rather be at your side," Opane insisted.

"If you sense something, come to me," Josephine instructed, "but give me a chance at privacy first."

Opane gave a simple nod, letting the sage walk right by her and exit the building. The regent gave her companion a reassuring look before following suit. Back outside, the sage led Josephine off to the side so they couldn't be heard and yet still be in the peripheral of the guards milling about the campsite.

As they found their spot underneath a giant tree, the sage looked down at a fallen log, once some prominent branch. He frowned and looked back up at Josephine. She hadn't realized it, but she was standing tall, with her arms guardedly crossed and a sour look on her face. The helpless expression in the old man's face made her feel like some sort of villain. As if reading her mind, the sage asked, "would you mind if I sat?"

Josephine let out a long sigh. "Very well."

The man let out a groan that spoke of elderly pains as he sat. His posture was slouched and it was clear that his back had given up on supporting him many years ago. Closing his eyes for one moment too long, Josephine could have sworn he had simply fallen asleep, but that was not the case. His eyes reopened, and a certain pain was found in them. "I suppose you're wondering why a Taglst sage is living out here with Yabban, or paleskins as the Empire prefers."

"I'll admit a curiosity." Something was off about this sage.

"Well, I guess you could say that I've been here a very long time."

"How long?"

The old sage met Josephine's eyes and squinted. "About twenty-three years, not too long before your first birthday."

That put a pause on the conversation. Josephine couldn't help but simply stare at the elder, letting the sounds of both the forest and site take over. She chewed on her cheek, knowing the answer to her next question. "What is your name?"

"Demitri."

"The Father Sage Demitri?"

He gaped for a moment, as if he had to think about it. "Once, yes. I haven't had any contact with the Cathedral for as long as my self-exile."

"Why?"

"I didn't think I needed to keep up to date on things if I was to be living—"

"No." Josephine waved her hands. "I mean why did you run away?"

Demitri pursed his lips and sat up straight. "I take it you know about my interactions with your father."

A stone fell in Josephine's stomach. Her eyes widened as Demitri's stare deepened. She asked, "what do you know?"

"You're asking about your early life, I wager, about your mother's illness?" Demitri furrowed his brow and wrung his hands nervously. "I'm sure you've heard every answer to those questions, and indulged every rumor."

"Tell me what happened." Her voice came out strong.

Demitri twisted his face into something serious, his own tired voice deepening. "I left so I wouldn't ever have to do such a thing." He stood up, legs shaking. "But I knew, I knew deep down you'd be the one to find me, and to ask me this question. I dreamed about many nights and woke up in sweats and shakes. I'll admit, I fear you."

It was Josephine's turn to furrow her brow. She leaned back, surprised and confused. "What?" Her voice came out like a hiss of air. "Afraid of me?"

Demitri's lip trembled and his eyes bounced with energy, as if he was dredging up some long buried task, some festering seed that he had tried to shove deep down. He breathed heavily. "Josephine." He grabbed her wrist, his old thumb pressing into her skin. Through the force of the grip, Josephine could feel her pulse rush under his finger. She looked down at him, her own fear growing. He gritted his teeth and squeezed harder, her pulse now struggling to push through.

"Josephine." He looked her right in the eye. "You are dead."

A glisten of moisture found Josephine's eyes, she didn't know why. Her emotions were empty, shocked even and yet tears were swelling. "What?" She ripped her arm free.

"I saw you." Demitri held up both his hands, as if cradling some unseen baby. "You died in my arms. I tried my best to keep you with us, but you couldn't—I couldn't. The sickness was too great. Your father was staring at me, his stare pierced right through me. You were there, dead, Sophia was on the bed, dead before even you. A mother and a daughter passed within an hour of each other. I did all I could." Demitri was babbling now, rivulets running down his own cheeks while Josephine just stared at him in complete teary-faced shock.

"You're a mad man." Josephine managed to croak. "I'm right here, alive."

Demitri winced, as if reminded of something. "You know it deep down. You're not. You barely belong to the waking world." Josephine touched her own face. Her finger glided under her eyes, where the dark spots of sleepless nights and terrible dreams had manifested. Demitri shook his head. "Your father..."

"No." Josephine shook her head.

"Your father," Demitri continued. "He asked her to bring you back. She said she would, for a price."

"No..."

"You already know this. It was fate. It was destiny that I would be the one to remind you."

"No!"

"Yes!" Demitri foamed from the shout, spittle on his bottom lip. "The Dweller herself breathed life back into you and your mother. I was there. I saw it, I heard the deal: your lives for his..."

"My father is alive!"

"Because he's a fool!" Demitri answered back. "He took the deal, but when has the Dweller ever told the truth? She took from him, sure, but what she took was his sanity, his control. Her arms pushed him into your mother, her hand stole his thoughts. Her grip isn't complete in this world, anyway... I'm sure you noticed your sleep getting longer, becoming more sporadic. Your father himself falls in and out and if your mother were alive—"

Josephine kicked a stone, sending the rock slamming into a tree. Her face was beat red. "Why?"

"Why?" Demitri parroted.

"Why!"

He narrowed his eyes and grabbed Josephine's wrists, pulling her down to his crooked height so their noses all but touched. He was staring at her with what energy he had remaining in his ancient body. "The Dweller wanted you alive, and your brother dead. The first will open the door..." He stared intently into her eyes. "And the second will lead them through; that's what the horned prophet had said."

"What door!?"

"The veil!" Demitri screamed. As soon as he said the word, a sharp and piercing ring blasted into Josephine's ears, as if trying to censor his words. Demitri's face turned a sickly color, his eyes staining red as if he too was hearing it if not a greater blast. "I saw it when she appeared, gah.." He closed his eyes in pain, the sound growing louder. His hands grew limp, letting go of Josephine as he slid down to his knees.

"The veil?" Josephine mouthed the words, but the ring was too great for her to hear her own voice. Her head was splitting with pain, her own knees wobbling.

"It's trying to... silence us..." Demitri's breathing turned heavy, his chest heaving with each word. "Find the horned... prophet... find the man of... runes." He gripped his heart. "The prophecy is already in... motion... this world is not..." The ringing grew to such a volume that Josephine could only stare in extreme pain as Demitri's mouth flapped, but she couldn't make out any more of his words. Blood started to trickle from the old man's ears and with a thud, he fell face first into the grass below.

Josephine let loose a breath she didn't know she was holding. Her body weakened and she fell flat on her back. Staring up at the canopy, her vision was stained red and fuzzy. The ringing was growing and growing and before she knew it, a rattling scream of pain shrieked out of her lungs.

Chapter 17
Wilhelm's Baby Brother

Caleb sat staring down at his plate. The wooden vessel held only a single dry biscuit and some browning apple slices. He was in his room and what sky that was visible through his window was a light purple, signaling the last few moments of sunlight for the day; a day just like the others. On either side of his dish, his hands were laid palm up, red rope burns and scrapes cut across his hands and marked his fingers. His gloves had long since been torn open, the undulation between horrible storms and maddeningly windless days had rocked the ropes of Catherine's vessel right through whatever barrier he put between himself and the coarse material. His fingers weren't the only thing that was sore.

Across the table, Catherine sat with half her food already pouched in her cheek, eyes staring deliberately at the man. Joining her in her gaze was Asharah, her plate already licked clean. It was a windless day, and the only storms were the thoughts in everyone's head.

"You should eat," Asharah broke the silence. Caleb offered her a dull look before picking up his biscuit and idly taking a bite. His teeth cut through the first layer, but he found he needed to chomp down with a snapping crunch to get through the staled interior. A sharp pain shot up through his mouth and he slapped the pastry back onto his plate and held his face in his hands.

Catherine's lips parted to speak but Caleb spoke first. "Don't say it." He removed his hands from his face and took a breath. "We can't."

"Maybe we should," Asharah braved. "Everyone is tired, you're tired."

"I've never seen you act like this," Catherine added.

"We can't turn back," Caleb answered, his voice groggy and cold. "We are close, I know it."

Caleb closed his eyes and spoke slowly, "I can't turn back."

"What about us?" Catherine added, keeping her voice slow.

"It's for the Emperor." Caleb was quick.

"Caleb..." Asharah sat up.

"It's for the Emperor."

Catherine tucked a frown into her cheek. "Wilhelm doesn't even know about this."

"It's for my brother." Caleb raised his voice slightly.

"Damnit, Caleb!" Catherine slapped a hand on the table. "How much longer are you going to rot for him?"

"He's my brother!" Caleb shouted back, rocking the table back into silence. He let out a long exhale through his nose and unclenched his jaw. "I failed him once, I'm not going to fail him again."

"Caleb... this is not your job, not your responsibility," Catherine answered. She looked to Asharah who nodded.

Caleb's voice fell soft, his eyes downcast as he thought for a long moment. "I want my brother back."

Silence again.

"Do you really think that the cure will be there?" Asharah spoke up.

"It can't be anywhere else." Caleb rubbed an eye and cleared his throat. Catherine stood up at that and ran a stressed hand through her hair before turning away and starting a pace. Caleb bit his thumb and looked down, taking a thoughtful pose.

"I searched everywhere else," Caleb said softly. "Every book, every scroll, for years and years. This is the last place to look, the last lead. I have to break the Dweller's grasp on him."

Catherine was pacing behind Caleb now, lost in her own thoughts while Ashallah stared at the man. "I owe it to him as well," Catherine said, "for all the good he did in his father's war, but we can't allow ourselves to fester in his place. He wouldn't want that."

"I know," Caleb sucked in a breath. "I had a similar conversation with my nephew once, of the same vein… but I can't help myself. He was always my best friend."

"Oh?" Catherine's voice was dripping with a snark that didn't fit the mood. She leaned over Caleb's shoulder. "What about me?"

The prince blinked, thrown off his rhythm. "Of course, you're one of my greatest friends as well."

"Then for the sake of our friendship, eat and think clearly." She grabbed the biscuit and held it in front of Caleb's face. Caleb recoiled.

"I am thinking clearly, what?"

"Eat!" She pushed the biscuit closer. "This entire trip has gone to shit, you clearly can't see it."

"I can—mm!?" Caleb was cut off by a sudden burst of hard old bread and dusty crumbs being shoved into his mouth. He did his best to swallow most of it but ended up coughing a cloud of biscuit before reaching out to grab Catherine and accidentally knocking the chair he was sitting in over. "What in the void, Cath?" He growled from the floor before rolling back to his feet only for Catherine to grab his collar with both hands.

She gave him a shake. "We are drifting in unknown waters with a skeleton crew, eating old bread and grainy apples." Her eyes were wild. "I miss my bed! I miss real food!"

Caleb grabbed her collar in retaliation and narrowed his eyes. "We still have plenty of water, and plenty of reserves. We will go until we can't go any more! Don't you think I miss my bed, too?"

"Not enough! Clearly!" Catherine hissed.

"Guys!" Asharah was standing now, just outside the spat. "I think we are all a little overworked!"

"Tell that to the crew!" Catherine shouted at Asharah.

Caleb frowned. "No need to scream at her!"

"I hate this!" Catherine yelled at Caleb.

"I hate it too!" Caleb yelled back. Asharah opened her mouth but then closed it and held her face in her hands.

"Heinrichs..."

"What!?" They both looked at Asharah.

The Stenling quickly recovered by changing the topic. "We might have more food if we weren't feeding the prisoners."

Caleb's face looked utterly annoyed and Catherine loudly agreed. "The two Tagists? Those ones? The two that tried to kill us? Weird they are still alive to begin with." Her eyes snaked at Caleb, sarcastic and frustrated.

The prince closed his eyes. "The battle is over, already. Don't ask me to kill outside of battle."

"I hope they feel the same way." Catherine released Caleb and Caleb released her in return. Asharah raised her brow.

"There, nice and calm."

The Heinrich's both shot the Stenling a death glare, one that was quickly interrupted by a stiff knock on the door. They all turned as the door swung open. A sailor stood at the threshold of the room, a look of absolute glee played in his eyes, though he was clearly putting on a serious face. "Prince, Captain..." He started, "you have to see this." Caleb shared a glance at the others before straightening his collar. The prince gave the sailor a nod, grabbed his heavy grey cloak from the chair it was draped over and quickly followed the man out of the captain's cabin.

Passing through the door, Caleb was met with a gentle heat he hadn't felt in quite some time. Above him, a perfect blue sky hung dressed with floating clouds and below him, the sea was calm and lapping. Every sailor of the vessel was standing at the bow of the ship in an awesome silence.

"What's going on?" Caleb asked as he stepped across the deck. His fingers unclasped his cloak, eager to feel the warmth on his shoulders. He was met with quiet and cautious mumbles. One Stenling looked back at the Prince and jutted his rugged chin outward.

"I'm afraid if I mention it, it will disappear."

"What?" Caleb stepped quickly to the railings and leaned over, eyes squinting. In the distance, a thin line of land marked the horizon. As the image sank into his mind, Caleb felt his heart leap, and a burst of energy flared up from his stomach and into his chest. He slapped the rails and smiled wide until his cheeks ached. His voice was quiet, in disbelief. "We did it."

***

As the ship sailed closer, an inviting canopy of Autumn-burned leaves came into sight. Crimson reds and glittering golds stole the vision of the crew, but even still, they were still quite a distance from landfall and it soon became apparent that they weren't going to be sailing much closer. The ocean floor rose drastically the closer they got to the island and before they knew it, the ship was forced to anchor about an hour's walk from the destination.

Thankfully, the colder winds of the ocean seemed to subside in this surreal place and when Caleb leaped over the railing and into the ankle deep water below, he found it warm and pleasant. His crew followed suit and with that, they started a quiet awe-stricken journey across the watery plain towards the forested jewel set in the center. The sky stayed a bright blue the entire trek, and the only breeze that shrouded the crew came from the island. The wind brought with it a sweet and warm sensation, like the first gentle breaths of spring. Asharah and Caleb shared a look at that, and the curious faces of the crew confirmed that everyone was feeling the oddity of the place.

When the salt of the sea faded into fresh water and gnarled roots, the sensation grew, and by time the trees were overhead, Caleb was struck with the alien beauty of the island. Dark barked trees rose from the shallow pool of water and the only other thing above the reflective waters were small bundles of moss that had grown over the serpentine roots, but further still, Caleb was struck by the water itself. The leaves of the yellow and red canopies not only bristled and covered the sky above, but had fallen to coat the water at every inch, and with every step, Caleb sent small ripples throughout the fluid sea of crimson and gold.

Another thing that hit Caleb as unique was the air. It had a crispness to it, like the beginning of an Autumn chill, and yet it also had a comforting warmth threaded through it, like the moment when the spring sun would first heat the morning. It was a primordial atmosphere, and one he felt intimate with, as if he had been here before, and after so many early springs and colorful falls he had experienced in his own life, maybe he had. But to experience it all at once—that was a sensation like no other.

"What is this place..." He could feel the question whisper through his lips while his eyes were long lost in the maze of trees and foliage. His question took his attention away from his vision and to his ears. He had missed it before but as he walked through the soft paddling of the water and moved under the swishing trees and raining leaves, a thick chorus of frogs sang through the mossy roots of the mystical land.

It was a soothing sound and not thinking anything of it, Caleb soon closed his eyes to take in all the sensations. The falling leaves brushed against his face and shoulders, the water tugged at his feet ever so slightly and his ears were filled with the sounds of the swaying forest and singing creatures. After spending so much time in a salt-ridden boat, he found a paradise, down to the plush ground under the water itself.

His eyes snapped open, something was coming. Jerking his head off to the side, he narrowed his vision and spotted two yellow eyes looking back at him. His hand snapped to his sword handle and a myriad more of the eyes appeared between the trees, their true faces hidden by the waving shadows of the leaves.

The foremost set of eyes crinkled with a friendly squint before stepping out from behind the veil of the forest. A creature with the body of a warty frog was walking towards the group. The creature walked on two legs with big webbed feet and had a face that reminded Caleb of an elder, with wispy white hairs hanging from under his chin. Stiff, reed-woven robes clung to the elderly frog's body and a mushroom-laden satchel hung from his shoulder. In one hand, he held a knotted walking stick that led him through the autumn waters until he stood two arm reaches away from Caleb.

At this distance, Caleb could clearly see the strange elder was only a few notches taller than his own waist, and with the elder's approach, other frog people of different ages and persuasions were peering out from the trees. Some even held martial looking staves with paddle-like ends and wore large, round hats of reeds.

"Who are you?" Caleb asked while keeping his sword arm ready by the hilt of his blade.

"…What are you?" Catherine couldn't help but add.

The elder frog held up a single bulbous tipped finger and gave a deep croak in some bizarre language. Caleb returned it a puzzled look, but before he could question further, the elder frog pulled a small wooden mug from his satchel along with a fuzzy bit of moss. Leaning on his walking stick, the elder flicked the bit of moss into the mug and then leaned to scoop up a hearty portion of the water below. He gave it a swirl before taking a gulping sip with his amphibian throat expanding in a way foreign to Caleb. A splitting, toothless smile formed on the satisfied elder's face as he held the cup towards Caleb.

The prince looked into the cup, the water inside was a murky green and to his knowledge, would likely still be salted from the connected ocean. He pinched his chin in thought.

"You aren't going to…?" Catherine made a face. "Are you?"

"When in Alconia…" Asharrah started.

Caleb closed his eyes and grabbed the mug. "Do as the Stenlings." With the speed a sober man seeking to dispel a disgusting drink, Caleb quickly tipped the mug to his lips and gave a wide mouthed swallow. His eyes opened with surprise. It was fresh water, and it was sweet. "What the..."

"Oh, that's much better," the elder frog croaked. Caleb's eyes snapped to the creature.

"I can understand you!?" Caleb croaked back.

"What was that?" Catherine stared pointedly at Caleb. "Oh Graces, please tell me you're not turning into a frog."

"No!" Caleb used the Imperial language. He looked at the elder. "No?"

"No." The elder answered, suddenly using the Imperial tongue as well. "Just a simple spell to make communication a lot easier."

Caleb let out a long exhale, having been more worried about turning into a frog than he'd like to admit. Regaining himself, he stood up straight and jabbed a finger into his chest. "I'm Caleb Heinrich, of Jerrovia."

The creature bowed his head low. "I am Master Frugi, grandfather of many here."

"Frugi..." Catherine gave Caleb a side eye.

Master Frugi peeked up. "Yes?"

Catherine quickly coughed. "Uh, well..."

"She is curious about who we are meeting," Asharah said. "We've never met anyone of your kind before."

"We are the Aquatids, an old and ancient people..." Master Frugi frowned slightly. "But we of course will be discussing that later."

"We will be?" Caleb raised a brow.

"Of course... it was seen." The elder frog shook his head. "Might I walk you to our village? I can only imagine how long a trip you must have taken to make it here, and I'm sure you have questions I can answer along the way."

"Yeah, firstly, how come the tides haven't taken this place?" Catherine blurted as they all started their trek through the waters. Frugi gave a ribbiting chuckle.

"You'll soon see."

***

Even at the heart of the strange island the waters never quite faded underfoot, save for the mounds of moss and black soil that broke the colorful pools here and there. Speckled with the leaves of Autumn and breathed to life with spring winds, the entire island never lost its magical luster as the group carried onward, a fact which helped Caleb ignore the fact that his feet were starting to get rather soggy.

The very existence of such a place kept his mind occupied, his finger perpetually pinched between his gnawing teeth as he thought and walked. Such a strange land so far away from Jerrovia, especially strange considering that it shouldn't exist. Only a single book in all his studies mentioned it and only due to desperation and the egging of Asharah did he even think to give it a try; never did he think he'd actually find such a place. Weirder still, were the Aquatids. They were such strange creatures, with not a single book dedicated to them or their like... and yet... he could have sworn he saw a grotesque somewhere that had frogmen carved into stone.

He shook his head. "Master Frugi."

"Hm?" The elder didn't look behind him, intent on leading his charges.

"What did you say the name of this island was again?"

"Buyan."

"Buyan…" Caleb felt the name on his tongue. "We aren't your first visitors are we?"

"Hm… no… I think you might be."

Caleb looked to Asharah who shared a surprised look. Caleb spoke, "No other travelers? No academic types? No one looking to write stories of their grand adventures even?"

"No… but long before my time, as old as I may be… one of our kin set out for your land on the request of Mondaral." Master Frugi kept his pace.

"Mondaral?"

"You'll be meeting her soon enough, though I ask you to keep your voices low when you do as she is not well. Ah! Home."

As if summoned by Frugi's voice, the trees seemed to open up to a comfortable oasis. Pools of water were cut off from the unending flood with small walls of sod, and hovering above the free water were wooden platforms balancing on thick stilts. Almost spherical houses of clay sat atop these platforms with conical roofs of thatch. A melody of ribbits and croaks filled the air as the aquatids of the village went about their daily lives.

Warriors in the wide brimmed hats walked the area with their bizarre paddle staves, while more gentle folk cleaned fish, fired furnaces balanced on platforms, or tended to strange tadpoles that lurked in the village-dotting ponds. Happy black tadpole eyes popped out of the water to curiously watch Caleb and his entourage.

The prince's attention was stolen almost immediately from the alien village when he spotted a large white stone that dwarfed the largest hut the Aquatids had to offer. It sat in the endless sea, its foot completely hidden from sight as water gushed out from under it. Watching the flow of the water through the movement of the layer of leaves that capped the scene, he could tell it flowed straight towards him and beyond outwards from where he came.

"Alatyr," Frugi said. "Stone of stones."

"Stone of stones?" Caleb gave the rock another look. It was a brilliant white, and yet held an ethereal blue hue to it as well. Instinctively Caleb gave a sniff, and the smell of a perfect summer's day filled his nostrils. He reached out, a curiosity burning in him, a desire to touch the strange relic, when a voice called from behind him.

"It all began here, in a way." The voice was old, tired, and yet held the rasp of a woman not quite done with her life. Caleb and his group turned to the voice, and there standing was a stranger creature than even the aquatids. She was taller than Caleb, but not by much, and in place of hair, she had long sapphire feathers trickling down past her shoulders. Her face didn't match her voice, being youthful yet sickly pale. Her eyes were sharp and black with a once brilliant white faded to grey and her lips in a forever frown. From there she was very close to being a human, if not for the feathers that cuffed her elbows, wrists, and ankles, but more strikingly was her extra pair of arms, settled right under where her fuller, more 'usual' ones were placed. She was dressed differently than the aquatids, wrapped in a close-to-form silk of sorts whose dye had long since faded.

She gave Caleb a thoughtful stare. "But perhaps not the story of Jerrovia."

Sputting, Caleb tried to find his words. So much was happening all at once and in such an alien land at that. Sucking in a steadying breath, he finally found a train of thought to hold onto. "Mondaral?"

The woman gave a soft smile, "Of the Sondoper. I pray our aid has not come too late but at least here we can speak without the veil interfering."

"Veil?" Caleb squinted.

"Yes, I will reveal everything," Mondaral answered. "I will reveal the truth of this world. Ironic that its true form shall only be known right as it is to end." Caleb froze at that, a fear in his heart. Mondaral's voice went low. "And it will end."

Chapter 18

Hinan

A terrible headache pounded through Josephine's head. The princess was cloistered away inside one of the yabban's yurts, fingers kneading her temples. She could feel her memories of her conversation with Demitri fogging, as if some thick blanket was covering them. The Father Sage himself was already tucked under a blanket and brought away from the scene with his corpse frozen in a state of absolute horror. Josephine knew she needed to work with the information she was given, and fast. Her hand gripped her chest; her heart was pounding, skipping every other beat. Could she really be already dead? Her narcolepsy episodes were increasing and the dreams were getting more intense; was she falling apart? A teardrop landed on her lap; what was going on?

Opane ducked into the yurt but Josephine didn't bother to look up from the dark spot where her teardrop had soaked through her pants. The Kafshe cleared her throat. "Regent."

"Please... just call me Josephine." Her voice was soft, shallow, sad.

"The shaman located the altar of the infiltrator—he has prepared a group to lead you there."

The regent stood up; her knees were weak. Looking up at Opane, she brushed her eyes clear. "Opane."

"Yes?"

"Do I look different?"

"What do you mean?"

Josephine shrugged, her chest was heavy and her body alien to her all of a sudden. "Nevermind." Sucking in a deep breath, she did her best to find her confidence and authority. "Send one of our riders north to contact my brother. I'd like him to rendezvous with us there, and maybe we all could get some answers."

Opane gave Josephine a concerned look, a look Josephine did her best to ignore. There was no way that anyone else could have heard what Demitri said, and yet Josephine couldn't help but feel like people knew she wasn't... normal. Maybe they always knew and always looked at her like that, and she just never knew to recognize it.

"Of course," Opane answered before ducking back out of the yurt. Josephine watched her leave. She chewed her cheek: something didn't feel right, not that anything could feel right at this moment. But something else felt off, as if something bad was about to happen. The regent closed her eyes and she could feel it in her gut, the same as she could feel the tug of sleep in the back of her mind. A whine escaped her throat—she didn't want to sleep again, not so soon, and yet, she could feel herself fading.

***

Jornho stood against the horizon, dark and quiet. Duke Peter and a large portion of his forces remained in the ruined city, keen on keeping the peace until a successor to Fenric could be decided among the surviving nobles of Gavaria. Fenric's body was never recovered, a fact that sat ill in George's mind and yet at the same time provided a strange sense of relief. With the city behind him and his troops, he couldn't help but feel the guilt of his brawl with Fenric seep into his gut. He hadn't planned on using the smokeform, nor did he expect himself to lose himself so completely. The fight was a memory of red and anger in his mind, with flashes of Hilda's tear-soaked face. George remembered when he had walked back down from the tower, how she broke from his soldiers and gripped him tight, screaming for her son—her voice still rattled in his ears.

George looked down at Oathkith, the pommel reflecting the dim evening sky. Esmachus' survival sat in his gut like a poison, but so did all this violence. The general sat on Ai, marching with his troops. Next to him was Williams and Rosaline, and on his other side rode the Commander of the regular forces that Duke Peter had sent off with George, Baldra.

"I can't imagine finding Esmachus will be easy," Baldra said, her eyes set on the sky above. She scoffed, "To think he escaped."

"He's a coward," George replied without much conviction. "His forces have been scattered and routed, though, I have faith that you and your soldiers will be able to clean the countryside... assuming you haven't changed your mind?"

"Regarding your aid? I think we can manage. I'd hate to burn Imperial resources on a manhunt. Besides, you have to get back to your sister at the capital, no?"

"Actually," Williams interrupted, "a rider came this afternoon, we are reorganizing our march towards the Imperial Forest to meet up with the Regent."

Baldra cracked a grin. "So formal, using her title."

"What else would I use?" Williams stared at the soldier.

"Everyone important already knows that the Regent has a secret paramour—myself included. Just call her by her name, lest you accidentally call her Regent while fingers laced." Baldra sat up straight and looked at George for support.

The prince pulled himself from his thoughts to offer a quick smile. "She's right, Williams, that's a quick way to ruin the mood."

"Josephine then." Williams rolled his eyes.

"Good," Baldra encouraged. "Life's too short to focus on trivial things like that..." A hurt look winced in Baldra's eye, as if she was remembering something.

Williams frowned. "You're not wrong. I think I've been being a bit of an ass."

"Tell her that, not me." Baldra found a small laugh.

George emphasized his smile for a moment before fading to a serious tone and looking at Baldra. "There was trouble at the palace and some criminal escaped the city with important information. My sister chased him down and requested my presence."

"Ah, I see." Baldra let out a long breath. "It never ends."

"No, I guess it doesn't." George folded his arms and looked straight ahead. The rolling hills of Caldora were mostly in sight, only cut by thick groves of pine. The sounds of marching were accompanied by errant crickets and spring-time frogs. He squinted at one of the hills, the crest being mostly cleared of trees by some long finished logging project which left only a cemetery of stumps and sprouts. George pointed his finger at it. "Let's take the evening and set camp there. There is no use marching at night when there are still Nachtists running about. In the morning, we can split our troops."

Williams nodded, and Baldra followed suit. "Good idea."

The two pulled forward on their horses, leaving George alone with a silent Rosaline. The ex-medic was staring at the prince. George furrowed his brow. "What?"

"You don't hate me do you?" Her voice was meek and uncharacteristically scared.

George paled for a moment at even just the thought. "Why would I ever hate you?"

"Because I'm a Tagist," Rosaline said. "Because Esmachus told you to watch out for Tagists. Because Tagists ruined your life. I can see it on you."

George held firm for a moment. She stared at him, her eyes so thick with emotion, George was forced to look down. His gaze found his bare hands, still stained red from the smoke form. His fingertips no longer faded back to normal, and he could feel it veining across his heart. His body couldn't drain the smoke as much. A grin found his face and he looked up at his lover. "I'm cracking at the seams," he said, "but I could never hate you. I love you."

Rosaline reached over to claim his hand. She brought his burnt fingertips to her lips and held them there. "Do you mean it?"

Her eyes were a shimmering brown and George's soul was a black swirl of anger and confusion. He could feel the bite of Oathkith on every bone he ever broke with it, and he could feel the sting of all the tears he caused. He could feel the strike of all his choices and the cuts of all his battles. The crimes of the Tagists sliced into his flank and the curses of the Dweller pinned his flesh. Above all, though, George could feel his love. His love for his father, his sister, and his friends, and of course his love for Rosaline. The broken prince squeezed her hands. "I mean it. There is nothing that would pull me from you."

Relief shined on Rosaline's face and it was George's turn to push. "Rosaline," he said, "what's bothering you? This isn't like you."

"I'm lost, I think," Rosaline answered honestly. "I can feel my faith shaking and the world under my feet shifting."

George chewed his cheek. "I'm not much of a philosopher, but I do know that the Tagist ideals don't match the Tagist actions. What's wrong with keeping the morals and ditching the sages?" Rosaline offered a weak smile at that.

"I hear you," She said, "but no, there is something more bugging me about it. I feel like something is amiss, as if I'm not the only Tagist to have lost their way. I feel like something is missing in the church, and that missing piece was replaced with all this political nonsense and evil deeds that plague us now." She sighed against George's fingertips and held them against her cheek. "What happened to the teachings I learned when I was a child." Another sigh. "As I said, the world is slipping under me."

George mustered a smile. "Maybe I should teach you Stromism, then! It's great for keeping balance."

Rosaline knit her brow, shocked for a moment before grinning. "It'll be useful, at the very least. Do you think I can learn it?"

The prince nodded. "There is only one way to find out!"

With a punctuating kiss, Rosaline let George's fingers free and projected her best face of contentment. "Then I'll be in your care."

***

The night quickly took over the evening droll of setting up the camp and Stromism practice with Rosaline. It was a quiet night, or as quiet as it could possibly be in such a settlement. George laid awake in his tent with Rosaline's sleeping form beside him. He was staring up at the fabric ceiling from his stiff mattress, listening to the sounds outside. Commander Maelinn was still barking at some poor auxiliaries to finish their duties, and someone to the south was singing a horrible rendition of an old campfire song, but still, it beat the sounds of war. George folded his arms, looking very much the part of a contemplative body shoved into a coffin. He couldn't help it, though, a heat was throbbing in his fingers, a heat that hadn't left him since his fight on the tower. He could feel the gateway to the smokeform growing bigger and bigger and his grasp on controlling it slipping. Fenric even managed to force him into it using only his words.

Pulling his hands to his face, he looked at his blackened fingertips, swirls of nearly invisible smoke trickling across them as if he was frostbitten by his own emotion, but better than red. George could feel his stomach churn with rage, sadness, anxiety, guilt, all the emotions he unleashed and allowed himself to feel back in the Ulmi shack. He let his hand fall to his cheek, brushing against the stiff scar that marred that half of his face. The doors were open, now he just needed to learn how to balance what he found inside, temper it, if not just for his sake—he looked at Rosaline's sleeping face—then everyone around him.

George rolled off his mattress and onto the cold, hard floor of his tent. He laid there for a moment, splayed out on his back and collected his thoughts before sucking in a determined breath and forcing himself to his feet. Franklin's cape was draped over a nearby chair, to which George threw it over his shoulders, giving him the look of a hero in their white cotton pajamas (which were little more than a set of quilted pants and shirt). To finish the look, George slipped on his tall black boots and strapped Oathkith around his waist. He scoffed at his own attire, which reminded him of a time his father attended a very important meeting in a similar fashion.

"Like father, like son," he said to himself. He grimaced and shook his head. "Well, hopefully not entirely."

A pause. "Though I am talking to myself... oh no."

"Hm?" Rosaline grumbled from the bed.

"Just getting some air, Love."

A snort as Rosaline sucked in a deep breath. "Mmkay..."

George cracked a grin, happy for the distraction and pushed out of his tent. The evening spring air hit him harder than he expected, with a breeze seemingly waiting for him and sending goosebumps up his arms. He wrapped his cape closer to his body, thankful for its heavy Gavarian knit, and started his walk.

Soldiers nodded at George as he walked by, with none really thinking much of their general's presence. Onward George walked, the orange flicker of campfires occasionally stealing his vision. The hushed clatter of an active camp trying to sleep mixed in his ears along with the chirp of nocturnal insects. George himself kept his mouth shut, save for the occasional return of greeting, all up until he made it to the perimeter of the encampment which was marked by a shallow palisade and watchmen. He approached one of the sentries: a short man that George recognized as a soldier of the 11th.

"Evening," George said.

The man turned to George and gave a respectful nod of his head. "Good evening, General."

George returned the nod. "I'm going to try to find some silence down at the foot of the hill, if I'm not back in fifteen minutes, come check in on me."

"Would you prefer an escort, sir?"

"I trust our scouts have the perimeter secured, and I'll be cautious. Just give me a heads up if it's been a while, okay?"

The soldier gave another nod. "Of course, sir, yes sir."

Again, George returned the gesture and set off away from the lights of the camp. As he walked down the grassy hill, he pulled one of his hands from under his cape and stared at his fingers once again; the joyful little distractions did him some good, but he could still feel the heartbeat in his fingertips. Onward he walked, until the slope evened out. There was a small meadow of springtime flowers ahead of him and then the darkness of a conifer forest. At a younger age he might have found the woods tantalizingly mysterious, but being who he was now, George knew he had his own scouts running around in them. Out of the corner of his eye, the prince spotted a dense log resting in a bed of moss and being that he came here to think, he quickly walked over to it for a seat.

He plopped down and his determined grin from earlier frumped into a frown for a moment and he reached under his rump to clear away intrusive vestiges that once were poking branches. Once comfortable, George closed his eyes and sucked in a deep gulping breath of night air. With a slow exhale, his mind's eye was transported to a vision of his altar of creation. A wondrous sea of mist battled a persistent and striking battalion of smoke. Where harmony was found between them, a thread of golden magic sparkled but ultimately, it seemed to be in turmoil. Feelings that George once resisted were now empowered with freedom: his anger, his sadness, the pains of the past and present. Regret and uncertainty fueled the mist, striking back at the freed feelings and in retaliation, the smoke would irritate and become frustrated, pulling in more energy to push an advantage. George's altar was a battlefield, a battlefield inhabited by two powerful opponents.

The prince furrowed his brow as he felt something else. His attention was pulled away from inside him and to his surroundings, though his eyes remained closed. There! In the trees he could feel the altar of another. It wasn't chaotic like a Nachtist's, nor was it quiet and balanced like a Stromist's. It was completely different, it felt old, haggard and ancient. It wasn't outrageously large like his own or Ai's, but it was big, bigger than most. He felt he knew it.

"Hinan."

George's eyes shot open; he definitely knew it. In front of him stood a beast draped in the shadows of the night. The beast stood half a man taller than George would have even if he was standing up, though not quite as large as a giant, but much more intimidating, with dense muscles, hair matted shoulders, and the head of a bull. The bullman stood strong, with a warrior's skirt of leather around his waist which hid muscled legs that tapered down into some strange amalgamation of cloven hoof and heeled foot. His chest was covered in a loose woolen shirt, though his hairy shoulders were noticeable through the amazingly large neck-hole which was likely made in such a way to allow his great curling horns to pass through. A metal strap tightened from shoulder to hip, holding a great metal cage to the beast's back, and even from George's angle, the prince could see the outline of the largest and heaviest book that he ever witnessed trapped in the mechanism. To add to the weight, a double-headed axe the height of George was strapped alongside it, though with an ancient leather bind.

At a loss for words, George sat there, looking up at the beast with his mouth agape. The creature's voice was definitely familiar.

George heard it in his dreams as a child and his dreams after the second battle of Kors. What stuck George the most, though, was how unthreatened he felt. The beast looked down at him with eyes not unsimilar to that of a kindly grandfather. Could this really be the beast that once chased him from his own home? Why wasn't he scared? He did once swear he'd never run from it again, but now, here he was, fulfilling his oath on his backside.

"Hinan?" George repeated at last.

"A Harnian word for one such as yourself." The Harnian's voice was warm like a hearthfire and yet held pounding consonants not unlike thunder. "Know me as Freg Gerntef."

George shot to his feet, his awe igniting into shock. He pointed a finger. "You're the horned prophet!" A deep grumble resonated from Freg's throat as if in thought but George continued. "Hinan! You've... You're! My dream!" It was all rushing to George. "You're the one who chased me!"

Freg sat down with a great shake of the ground as George continued, playing off his fingers as he recalled his life. "Your shadow was in my dream as a kid, you were the figure that ran me out of my bedroom, you were in my dream after the battle of Kors." His eyes widened. "You were there at the camp in Caldora, with me and Lawrence and the others!"

Freg nodded along as George slung his accusations until finally George found his stern will and puffed up his chest. His mind was a scramble, but a single question came to mind as he realized how closely this creature had been following him. "Why?"

"Why, what, Hinan?" Freg rumbled.

"What's the meaning of it all? Why were you in my dreams, why are you the horned prophet, what do your prophecies mean and most importantly." George felt a long buried question emerge from his gut. "Why did you save me, only to drop me off into the hands of the Ulmi?"

The great Harnian gave George a silent gaze, his dark bovine eyes looking the prince-turned-general up and down. Finally, Freg let a long flapping breath through his lips and shook his head. "Very soon, I will be able to answer every last question you might have, but for now, I'm afraid I bring only a small offering."

"What?" George frowned. "You finally reveal yourself after all of this, after all that happened, and that's it?"

Freg held up a rough palm, as if asking for silence. "You've been patient, Hinan, but you're not yet ready—the world is not yet ready."

George narrowed his eyes. Freg spoke of patience, but all he could feel was a sudden ping of frustration. An angry pulse started up in the prince's fingers again, forcing him to clench his teeth. It was so easy to feel angry now, and just looking at this bullman who held all the answers whipped it throughout his chest.

"You see?" Freg's thick finger prodded George right in the chest, knocking George a step back. Instead of feeling anger at the gesture, George was struck with a realization. Freg continued, "Your smokeform has been unleashed, but you have not mastered it, Hinan. If you have any hope of defeating the Dweller—which you must do—then you will have to learn to balance it and perfect it."

George loosened his jaw and let out a calming breath. "Do you know how?"

Freg tipped his head forward. "I do, though I had hoped you would have figured it out on your own."

"I'm dense," George said in both irritation and instinct. "Or so I've been told."

Freg just snorted at that. If he was amused, it didn't show. "You've learned from your time at the Ulmi village how to allow the emotions you've bottled up to flow, how to let loose the chaotic nature of such feelings deemed unacceptable or perhaps negative by the Tagists. Through that, you learned to unleash your inner smoke, harness the smoke around you, and bring forth a great power. Now to balance it..."

George slowly sat back down on his log, listening intently.

"...You must learn to balance the smoke with the mist within, and create harmony. Anger, sadness, rage and pain, are all functions of life, but should you let them control you, you will be blinded; however, should you control them with reason, wisdom and temperance, you will leash the power of the former with the tranquility of the latter."

"How do you do that?" George furrowed his brow.

"A great decision will come to you, sooner than either of us would like." A sadness laced Freg's voice. "In that time, you will be in great turmoil, more than you have ever felt thus far, and inside this depth of pain and chaos, you must make your decision to be wise, to be tempered, to make a decision your father could not. Once you have made this great sacrifice, the rage of the smokeform will be tethered."

George narrowed his eyes. So many questions were forming, so much he couldn't pick what to ask first, swelling his throat. Freg gave a slight sigh, as if stressed himself, before standing up with a great heft. George followed suit, and a simple question slipped out.

"If I can't control the smokeform, I'm lost, aren't I?"

Freg spoke slowly. "You've seen the cracks yourself."

George looked up from his fingers and at the bull man. "You can't tell me any more, can you?"

"Not now."

The prince bit his cheek. "Why are you telling me anything at all?"

"Because, Hinan," Freg started. "I have been rooting for your success long before I ever laid eyes on you. I will come to you the day of the decision, I pray you forgive me enough to allow me to be there."

Dread was seeping into George's veins, sending a chill down his spine. "Forgive you?"

"Take heart, Hinan." Freg seemed sad, his forlorn face turning away as he took a few steps back into the forest. "The curse of mortality is not knowing whether a dark day leads to a brighter tomorrow or if a bright tomorrow leads to a dark day. We cannot see the consequences to come; most of us." With that, Freg started his walk back into the woods, twigs snapping and branches yawning as he made his way. George was left to the cacophony, staring in thought, with his fingers still hurting just a little.

His reverie was broken by Williams' voice, the knight standing behind him. "George."

The prince turned, silently answering.

"I was thinking, and if you'd permit it, I'd like to ride ahead. I have a few words I need to share with Josephine, and having them sit in my chest while we march is torment."

"Williams, are you fucking blind?"

The knight blinked and looked around. "What do you mean!?"

"The bullman?"

"What?" Williams winced. The knight stared at George in confusion long enough for the prince to drop it with a sigh.

"Nevermind, er, what were you saying?"

"Josephine?"

"Oh, right." George was distracted with his latest batch of questions, courtesy of Freg, but nodded along anyway. "Yes. Ride safe, we will be right behind you."

"I'll take a couple scouts with me."

"Good idea." George felt he was talking mechanically, mind wholly occupied on my bovine issues.

Williams nodded "I guess I'll leave you to whatever this is." He waved a hand over the scene. George cracked a grin.

"I won't be much longer, tell the sentries."

"Sure."

Williams' steps receded, leaving George once again alone in the woods. His thoughts once again found their way back to the fore of his mind.

Chapter 19

A Lost Son

It was many years ago, but the glow of the fire still stained Fenric's memory. He stood there as the sages sang a hollow chant, their song bouncing through the open courtyard. It was a dark night, without a moon, and his young body was shivering under his dull blue cloak. Even though his toes and fingers had gone numb and his cheeks stung from winter's breath, all his attention was on the fire that dominated the courtyard. Mourners gathered in circles around the fire: weeping, singing with the sages, or staring in silence.

The acrid smell of burning flesh filled the air and before long, Fenric was forced to pinch his nose shut. Only then did he realize he was crying, the shock of losing his older brother not as thick as he thought. The smell, that was Frodnir's body. He felt his knees go weak at the thought. A rough hand grabbed his wrist and pulled his arm back down to his side, while another gripped his shoulder and steeled him, forcing him to face the fire once again.

"Do not look away, boy," Duke Osbert harshly whispered from behind Fenric. His father's voice was stern and yet laced with pain. "That's your brother."

Hot tears rolled down Fenric's cheeks. He knew that was his brother, he also knew that wasn't him, and more importantly, he knew who his father would have rathered to be in the pyre.

"Pigguts," Fenric managed to burble, as if trying to shift the blame.

"Sh." Osbert corrected. "Just watch; you have to live for both now."

***

A horrible pain ripped into Fenric's right arm, forcing his eyes wide open. Something was sawing into his very flesh, the pain screamed through his mind until it was a blank white. His jaw clenched, biting into something wooden. The pain reddened his vision and stars blotted across the scene. He was restrained. Fenric tried his best to jerk free but an old wrinkled hand came across his face and held his head down. The sawing continued.

"Easy," an old woman's voice managed to pierce his tormented ears. He could hear his flesh snapping, the scraping of metal on bone until Fenric let out a shaking scream. The pain in his arm was replaced with a burning nothingness—something indescribable. A wet cloth was pressed against his nose and something sweet entered his lungs. His vision blurred again and he fell into darkness.

That time, Fenric didn't dream.

***

Fenric's heart pulsed and sent thin blood through his body. His eyes didn't need to open as his lids were lazily parted and only twitched when his consciousness regained control. Immediately he was struck by the dryness of being unblinking for so long but before he could register it completely, a sharp and terrible pain pulsed across his body. A displeased groan passed through his throat; his body felt destroyed or at least most of it did. He couldn't feel past his right elbow.

Weakly, he lifted his arm, just now noticing the bed of straw he was laying in. His pale eyes soaked in the sight of his arm: beyond his elbow, there was nothing. Despite that, he tried to move his fingers, but there was nothing to move. He stared in quiet shock, until the voice of that old lady rang in his ears.

"Have you awoken for real this time?"

The voice bounced off the walls of a cave, the entire scene finally registering to Fenric. He was alive, laying in a bed of straw, hidden away in some dark cave that was lit only by a pair of lanterns. An old, itchy blanket covered him from the chest down, and yet he was still cold. There, off to the side, opening a steaming wicker basket, a woman was staring at him. He recognized her wrinkled face and sharp eyes.

"Kilnsdot." Fenric said, the words pushed through a hoarse throat.

"Gretchen is fine," the old surgeon corrected.

Fenric let his head fall back into the straw. From there, all he could do was watch the light flicker off the cave ceiling.

"You took my arm."

That elicited a laugh from Gretchen. "That's the first thing you wish to say? It was bound in tainted metal. I was surprised that you yourself didn't turn completely tainted or that your heart didn't explode."

"Maybe I am recusant," Fenric croaked from his bed.

Another laugh. "Not many people survive the taint enough to become recusant to it, and you are no exception. You should be thanking me. I saved your life."

"Maybe I don't want to live."

No laugh this time. "Then you should thank me doubly, for giving you a chance to change your mind."

"My mind won't change."

Gretchen grabbed Fenric's chin and tilted his face so he was looking right at her. Her expression was focused rather than serious. Fenric expected a lecture but instead Gretchen pulled out a dripping rag and pressed it roughly against his right cheek. Immediately, a rush of stinging pain shot through an open wound he didn't know he had.

"Ack!"

"Hold still, baby duke," Gretchen scolded. "I had to cut some off your face as well. If you don't want an infection, it needs to be cleaned."

Fenric winced but accepted the pain. "Where am I?"

"A cave not far from Jornho."

"Why?"

"I couldn't rightfully keep an enemy of the Empire in my home, now could I?"

She let go of his head and this time he leaned up, propped on his good arm to look at her. Pain rippled through his body, but he bit his way through it. "Why," he started," why bother saving me at all?"

"Believe it or not, Fenric, you're still a person, and when I see a person crumpled at the bottom of a tower, dying, I make sure they don't." Gretchen pulled out a steaming loaf of bread from the basket, ripped off a piece and shoved it into his mouth. A buttery goodness contrasted the scene and separated the pain of his body from the joy of his tongue. Tears welled in his eyes and confusion welled in his head.

"Fank you." He finally said through the bread.

"That's a start." Gretchen sat back and let out a long sigh.

Fenric swallowed before pushing himself to fully sit up. As he did, a ripple of pain gripped his entire right torso. Before he could even ask, Gretchen spoke.

"Your ribs still need to heal but be thankful it wasn't your head. I'll give the tainted metal some credit, it did take most of the blow."

Gretchen stopped to cross her arms and give Fenric a look. Her eyes were studious if not judging. Fenric finally broke the sudden silence, "What?"

"Well, now that you're awake and your face doesn't look as pitiful as it did earlier, I can't help but recognize you as the ass who turned Gavaria into a den of Nachtists."

The tears that welled from earlier started to drip and Fenric furrowed his brow, his face not following suit. "I'm a fool."

"No question."

Fenric gave a grim smirk at that before frowning. "I didn't deserve this kindness."

"No one has to deserve kindness, those who think otherwise, might not be dishing out kindness." The old surgeon let out a long sigh. "I don't like you, Fenric, in fact I'm pretty sure I hate you, but I'm old and I learned the rules of kindness long ago. At the heart of it all, you were someone's baby and I wasn't about to let someone's baby die in the dust."

At that, Fenric looked down, wet splotches were dripping onto his blanket. "I don't have time to be a child."

"Then go be whatever you think you have to be." Gretchen stood up. "Or you can stay here a while longer, I recommend that."

Grunting with each movement, Fenric wrestled himself to his feet to stand beside Gretchen, wobbly as he may be. "I need to go."

"And do what?"

"I don't know." For once, the voice of the Dweller wasn't cast inside his head, the whims of Esmachus were nowhere in sight and the expectations of his father weren't burying him. Fenric stood there alone, for the first time, a ragged blanket hanging off of him and his right arm missing. His face was scarred, his body was broken and he had fallen from his own tower, but there he finally was, simply Fenric: a man who didn't know anymore.

Gretchen offered the broken man a pitying look. "I won't stop you, just please, do better."

Her plea was like an arrow, one Fenric felt in his heart. He nodded, though, unsure.

She turned away but he held out a hand. "Gretchen...?"

"Hm?"

"Can I keep the blanket?"

"Why?"

"I'm cold."

Gretchen turned to look at Fenric, giving him an up and down before shaking her head. "Take it, you fool."

***

Stiff winds were rushing down from the slopes of the arctic mountains. The stalwart icons of the north stood in the blue distance, directly across a low valley ringed by rocky hills. Patches of farmlands and pastures quilted the small lowland, and through its fields, Fenric walked. Gretchen was nice enough to give him a sack of hard bread and cured meats, that of which he now had over his shoulder, but other than that, he wasn't weighed down by any possessions. His tattered gambison he had worn on the tower was replaced with the simple beige tunic and hose of Gretchen's late husband, and his feet were wrapped in thick socks tied to leather soles. He would have looked normal, perhaps even passable as a farmer, if not for the old blanket he wore around his body to fight any spring chill and to admittedly hide his missing arm.

Fenric's face wore an expressionless look as well as a grotesque wound wrapped in linen bandages. Despite the circumstances, what remained of Fenric's pride emerged enough for him to have stolen a farmer's hat to hide his face under the brim. With aimless resolve—if it could be called resolve—he made his way north.

He wasn't quite sure what his plan was. He held the blanket close. The arctic mountains had always loomed over his home, and now that he had basically died once, he figured it didn't hurt to walk into them to meet whatever fate wanted to greet him. As the ground turned from road to rocks and the fields to slope, Fenric furrowed his brow; he was due his punishment.

Gretchen's words bounced around his head, he liked how they sounded but his heart turned away from them—he couldn't believe he deserved kindness. His eyes glinted down to his right side, it was his right hand that killed his father. A heat started to well in his eyes. He couldn't feel his right hand, he couldn't feel the fire he had when he did it—the anger. All he felt was a deep ocean of sadness and defeat. He closed his eyes and continued into the mountains.

Hours passed but Fenric couldn't help but relive the same memories all over again, from the first time the Dweller whispered in his ear, to the fateful night of his father's demise and the wicked grin of Esmachus when he reported the news. He could see his mother's eyes when she heard of Osbert's death, they looked nothing like Esmachus'. The peace the Dweller promised seemed distant then, he saw her heart break, only to notice his own heart just as broken.

Fenric remembered when George appeared a few months later, how they stood in the Tagist chapel, as if Fenric could find redemption in there, as if George's virtue would rub off on him. A tear fell off his chin, he didn't know where he was going, he never did.

The sky was orange. Teal reflections outlined the peaks in front of him and behind him. Fenric's feet were sore and dusted with what snow remained from the winter. His stomach was rumbling and his throat was dry, but he didn't care. His boots scuffed to a stop, and the distinct wind of a high altitude bleed through his clothes. Looking up from his feet, his vision spilled out over the scene before him. A wonderland of nature was spread out underneath, just a touch away from the cliff he stood on. Endless pines and patches of snow and moss. Fenric looked directly down off the cliff, to the forest below. The setting sun caught a glisten as he watched one of his tears fall into the distance.

The dizzying sight stole his attention and in his deep sorrow and confusion, he stepped off after the tear. Fenric closed his eyes and let his body fall, but just as the wind enveloped him and he felt his body leave the cliff, the very ground moved under him with a great and thunderous rumble, catching him in the same bed of moss and snow he had stepped from. Not expecting it, Fenric yelped and fell face first into the snowy undergrowth.

"Careful." A booming voice not unlike a rolling boulder pounded through his body.

Fenric opened his eyes, blinking through melting ice crystals and rolled onto his back. His heart seized and his eyes widened. The side of the mountain was looking down at him with big eyes—no. A face peering out from the rocky side of the mountain was looking down at him. The face was massive, yet human, with rock and vegetation masking it. Fenric's vision traveled down, following the hidden lines and bumps under the peaks and valleys of the mountain, slowly realizing the very human shape of the landscape, if only accumulated with soil, rock, and forest.

"You... you..." Fenric sputtered, his sorrow knocked away by intense surprise. Such a creature only lived in the ancient legends of the giants.

"You almost fell off my knee," the Titan bellowed.

First Gretchen, now the very landscape. Fenric let his head fall back into the wet moss. "I didn't fall, I stepped off on purpose."

"Oh..." The titan's voice rumbled through the valley. "Now why would you do that?"

Fenric crossed his arms, still laying on his back. His vision was stuck on the orange bruised sky above. He opened his mouth but then twisted a frown, why would he spill his heart to a random talking mountain creature?

"It's okay," the titan bellowed, "you needn't speak. Rest if you'd like. No harm comes to any guests of mine."

Fenric closed his eyes, and when he did, he felt hot tears squeeze down his cheeks.

Jornho's castle had a cavernous dining hall. Despite the impressively long table, only two seats graced its length anymore. There were no windows, being situated in the heart of the keep, but rather the lighting was reliant on the effect of braziers that now only cast a dim glow. The plates were cold, and dinner had long since staled. No visitors, no witnesses, no company but a blank faced Fenric and oppressive Esmachus. They sat over a bland dish of boiled fish and yam.

Only a few bites were missing from Fenric's meal, his face gaunt and eyes distant. Esmachus, however, had finished half of his and now stared hungrily over at Fenric, a wolf's grin on his metal freckled face. Every time he spoke, a puff of smoke would exit his cracked lips and call Fenric's attention.

"You've done well, you know..." Esmachus said with as much joy as such a man could muster from the depths of a grave-like personality. Fenric stared back at Esmachus, unsure of what to say, or what could be said. Guilt battled in his chest, and a cold numbness was all that acted as a membrane over his sanity.

"We are one step closer to world peace," Esmachus continued, idly scraping his silver fork at his plate, pushing the bits and pieces of his food here and there. "Tobias has sufficiently been blessed by the black smoke and most naysayers have found... An early exit from this existence." He lifted his fork and placed it down on a silk napkin. He gave his dining companion a long look. "You're rather quiet, Fenric."

"Um." Fenric blinked, finding words to answer with.

"Oh?" Esmachus tilted his head. "You don't seem very happy, dear boy."

A cold wave of fear permeated into Fenric's gut as he stared back at the wicked man. It was an odd fear, knowing he was the one who invited Esmachus into this place much like a victim inviting their murderer to bed. Fenric twisted the worst smile and shook his head. "I'm just eager, I suppose, to see the end result."

Esmachus didn't skip a beat. "Not a fan of the means?"

"I... um..."

"Just remember," Esmachus interrupted. "All you've done is purge the world of undesirables. There was no room for the greedy and for obstacles in the world the Graceful One will bring. Even a failure such as yourself will find redemption."

Fenric winced. "I'm not a failure."

"Mm." Esmachus rolled his jaw. "Soon enough, you won't be. But as it stands, you failed to kill the Cursed One at Kors." He raised a finger. "But, this is the Grace of our Dweller. In due time, George will be forced up here and you will kill him then. Then, onto his Sister, and then the door will be open for paradise. A world with no pain, no stress, no anxieties or worries." Esmachus' eyes looked into the dark distance as the soft orange flicker of the lights around illuminated his mutilated face. "A world without war, without sadness."

The man's voice carried across the room until it faded into the soft crackle of the surrounding fires. The popping and flickering of the tinder filled the void, while Fenric sat unsure, across from his own predator. Fenric could feel his blood pulse, pushing away the chill of fear long enough for his jaw to loosen and his voice to sneak out. "I'm unsure."

Evil eyes snapped to Fenric as Esmachus glared. Eventually, the deadly stare turned into a soft facade that a teacher might offer a troubled student. "You no longer need to be, you'll leave it all to me from here on out. You just stay here and wait for the Cursed One to come and I'll take care of the rest."

There used to be honey in his words, seasoned with the sugary affirmations of the Dweller, but now as Fenric sat in the hollow halls of his murdered father, all he could smell was corpses and all he could taste was blood. All he could taste was blood.

***

Fenric's eyes slowly opened to the twinkling of the night sky above. An iron taste was on his tongue as his teeth had chewed into his cheek while he slept. He swallowed the blood and let out a long sigh, punctuated by a poof of frozen breath. He watched his breathy steam dissipate into the night air and just as he pulled in another breath, the rumbling voice of the Titan shook his mossy bed.

"Awake again, are you?"

"I am." Fenric's voice was quiet, defeated.

"You dream so vividly, you know?"

"Do I?" Disinterested.

"I couldn't quite see into it, but I could feel it, as sure as the finches and weasels on my back, I could feel it."

Fenric closed his mouth but didn't move from his position. "And what are your thoughts?"

"A dark woman and a sinister priest," the titan said with as much softness as a boulder could offer. "The wicked have a way of finding the most malleable hearts, when the walls are down and the

232

doors are broken. The question is, what does the boy do when he finally realizes he isn't who he wanted to be and he did what he didn't want to do?"

"What does the boy do?" Fenric could feel a tear roll down his cheek.

"Maybe you should tell me?"

Fenric folded his one good arm under his head and stared at the sky. A stiff night breeze washed over him. It was unreal. No matter how much he had changed, the feeling of wind never quite does, and it always seems to hold nostalgic scents, but now in such an unchanging world under an unchanging phenomena, he suddenly felt alien. He turned on his good side, the plush moss tickling his nose as he thought, what does he do now?

In time, the Dweller will come for him, be it in his dreams, or when her plans come to fruition. Plans he set forth for her, plans he helped her complete in exchange for temporary relief and echoing promises. This world she offered, suddenly didn't feel real, and now he didn't feel real in the world at present. What does he do?

"Titan," Fenric said.

"Hm?"

"If I asked you to charge with me into battle and to destroy those I once helped in some vain attempt at redemption or perhaps peace of mind before death, would you?"

"Oh..." The titan thought out loud. "I'm afraid there are too many things on my back and on my knee. I'd feel guilty to stand after all this time. Long ago, maybe, before I fell asleep that is, but, if perhaps I could offer you something else?" Fenric sat up and the Titan continued. "If you helped break the world and set people against each other, then maybe you should set them back together."

A pause. "I would wager, such people would do what I cannot for you."

The duke looked down at his missing arm and then up at the kind face of the titan hidden in the stone. "If I walk off your knee, would you catch me again?"

"Until you learn to walk straight."

He bit his swollen cheek. To put right what he had broken. The chirping of birds and the gust of wind accompanied his thoughts. Visions played across his mind, memories really, of all the pain he had caused, and the flimsy justifications he told himself while he did it. The people he betrayed and the people he killed. The wars he prolonged and the wars he started. He pictured it all until the titan's voice cut through the myriad of pictures.

"Bring them here."

"Huh?" Fenric questioned.

The titan spoke, "the chieftains you have wronged."

Chapter 20

Under the Old Oak Tree

Josephine was laying on her back, confused. She was staring up at the ceiling of the Imperial palace, her plush pillows in her periphery and her blankets weighing heavy over her. Her body was hot and her head was groggy. She mustered her strength and went to push her blankets off of her, but her arms didn't move. She kicked with her leg, but that too didn't move; Josephine couldn't even turn her head. Her eyes widened with panic, only to sting as black smoke started to rise from below the bed and encase the scene.

Something rubbed against the back of the bed's headboard and the sound of hands gripping the top caught Josephine's attention. A familiar face leaned over her, smiling. The face had two cold eyes, both an icy grey-blue not unlike the magical mist itself, but the rest of the woman's face was pale and laced with tainted metal and flakes of gold. It was the Dweller.

Josephine squirmed, or at least she tried. A slender, almost caring hand gently held Josephine's cheek. The princess and the devil's eyes were locked.

"You're my last hope," the Dweller whispered. "Come home to me soon. Your world needs me. Just open the door." Hot tears started to patter down onto Josephine's face and for a moment, the regent could see a deep pain in the Dweller's eyes. "Please, Josephine. I've been stuck for so long. Please."

***

This time Josephine opened her eyes to reality. She was tucked into a fur-filled cot. A wet rag lay limp across her forehead and smelled ripe with some awful rotting juice. Her nose crinkled in disgust but before she could shake the rag off, a pale-white hand snatched it from her head. The owner of the hand, the shaman of the Yabban, inspected the rag before tossing it into an equally rank bucket of strange liquid. The rag immediately dispersed a gross film across the concoction and the shaman made a face.

The shaman began to speak and a nearby Lor Kabblest translated. "I'm sure you know that my people are not strong in the ways of magic, and so we scour the world, our shamans reaching out with what alters they possess in search of Kafshe to represent us and give us our connection to the spirits." He let out a long breath and looked to Josephine. "But as you can see, some old medicines of the far away times can suffice. You have been asleep for quite some time, wracked with nightmares."

"I assume that stench was my cure." Josephine let her courtesy slip. Lor quickly translated for the shaman.

A toothy grin. "Indeed. Your people are waiting for you, as I have told them the location of their quarry."

Josephine sat up on her own now, more used to these abrupt awakenings of late than she'd like to be. "Can I ask you a question before I depart?"

Lor spoke between them and the shaman nodded.

"Why would you help me?"

"Ah..." the Shaman scratched his head. "This village has a Kafshe, you see. He is an old man now, barely spry and yet despite his inability to live the wild ways, the spirits still whisper to him even in his bed. He had told me that you would appear, and that you must find your quarry, and when the time comes, you must assist your brother."

"George?"

"Yes." the Shaman wagged a finger. "The threads of fate rely on a single instance of destiny, that's what I was told, that you must find your quarry and after, you must help George make his choice."

"What choice?"

The shaman hung his head. "That, I do not know, but the sake of my people and yours appears to balance on the edge of that moment to come."

Josephine bit her lip in thought, this was all becoming too much. She let silence permeate for a moment before realizing she wasn't about to get any more clues, or at least any clues that didn't bring more questions than answers. Slapping her lap, she gave the shaman a steely blue gaze. "Off I go, then."

Without much more to say, Josephine found her feet and stood tall. The shaman didn't rise, but rather looked up at her with a curious gleam in his large eyes. They shared a gaze for a moment, as if trying to read each other's thoughts before the regent frowned and the shaman spoke one last message. "Be safe. It's rare enough to find an Imperial as collected as yourself. I'd hate for both our peoples to lose such an asset."

"I will do my best," Josephine offered a weak grin. As much as she'd like to reassure the strange creature with more confidence, everything seemed to be slowly constricting around her, and she wasn't sure she had enough metaphorical space to breathe let alone comfort the concerns of another. With little else, she passed through the hovel's quilted door.

As she did, a stiff breeze was pushing through the canopies above and dipping down into the small glade of the village. The warm spring wind threaded past and rumpled the heavy quilt behind her. It was a comforting wind and yet a dense cold pit was still festering in Josephine's stomach. She could see the eyes of Demitri and hear his words—the dreams were getting stronger, more frequent. Even now, her eyelids were heavy and she could feel the exhaustion under her eyes.

"Are you ready?" Opane's voice pierced her thoughts and she turned to the Kafshe. Contrasted to Josephine's olive travelers tunic, Opane looked more ready for a hunt than Josephine ever would, who looked and felt more ready for bed. Still, it reminded Josephine that she should probably put on some protection before heading out.

***

Dressed in a black jack-of-plates with Flaretongue, Josephine's long and wavy-bladed sword, strapped to her hip, the Regent crouched in the shadows of the forest. Across from her, covered by bushes, was Opane, her fingers shimmering with the promise of frost. The pair stared into a small mossy glade that the Yaban shaman had described. Along with the pair were Josephoine's soldiers, forming a secret ring around the glade. Up ahead, a large pine tree dominated a low impression in the ground and its thick boughs hid a small woven hut, fit for one person to sleep in and perhaps store a few things. Outside the hut was a blackened firepit and stove. Nothing looked very old or even settled about the place, as if it was only built a month or two ago, after the winter had faded.

Even in the shadows of the foliage, Josephine could feel a pair of eyes staring right through her. She clenched her teeth before calling out, much to her soldier's surprise. "You already know we are here!"

The forest answered with a rustling breeze and a few errant bird songs before the voice of the runic man called back from the exit of the hut. His voice was melodic, yet deep and bold, twisted with an unknown accent. "I do."

"Then you know you're surrounded." Josephine stood up. As she did, the other soldiers did as well, punctuating her statement.

Ambient sound once again reigned, only to be broken by the crunch of a few leafy steps. The runic man dipped out from under his hut and stood tall in defiance. A set of sunny gold eyes glared at Josephine. As much as she wanted to, Josephine found herself physically unable to hold his stare and flicked her eyes away to his general visage. He was a well proportioned and aligned creature, almost as if he was carved rather than born, with curly black hair and golden skin, but more importantly, the runes carved into his flesh hurt to look at more than his stare. A dense ringing started to form in Josephine's ears whenever she stared in one place too long, her eyes almost wetting as if she was cutting onion.

Even if the ringing was familiar to the kind she experienced with Demitri, something was different about it now. Instead of a blackening and hollow fuzz, it was almost as if beyond the ring were words, and as if the headache that ensued was trying to paint pictures. Josephine forced her eyes back over the runes and asked. "Why don't you run?"

"I'd like to, but I know you'd catch me," the man answered. He stepped forward. A crowded rasp of steel sounded as everyone pointed their weapons at him, Josephine included. Holding up his hands in surrender, he spoke again, "Know me as Tomko, and know that you must leave this place. I am not the threat that lurks here."

"Then who are you?" Josephine drew closer, Flaretongue pointed straight ahead.

"I already said, I'm Tomko."

The regent knew that wasn't what she wanted, and she figured Tomko knew that as well. There were enough secrets, it had to end here. "What did you want with my father?"

"Please, Josephine," Tomko spoke with undeserved familiarity. "I can't answer the questions you have, there is a balance to uphold."

"What balance?" Josephine narrowed her eyes, edging ever closer.

"This isn't about me, this isn't about you," Tomko took a step back, hands still up. "This is for the sake of everyone. You have to leave this be and let me go."

As she stepped closer, the meaning behind his strange runes were starting to become clear through the ringing sound. Josephine's eyes flicked to his bare arms and she scanned the alien words. Tomko seemed to notice and crossed his arms in an attempt to hide them, but it was too late. "Ritual..." Josephine recited. "Blood of the elmborn... the shard dagger of sol"

"SH!" Tomko hissed, but Jospehine's eyes went wide as she studied the runes on his cheeks.

"Keep the evil ones at bay... Renew the veil..." Upon saying veil, a blast of sound seemed to ripple among everyone present and the ringing took over once again. The sharp screeching roared across the grove, and sent the soldiers to the ground, writhing in pain.

Opane wasn't safe, either, her knees buckling suddenly before falling face first into the moss below. Only Josephine and Tomko were left standing. The two stared at each other hesitantly. Tomko was on his back foot while Josephine was about to advance. She didn't know why she was still standing, but she couldn't let him get away.

Josephine sent a blast of Stromist magic down her leg and launched towards Tomko, but he had anticipated it and with a swirling ribbon of his own magic, he launched into the trees. Branches snapped and leaves were kicked up into a whirlwind as Josephine launched after him. The two barreled through the forest at incredible speeds; their feet landed only to kick against the ground or the very trees themselves, leaving large pits and broken branches in their wake. The world turned to green pinstripes, tunneled around her prey as Josephine sped through. The wind was roaring by her ears and her heart was pounding as she knew that this would spell the answer or the end to her questions.

The noise of the chase was abruptly punctuated by the sound of a dead tree snapping. Tomko had landed across the trunk of the tree and misjudged its strength which sent it exploding into a cloud of splinters. Tomko yelped and Josephine sucked in an anxious breath, her own weight unable to stop so suddenly. Her vision blinked white for a moment as she slammed into an ancient tree; her lungs emptied and left her gasping.

It only took her a split second before she forced her lungs full again and in spite of the pain in her side, she spun in place, looking for any sign of Tomko. She chewed her cheek, heart in her ears and throat.

"Josephine! He went this way!" Gennisberg's voice rang through the trees, out of sight but clearly moving fast. Too drowned in energy to be confused, Josephine twisted to face the voice, catching a glimpse of the man sinking into the trees. She readied Flaretongue, adrenaline zapping through her veins, and launched after the Count.

Flinging herself in the direction Gennisberg ran off to, she was met with only a path of wreckage, clear signs of someone zipping through the forest with immense magic. Josephine couldn't remember if Gennisberg even knew Stromism, let alone a type so fast, but kept after his trail.

The trees whipped by and debris kicked up behind her as she snapped through the woods, only slowing as the tunnel of trees gave way to a clearing. A flash of metal glinted before Josephine and at the last moment, she brought Flaretongue to bear. Her blade reverberated off of Gennisberg's own sword and she went glancing off to the side. The dust from her sprint came blowing through, settling to reveal the scene.

Gennisberg stood under an old oak tree, impossibly prehistoric and gnarled. A green meadow marked the area around the tree, but a grisly scene disturbed any sense of serenity. A pile of human bones littered the base of the tree. Gennisberg looked down from his nose at Josephine, his usual smile replaced with a sinister grin and all light drained from his face as smoky wisps hissed from his body.

Josephine put both her hands on Flaretongue and held it towards him. "I'm going to take a guess and say pigguts aren't responsible for this massacre."

"So many years," Gennisberg said cryptically, almost longingly. "We brought so many scions of the Heinrich branch here, scions long since lost to history, but none of them took." Twisted delight played on his face. "But now I know why. They weren't 'elmborn'... They weren't you."

Josephine scrunched her nose in disgust and turned her legs to take on an offensive stance. Pushing off with her backfoot, she charged in. Flaretongue came curling in at a wide arc but Gennisberg quickly brought his own blade up and deflected it, only for his eyes to widen with surprise.

Like an echo, Josephine's strike doubled as her arm turned into a blur, the same strike curling in again, but at a lower angle. Gennisberg let out a sharp screech, sending a plume of black smoke down his arm and moving out of the way just in time to save his hand from being severed.

Gennisberg was reeling now using his smokescreaming to keep up with Josephine's flurry of blows. Whenever he attempted to predict where her strike was going to land, it would strike twice and in places he wasn't expecting. He clenched his jaw, but Josephine kept her cold stare as she swung, using impeccable footwork not unlike her uncle's.

Finally, one of his parry's took, her blade bouncing off of his, but just as a smile started to stretch on his face, Josephine's knee came rocketing up and slammed into his gut. She could feel his ribcage bend back under her blow before he went flying backwards. The duke slammed into the oak tree with a crunch. Swiping her blade a few times in the air, Josephine narrowed in on Gennisberg, eyes flicking to his throat.

"I won't lie," Josephine started, "there is something rather cathartic about this."

She hesitated. A dark pull drained on her for a moment—no. Josephine knew this feeling; it was her narcolepsy. She felt heavy. Gennisberg's shocked face turned into a wicked smile.

"You feel her presence, don't you?" He picked himself up. Josephine held her head with one hand, any fear she might be feeling was replaced by a sluggish and tired anxiety. Gennisberg let out a screech and black smoke enveloped his body. A shimmering blur, he launched forward. Josephine could barely follow the attack. Deep inside, Josephine pushed on what magic she could and summoned a golden ribbon to her sword arm, placing Flaretongue in place just in time for Gennisberg's blade to spark off of it. Still, the force knocked her on her back foot, wobbling as she further felt drained. The Dweller's voice was whispering in her head as dreams tried to take over.

Another swing was heading towards her, shrouded in black smoke. It was too fast.

A rune covered arm appeared holding a golden dagger. The small blade managed to deflect Gennisberg's swing and Tomko landed between the two combatants. No words were said, but Gennisberg let out another scream of smoke, his body blinking through the haze as a whirlwind of attacks.

As fast as Tomko' Stromism was, Josephine could see he wasn't much of a fighter. Her vision was blacking in and out of reality, but each time she could see ahead, the fuzzy image of Tomko using his small golden knife to deflect an attack was getting closer and closer. The last image she saw was Gennisberg's blade cutting into Tomko's wrist at a grisly angle and the golden dagger fall to the forest floor.

A horrific scream led Williams charging through the woods. Opane was right at his side, having been woken by the knight; both had their weapons in hand as they followed the sound of the smoke-screaming in the distance. They were close and yet only grew anxious once the screaming stopped. A terrible feeling twisted Williams' gut and he tightened his grip on his sword. Together, the pair broke through the treeline and entered the glade of the old oak tree.

There Williams was struck with a sight that froze his heart. Tomko lay on the ground holding his bleeding wrist with pain etched on his face, while Gennisberg stood by the oak tree holding a strange golden dagger. Pressed against the trunk of the tree was Josephine, eyes closed, and just as Williams entered the grove, Gennisberg slammed the golden knife into the middle of Josephine's chest, pinning her to the tree. Her eyes shot open, ripped in pain, but no sound came from her mouth.

"No!" Williams rushed in, and the ground started to shake. An eerie screech started to ring from the oak tree as Josephine haggardly breathed against its bark. Gennisberg turned to Williams and just as they met eyes, a blast of light shot from the oak tree and hit the sky above, rending a sickly red crack through it. The crack grew and grew, until a loud thunderclap sounded, and the sky shattered into an abyssal swirl of black and red.

Opane's eyes widened in shock and nearly fell back with what looked like sudden vertigo, but Williams was too focused on Gennisberg, a fire roaring through his veins. He charged. Gennisberg was quick, and with a blast of smoke, he ducked Williams' swing and sliced his side with one of his own.

Above the fight, streaks of blue mist were showering down like comets into the unseen distance, while other comets of black smoke were following. Something was coming through the sky. Williams focused on Gennisberg, his side now hot and sticky with blood. The power of Gennisberg's swing had sliced through a weak spot into his armor. Biting through the pain, Williams swung again but this time, Opane jumped in from the side. Coordinated, they both struck at Gennisberg.

With a blast of smoke, Gennisberg seemed to dash completely backwards, both Williams' strike and a blast of cold magic missing, before he moved in and struck with a whirlwind of attacks. Opane deflected one or two with expert puffs of ice and Williams managed to as well, but soon, even between the both of them, they found themselves outmatched. Gennisberg let out a roar and swung down at Williams. The knight brought his sword to bear but the force of Gennisberg's blade sent Williams buckling to the ground, his sword snapping out of his hand. He rolled out of the way and bumped into the discarded Flaretongue.

Gennisberg wasn't done, and went in for a final blow but Opane let loose a torrent of frozen air from her palms. Gennisberg spun out of the way, but not before razor shards of ice sliced up his shoulder and the side of his neck, rendering a trickle of black blood down his body. That was all the opening Williams needed. He grabbed Flaretongue and stabbed the blade forward. For a moment, he and Gennisberg met eyes and at first, the anger in Williams' face was met with surprise from Gennisberg, which then turned to sadistic amusement. The Count exploded into a puff of smoke only to spiral away from the blade, unharmed, before reforming.

There was a snap from the side, and with a loud bang, the Stromist soldiers that had accompanied Josephine came hurtling from the tree line. They were slightly dazed from earlier, but armed and shouting. Gennisberg's eyes flitted all around before he gave a final grin to Williams and then with a blast of black smoke, he escaped through the other side of the treeline, his body a chaotic blur.

Williams stared at the place Gennisberg had escaped only for a moment before blurting, "Josephine!" And jumped to his feet. With a slight limp he ran to the oak tree, the ancient wood now crackling with magic energies. He placed both his hands on the golden dagger that pinned Josephine to the tree. She was looking down at him with a pale and lethargic face, but still she breathed. A steady trickle of blood was pouring out from behind her back and threading along the tree bark.

"Don't!" Opane barked, running to Williams' side. "She'll bleed out if you remove the dagger. Here." The Kafshe swiped Williams' hands away and held the knife steady. "You pull her from the tree, I'll follow in such a way the dagger comes with her." Opane's face was twisted and disturbed.

Williams nodded, his own face turning pale the longer he looked at his dying love. The crackling abyss that was the sky reflected off of Josephine's eyes. WIlliams felt a heat on his own and gave her his best reassuring smile. He didn't mean to ask. "Will she live?"

Opane didn't answer, she didn't even look over at Williams and then with a yank, they both took Josephine out from under the old oak tree.

Chapter 21
The Emergence

The sky above the Imperial palace was a bruised black and red. There were no clouds, and staring straight up gave a sense of vertigo that made one think there wasn't even any sky. Flashes of light not unlike lightning blurred the colors and with each flash a comet of mist or smoke rocketing down into the unseen distance. Hector himself stood in the Imperial gardens, looking straight up at the stormy void of a sky. He couldn't even fathom what was going on and yet he felt like a long forgotten weight was removed from his mind, a weight he had unknowingly lived with his entire life.

An eerie breeze rushed through the gardens and sent a chill down the man's back, and brought with it the scent of fire. His eyes widened, one of the comets of black smoke was heading straight down. He could hear it ripping against the wind as it fell and the closer it got, the more the hair on his arms stood up.

Snapping to his senses, Hector burst from his spot and started to run towards the closest entrance to the palace. His boots ripped at the grass and loose pebble paths while the other palace guards in the area rushed with him right until the comet slammed into the gardens behind them. Brick cracked like thunder under the impact and a large chunk of the palace wall came crumbling down. No one had any time to adjust to the suddenly dusty air before the sound of clashing metal took over the scene. The verdant gardens quickly turned into a battlefield against an unknown enemy.

Hector spun in place until the face of one of these enemies came bursting through the dust. It looked human, at least in shape, but had the metal plates associated with tainted smoke-screamers splotched on its skin. Curiously, tiny dots of blue crystal also stained their bodies and while black smoke seemed to puff with every breath, their eyes were a pacified blue not unlike the highest of sages. In the beings hands was a spear made of the same blue crystal, pointed menacingly at Hector. It was a tainted person, corrupted by the smoke to the point of insanity, and yet something mist-like yoked them.

The Stromist Marshal quickly snapped his eyes to either side of the opponent; the palace guards were in a tight spot, with this sudden enemy standing on top of the corpses of those caught off guard by the crash. Some of the others were still coughing the dust from their lungs while trying to deflect spears with their swords. Hector curled his bare hands into fists and took on his stance, giving his attention back to the enemy in front of him.

Silently, the tainted creature lunged, but with a flash of magic, Hector juked to the side, placing himself right next to the now surprised opponent. Hector's eyes were already on his next enemy, the Marshal snapped his arm back, a magic imbued fist slamming into the spear wielder and sending them cracking to the rubble underfoot.

Another spear came stabbing in, but Hector grabbed it with his open palm and yanked the owner right into his free arm, clotheslining them as he moved forward. The next enemy put a shield in his way, but with a swift kick to the knee and a following uppercut, Hector was already past them while simultaneously yanking another one of the creatures off of one of his comrades.

Wrenching the palace guard free, Hector tossed the assailant into a crowd of the beasts. Despite the emotionless visage of the tainted, Hector could tell they were starting to show him caution. Taking the seconds offered to him by their hesitation, Hector bellowed with a blast of Stromism. "For the Emperor!"

"Hoo-Ah!"

One by one, the Imperial guards fell into line by Hector's shoulder, reforming into a proper unit. Both sides started to lurch but were cut off by a loud and alien voice.

"Stop!"

The tainted creatures froze in place, obedient. Their blue eyes seemed to shine as they did. The Imperials themselves stood their ground, cautious to the scene before them. Hector chewed the inside of his cheek but didn't let his fists fall from a fighting position. He had never known those completely tainted by the smoke to follow commands so readily, and there was no way they were all recusants. It was rare enough to find one smoke-screamer still sane of mind, let alone many non-smoke-screamers who adapted to the taint.

Hector's attention was yanked upwards and his eyes widened. There, floating above the rubble was a figure unlike any he had seen before. She was a tall woman, draped in flowing blue cloth that glimmered with ethereal qualities, sifting in and out of existence right before Hector's eyes. Whenever it faded, Hector witnessed a body quilted of crystalline blue and pale skin freckled with tainted black metal and flakes of gold. Some of her flesh didn't seem to be all there either, nearly transparent and instead held the consistency of mist. Even still, she was a graceful creature, with no sign of injury or malice beyond the twisted scars of black metal. The most alien thing, however, was her face, or lack thereof. It was a flat sheet of blue crystal, smooth and perfect, and yet Hector knew that the strange sing-song voice he was hearing was coming from her.

"Know my name for I am the Graceful One, long since lost from Serenity." Her words seemed to mesmerize those around Hector, and even he had to admit she had his utmost attention. He could feel a strange empathy or perhaps sympathy towards the self-proclaimed Graceful One, as if she had gone through enough pain to make it palpable.

"I will not deceive you," she continued, "many of you know me now as the Dweller, but I am anything but simply here to dwell. I have felt the pain of this world, watched it suffer for countless years. I was forced to sit in a prison of silence and torture, my vision stuck on a land of violence, hate, sadness and loss. But now I am here, and I will deliver you all, I will save you all from this pain."

The gardens fell to silence as she finished her speech. Hector could barely think as he stared up at her, his magic waning as confusion set in. He had no right to be confused, nor should he be hesitating. The marshal knew she was his enemy, after all, she just invaded the palace, and yet he couldn't help but remain still, stuck. His eyes were glued to her crystalline face and her words rang in his ears. The sound was hypnotic and warm and his mind started to play memories of happier days, days before the wars. He saw things he lost, he saw Franklin. Tears started to well in his eyes and without thinking, he fell to his knees. The only things that mattered were his eyes and her face, and a lifetime of memories between the two. Could peace ever be real?

"Absolute peace..." The Dweller whispered in his ear, her voice dripping like molten honey. Hector furrowed his brow.

"How?"

Her breath spilled against his face. "I'll take it all away, just leave it all to me. Give me your burdens..."

In his periphery, he could hear the rasp of someone's blade free from its scabbard, a short slice and then the sound of a body hitting the floor. Hector's mouth hung open, slacked, but instead of anxiety, the Dweller filled his heart with promises. He could hear the sound of mist hissing across the garden, the gagging sound as people choked on it, but he didn't mind, he could feel it tickling his own nostrils. Hector smiled.

It all came to a sudden halt. The Dweller's attention was ripped away from the troops and Hector felt his senses come flooding back. He could hear the pounding of someone's footsteps far above and looking upward, he could see Emperor Wilhelm sprinting across the roof of the palace, sword in hand.

"It's the Emperor!" Someone shouted.

Wilhelms boots crashed heavily across the tiles of the roof as he huffed hot breaths. Hatred burned in his eyes, and the armor of a palace guard rattled over his frail frame. Wilhlem's wild golden hair waved all around him, liberated into the evening wind. The emperor's mouth snapped open with a chest shaking roar. His eyes were lucid, his eyes were fury. Frozen by the sight, Hector could feel the pain in his voice.

With a powerful stomp, the emperor kicked off the lip of the roof. The wind caught him as he flung through the air towards the Dweller. Before the floating figure could react, Wilhelm's blade sunk deep into her chest, and the two plummeted to the ground. Wilhelm screamed angrily in her ear as they rocketed down towards the garden floor and a massive plume of dirt exploded from the impact.

Hector looked back at his troops as the tremendous bang rolled over his shoulders. The palace guards looked back at the man as a strange blue faded from their eyes and were replaced with a sense of duty. Clenching his fist, Hector turned to point back at the enemy. "For the Emperor!"

A roar shot to the skies and the guards rushed in to continue the battle. The strange minions of the Dweller responded with an aggressive and eerily silent charge to quickly match the renewed guards.

With a blast of Stromism, Hector weaved through the scattered fighting, slamming and smashing the heads of each passing beast, eager to reach his emperor.

It didn't take long before Hector managed to fight his way to the clearing where the two had fallen. In the crater of the impact, Wilhelm was dueling the Dweller, his body shimmering a long repressed gold. The sheer brightness of the emperor's magic forced a squint from Hector.

Even with echo Stromism, the Dweller was deftly and easily beating the emperor back with a long spear made out of strange blue crystal. Wilhelm was on his back foot and the Dweller didn't seem any worse for wear from the emperor's first stab, her wound not even bleeding. Hector took a step forward, eager, but Wilhelm suddenly looked at him with wide and lucid eyes.

"Go, Hector!" His voice had a strength behind it that the young marshal had never heard before. "Evacuate and join forces with my daughter." The Dweller's spear just missed Wilhelm, slamming into the ground. The emperor gritted his teeth and shouted as he turned back to his opponent. "Don't let my sacrifice be in vain! Find my daughter!"

The Dweller's spear came thrusting in again, but Wilhelm just managed to bounce it off the blade of his sword. Wrenching himself from his spot, Hector started to back away. Just as he was about to take his eyes off Wilhelm, the Dweller sent out a blast of blue mist, encapsulating the emperor, only to follow up with a powerful punch of her spear. Hector saw the blue tip of the blade carve right through the Emperor's chest and rip out through the back. Wilhelm's fingers slacked and his sword fell to the ground. The faceless visage of the Dweller shifted from Wilhelm to Hector, and feeling an intense fear, unlike any he ever felt before, Hector summoned all his magic and started his escape.

His legs erupted with golden ribbons and he shot backwards just in time to avoid the Dweller's thrown spear. The strike kicked up a cloud of dirt and debris. Hector scrambled, pumping his legs and darting back across the garden.

"Retreat!" He managed to bellow as he wove through the battle, all too aware of the Dweller. Three crystal spikes came spiraling at him, but Hector skidded behind a tree; the javelins slammed into the trunk and blasted it into wooden shards. A piece of wood slashed across Hector's cheek and dug into his arm. Not losing momentum, the marshal dove for a window of one of the garden patios.

Hector tumbled through the thin glass with an immense crash and drips of red formed on his growing cuts. He peeled his face from the marble floor and scrambled to his feet. The fighting had spilled into the halls of the palace and as he stood up he found himself face to face with a crowd of the strange beings, embroiled in combat with some guards.

Tapping the closest allies shoulder, Hector dove into the fight. Managing to push into the worst of the fighting, Hector's presence naturally formed an anchor for the guards to rally around.

The enemy horde started to thicken and the Marshal's brow furrowed with worry as he continued. He struck out with his fists and he stomped on the fallen bodies of the twisted beasts. He dodged serrated axes and swords, and ducked under thrusted spears and darting arrows. He stepped to the side to avoid enemy charges, and he rolled under swings of halberds.

Onward Hector fought, his collection of followers growing as he forced his retreat through the enemy forces until finally they broke through and spilled into the palace's main foyer. There, the palace guards present had already secured the area, save the hall to the Eastern wing, which still swarmed with enemies, held back only by well placed spearmen. The marshal sucked in a balancing breath; he was going to need as many guards as possible to get through the city below.

Two big flashes of fire bloomed behind the enemy and the smell of sizzling flesh grew, another flash and the enemy was blown back into the foyer, charred and lifeless. The spearmen were shoved back by the blast as well, but landed otherwise unscathed. Through the now opened path came Reginald and Cassandra. The servant held a kitchen knife in both hands, a crude black blood staining it and her cheeks, while her dress was charred and burnt. An old book hung partially out of her pocket. Reginald, conversely, looked spotless, with only worry in his eyes. A strange sword hung on his hip, the blade welded shut inside its scabbard.

"We have to withdraw," Hector said as soon as the others were within earshot.

"The Emperor?" Reginald asked first.

Hector furrowed his brow. "His orders, we abandon the palace and regroup with Josephine."

Cassandra signed frantically. "What about the city? The people?"

Hector stared, unknowing, then looked to Reginald who translated.

"We cut our way to the docks and take as many as we can with us. We can't afford to lose our forces here and now... are you ready?"

Cassandra gave a grim sign. "Well no, but none of us are."

Hector gave an appreciative snort and then nodded to them and the onlooking soldiers. The clash of battle rumbled in the distance like thunder, giving Hector only a few moments to find his second wind. As he breathed, the horrors of what was happening started to creep into his mind, but with a soldier's defiance, he cast it away—that was something he would have to come to terms with when lives weren't on the line. "Right then, we cut a path to the docks, collecting as many as we can and then take the largest boats out of the city. If we get split up, let's all plan to sail west and reconvene at the Forest Garrison."

There was no big "hoo-ah" this time, but rather a quiet understanding that passed between everyone.

Chapter 22
The Escape

Reality was crashing all around Cassandra. She felt the weight of the world in her chest as she ran with all her might. A kitchen knife lingered in her hands, her fingers numb. She could still feel the pull of the flesh as she claimed her first ever life, and the deadly fear she felt before and after. The world was a spinning mess of black, red, gold, and blue and as her shoes stomped on the flagstone streets, the only concrete things she knew to be real was her weapon, her fear, and the bouncing weight of the Father Sage's book in her dress pocket. With the shock of the invasion, Cassandra held dear to these three things, as they were the only rope she had as her mind dangled above an endless pit of despair.

In front, Hector led the charge down a winding road which eventually spilled into the upper reaches of the Imperial city. To her left, Reginald ran, stoic and alert with his hand on a sword welded in place. That sword—Cassandra had seen it unsheathed twice, and knew that it was only a matter of time before it came undone again.

The flanks of the retreat into the city were a swirl of fighting, with the tainted creatures embroiled in war against the city guard and preying upon the helpless citizens. Screams curdled next to shouts and grunts, and sounds never to be repeated plagued Cassandra's ear. Worse still, the comets were still falling from the skyless sky, each impact sending shockwaves through the ground and reminding Cassandra that there were ever more of the enemy.

Cassandra's wedge of allies managed to penetrate into the merchant's district before they were stalled by the fighting. Crowds of civilians were started to conglomerate into their ranks and as the formation swelled and the battle quickened, Cassandra was forced to the fighting edge.

Now standing beside Imperial guards, and desperate palace staff, Cassandra was face to face with the endless swarm. Her hands were shaking and her knife reflected dull flashes of the fight around her. The guards were doing their best against the strange weapons of the enemy, but with every tainted creature struck down, another took its place. Between the snarling and the sound of flesh ripping, Cassandra's mind was taken back to a time she had tried to forget.

An enemy burst past the guards to her left and right. Dull eyes stared at her as the creature lunged with metal claws and a broken jaw. Panic shot up Cassandra's spine and with a wordless scream, her arm shot out. Her knife slammed into the creature's gut and ripped down, tearing the fat and releasing the innards, but instead of gore, Cassandra was met with clusters of blue crystal and gooping black sludge. A grimace ran up her arms just as the guard next to her stepped in to finish the tainted beast.

The screams of the civilians were shaking the air at this point and the city was aglow with so much orange and fire, Cassandra's vision was a blur of movement. Their little bubble of warriors could barely cover the people they've saved at this point and the fear of being scattered entered Cassandra's heart.

She bit her cheek hard enough that she tasted iron. She couldn't be thinking like that now, not while people were depending on her. With false confidence, Cassandra stepped out from behind the guard that had aided her earlier, and let out a swift stab to help the man finish off another silent beast before falling back into safety. Again, Cassandra did this, and again.

***

At long last, the smell of blood and fire mixed with the stout winds of the Imperial Lake, promising some semblance of hope to the city's refuges. The growing stench, save the salt, was all too familiar to Cassandra. As a prisoner of Esmachus freed, she hoped she'd taste this scent ever again. She shook the thought out of her head, it had been a long road to now but she had to keep going. All around her, everyone's faces wore fear, save for Hector and Reginald. Hector held the face of a father, as if all the civilians following him were his children. It was stressed, but eerily calm and composed. Reginald on the other hand wore the same face as always. His dark eyes betrayed that he had seen many things in his life, perhaps enough that this invasion barely pierced his psyche.

The fighting was less intense by the docks, with the worst behind the refugees but that also meant the fighting was worse in the rear. As the group clamored across the wooden piers of the dockways, the sea reflected the sky above and gave its lapping waves a certain emptiness. People were already leaping into the water, swimming this way and that, but Cassandra took note of the largest boat right away. It was everyone's best chance at survival.

She opened her mouth to shout orders, but felt the wind in her empty mouth. Her eyes watered and she noticed the people who had split off were already being hunted down. No. The formation was falling. Her eyes flickered to Reginald and Hector, but they were busy trying to cover the retreat onto the docks. Cassandra let out a wordless scream, perhaps of frustration or maybe anger and sprinted down the docks. With all her weight, Cassandra threw her body into one of the many flag poles that marked the port and with a thunderous crack, one such plum and wine banner collapsed into her grasp.

The kitchen knife was tossed into the water and with another scream to the horrid sky, Cassandra waved the banner of the Empire high. Faces turned to her, feet ran to her, the citizens flocked to her. The maiden of the dock, Cassandra screamed again and now the rush of refugees were collected behind her like sheep. Hector fell to the flanks with Reginald and the last of the guards, becoming the final membrane between the helpless and the enemy.

Stomping, Cassandra led her group to the largest boat, but before she stepped foot, her eyes shot back across the planks to Hector. He looked back at her for a moment and mouthed some words. "Go on!"

Cassandra threw a sign, not that he knew her language.

"Go on!" He mouthed again, though he very well could have been shouting. "We'll cover! We'll find a smaller boat! We'll follow!"

Cassandra barely knew Hector, and yet she couldn't help but frown in sympathetic worry. Instead of arguing, she nodded and looked at the many startled faces of the civilians already saved. They were staring at her, and they weren't looking at her as if she was just the outcast servant girl covered in salacious rumors, but as a savior. Cassandra put on a stern face and slammed her banner down before pointing to the boat.

The stampede began and the wood of the dock yawned and protested the weight, only to crack with relief as the refugees started to pour onto the boat. It was a large vessel, probably used for shipping cargo to and from Barcena, but with the amount of people being evacuated, it felt infinitely small. Funneling onto the deck and to the hold below, the surface of the boat was already shoulder to shoulder with people, bleeding and frightened. Soot covered the faces of the survivors and guards who had been fighting for hours now lay slumped over, their adrenaline leaving their broken bodies. Some Barcenian sailors were found holed up, shaking and frightened.

Cassandra watched it all from the boarding planks, all too aware that they would need to take a second boat. Once the first was full, she ordered the helm to leave with a snap of her flag and ran over to the next boat, to once again funnel the people onboard. The first boat had just unfurled its sails when Cassandra looked back to the line Hector was holding. He was fighting with all his might alongside other brave soldiers, but the enemy line was growing darker and thicker. She recognized the man at Hector's right as the Hero Harris, deftly aiding the Marshal. Reginald was nowhere to be seen and Cassandra could only hope he had made it to one of the boats, but something in her gut told her otherwise.

Startled people ran by Cassandra as she coordinated the filling of the second boat, but her stomach sank as she realized that this boat wouldn't be as packed full as the first. Was this really all the people of the city that they had managed to save? This few?

With the final people scrambled onboard, Cassandra ran after them and up to some poor man standing by the helm of the boat. Each of them shared a look of confusion, and whether or not the man knew what he was doing, Cassandra pointed her flag as if shouting, "Follow that boat!" Her banner pointed to the first ship, which had already started its journey. The man fumbled with the ship's wheel and started to shout at others to deal with the ropes, all the while Cassandra retreated to the side of the boat. She slammed her gut into the railing and lurched over the edge to look down the port. She yelled with all her might, hoping Hector might find some meaning in her wordless scream.

The man didn't respond, himself deeply engrossed in battle. The ship lurched and started to peel from the port. Cassandra gnashed her teeth in frustration. The enemy was growing thicker and the battle was growing more and more violent. Hector was doing his best to fight backwards and towards the dock, but there was no room to breathe, no room to withdraw. A sword came slamming down and Cassandra could feel the impact from where she stood. Hector went toppling to the wooden floor. Cassandra didn't realize it before, but her heart was pounding in her ears.

The Hero Harris stepped in, swinging his own blade to engage the monster that had toppled Hector and while he fought, Cassandra rediscovered her breath. Hector was squirming on the ground; he was alive. Slowly he shuffled to his feet, holding his shoulder, but now Harris was stuck where he once was. *Shit.*

Cassandra closed her eyes and her mind screamed in prayer, to anyone, to someone, something greater than the Graces themselves. A flash of pink leaked by her eyelids and forced them open just in time to catch the mangled bodies of the enemy scattering through the air, chased by a mighty fireball as Harris and Hector made their limping escape. What soldiers remained followed suit, with Reginald holding one up from under the arm, a stern and unphased look on his face. His free hand held his blade, the metal red hot and dripping something molten. Even still, the enemy was not gone and they had already started to regroup. Cassandra furrowed her brow and held her breath again, only releasing it as the survivors scrambled onto a small oar boat and started their escape from the scene. With everyone in the water, Cassandra slumped against the railing—they made it.

A great horn-like sound loomed through the air, shaking the stormy waters and rattling Cassandra's chest. Her eyes shot upward, spotting a great ball of flame and black metal roaring through the broken sky. She had never seen the likes of it before. It felt like smoke-screaming and it was heading right for her ship.

The great ball of metal and flame clipped the top of the forward mast, snapping it in half but otherwise missing the rest of the boat. The mighty lump slammed into the hissing ocean and conjured a wave that nearly saw the boat go horizontal. A gusty spray of salt and cinders washed over Cassandra, soaking her to her bruised skin. She didn't have time to react before another horn blasted and then another.

Cassandra's eyes snapped to the shoreline, and there, the enemy had mighty beasts in a shape she had never witnessed before. Each had four legs the thickness of ancient trees, wrinkled grey with splotches of black metal. These four legs held up a lump of flesh the size of a carriage with no face or eyes, and from this flesh spouted metal pipes, with no clear uniform or order, much like a chaotic organ piano. The sound was coming from them as they slowly walked, and then with exploding blasts, they launched more and more of their barrages from their organ-like pipes.

One by one these fireballs rained down until it became a storm. The larger ones were thankfully missing, but the ship was considerably slowed down from the first strike and loss of one of the sails. The ship in front of Cassandra cracked as a ball of metal rammed into the side. She could hear the screams and put away the thoughts of who might have been hit in such a packed vessel.

Hector's smaller vessel had it the worst, being the closest to the shore, and while the barrage over her own boat and the one in front was lessening as they grew more distant, that meant the enemy was refocusing on Hector.

With her eyes, she could make out Hector lying down between Harris and Reginald who manned oars, the marshal was alive but hurt. The other soldiers were rowing madly, eyes wide with fear. Her gut twisted and she heard the bellow of the enemy beasts hit the wrong tune. Snapping her eyes upward she saw one of the fiery projectiles heading right for Hector's boat but there was no way they could row out of the way in time. Even Reginald's face seemed to twist with concern.

Reginald dropped the oar and put his hand back on his hip. The world seemed to freeze for a moment and as Cassandra watched on, panicked and frozen, she recognized the face Reginald wore. It was the same one he wore back when he was a knight of Wilhelm's coming to rescue her and the others from Esmachus. It was a face as fierce as the son of a dragon. For a fourth time, Reginald pulled at his sheathed blade, and like all the other times, the metal seal that held it shut glowed red and dripped hissing into the sea air. A chest ripping shout boomed from Reginald and with a rip of his arm, his sword came shrieking free.

An inferno in the shape of a cone came blasting from the man. The immense force of the spell nearly toppled the oar boat and sent a shockwave so powerful, it knocked Cassandra off her feet and onto the salty blood ridden planks. Tears of pain wetted her eyes and as she looked up from her fallen position, she watched Reginald's spell crash into the metal ball of the organ beast, ripping it into a sparkling explosion.

The water ripped and the sky revolted with smoke, but then harmless sparkles trickled down into the water below. After that, there were no more blasts, no more fireballs. They were out of range.

Letting out a relieved breath, Cassandra closed her eyes. She was spent, her body could do no more and her mind couldn't worry a second longer. Each beat of her heart sent a pulse of pain to every muscle and for the first time in years, her throat was hoarse, but at least the hum of the enemy was growing further and further into the distance. After such an escape, Cassandra laid there confident as the sounds of battle diminished and the slap of Hector's boat's paddles overtook the stormy waves. Minutes later she could hear the soldiers from the dinghy boarding her crippled boat. Footsteps shuffled all around her but she didn't bother to get up or even open her eyes. The sound of Hector's voice and the chatting laugh of Harris was all she needed to hear to know that everyone had made it. With that, and her energy burning from her body, she let herself slip into some sort of unconscious state between anxious and asleep.

Chapter 23
Pain and Temptation

George's company of soldiers were in an uproar. Medics were rushing every which way and orders were being howled into the pained sky above. The prince himself held Josephine aloft, using his unworn cape as a makeshift stretcher. While he held the upper side, Rosaline carried the lower. Opane and Williams rushed alongside them and medics crowded as they laid the Princess on the flattest ground they could find.

Josephine's eyes were closed and her breathing was faint. George's own breath was hot and rapid, and his heart was about to break out of his chest. Tears were already blurring his vision and soft "no's" slipped through his lips. Smoke, imperceivable, swirled at his fingertips and his pulse quickened with panic.

"I'm sorry, George," Opane whispered. Her usual face of stoicism was etched with worry and shame.

A medic growled in frustration at the wound, old blood seeping past his fingers as he inspected her wound. "This doesn't make sense. She isn't bleeding fresh." He went to pull the dagger, but before he could, Rosaline knocked him back.

"Idiot," she barked, emotion stained on her face. "Take the blessing. Maybe the bleeding is stopping." She pressed the cleanest part of Franklin's cape around the dagger, using her full weight to add pressure to the stab wound.

"She's anemic," the other medic barked back. "She has no blood left, it went through her heart. She shouldn't be alive."

George's eyes flared. "She's my sister," he growled through his tears. "And your regent."

The medic backed off and Rosaline continued to add pressure to the wound. Josephine didn't stir. For a moment her eye twitched, but then her breathing shallowed further. Every shuttering push of her lungs sent anxiety in George's chest. Every glint of his sister's murder weapon sent anger into his heart. Behind them, soldiers had Tomko bound, swords pressed against every inch of his throat.

"Hinan." A familiar voice rumbled from the tree line. The bull man, Freg, walked through the shadows, and sent the soldiers into a flurry of shouts and drawn swords. Freg stood stoic at the end of the scene, his massive book ever-present on his back, and a hand on the pommel of his axe. "A choice has come to you."

George stared at the bull man, eyes wide and unbelieving. "Choice? What choice!" He shouted, angry. "You're a madman if you think there is a choice here!" He remembered his last conversation with Freg and a fresh rage hit him square. "You knew this would happen."

"I did," Freg answered.

George gaped for a moment and the smoke started to swirl even stronger around his fingers and up his arms. Desperate, George shoved his fingers into his pocket and felt for his raindrop. He tried to roll the wooden bauble in his hand. He had to regain control. His mouth moved without command. "You did nothing to stop this."

"I did not," Freg concurred.

"Bastard…" George's voice fell low. He was losing, his head was fuzzy. George squeezed the raindrop, but the smoke was speaking. "She's dying because of you."

Freg remained silent this time, but simply stared with sad eyes. "A choice has come to you."

Oathkith screamed out of its scabbard. "Quiet." George's words dripped with otherworldly anger, his skin stained red and his hair shocked white. The bauble was ash in his pocket, burned by anger. George felt untethered, his rage pure and foggy; there were no more thoughts. Freg held up a hand, as if to calm the man, but before he could get a word out, George blasted forward.

"George!" Rosaline shouted and a yelp came from Williams, but the prince was a blur. He crossed the distance in a blink of an eye. Oathkith flashed at pinstripe speed and just as fast, Freg threw up the face of his axe. The sword slammed into the ancient bull man's weapon and its enchantment erupted into a ball of flame. The shockwave sent George's own soldiers tumbling to the ground.

Flame licked but George didn't relent. Freg had his axe in both hands and another strike came shooting from the prince. Another explosion, this one singed the prince's clothes. Another strike and another blast, with Freg no worse for wear, from the flames at least. George's strikes grew in speed, and Freg kept up with every one of them, his arms golden ribbons, but his face strained, until finally a loud sob choked from George and the prince slammed Oathkith into the ground with a crack.

Falling to his knees, George let out a shaking roar of pain to the sky. Tears rolled down his cheeks. He had shattered. He had broken. This was it. He had lost, he was losing. The red deepened and the smoke stained his heart.

"My boy," a motherly voice sang in his head and echoed off the trees. "I can feel your pain in my own stomach." It was the voice of the Dweller. Freg stood still, face pursed, while the soldiers whipped around, as if expecting the devil to appear. Rosaline stared in silence, hands over Josephine's heart, while Williams had his cheek to his lover's lips, attempting to find her breath.

"Look down," the Dweller commanded. "See your tears?" George did so and found himself staring at a small puddle of his sobs, the blurry face of the Dweller staring back up at him. "See?" She soothed. "We even share in our tears."

"What more do you want from me?" George choked. "You've taken almost all of it."

"I don't mean to," the Dweller admitted. "I love you, George, but I also love this world. I need you to put up with me just a little longer, I need you to embrace me so we can end this—as a family."

"Damn you," George growled at the puddle. "You liar. Damn you!" His hand lashed out and scattered his tears. The Dweller's voice scattered with the droplets.

"I was trapped between the worlds for so long, I could feel every ounce of pain you all felt," she said. "But I can end all the pain forever. I won't need to feel it in my chest, and you don't need to feel it in your hearts. Just stop, that's all you have to do. Just stop, don't oppose me, let me take over. I'll make all the choices, all the decisions, all the goals. No more pain, no more worries, no more anger or sadness, just me and my love. If it's all just me, there is no pain."

George stared at the empty ground, his mind abuzz. Everyone looked on, and the Dweller quickly added. "Think about it. Think about all the pain that could have been avoided if I was in control. There wouldn't be any wars, any murders, any prejudice or hate. I can save you all, I can even save your sister."

The prince's eyes widened. He knew her words were honest, but he also knew she was the cause of a lot of the pain, or perhaps you could say she used the pain to her own ends. Her voice was sincere, though, she truly regretted pain and wished for a certain kind of peace. A peace that could be found by running back from decisions, avoiding choice, and letting her take total control. It would be easy, to just become blank, to just live in a world where he didn't have to remember all the names he put on the edge of his sword, or the tragedies of the past. But to run, to run from pain, would be to run from what shaped him, wouldn't it?

"I ran once," George muttered. "I ran away from my home, scared." His eyes flicked up to Freg, the creature who ran him down the halls. "Then I swore never to run again, but then I ran as soon as I saw him once more. That second time, I said that I would get stronger so I wouldn't need to run ever again. Ironically, I ran again, this time chasing strength, and only after did I find out where strength really lurks." George pursed his lips. "It's silly." Magic sparkled on the tips of George's fingers and he looked down. "Chasing and running, applying this and determining that. All these outward solutions to the world, when the thing you're chasing or avoiding is inside you." The smoke in George's heart stilled, as if it found direction. "I won't run and I won't chase, not again." His eyes fell to his sister's pale face and heat rolled down his cheek. "I'm going to march forward, as myself, into a world of grief, not because I welcome it, but because I know we won't grow, become better, and learn to control ourselves if we ignore it. I'm not going to fall down now, I can't. The world needs every good idea and every sudden revelation, not the promise of one Dweller. The world needs a chance to break from its own shed."

Smoke swirled around George, as did flakes of blue mist. He could feel his anger and sorrow temper, he could feel it find a direction. It didn't want to lash out, it wanted to pull forward, to dig. Sadness still cracked George's brow, and his eyes shimmered over his sister. Before he could say anymore, the Dweller spoke again.

"So you'll oppose me and my plans?" Her voice was sad.

"You always knew I would," George answered.

"If you go after me, your sister will die," She warned.

George was silent at that. He wished he could say he was silent because he was unbroken and unwavering, but he was silent because he was human.

"It will be your choice." The Dweller echoed.

"It was your hand that held the knife," George whispered. "My father had a price, but I won't sell a soul to you."

The Dweller's voice didn't come again, but George didn't feel any regret, just grief. The crowd grew silent, watching the Prince stare at his dying sister. A long moment droned before George spoke softly, his body draining of smoke and returning to normal. "Freg."

"Hinan?"

"There is a lot that you know that I don't." George looked up at the bull man. "It's high time we all step out of the darkness. Tell us all of it—the whole story."

Freg pulled a latch and his mighty book unclasped from his back. The ground shook as the monsterous tome slammed into the forest floor. Without ceremony, the bull man yanked the cover which carried only the words "The D'sastr" on it, and began at the first page.

***

"The secrets of the cosmos?" Mondaral of the Sondoper nearly tripped over a root at the request. She was leading Caleb and his companions through a gnarled and ancient forest. The pooled lands from before had given way to this darker, autumn filled grove where the bark was nearly black and the ground a mixture of cobble, soil, and moss. Caleb couldn't quite remember when they started walking through this strange land, but he remembered Mondaral mentioning that it was the best place for them to speak.The smell of twilight was thick in the musty air, and fireflies flitted all around them. The Sondoper raised a feathered brow. "You certainly get to the point without much fuss."

Catherine gave a nod. "You'll notice he isn't married."

Caleb ignored her. "I'd be happy to learn anything you might know."

Mondaral looked up through the canopy and to the broken sky. "I know all of it."

"Can I hear it?"

The Sondoper stopped just as the group spilled into an open glen. In front of the group was an orchard of stone statues, with no theme or rhyme. Some were large toads with their mouths open, some were kings holding open bags, or others still were stone tree stumps, hollow and open as well. In some of the mouths, bags, and otherwise, small glowing orbs of ethereal light floated. Mondaral caught Caleb's gaze, a small prideful grin on her lips. Between herself and Caleb, small motes similar to the orbs floated, each reflecting a memory of Caleb's or Mondaral's.

"Long ago, people used to come here to exchange their memories or perhaps lock them away..." Mondaral looked away, through the trees. "Come, let's keep walking, I'll tell you all you wish to know on the way... but where shall I start?"

Caleb swallowed hard, knowing very well he was about to hear everything he wanted to know. He opened his mouth. "Start from the beginning?"

Another prideful smile. "Very well...

"In the beginning there was an infinite emptiness filled only by the smoke and the mist. The ethereal smoke swirled and spun, chaotic and free, while the mist hovered and expanded, pacified, stagnating and orderly. Naturally, the smoke and the mist were enemies, and at their border, a great many beings were born. Warriors of smoke rose up as smokeborn, and clashed with the mistborn soldiers. The fight was equally matched, and where a smokeborn died, a mistborn was also slain, and when a new life was born on one side, an equal life was created on the other.

"For countless eons, the fight was without end and a great pile of the dead grew at the border, the fallen smoke swirling with the slain mist. From this macabre mixture, two brothers were born. They were not smokeborn bent on chaos and freedom, nor were they mistborn indentured to order and stagnation, but they were born of both. Because of their equal birth, the brothers of both were named The Brothers Harmony and their names were Prax and Solam.

"All around them they witnessed the carnage of the primordial war between the smoke and the mist and to their surprise, a great voice called out to them. It was the quiet creator, Iac, the God beyond it all, and in simple words, Iac instructed the Brothers Harmony and taught them to wield the magic of creation. The reason was simple: they were to create a new land and end the war.

"Calling upon a great magic embedded within them as living altars of creation, split between the first smoke and the first mist, the Brothers Harmony crafted a world from the pile of the slain. They twisted the smoke and molded the mist until they balanced endless motes of smoke and mist together, bound by imperceivable, miniscule altars of creation. Together they named these building blocks 'matter' and from matter, they carved the world of Ampexida.

"Knowing both the mist and the smoke would lay claim to their new land of harmony, they called forth another great magic and crafted a seamless firmament. With this firmament they separated the smoke and the mist, trapping each into a realm of their own; however, the great void left behind threatened to swallow Ampexida whole, and so the Brothers Harmony wrapped Ampexida with another firmament, making it a realm of its own, but not before losing some matter here or there to the great expansive void. Thus four realms were born, one of chaotic smoke, one of pacified mist, one of infinite void and potential, and one of blissful harmony.

"The Brothers Harmony were happy with their work so far, but the itch of creation kept them busy. Out of the smoky and misty surface of Ampexida, the Brothers Harmony crafted rock and ground to hold them. Shortly after, they raised the ground on both sides so as to make a special valley for them to live. They named this valley 'Unifax,' and inside it they continued their crafts.

"First the brothers ignited a sun far from the ground, so as to see their creation unfold. Second they watered the ground from a stone, as to make seas, rivers, and oceans, they then decided to clothe the rest of the world in vegetation, clouds, and sky; marveling at the beauty of its many colors. Prax looked at Solam, and Solam looked at Prax, and together they both were content with their creation.

"Despite their success, the two brothers grew lonely and then, they had a new idea. Together they forged two new objects, an orb of glassy black and one of pearly white. Through the black orb the brothers could communicate through the Firmament and into the realm of smoke, and through the white orb the brothers could communicate with the realm of mist. As one might expect, the respective leaders of each realm, the smokeborn known as the Liberated One, or sometimes the Tainted One and the mistborn known as the Serene One or Stagnant One, were not pleased with the brothers, and so reception was soured.

"Disregarding the distaste of the Liberated and Serene One, the Brothers continued their conversations with each realm, talking with lesser beings of each. Unfortunately the conversations were limited, as the Brothers soon found each realm to be obsessed, with the smokeborn constantly erratic and chaotic, spouting the necessities of untethered freedom, while the mistborn were refined, orderly, and constantly preaching about total pacification and unification. Some smokeborn in particular even threatened the Brothers Harmony, intent on freeing the trapped smoke inside the creation of Ampexida and inciting it to rebel, while some mistborn expressed the desire to completely control the new creation and envelop it in unending stagnation.

"The Brothers Harmony were distraught once more, and even considered making a third orb to converse with what strange beings and monsters may have been born in the swirling infinity that was the void, but ultimately decided against it. Displeased with the results of the orbs, they crafted a fine beechen chest and stowed the orbs away. After this, the Brothers Harmony retired to their cottage in the valley of Unifax to contemplate their next step.

"Almost instantly Solam had an idea, and then Prax had an idea. They weaved their magic, and together they crafted a perfect being. Its skin was a golden hue, and its body was of perfect symmetry, with eyes radiant like the sun. The Brothers Harmony named their creation Stenmur, first of their living creations.

"Excited, the brothers quickly crafted more like Stenmur and named them the Precursors, or the first beings, but not all was well. Stenmur and the Precursors stood as statues, perfect but without life or movement. Solam thought, and Prax thought, and together the Brothers Harmony decided that they must act. Solam took a branch from a maple tree and spun it into a staff, marking it with intervals and dates, thus creating time. Prax took a branch from an oak and spun it into a staff as well, imbuing it with the essence of life and creation. Together the brothers brought their staves upon their creations, granting them not only life and the ability to create, but also time to move and live through. Solam was happy, and Prax was happy. Yet, Solam, knowing the Precursors to still be incomplete, taught them to think for themselves, to speak, write, read and live, while Prax taught them how to create, mold Ampexida through magic, utilize altars of creation and otherwise bring forth new crafts to the world.

"Stenmur quickly grew to love his creators and followed them throughout the valley, soaking in the lessons they taught. Eventually, Stenmur approached the Brothers Harmony and requested a means of which to create as they do, for the Precursors were a lonely race, kept company only by themselves. Solam and Prax agreed and presented Stenmur with a hammer and an anvil to create new life.

"The first born dove into his work, his hammer swinging wildly against the anvil. First he created the animals and other creatures of the ground, sea and sky to play with. Second, Stenmur began to create other beings similar to the Precursors, the first being unique sparsely feathered men and women named the Sondoper who inherited his love for craft, the second being the Harnians, a race of great bull men who quickly settled across all of Ampexida and built mighty societies, and the third being the Aquatids, a race of wise frog people who quickly took to riddles and ascetic life.

"Some Precursors named themselves the Sten, and apprenticed under the first-born, Stenmur, while others crowded Prax and Solam for their knowledge. All lived in unity in the Valley of Unifax, and those who dispersed to other lands lived in harmony wherever they went. The Sondoper crafted great canals across deserts, mighty sea walls, and even painted the sky so beautifully with stars and heavenly bodies, it was decided to be shown every night. With the void so close to Ampexida, the Sondoper even figured out a new magic, in which a sleeping mind could create, twist and imagine infinite possibilities as if it was in the void, but trap it just for a night. They called this new magic dreaming, and gifted it to all other beings. Ampexida was a paradise, but its perfection would not last.

"One day Stenmur was out looking for the Brothers Harmony, and happened upon their cottage. Being their favored student and firstborn, Stenmur let himself in. He called out to the Brother's Harmony as he stepped inside, but all he heard in response was a strange song being hummed by a voice he did not recognize.

"Quickly identifying the culprit, Stenmur noticed that the staff of life had fallen from its place on the wall and was now leaning against the beechen chest that held the orbs. The chest itself was the one humming, its lid acting like a mouth, and the song it sang was an old battle hymn from the long since ancient war of the mist and the smoke.

"The humming stopped as Stenmur approached the chest. After a short introduction, the chest revealed the magical orbs to Stenmur. The young prodigy first picked up the orb of smoke, and as soon as it was in his hands, the Tainted One began to speak with him. Through silver tongued words the Tainted One convinced the naive Precursor to take up the orb of smoke, along with the two staves of life and time. With these items the Tainted One instructed Stenmur on how to sap the power of the Brother's Harmony from the artifacts and use it to open the Firmament.

"Being the quick learner that he was, Stenmur easily ripped open the Firmament to Ampexida, and to the realm of smoke. Almost instantly the smoke poured into the valley, and Stenmur was drowned in the onslaught of chaos. Stenmur's body twisted and changed and his mind bubbled and malformed as the smoke that was used in his creation was irritated and brought out of balance. In the end Stenmur was no more, but replaced with a tainted version of his former self, known as the Changed One.

"The Tainted One took the Changed One as one of his new Generals, alongside his faithful first general who was known as the Fellowed One or more commonly, the Smoke King, and together the three laid siege to Ampexida in an attempt to liberate the smoke trapped in Ampexida's creation. The Brother's Harmony was depressed at the loss of their first born, but more horrified at the sight of the primordial smoke oozing across their land of balance.

"Born from the great smoke itself, the smokeborn entered Ampexida. Their chaotic forms of smoke were held together by a strange black metal born of the realm of chaos, and anchored in the mortal realm by a single heart of twisted black and hazy smoke hidden in their metal wrapped chests. From their smoky wisps they summoned mighty weapons and shields of their alien iron, the same primordial weapons once used in the war before time.

"Alongside them marched mighty beasts of war, twisted and chaotic in creation, plated with that same metal formed of smoke. Wherever this great army marched, so too marched the taint as the smoke that once lived peacefully inside the creation of Ampexida was awakened once more, destroying the balance of harmony and twisting creation into disfigured chaos.

"Quickly the Brother's Harmony called their creation to arms, eager to snuff out the encroaching taint. The Harnians were the first to answer, and the first to taste the corruption. Their high king was one of the first to be twisted by the smoke, and their ranks were in chaos. The Harnians held firm though, being one of the few races with a martial history despite never experiencing war.

"The Sondoper and Precursors aided second, followed by the rest of the newest and youngest races. The smoke itself twisted a few of these races, forming even newer races. Despite the chaos, however, the creations of Ampexida stood together against the Tainted One. The artifacts of power were taken back from the Changed One and the Chest by a Harnian, who then gave them to the Brothers Harmony.

"Despite recovering the artifacts, the Brothers were unable to close the rifts in the Firmament, in fear of trapping the taint in Ampexida forever. Another problem arose, with the taint roaming unchecked except by battle, the balance of Ampexida was beginning to fail. The only option the Brother's had was to allow the mist to also invade, in hopes of rebalancing the land.

"Striking a tentative deal with the Serene One, the Brother's opened the Firmament to the mist, and soon Ampexida became a land of war, but at the very least, the fabric of its balance was secure from total takeover of either mist or smoke.

"The Serene One brought in its two generals, the Graceful One and the Ordered One. Together, the three aligned themselves with the Ampexidians in an attempt to stem the growing horde of tainted beings and smokeborn, and to possibly reclaim their lost mist, and bring Ampexida to pure order.

"Similar to the smokeborn, the mistborn were also anchored, but by strange crystals that served as hearts, their misty forms held in place by a pure translucent metal and from their mist came their own primordial weapons. Likewise, wherever this army marched, the mist that was bonded with the smoke in the creation of Ampexida and its children was awakened and threatened to bring perfect stillness, called the pacification.

"With the taint challenging the pacification and the pacification challenging the taint, there was yet hope for balance. Despite this truth and even with such an alliance, the Brother's Harmony knew that they alone could not defeat the Tainted One, close the rifts, remove the pacification of the mist, and the taint of the smoke all at once, but neither were their children yet able to face a being such as the Tainted One alone and remain balanced.

"Ampexida needed a champion. A champion of both the smoke and the mist, but one who could not be corrupted either way: a champion greater than the Brothers Harmony, and one that would never stray from their duty to protect the harmony of Ampexida from outside forces.

"Together the Brothers used the anvil of creation they had gifted to Stenmur, and together they bled upon its surface. Striking their essence with a hammer each, the Brother's crafted a being that could be everything they needed. As the being was crafted, sparks of the blood flew from the anvil, and where it landed, new Precursors were born. These new Precursors were called the Jerrovians, your ancestors.

"The newly born Jerrovians were scared, having been born in the middle of such a war; however, shortly after this, the Champion was finished. The Champion was a being of pure harmony, radiant like the sun, and traveled on angelic wings while plated in an armor colored like the stars. This Champion was named Sosolam, after Solam, whose blood was used to create this being. As for the blood of Prax, a second creation was born on the anvil, the Sword of Prax, sometimes referred to as the Blood of Prax.

"The Sword of Prax was gifted to Sosolam, and was to be used by this Champion to be the tool in which to protect Ampexida. The blade itself was given a life, so that it may only be used by Sosolam, or those deemed worthy by the Champion to handle it. This blade was so sharp and so imbued with the power of the Brother's Harmony, that it alone could tear and mend the Firmament with a simple swing, and it alone could destroy the anchored hearts of the greatest beings in a single blow.

"During the process of creating the Blood of Prax, a single shard sparked from the anvil and landed with the Jerrovians. This shard of the Blood of Prax was taken by the Jerrovians, and while it did not hold the power or safety of the Sword of Prax, this Shard was used by the Jerrovians to escape Ampexida.

"By concocting an elaborate ritual involving the shard, the Jerrovians in their terror ripped a mass of land from Ampexida and flung themselves into a new realm of their creation, which was named Jerrovia and surrounded by a new firmament they named 'the veil'. Upon witnessing this ritual, the Graceful One greedily attempted to intercept them, as to rule over Jerrovia. Unfortunately for the Graceful One, their timing was wrong, and they were trapped outside of Ampexida as well as Jerrovia, wedged between two firmaments and trapped in this odd, insular space of the void with other mistborn, as well as an overwhelming amount of smokeborn. In this prison between realms, The Graceful one was eventually tainted by the smoke, twisted into flesh and stuck between pacification and taint, thus becoming the Dweller. A primordial being haunted with sudden mortal emotion."

Mondaral pursed her lips in thought at her final words, holding everyone's attention as she chose her next carefully. "My time on the island Buyan has granted me an odd angle in which I could see the shadows of between the veil and the Firmament. Be it a gift of my Sondoper eyes or an innate magic I don't know, I could see the Dweller squirm. Emotion seemed eager to burn across the veil and the worse they are, the hotter, and she struggled against it. I say she, for she has taken a motherly form, burned into nearly flesh from centuries of pain. I admit a soft spot for her, but she is not reasonable. Loving, perhaps, selfishly in a twisted form, but not reasonable."

The Sondoper looked at Caleb. "You cannot bring her back to Ampexida with the rest of Jerrovia."

Caleb flinched for a moment at the thought. "But why go back at all, is Ampexida still a land of primordial war?"

"No." Mondaral shook her head. "Such war was given a name, 'The Cacophony,' and ended long ago. Both the young races and the old managed to end it with Sosolam leading them to victory."

"If you think it would aid us now, tell me how it ended," Caleb said.

"Armed with his sword, Sosolam led the armies of the Brothers into war, as I said," Mondaral continued. "The Harnians, The Sondoper, The Sten, The Aquatids, and the Praxian Storm guard all fought under the banner of Sosolam, alongside whatever extra forces the younger races could muster.

"Sosolam met the Changed One and the Smoke King in battle, and with the Blood of Prax he cut open the barrier to the void and cast them into the infinite darkness. Without the generals present, the Smokeborn army capitulated before the combined army of the Brothers Harmony, leaving the Tainted One open for a final battle, and since the generals' anchors remained intact, the Tainted One was unable to reform new generals for protection.

"What remained of the Tainted One's army rallied against the Brothers Harmony and their champion. Fearing that they may lose, the Tainted One guarded the original tear in the Firmament, hoping that his generals and reinforcements may emerge. The Brothers Harmony heard of this plan and decided to attack immediately. Prax and Solam gripped the edges of the tear in the Firmament, and together they held it as close as possible, to stem the time of reinforcements. The Praxian Storm Guard received its name as it too guarded the Firmament, protecting the occupied Brother's Harmony and standing in the gap to prevent enemy recruits from emerging from the void.

"While the Brothers and the Guard did this, Sosolam engaged the Tainted One in mortal combat, and the remaining army of the Brothers Harmony defended the champion from interference, augmented by the army of the Serene One. The fight was grueling, but in the end Sosolam struck true and the blade of Prax cut through the Tainted One's heart, destroying them until such a time the primordial smoke could form anew.

"Immediately the Serene One betrayed the Brothers and as Sosolam was busy finishing his fight with the Tainted One, The Serene One attacked the occupied Brothers. Unable to defend themselves, as they were busy holding the Firmament, the Serene One managed to inflict heavy wounds upon them, blinding them on the spot. The Storm Guard rallied against the Serene One, protecting their creators against further injury as much as they could. They managed to stall the Avatar of the Mist long enough for Sosolam to arrive, and defeat the Serene One in combat.

"With the forces of the Mist and forces of the Smoke defeated, Sosolam slipped through the rip in the Firmament, and sealed all the realms from the void, to ensure the strength of the Firmament and to guard Ampexida steadfast until needed once more. Jerrovia was left alone as the Firmament was too weak from the Cacophony to endure the power of returning to Ampexida so soon, and so it was forced to stay separate until such a time was deemed for it to return. The Brothers Harmony, in their blinded state, were forced to hide away in the Valley of Unifax, their injuries far too great for them to be the creators they once were. The Valley disappeared with the Brothers, or at least was lost to time. Though it is said that all who pass their mortal coil find it.

"While saved, Ampexida would never be the same, just as a still pool of water splashed with a stone will never still once more, Ampexida was now in turmoil. The Precursors and the other races now knew chaos and order. War was born and the land was forever stained with imperfection, and slowly the children's children of the once flawless races grew imperfect. But the Brothers Harmony remained in Unifax, hidden away from the rest of Ampexida, where they would welcome those who had died back into what remained of the land of Balance—until they deemed fit to straighten the world once more."

Caleb stood with wide eyes. The trees from before were now behind the group and in front was an impossibly green upward slope that led to a cracked sky. There was no indication of what may be on the other side of such a monument, but where the sky met the horizon, promises of an azure blue leaked. The prince was stammering, incoherent, until finally he said with purpose. "I need to get back to Jerrovia. I believe the Dweller might be making her move."

Mondaral looked up at the sky. "I believe she already has."

"What!?"

Shaking her head, she looked to Master Frugi. "I can get you and your friends back home, but please, I have some items I must give you first, stored here in wait for this very war. Most notably a book penned by your own IAO."

Caleb opened his mouth at the name, but the story before was more striking than the promise of a new tome. Catherine interjected on his behalf. "Not sure if you knew this part, but we are a little too short handed to be sailing any boat."

Mondaral laughed. "I am Sondoper. Distance is a trifling, you won't need the boat."

Caleb turned to Mondaral, a steely look on his face. "Then see us back, my family needs me."

***

"But what of my father?" George looked up from the pages of the book. "What of me, or my sister, what of all of this!? What of IAO or the Sages and the... everything!"

Freg held up a hand. "I believe your prisoner might be able to field those questions."

All eyes fell to Tomko. The Precursor held his head in shame. "Long ago, me and the others escaped to this land by cutting it from Ampexida."

There was silence and Tomko continued. "We used the Shard to create a ritual in which we bound Jerrovia inside its own veil to protect us from the war. Unfortunately, our veil was unlike that of the Brother's Harmony, and actively censored all thoughts and knowledge of existence outside of our new home. While some of us were put off by this sudden side effect, others were glad, hoping that ignorance would be bliss and save them from future conflict."

Tomko gave a thoughtful look, "I suspect someone added it to the spell on purpose, but purposeful or not, the veil would not last unless it was renewed every so often. That was easier said than done, as with the veil beginning to actively censor the knowledge of Ampexida and the other realms, the others would soon forget the renewal spell unless measures were taken. In preparation I was picked among the survivors to be embedded with magical runes in my skin that could bypass the censorship and depict the instructions on how to renew the spell, so that the knowledge may never be forgotten."

George gave an impatient look and Tomko sighed. "When the veil was created, so too were two beings that represented it. An oak tree and an elm tree. Whenever the veil starts to weaken and the influence of the Dweller drips into the world, the blood ritual has to be performed on the elm tree to renew the spell. This is the same elm tree that we built our first city around. You know it from the garden." Tomko stared at George. "We made the provinces and we set up the noble families including the Heinrichs long ago in an attempt to keep track of our bloodlines so we could renew the spells, but little did any of us know how quickly the veil would censor our understanding of it all and even less did any of us realize that the only blood the elm tree would accept would be that of one of the original dynasty—the Heinrichs—so long as said individual entered—or well, was born near the tree and thus blessing their blood."

George looked down at Josephine, his sister deathly still. "And," George said out loud. It hurt to look at her this way. "What of the oak tree?"

Tomko frowned. "As the elm renews, the oak undos. Similar to the elm, it needs a Heinrich born near the elm tree. Extant branches don't work. If they did, I wouldn't be risking my life every so many decades to try and talk to the Emperor or Empress."

"Just as Josephine's life was used to break the veil," Freg started from his spot, "if the life of another of the original Jerrovian bloodline is cast against the elm tree, we can bring Jerrovia back to Ampexida. But first, the Dweller must be defeated lest we bring her with us."

"First, tell me the rest of the story," George looked sternly at them both. "Of IAO, the sages, and my father."

Tomko bit his cheek. "Despite being trapped, the mistborn and the Dweller continued to influence Jerrovia. The former founded the Tagist religion sometime over seven hundred years ago. Using this new force, they incited a rebellion in the north, causing a schism between the empire and the northern people now known as the Vagrants. Their goal was simple: replace the Heinrich line so the veil couldn't be renewed any longer and spread their total control over the region. They were taught mist-talking and if not for the intervention of Freg, I don't know if your ancestor, Victor, would have been able to maintain the order my siblings put in place."

George looked at Freg. The Harnian bowed his head. "I taught a young warrior who eventually was to be known by the name of IAO how to harness his altar and instilled upon him the Harnian knowledge of Stromism. Sadly, I'm not sure it mattered generations later, when the Tagists hijacked the existing Imperial Iacine Church and slowly rewrote its own history."

At that, Rosaline perked up from her seat, but remained silent.

Crossing his arms, George jumped to the final topic. "And the truth about my father and mother?"

Tomko and Freg shared a sad glance. "Your father gave in to the promises of the Dweller when your sister and mother passed from disease. Using her power, the Dweller gave a piece of herself to bring them back in the hopes of circumventing the prophecy."

"Prophecy?"

"That the first born of Wilhelm would reopen the veil and that the second would lead Jerrovia through it safely." Freg pointed a meaty finger at George. "You were but a baby, in the womb of your mother, when the Dweller thought to destroy you by using her deal with your father to force him to push her. But you survived, and then you survived her attempts to kill you up north, you are a curse to her, a bane, but to the rest of us, you are our hope. Deny the Dweller, Hinan. Let's put an end to this cycle."

The Dweller's voice rang inside George's head. "The only way to bring a true end to the cycle of pain is my solution. Under my guidance, I will lead all the worried heads of the world through peace. I will decide, I will choose, I will take the burdens. We can be free from Ampexida and the troubles there, we can make a paradise here!"

"Enough." George's voice was stern. With the stories over, the reality of the situation was sinking in. He still sat beside his dying sister while his lover and friends stared on in shock. George's own body threatened to teeter back into the rage of the smokeform, but his sense of direction, his sense of righteousness kept it focused, if only barely.

"George," the Dweller started again. "If you refuse me, if you come to me with violence, I won't save your sister."

"Quiet." George hissed. His fists stained red and his hair jumped white for a moment. The Dweller went to speak again but George shouted, "No!" He could feel his rage coming back. "You took my father from me, you don't get to speak!"

"George please!"

"No!" George growled.

"My mist lives in you, given from your damned mother; you cannot deny me, you are half my son!" The Dweller's voice, no longer sweet, rang from George, loud enough for everyone to hear. George's eyes swirled with rage. Without another word he walked back to where he plunged Oathkith into the ground and yanked it free. With the sword of his father in hand, he pointed it at the broken sky. He shouted, he screamed and a rippling wave of powerful magic blasted with pained roars, sending the trees into a quake.

George stayed in that position, his smokeform taking over his body, but instead of falling to the flames of rage, he stood still in his position. Hot tears rolled down his cheek. "I will not take your deal." His voice was hoarse. Josephine gasped, as if in pain, and then tears ran freely down George's chin. "I will come for you, Dweller. I will end this."

Josephine whispered behind George. Williams stood by her face, ear to her lips, and together they all heard Josephine speak. "I love you." George swallowed hard and turned to look at his sister. With broken sapphires, she stared at him. Her hand moved weakly from her stomach and slapped the ground in George's direction, motionless and pale. "I don't know... if I'm going to wake up... this time..."

Her voice stopped and tears streamed down George's red face. Even still, he stood there resolutely, if not for his sister, then for everyone else. He will see Jerrovia safely through. He looked down the blade of Oathkith, the sky reflecting off of it. He has to. He can't let the Dweller claim anyone else. She clutched her means with death's fingers.

As George stared, the flat of his blade reflected the sky, catching his eye. Looking up to confirm, there in the sky, a golden dot was wrestling against a wave of nothingness. He could barely make it out, but he swore it was there. Freg's voice came over his shoulder and answered his thoughts.

"Sosolam."

Chapter 24
The Emperor of Jerrovia

George sat in the clearing, his body worn from emotions. This time, he had asked to be alone and while he wished to recuperate from his day, he knew he had one last conversation to engage in. In his lap he held the weapon that stabbed Josephine, the shard of Prax. It was an ornate yet small dagger with runes covering it in a language long since lost to time. He hated the shard; it caused so much pain, and not just to him and Josephine, but to every Jerrovian.

The sky above was still broken, the same as it had been since Josephine was sacrificed, but George's eyes were focused on the golden speck in the infinite distance. "I want to talk to you."

Almost immediately, George felt a tug in his mind and gave in. His vision blurred, only to refocus in a completely different place. He wasn't there, but his mind was, floating in a splitting nothingness. In front of him, the mighty Sosolam was hovering. The image of the Champion left George speechless. Sosolam was imposing, dressed in seamless armor colored the cream of the stars, with billowing wings of golden light. The only hint of a person beneath the armor was the slits where two sun-like eyes peered out from Sosolam's helmet. In each hand, Sosolam was holding tight some velvety fabric that George's mind could only register as the sky itself. Behind Sosolam, beyond whatever trench the champion was holding tight, George could hear the sounds of an intense battle and every now and again, Sosolam would jerk in place as something struck their back.

"What are you doing?" George heard himself ask.

"The generals of the Tainted One, long since banished into the void, now see an opening. I must keep it closed or all will be lost." Sosolam's voice was strange, alien, yet imposing.

"Your sword?"

"I have laid it at your feet."

George felt confused. "What?"

"You will need it to defeat the Graceful One. You are not strong enough alone, nor does your home have the time needed for you to grow to such a strength. Listen closely, I cannot withstand the attacks of the Fellowed One's army forever. You must go to the Graceful One and defeat her in combat. When there is an opening for a final strike, take up my sword and I will become one with you. Though my body that you speak to now will be forever destroyed, together we will destroy the Graceful One. Be wary not to take up and summon me before that vital moment. Even with an altar the size of your own, I don't think your body would survive more than a few minutes surging with my power."

The prince went to speak but Sosolam interrupted him and at the same time a large thwack sounded across the champion's back. "After this is done, the final ritual to send Jerrovia back to Ampexida must happen or else this realm will remain at the whim of an opened void and be destroyed."

"The sacrifice at the elm tree?" George asked, both eager and worried.

"Seek the counsel of the first Jerrovian. Go, and do not forget my words..."

"But wait!" George held out a hand and Sosolam stirred. The silence of Sosolam was a deep rumble, as if a sun was sighing.

"Why don't you take up the sword and destroy the army behind you, then we can fight the Dweller together."

"A primordial lives in the realm of mortals by their anchor, the void has no such anchors to hold them, I'm afraid it would be an endless battle. Neither could I let them into Jerrovia first, for I fear your realm would not survive such an imbalance. No, our only option is for me to sacrifice myself here and for you to take up my blade. This is for more than just Jerrovia, this is for all of Harmony." Sosoalm's voice boomed. "Do not forget, and seek out the first Jerrovian!"

George's eyes snapped open. His fingers were still twiddling with the shard of Prax, but now in front of him, a sword was thrust into the ground next to a fitting scabbard. The blade was the same starry color as Sosolam's armor, and the ancient script found on the shard adorned its double edged blade. The hilt was in crucifix similar to Oathkith and the handle was comfortable in both one or one and a half of George's hands. By all means the craftsmanship looked immaculate. George rose to his feet and placed a hand on its pommel. It was warm, similar to the warmth of someone's breath. "That's right, its alive," George thought to himself. The prince went to wrench it from the ground, but it came free with ease, slicing the ground as if it was foam. George now held the blade in his hands, admiring it, but the longer he held it, the more he could feel a tingling sensation rising through his hands and into his arms. Remembering Sosolam's warning, George sheathed the sword, the Blood of Prax, into the scabbard that was next to where he found it and tied it to his belt, right below Oathkith. Taking a long look at the Shard of Prax in his other hand, George reluctantly tied that to his belt as well.

The next morning, the group, along with George's vanguard, took to the many winding paths of the woods with the goal of making it to the forest garrison—the largest Imperial presence in the province—to properly plan their next move. Josephine's body was placed on a cot in a wagon with three guards and a medic watching over it. By all means it seemed she had succumbed to her wounds with her limbs cold, lips blue and blood still. Yet every now and again, a stray, almost dying heartbeat would pang against her ribs, even if her lungs were empty. This was enough for George to hold on for her, even if he was half convinced he was imagining it. Her life was supernatural, so why should her death be any different?

As the group marched, George couldn't help but notice how quiet Williams was, quieter than usual, with a face stained red from a sleepless, tear filled night. George didn't find much sleep that night either, but a small piece of him felt guilty standing next to Williams. His friend had cried more than he had about his own sister. He wasn't sure why, but despite the aching pain in his chest, the sadness never found its way to his eyes. It was as if a stern goal was there instead. Maybe something in him snapped, or maybe he was just pretending to be numb.

"Tomko." George turned to the golden-skinned Precursor. The man was walking alongside the others, but he was free only in appearance. George had no intention of letting the man out of his sight. Hearing George, Tomko looked over. With the veil destroyed, the runes on his face no longer bothered the prince, giving George a chance to look deeper into the man's visage. Only an oozing guilt lived in those eyes.

"Yes?"

"Why did you come back to my sister?"

Tomko looked down. "I couldn't just watch."

"And yet you brought the shard with you," George pushed, "the shard Gennisberg needed to perform the ritual."

The Precursor's face twisted at that. George knew he had caught him.

"Maybe..."

"Maybe?" The prince pushed.

"Maybe I wanted this all to end, too." Tomko refused to look up.

George felt his anger rising at that. He wanted to grab Tomko and shout, "that was my sister!" but instead he clenched his jaw and kept walking, fingers curled. "The final ritual," he eventually said. "To send Jerrovia back to Ampexida, what is it? I need every detail."

Tomko looked up at that. "Similar to the oak tree, someone of an original Jerrovian bloodline needs to be sacrificed with the shard to the elm."

"Another elmborn, as Freg said?" George probed. Tomko looked away, as if processing the question. A breath hesitated on the man's lips, but then he gave a weak, "yeah."

Scuffing to a stop, George looked the Precursor over. George and his father were the only ones left who matched that description and George couldn't ask his father to do that. He frowned, knowing exactly what this meant. "Okay."

After that, a somber silence overtook the march, a silence that was only broached by the crunch of leaves underfoot and the swaying of the trees. No birds were singing, or even flapping about, as if they themselves were mourning Josephine. It was every bit a funeral procession.

George did his best to keep his mind off of it, and his efforts were helped dramatically as he and his troop approached the forest garrison. The wooden walls of the fort loomed through the trees of the forest, standing as one of the few symbols of Imperial control in the wild province. Its snapping banners and towering outlooks were usual enough, what wasn't was the fact that not only were the gates wide open, but they were stuffed with soldiers of countless stations, most of which didn't bear the green badge of the forest garrison. But it wasn't just soldiers crowding the area, but civilians.

"Isn't that the palace guard?" Rosaline pointed to a group of soldiers in the regalia of the palace surrounded by desperate looking civilians.

George furrowed his brow and started forward. "Y-yeah..." He put all his thoughts to the side and beelined right to the closest Imperial guard. She was favoring a leg as she stood, clearly injured. The grim of bloody battle still stained the sleeves of her hauberk and dark bags were under her eyes. She was trying to get someone's attention when George called out. "What's going on here?"

She turned, frustrated, then surprised as she realized who was talking to her. With eyes as wide as saucers, she stumbled on her words, not getting anything fathomable out.

"More refugees?" An oblivious soldier nearby called out as he looked down the road, now littered with George's combined forces. Commander Maelinn, who was in earshot, frowned, while Commander Darius beside her shook his head.

Faces turned towards the new party and murmurs started, only to be quickly silenced by Baldra, who stepped out of line and announced, "Presenting the Combined Forces of Prince-General George 'Iron-Will' Heinrich."

A voice called back and Hector stepped out from the desperate swathe of soldiers. "Presenting the forces of the Imperial City and Palace, marshaled under Imperial Marshal Gregory-Hector Von Imperia." He and George met eyes, and when they did, Hector flinched—he had bad news.

"Presenting..." Another voice called out further towards the walls of the fort. It was an old and irritated voice that reminded George of Dame Honora, if only more pleasant. The crowd at the mouth of the walls split to reveal an old General in all her regalia. Her hair was a wiry nest of silver, and her face deep with wrinkles. Despite her gilded uniform and elderly appearance, the deep tan of work still played on her face, and her dark brown eyes flickered with the energy of a fresh soldier. She continued, "the Imperial Forest Garrison of General Tamara Von Fan... a very confused General Tamara Von Fan."

Maelinn muttered under her breath, "I second that."

George chewed his cheek and nodded at Hector. "Perhaps some explanations inside the walls are in order."

***

The inside of the fort was no less busy than the outside. The citizens who had flooded the garrison were in haphazard lines, each being checked by doctors while other auxiliaries were handing out bits of bread to children. Testimonies were being crudely recorded by scribes or just being vented at the closest soldier. George could smell death and brimstone clinging to the singed clothes of the survivors, his nose itching from the stench. He recognized the most pungent smell among them very clearly: smoke-screaming. George's face apparently wasn't subtle, and as he walked beside Hector and the others towards the center keep, the marshal explained. "Tainted creatures stormed the capital and palace. We were forced to evacuate by sea."

George furrowed his brow and shared a worried look with Rosaline. She walked a step closer to the prince, her shoulder brushing against his, and yet her face seemed just as worried as his own. Tamara cleared her throat, taking everyone's attention. The general stood in front of two mighty doors, the great entrance to the wooden keep of the forest. "This way."

Two soldiers armed with spears pushed the doors open and a cold air flushed through the vacuum. George blinked through it, only to be reunited with a vision of the interior foyer. The entrance hall of the fort was plain, but big, like a great wooden maw. Arrow slots were strategically placed to light the area nicely, giving a clean view of the survivors hiding inside among the soldiers and hurried doctors.

Cots and makeshift beds of injured people, both bloodied and beaten, littered the majority of the floor. The grim look carved in Tamara's face was easy to interpret that the usual medical facilities were already overrun.

"Father!" Rosaline suddenly shouted, and the Hero Harris perked up among the crowd. The man was healthy, if not a little bruised in the neck and face. He flashed a smile at his daughter and came walking over as fast as he could without running. Rosaline slammed into his chest with a wrapping hug, nearly toppling the champion. The worry that was in her face seemed to fade into relief, doubly so as Harris betrayed a few tears. George couldn't help but smile out of sympathy, only to frown as the groans of the injured entered his ears. A thought hit his chest and it hit it hard: what of his own father?

George furrowed his brow and looked to Tamara, who simply offered a frown. He looked to Hector, who looked down at his feet. Despite the noise around him, George found himself in silence. He could hear his heartbeat and that was all. His sister lay lost in death outside the fort, his father now gone, Uncle nowhere to be found and here he was alone in a room of pain. A gentle hand grabbed his arm. He looked up.

Cassandra was standing in front of George, her eyes puffed from tears. George felt a heat hit his own at the sight. George swallowed a dry swallow. "My father..."

Rosaline took George's other hand and gave it a squeeze, but George stood frozen.

"He sacrificed himself so we could escape," Hector said, any sense of strength gone from his voice.

"No..." George said under his breath. He could feel the smokeform deep inside his chest, but his determination kept it from appearing, he wouldn't let the Dweller win. Looking over at Rosaline, George pulled her into a hug. A tear burned out of his eye just as she squeezed him in return. Sadness wasn't on his face despite the tears. The Dweller will take no more from him, or anyone.

Hector put his hand on George's shoulder and Cassandra took the other. George's strength shattered and the tears began to flow freely.

Another set of arms came out of nowhere, embracing George as well as Rosaline. George knew this hug from when he was a child, the embrace of the man who raised him, who taught him everything he knew, the embrace of his nanny, of his free-time-nemesis, of his teacher and oldest friend.

"There you go," Reginald's voice hummed over the scene. "Let the grief flow out so the peace can flow in."

George gave a sobby snort and cleared his throat. He disengaged from the hugs and wiped his face with his arm. "Proverbs, even now?" He did his best to try and smile at Reginald, who seemed to be able to find a smile with much more ease. The prince held it for a moment before losing it again. "Josephine is..."

Reginald's smile faded and he furrowed his brow. "She is?"

George closed his eyes, tears squeezing out of them as he nodded.

"Look at me, then."

The prince split his vision open to stare at his teacher. Reginald nodded at him and looked around. "Everyone look at me!" It was the first time George ever heard Reginald raise his voice despite all the years he spent with the man. The room fell to a creeping silence, no one refusing the demand, save the most injured. With all eyes on the old steward, Reginald looked back at George.

"Before us stands a prince or general no longer." Reginald slowly bent down to one knee. "But Emperor George Heinrich of Jerrovia."

The emperor blinked and took a step back. Now all eyes were on him and a pregnant pause of respect and perhaps desperation and reliance on George seemed to thicken the air. All these faces and all these eyes were studying George, looking for the hope they desired or perhaps the answers they needed. Even Rosaline stared at him with a new view, not diminished from her loving stares she often sent his way, but rather augmented now, with a new sense of determination on his behalf, as his partner.

Tamara cut into view. "Then emperor, let me be the first to request an audience as we figure out this catastrophe." George opened his mouth and then closed it. From boy to man to emperor, he stood. He knew very little, but he knew the way forward. He steeled himself in the face of the request and dipped his head.

"Of course."

Chapter 25
The Resistance

While not small, the forest garrison's central keep was not designed to house several armies, nor was it equipped with an appropriate room for the level of meeting that was about to happen. In response, Tamara had the keep's supply room cleared enough to stuff as many chairs as possible inside, leaving old grain and boxes of dried foods littered in the hallway. The room itself was as dark and dank as expected of a storage room, with it partially buried under the hill the keep was situated on. Due to the depth of the cellar, there was only a single small window near where the wall met the ceiling for light to enter, calling for the need for candles. Since wax was out of the question, smoky lard candles lined the walls, completing the feeling of desperation as some of the most powerful people of Jerrovia sat in their own self-made prison cell.

George was the first one there, of course, along with Williams, who had yet to speak since Josephine had been stabbed. To both their rights sat Rosaline, Harris and Hector, and to the left of them was Reginald and Cassandra (now hailed among survivors as the Lady of the Docks). Beside her sat Dame Honora, the general of the auxiliaries no worse for wear. Surprisingly, the Dame held no qualms with who sat next to her, Isabella Heinrich—though this was likely due to Isabella wholly ignoring Honora to complain about the meeting location from behind a silk cloth that she had pressed against her mouth and nose.

Beside them were Baldra, Darius, Maelinn, Opane, and of course General Tamara herself, completing the response team and forming the impromptu chairs of leadership during the sudden catastrophe. The most notable absence from the scene was the lack of any Tagist Sages, an Imperial staple at any high end meeting of the Empire in living memory, but curiously, none had made it to the garrison, nor were they exactly welcome.

"The forest garrison cannot field this many troops all at once, let alone the refugees," Tamara was saying. George looked past clasped hands that he had pressed against his nose. His eyes flickered over to Baldra, the commander piping up.

"Word from Duke Peter has trickled to a stop these last few days, but we hope to reconnect with him soon and reinstate our supply lines from Caldora and Gavaria." She didn't sound convinced.

"Excuse me, dear, but I'm not so sure we can rely on any unknown variables at this time," Isabella tuned in. "If the enemy has such a habit as falling from the very sky onto cities, I'm not sure the other provinces are faring much better than the Capital. We will have to take stock of what we know before we start making speculations."

"Astute observation..." Honora begrudgingly admitted. Isabella dropped her silk below her chin to give the general a twinkling smile that seemed to only deepen Honora's stress lines. Commander Maelinn cut in.

"Regardless of logistics, we can't give up any advantage of numbers or troops available to us. It's impossible to say entirely where the enemy is or how many there are."

Darius chewed his cheek. "I suppose we could divide our forces, or at least spread them out to lessen the burden on the garrison but keep them close enough to react to one another."

"I'm sure we can hash out the logistics of it all later," Harris said, "We do have the best minds in the Empire for it." He gave a nod at Honora before continuing. "But I think we should discuss exactly what we are going to do."

"Allow me to answer that question," George finally said. All heads turned to him. Before the meeting had begun, he briefed the group on what he learned from Freg and Tomko, save the need for his own sacrifice to end the ritual. The new emperor looked to Williams, who gave a shallow nod before rising to his feet and walking out of the room. George continued, "while we are unaware of the exact condition of the rest of the Empire, we do know that the leader of the enemy forces, the Dweller, is situated in the Imperial Capital. I propose that if we eliminate the Dweller, we will be able to more easily scatter the rest of the enemy forces."

"Indeed, Hinan." Freg's voice boomed into the room as he came walking in barely fitting through the door. Williams was leading him and Tomko. The Precursor was silent, his eyes on the floor as the knight led him in. Everyone seemed to sit straighter at the sudden presence of the Harnian. Some, such as Darius, looked as if they were about to leap out of their seats. Isabella stared with saucer-wide eyes.

"And who is this?"

Baldra looked at Darius, a long held cathartic smile curling her lips. "The Horned Prophet, Freg." Darius winced, suddenly remembering an event between him and Baldra long ago.

"From your story..." Tamara steepled her fingers. "Very well, I assume you had something to add?"

"Yes." Freg stood in the corner, trying his best not to take up any more space than he already was. Failing that, he continued, "in support of the emperor's plan, I will add that the tainted forces of the Dweller have long since been pacified by her abilities as a general of the mist."

"Meaning?" Tamara asked.

"Meaning that if she were eliminated, her sway and the tainted beast's ability to organize would both be destroyed."

That got a chorus of opinions and agreement, only to be hushed by Tomko's voice. The Precursor stood in the corner, arms crossed and face grim. "That's only half the problem."

All eyes were on him. George narrowed in on the Precursor, trying to read his face. Tomko continued, "the mistborn, your worshipped Graces, do not follow the command of the Graceful One any longer. Since Jerrovia had formed, they worked to pacify it in the name of the Serene One, a land of total stillness, of pure mist. Even now they strive to do that, and said mistborn have been released along with the Dweller—as was their plan all along."

Darius spoke next, "what does that mean for us?"

"It means they will need to be taken care of, or at least scattered. We should keep an eye out for such an opportunity while we march on the Dweller. I wager there aren't many, not after all those years trapped in the Jerrovian veil, but I'd be surprised if they couldn't field an army."

"Then it's settled," Rosaline finally spoke and looked at George. The emperor nodded at his partner and stood.

"We will plan our counter attack to retake the capital and slay the Dweller, all the while keeping track of the movements of the mistborn and any other enemy forces. We will take the rest of the day to merge our logistics, distribute our forces, and reconvene tomorrow afternoon for planning our strategy. All in agreement?"

"Spoken like a Heinrich," Isabella gave the new emperor a wink, who offered a concerned smile to his cousin. Everyone else nodded along and in the end, everyone agreed, but before they could all funnel from the meeting room, Opane pulled George aside.

Her eyes still wore the pain of guilt for Josephine's demise as she approached her student. "George."

The emperor regarded her with kindness. "Yes?"

"I wanted to tell you, I'll be leaving now." Before George could ask, Opane quelled his panic. "I'll be back. Don't you worry. Something in the spirits is calling me north, though, and I intend to meet the call."

George cocked his head at that. "What do you mean?"

"I'm not sure." Opane bit her lip. "I can feel an ebb and flow in the air. The spirits are calling me as a Kafshe. I need to see what they desire." Silence. "Though I understand it may seem like I am running after my failure to protect your sister."

"No," George felt his heart hurt at the idea. "I know you well enough. Go on your journey, I'll welcome you back when you return."

The kafshe offered a smile and in a rare show of affection, she gave George's shoulder a pat. "Thank you for understanding. I am proud of how you've grown."

"I'm doing my best." There was a hurt in George's voice.

Opane turned to the door. "You're doing well."

***

With the hardest parts of the day done and everyone split up to do their part, George found himself alone. The world around him was a storm, and he would have been a liar if his heart wasn't equally in turmoil. He lost the rest of his family today; his entire people lost their family today. George stood outside the keep and after a bit of a walk, he found a small nook of grass wedged between the garrison kitchen and barracks. It reminded him of the nook he used to escape to back at Torskyla. Without much more thought on the matter, the new emperor slipped into the grassy gnoll, eager for the quiet space.

A piece of George felt like he should be beside his sister, grieving over her, but he couldn't bring himself to do it. He hurt too much. The emperor let a tired sigh cut through his lips and fell backwards until he leaned against the rough wooden wall of the barracks. The clank of his armor hitting the wall reminded him that he was still in gear. The day had been so hectic he didn't even realize the extra weight of his hauberk and plate. Too tired to deal with it now, he undid his sword belt and slid down the wall until the vision outside the nook was hidden by his knees. He looked down at Oathkith.

"It's just you and me now."

Oathkith didn't respond.

George looked over at the sword of Prax, ignoring the shard. "Oh and you."

The sword of Prax didn't reply either.

"And me?" Rosaline's voice caused the man to flinch, inciting a well needed laugh from the soldier. George nodded.

"Of course," he answered.

Rosaline crooked a simple grin and sat next to him, also still in her armor. She took in a hefty breath, reminding George to do the same. The fresh forest air soaked in his lungs just as Rosaline said,

"I'm sorry, you know, for everything that's happened. I know I can't feel your pain as sharply as you, but I'm here for you."

"I know you are." George let his head fall back onto the wall. "I appreciate you."

"I love you," Rosaline quickly responded. George blinked and looked over at her.

"I love you too..." George furrowed his brow, remembering Sosolam's warning and Tomko's answer on what he needed to do to end the ritual.

"What's wrong?"

"Remember how you told me you detest war and battle?"

Rosaline cocked her head and narrowed her eyes in suspicion. "Yes?"

"Should I feel guilty asking you to fight alongside me, teaching you Stromism to hurt?" He put a hand between them.

Rosaline let out a long sigh and put her hand on top of George's. "I detest war because of all the pain it brings, both the immediate pain and the pain of the survivors. That said, I'm not stupid or so bent on my philosophy that I can't see why we need to fight this fight—and I *will* fight it, whether you asked me to or not. This isn't about me, it's about the people of Jerrovia."

George smiled at her resolve. It wasn't a brilliant or bright smile, but a smile nonetheless. Rosaline looked him over, unconvinced. "That's not what's bothering you, though, is it?"

His smile faded. "I just... I don't want to cause you any pain if something were to happen to me."

Rosaline pursed her lips into a serious line, George opened his mouth to continue but Rosaline stopped him. "Stop right there." She shook her head. "You know who I am George, this is my choice and I'm choosing to stay beside you. I already know the possibilities." Her brow furrowed. "But I made the choice to see our relationship through it in spite of what could happen." She paused. "This isn't like you, George, what's bringing this on? Did I scare you with my love confession, because I'll be honest, I didn't see it going this way at all." She let out a single laugh devoid of comedy.

"No!" George waved his hands wildly. "Your words are the sun to my day-"

"More of Caleb's poetry?"

George gave a genuine chuckle at that, putting a smile on Rosaline's face in return. It quickly faded from both of them as they returned to their serious nature. "No. I do love you, and I'm glad you found it fit to tell me the same. I'm just concerned I might not be making it out of this conflict alive."

Rosaline was taken aback. She scrunched her nose and frowned. "Why would you say something like that?"

A nervous red took over George's face and emotion swirled in his eyes. "The final break of the ritual, to send Jerrovia back to safety, requires a sacrifice on the old elm tree. It has to be me."

She sat up at this. "No." She shook her head. "There's another way. There's always another way."

"I don't know of it." George closed his eyes, struggling to keep the growing feeling of tears inside. Rosaline put her hand on his cheek. It was cold against the heat of his face. Her thumb grazed under his eye, collecting a hot tear he didn't even realize had escaped.

"Well then we will have to find it, right?" Her confident voice betrayed the sound of sadness. "And besides, we've all had enough grief for one day."

George cleared his throat and sniffed in. He opened his eyes to meet hers and nodded. "You're right, let's enjoy what we have." He looked around him. "A foot hold."

"And that's all we need to spring back," Rosaline encouraged.

They shared a look until George started to nod.

"What?" Rosaline cracked a smile.

"I'm forever amazed at your ability to see the light," he said.

Her smile split into a short gasp of a laugh. "The world is brighter when your head isn't stuffed in a cave of sorrow." She stood up and wiped her knees free of loose grass. She extended a hand. "Now maybe some training will get us out of this funk?"

He took her hand. "With you? Deal."

Rosaline squeezed his hand and probed gently. "I love you."

"I love you, too."

A short, quiet 'yay', broke under Rosaline's breath and she tugged him along.

***

Williams was outside the walls of the fort. Birds were chirping and squirrels were chattering above him, leaving him lost in his thoughts under the emerald canopies of the forest. He sat in the dirt, facing the fort itself, a line of people still clamoring in the distance to get in, but he wasn't focusing on that. Across his lap was Flaretongue. He could see the outlines of Josephine's fingers on the leather wrapped hilt from where she practiced with it. He placed his fingers over hers and closed his eyes, a tear dripping down his nose.

There wasn't much in the world that moved Williams, not much that he cared about. His friends, of course, were one, but Josephine was the star above all of it. Ever since he first got lost in her sapphire eyes or dazzled by her strong voice and sharp grin. It was gone now and he could feel the hollow in his heart. When George confronts the Dweller, she will be gone forever. Worst still, he could feel the frustration of his defeat agitating the void inside him. He not only lost the fight, but he lost Josephine because of it. He couldn't save her, he couldn't even avenge her. Another tear dripped down his nose and onto the blade below.

"Hinan." Freg's voice wrenched Williams' eyes open and attention forward. The Harnian was standing in front of him, somehow going unnoticed despite his size. "Why do you cry?"

Williams pursed his lips. "Why do you call me Hinan?"

That elicited a small sound from Freg not unlike what a bull's laugh might sound like. "Harnian for hornless. Saying it gives me some memory of my homeland."

Williams looked disappointed, "and here everyone thought it was some great codeword or grand mystery."

Another bull-laugh. "But why do you cry, Hinan?"

"Like you can't tell on your own."

"I make it a habit not to assume." Freg unlatched his mighty book and slammed it onto the ground with a gust of air and shaking bang. Williams nearly jumped from his spot and a scattering of leaves came fluttering down. The Harnian sat on top of his book and folded his hands between his knees.

WIlliams, disturbed from his earlier thoughts gave up with a shake of his head and nudged his chin at 'The D'sastr'. "I don't suppose there is anything in there on how to beat a smoke-screamer without Stromism."

"Gennisberg, you mean?" Freg leaned in and Williams subconsciously mirrored him. Without a response, Freg continued, "He is an exceptional smoke-screamer. Recusant, and hides it well. You, on the other hand, have a very very small altar of creation, even if you learned how to harness it, it may not be very strong."

Williams' eyes dimmed and he looked down at the tear spotted flaretongue. "That's what I thought."

"Hinan." Freg shook his head. "There is more to a fight than who has the stronger magical bits, and something you have naturally is something not even George has. A sharp wit, quick to adapt, and a determination rooted from the life of an abused young boy looking for justice."

"How do you know that?" Williams snapped his eyes onto Freg's.

The Harnian raised a bovine brow and pressed. "Ask the question."

"How can I beat a man who can change where he is going to be, and at such an incredible speed that I cannot physically keep up?" Williams pursed his lips into a straight line. A simple silence fell between the two as Freg began to twist something of a smile.

"Be there before him."

With that, Freg stood up and hefted his book up into his arms with great strain. Despite being planted in the grass and moss of the undergrowth, not a stain defaced the metal bound tome. Williams was caught in the words of Freg, swirling a thread of hope into his pit of despair. He looked up at the Harnian and nodded. "Thank you."

Freg let out a hot stream of air through his nostrils and sighed. "It is really the very least I can do. It's not much, Hinan, but I offer my sympathies and further my apologies for those who got caught up in the threads of a cruel fate."

"She's a wonderful person," Williams said.

Freg nodded his great horned head. "I have no doubts about that."

"I love her."

"Even when it hurts," Freg said solemnly, "love can guide you forward. You'll find your peace, just as she may find peace in the Valley of Unifax." The Harnian latched his book to its harness and heaved it over his back. "Look forward, and she will be looking with you."

Williams felt a tear drop from his chin. He gave a nod, fingers curling around the handle of Flaretongue. He swore he could feel her fingers squeezing back.

***

The armory of the garrison was nothing special. It was a musty and crowded room that smelt like earth and wood. The walls were thick logs, long since sanded down to create a seamless barrier between the hanging mail and the conditions of the outside. The floor was raised wood as well, keeping the place dry and insulated from the forest ground. A side effect of the floor being built the way it was, and perhaps a beneficial trait, was that it creaked loudly whenever anyone walked over it.

Reginald stood with a heavy clipboard and a stick of charcoal, marking down the helmets he was counting off the shelves.

The only light that aided him came from small double paned windows, the shafts of sun illuminating the many particles of dust that danced around him. His mind was on his duty, not giving it any room to think too long about the events of the day — though he'd be a liar if he didn't feel like he lost both a son and a granddaughter in one fell swoop. Reginald was the type to find himself too old and battered to cry, but if he could, he knew he would. He remembered Wilhelm's eyes as a toddler, and then seeing them once again when Josephine was born. Deep down he always knew her life would be fast and short, but he cared for her as if she was going to outlive himself. The old servant shook his head at the thought; to outlive himself.

As he was wrapping up his thought and fitting to place it in a velvet box until he was ready to approach it, the sound of the floor creaking made his ears perk. Reginald raised his brow at the unexpected guest.

"I'm surprised to see you roaming freely."

Tomko, bruised with a certain depression, gave a weak curl of a smile at that. "The cells are all in use, and besides, I wouldn't call this freedom. There are eyes everywhere on my back right now."

"Eyes that don't mind you wandering into a storage room?" Reginald clicked his charcoal stick against his clipboard.

Tomko shrugged and stepped further into the room, idly dragging his fingers across a metal cuirass. "This might be a weird question, but since we are here, I have to ask: have I seen you before?"

Reginald turned to face Tomko squarely, and despite being a gentle old man, his posture put something of a fright into the

Precursor, who shriveled. "If you have been sneaking around the palace for as long as you have, then you likely have seen me."

"I remember you during Frederick's reign."

"Emperor Frederick," Reginald corrected.

"But you were old, even then," Tomko braved further probing.

"Indeed I was," Reginald agreed. "But not as old as the first Jerrovian." The old servant glinted a polite smile. "In fact, for once, I feel like I should be the one asking questions."

The Precursor nodded and leaned against the wall, fidgeting under Reginald's stare but otherwise cooperating. "I might have answers, what do you want to know?"

"Esmachus," Reginald said the name with no emotion. "Long ago, or perhaps not long compared to either of us, I chased him and rescued a girl from his clutches. He was trying to break the spell on the oak tree, but it was your testimony just recently that revealed he would have always been unsuccessful unless an elmborn was sacrificed against it."

"That's true..." Tomko answered slowly, cautious.

"Why do you think that is?" Reginald's lids fell to a stoic stare.

"What?"

"I mean to say," Reginald continued. "Why an elmborn, why not any old Heinrich?"

"I suppose," Tomko was careful with his words now. "I suppose that the blood in question needed to have entered Jerrovia by the Elm to count as a variable for the original spell."

"Blood related to the original casters, at that," Reginald clarified. "'Entered Jerrovia by the elm,' an interesting term for birth, but I suppose that it's correct."

Tomko cocked his brow. "You're awfully curious."

"Oh no," Reginald shook his head. The old servant forgot his manners for a moment, or perhaps he simply discarded them as he began a walk to leave the storage and this conversation behind. "I'm satisfied with my understanding of the oak. Now it's the elm I worry about. What rules dictate that tree, I wonder." He stopped at the threshold to the outside and clasped his hands behind his back, clipboard entwined. "A funny anecdote enters my mind."

"Hm?" Tomko gave the man's back a wary glance.

"A dragon," Reginald mused. "Long ago, she was reluctant to see her clutch suffer, and so did the impossible for them. Some days I wonder what I'd do to protect my own clutch, should I have been born a dragon." He looked back over his shoulder. "But such is the fancies of the imagination. Good day, Tomko of the Trees."

***

Cassandra sat in the impromptu meeting room. It was empty, save for the company of some chairs and a table. The room smelled like grain and old bread, with a hint of sweat—though admittedly that last smell might have been her. She was still in the dress she had worn when the palace came under siege, a black stain across the front and her left arm bandaged in linen. Her fingers hadn't quite stopped shaking since the attack, making the small drawing she was working on more of a mess than her mind currently was. Cassandra had lost Sophia, then she lost Wilhelm, and now she's lost him for real. On top of all that, George was calling an early meeting and had asked her to join for one particular reason that she felt uneasy about — there had been a sudden update on Esmachus.

A hand tapped her shoulder, and she turned. Her eyes studied Hector's face and fell to his eyes where she could see a deep compassion.

"Are you alright?"

Cassandra nodded and signed. "Yes, how are you?"

Hector stared at her in confusion. "I'm sorry."

Cassandra looked down at her doodle and flipped it over to a fresh side and put her charcoal to it. She wrote. "It's okay, how are you?"

Hector sat down on a chair close enough so he could see her paper. He gave her a stern look and said with conviction, "I wanted to see how you were before the meeting began. The flight from the palace was anything but easy, and I can imagine it was harder on you than most. We all owe our lives to your bravery."

Cassandra closed her eyes, but only found flashes of a tainted creature's face. Shaking her head, she opened her eyes and quickly jotted down. "What was I to do but what I did?"

"Humble," Hector grinned. "But really, I wanted to thank you. Those creatures were nasty, if nothing else."

Cassandra nodded in agreement at that but wrote. "I've met worse."

Hector spoke, uncertain—hesitant. "Esmachus?"

Cassandra nodded and wrote, "an evil man like no other."

"What makes him so evil?"

Her hand took to the paper and scribbled quickly. "He did what Gennisberg did to Josephine to countless of us."

"Us?"

Cassandra looked down at the paper then at Hector before writing. "I'm George's cousin, removed by many generations. No longer a Heinrich, but related."

"He didn't know the ritual wouldn't work on someone not born by the elm tree..." Hector pinched his chin in thought.

"That didn't stop him from trying," Cassandra wrote. She hovered her charcoal above the paper, nearly full of her words, as she pondered what to write next. She had so much she wanted to say, but in her mouth she could feel the remains of her tongue tap the back of her mouth helplessly. Frustrated, she opened her mouth and with a hoarse, distraught voice, she said, "I *haa* him."

Hector seemed taken aback but Cassandra kept her eyes pinned on his face. She put in the last space of her paper, "he was mad at the world for taking so much from him, but he took more from so many people." She opened her mouth again. "I *haa* him." Her eyes were wet with tears. Between knowing Esmachus was out there and that Wilhelm was gone, she couldn't stop the tears any longer. Her hands clenched and snapped the charcoal in half. Tears tacked onto the paper, muddying the words.

Cassandra couldn't see Hector anymore, but she felt a cloth be put into her hand and she could feel the air change as the door opened, and stayed open. George's boots scuffed behind the pair and they both turned.

The emperor wore a sad look in his eyes and he twisted his lips in thought as he studied Cassandra. She studied him back. This was the boy who used to pick on her and now here he stood, a completely different person now.

"Will you be okay attending the meeting, still?" George asked.

Cassandra wiped her face with Hector's cloth and gave the emperor a sturdy look and signed. "Anything to put an end to this."

A few moments passed and the room was full of every big name in the fortress once again. Compared to them all, Cassandra couldn't help but feel insignificant, and yet George would look at her now and again and give her an approving nod, as if she being there was somehow a comfort to him. Maybe it was because she was in a way, like a strange sibling of his, or maybe it was because they both shared a deep connection with Wilhelm, now gone. Whatever it may have been, it gave her hope for the days to come.

"So that's it then," Tamara steepled her fingers. "Esmachus rears his head again."

Maelinn groaned. "At least we can rest assured he will be considerably weaker than before."

"I wouldn't underestimate smoke-screamers," Darius added. "We'd be best to approach them cautiously but strongly."

"We have no choice," Rosaline threw in. "If Esmachus is approaching from the west and..." She pointed at the map of the Empire that sat center on the table, a blue stone to the Northeast. "...with reports of..." She looked to Tomko who finished her thought.

"Mistborn."

She gulped. "Mistborn... approaching from the East with Tagist rebels, we have to finish off Esmachus once and for all. The sooner we end his faction, the sooner we can focus on retaking the capital and ending this war before it gets too fired up."

Emperor George nodded. "I concur. Unfortunately, the mistborn will not wait for us to finish off Esmachus and are moving rapidly to our location."

Freg snorted. "The mistborn are forever tactful if nothing else."

Another nod. "We will have to meet their forces to stall them or better yet, destroy them before they gain momentum in Jerrovia. This will clear the way to the capital."

"A risky proposal," Dame Honora added. "Splitting forces is always a risk, we will be piecemeal."

"Do we really have any other options?" Duchess Isabella threw in.

General Tamara closed her eyes and sighed. "Not unless we know of any active allies to call on."

Commander Baldra spoke up at that. "I still haven't received word from Duke Peter, or any other vanguards for that matter. I think it's safe to say they are all preoccupied with their own invasions."

Cassandra's head was spinning at the discussion, when something finally occurred to her. She stood up and everyone fell silent to look at her. A red burn went over her face, putting heat in her cheeks. Now already in the oven, she signed. "If Esmachus is showing himself and looking to fight head-on in the field, then we know he is desperate. He has failed the Dweller multiple times and his force of smoke-screamers is greatly reduced. I don't think we should underestimate him, but I also don't think he is in his best mind."

Eyes fell to Reginald, who explained. There was a soft murmur.

"What if," Rosaline started, "he is acting boldly because he expects reinforcements?"

Cassandra shook her head wildly and signed. "The mistborn are in the way. He is isolated."

George blinked and looked at Darius. "Send out some riders to verify if he has any movements to the north or south of him." The commander shrugged.

"Easy enough, Georgie boy."

Everyone looked at Darius and he scoffed. "Force of habit. Sorry *Emperor*."

George cracked a smile, and seeing him smile made Cassandra smile. Maybe everything was going to work out after all.

"If what Cassandra says is true," George looked to everyone. "We will split our force with a larger portion heading to meet the mistborn while a second force meets Esmachus. A third, smaller force, will remain here. Objections?"

Hector raised a hand and George nodded his way. "If permitted, I would like to be a part of the forces to remain here. I feel it is my duty as Marshal to help the 1st Vanguard regroup and reorganize after our losses, to say nothing of the civilians."

George looked away from the faces of those at the meeting. Thoughts and possibilities flashed behind his eyes, and while he would prefer to have Hector on the front lines with him, he knew the man had just spent his energy escaping the capital and if nothing else, the palace guards of the 1st desperately needed his leadership. Finally, he nodded "Very well. Anything else, anyone?"

"I have a request," Rosaline spoke up. "Allow me to be in the force to engage Esmachus."

The Hero Harris piped in at that. "Rosaline, why?"

Rosaline said clearly, "From stories from your past, Father, and from my own experience on the tower of Jornho, I've seen the chaos he sows. I would feel better knowing I helped end his campaign." Rigid determination was in her eyes, and no one objected to her wishes.

"Does anyone else have any input?" George addressed the room. Everyone shook their heads and George gave his best face of determination. "Then let's take back our peace, and avenge our fallen."

"Hoo-ah." Darius agreed.

"For the Empire," Maelinn threw in.

"Foa Wiihem," Cassandra forced.

"For all of them," George said softly, a tiny break in his voice.

Chapter 26
Taint

Baldra was put in charge of the portion of regulars sent west to intercept Esmachus' smoke screamers. To assist the regulars against the magical enemy, Commander Maelinn with the 10th Stromist Vanguard as well as Rosaline were also dispatched. Reginald, by his own accord, also joined Baldra in her march. It took little convincing to get George to agree with his deployment. Although Reginald could see that the Emperor was uneasy with the idea, nearly two decades of being under his tutelage made it hard for George to go against him. Before George it was Wilhelm, Reginald felt a tug deep inside him, and now Wilhelm was gone.

"I'm sorry, Frederick," Reginald whispered to himself.

"What?" Rosaline looked over at the servant. The two were in the spotted shade of the forest, surrounded by tents laden with branches and leaves for camouflage. Around them, soldiers prepared in silence, or as much silence an army could muster. Beyond the trees to the north was an open meadow that stretched into the border of Caldora. Scouts dispatched by Baldra had already confirmed that the enemy army was going to be marching through that area and knowing that the smoke screamers would likely have the upperhand in the forest proper, Baldra and Maelinn agreed that it was best to intercept them before entering the wood.

Maelinn was also there kneeling by a bundle of personal items, her hands on a chest wrapped in a deep red sheet. She had been gearing up outside her small tent while Reginald and Rosaline stood against the trees, watching the troops. The soldiers' faces were grim, and Reginald could tell their overall morale was low with the news of the capital's demise and impending doom on all sides. Sucking in a large breath of fresh forest air, Reginald answered Rosaline. "I'm just thinking about the late Emperor," he admitted.

"I'd be more focused on the enemy forces headed our way, personally." Maelinn pushed the red sheet out of the way and popped the trunk open to reveal a circular shield adorned with a long, deadly spike jutting from the center. The surface of the laminated wooden face was long since scarred and scratched by battle. She threw it over her shoulder, talking under her breath. "Stromist scouts, paleskin scouts, all just reporting a big blob of trouble."

"Yagan." Reginald corrected.

"Hm?" Maelinn looked up at Reginald before closing her chest. He shook his head and she shrugged. "I don't know how Emperor George convinced them to help, but I'm not complaining." Her eyes met Reginald's and she stood up straight. Tucking her hands behind her back to hold her elbows square and get a little extra height, she scanned the old man. "But I am wondering why you're here on the front lines with us."

"I just want to make sure it all goes smoothly," Reginald answered.

Maelinn cocked her head to the side. "Do you have some sort of stake in this?"

"You mean beyond my allegiance to the Empire?"

The Commander gave a shallow nod.

Reginald couched his chin between his fingers and sighed. "It should be no surprise that Esmachus has been a thorn in the Imperial family's side for quite a long time. I'd like to confirm for

Emperor George that he is defeated without any chance of reprisal once and for all.”

“I second that,” Rosaline cut in. She had been silently watching the exchange, but upon mentioning reasons and motivations, Reginald saw her tense up. “His past scarred my own father and his present scarred George’s family as well as the people of the Empire. Besides, I noticed him shrink away from me when I last saw him.” The champion of the North fell silent for a moment. “I suppose he should be scared. He tried to drive a wedge between me and George as well as hurt my father long ago.”

“I didn’t take you as one for revenge,” Reginald offered with a perched brow.

Rosaline blew a sigh at that and smiled, if not a little forced. “Oh, I’m not.” She looked forward to nothing in particular, her vision clearly lost in a thought. “I never was one for hurting others, but I suppose I’m good at it. Esmachus needs to be stopped, and I strangely feel obligated to do it.”

“I understand,” Reginald answered. “I feel that obligation as well.”

“Well, you can count on the 10th,” Maelinn offered a smile. “We beat his forces once, we can do it again.”

Reginald tipped his head in return. “I appreciate your confidence.”

Maelinn gave another smile before looking around at the hustling soldiers and auxiliaries until finally her eyes fell on an active campfire. She chewed her cheek for a moment before looking back at Reginald. “Pre-war pancake?”

“Excuse me?”

“It’s for good luck.”

Reginald chuckled. "Then I think it might be prudent."

"No, it's pancakes." Maelinn pointed a fork at Reginald, the old servant not too sure where she got it.

"I like this Commander," Rosaline said, though her usual cheer was sobered.

***

Three overcooked pancakes and five hours later, the troops of the 10th and Baldras regulars were in their positions throughout the wooded border of the hills. A small, elite force was stationed behind the steepest hill, ready to pin down the enemy for the ambush. Reginald watched the army from back in the woods at an elevated position along with the auxiliaries who were guarding the camp supplies. Something inside his gut doubted this plan would go exactly as planned, Esmachus was too tricky to go down easily; a fact that Reginald knew that all too well.

He looked back at the auxiliaries around the supplies. They wore anxious expressions and some looked like they barely slept. Reginald turned back to the look through the trees, and now he could see a dark line appear on the hilly horizon. The smoke-screamers were approaching in lines. They were adorned in black painted breast plates and greaves over tattered robes of the occult. Reginald's fingers found themselves down to where a sword should be, but grasped nothing but air. He tightened his jaw; the enemy was already organized, they definitely knew there was an ambush waiting for them and yet they were still advancing.

From his angle, Reginald could make out Maelinn's column behind the hill. They were still as stone, despite everything, and as the enemy passed the hidden troops in the woods, they sprang over the hill, taking the high ground. A horn blasted from Maelinn's command and the troops on the hill unleashed a volley of arrows. At the same time, arrows whistled from the wooded sidelines, sending missiles at three angles. Reginald could feel his knuckles turning white as he watched in anticipation.

The arrows from the sides slammed into the blob of Nachtists, but as the arrows from the hill closed in, the front lines of the enemy burst into smoke, their forms dashing forward before rematerializing. These were skilled smoke-screamers. Reginald chewed on his cheek, the dashing smoke-screamers were making quick work of the hill slopes. There wasn't time for another volley before the enemy crashed into Maelinn's forces. At that, the troops from the wooded perimeter came charging out to hit the flanks of the enemy.

Baldra was leading the troops on the far side, the commander rallying her troops into Esmachus' soldiers. The swift strike of Baldra's line and the other flanking force charged into the smoke-screamers, but instead of a shaking crash of soldier against soldier, the smoke-screamers exploded into clouds of smoke, their forms shifting through the Imperial lines before materializing behind them. The pincer movement was now engulfed by the Nachtists. Screams of surprise and panicked commands shouted over the roar of the battle. The enemy was taking advantage of the chaos, thriving in the environment while the Imperials coughed and choked on the smoke between swings.

Things looked dire and while Maelinn's troops were holding steady on the hill, Reginald could see the other sides of the Imperials wavering under the brute force of the smoke-screamers. The

Imperials needed a push to turn the tide of the battle. The old servant pulled his eyes from the violence in front of him and back at the auxiliaries and the supplies. His eyes fell to his own trunk, then to the red wrapped trunk of Commander Maelinn, and finally to a horse.

***

Esmachus' eyes were smoldering with chaotic energy. He stared up the hilltop that the Imperial forces made their frontal stand. All around him, his army of smoke-screamers were screeching their power and slaughtering the Imperial soldiers. Glimmers of Stromist magic retaliated, but even Esmachus could see that hope fading from his prey, the feeling not unlike a mouse caught in a snake's grip. Of course he knew that those of his forces not recusant to the side effects of the smoke were quickly losing their minds from the intense use of the magic, but he also knew the Imperials wouldn't last long enough for that to matter.

Shielded on both sides by his fighting soldiers, Esmachus made his way up the hill—intent on destroying whatever held the Imperials together—when he spotted Rosaline Von Rugosa. His eyes widened and an old wound crackled in his blackened heart.

The warrior scion was beset by Esmachus' forces. Her spear had long since shattered and she was reduced to using her sword and shield. A screamer darted to her right, but she moved with a dancer's footwork and slipped her blade through the armpit of the assailant. It was a silent kill with the backdrop of the screams of battle, and with a glint of light, her blade slipped free. A black ooze leaked out and just as another enemy came charging towards her, Rosaline booted the first to the ground. To avoid tripping, the smokescreamer burst into a cloud of smoke before reappearing on the other side of their fallen comrade, but Rosaline's eyes were sharp and her blade cut the spear from her enemies hands before slicing the jugular open in two precise swings.

Clenching his teeth, Esmachus couldn't help but see the style of the Hero Harris in her every move. With a blasting scream, Esmachus roared up the hill, eager to snuff her out. A dark cloud of smoke engulfed his legs and the wind split around him violently. A shimmer of magic flashed across Rosaline's arm and she managed to catch Esmachus' saber on her hilt before parrying it away. It was a weak magic, Esmachus felt it, but it was enough to speed her movement. The wind whipped Rosaline's black hair into a storm and Esmachus found his footing. He couldn't help but bare his teeth at the heir of Harris. She stood there, a paragon, a saint, untainted so far by war, or so at least Esmachus pictured her. She was her father, she had to be. The smokescreamer dropped his sword—he could never beat Harris with that anyway—and with a swirl of his hand, he summoned a flanged mace of black metal from the air.

The two shared a look, and Esmachus could see hesitation in Rosaline's red-flecked stare, or was it ambition? He cracked a wicked grin. His breastplate and helmet were still clean, his mace ready, while her spear lay broken on the ground, the churn of grime and dirt crusting her armor and dulling her sword. Esmachus went to speak, but before he could, Rosaline charged, silent and clinical. Her arms summoned a magical light, and the ribbon of Stromism traveled up her sword until it reached the tip, where it flashed like a white sun. A simple trick of a weaker form, and yet he fell for it.

Esmachus' eyes burned negative and he was forced to blink. He could feel the danger, and sucked in a deep breath of battle gritted air before letting out a piercing screech. His eyes peeled open to see a torrent of black smoke shoot out of his mouth and push Rosaline back, small black shards of metal cutting into her armor and creating a cacophony of steel against steel. She brought up her shield against the onslaught and just as she was about to lose her grip against the powerful stream, the warrior found her footing and spun to the side.

"Harris!" Esmachus cursed, but Rosaline was already back in the fray. She was quick, and with small specks of magic, her legs danced.

"Rosaline!" The warrior broke her silence, and with soft counting under her breath, she thrust her blade. Esmachus' chest burst into smoke to let the sword through. He could hear her tricks as she breathed.

"One..." The sword sliced at his throat, but he dodged backwards in time.

"Two..." A sweep of his legs, but he was too quick.

"Three." Her arm thrusted under his own just as he poised to strike. The blade completely missed him but as she bent her elbow up, she had him grappled. Again he burst into smoke, his whole body this time.

"Seven." The announcement confused Esmachus as he reformed behind her, and her blade thrusted in reverse under her own armpit, nearly impaling him by surprise. Her style was tricky, another flash, another number, the order reversing, the numbers jumbling. A thrust here and a thrust there, never where it was expected and always dangerous. This was the duelist style of the Rugosa, augmented by a smidge of magic.

But it wasn't enough.

Esmachus' mace slammed into Rosaline's chest. Her breastplate took the blow and she had angled herself to have it glance off. It wasn't fatal, but her breath popped for a moment and Esmachus threw forward a hand, screaming a blast of smoke at her gaping mouth. Her eyes watered as the pillar of evil blasted over her face, her skin was starting to bubble painfully by her jaw. A shimmer of gold. She was trying to stabilize. Esmachus' eyes widened. No. He pulled away just in time and Rosaline's sword caught the air where he once was. Her arm was swirled with magic, broken from the grip of smoke.

With red bursted eyes, Rosaline stared as Esmachus and the two collided again. Esmachus was a swirl of chaos and Rosaline was a dance of refinement. This time she avoided his weapon entirely, her strategy had changed. She no longer grappled, she no longer played squirming tricks, she no longer parried or deflected. At the drop of a hat her entire style was different and changing again and again until at last Esmachus saw his opening. Her sword had missed him, her shield had fallen from her other arm. Esmachus turned into a wave of smoke and juked to her side, but as he reappeared, certain her gaze was still on his prior position, two gauntleted fingers rammed into his eyes. She had predicted it? No! Pain ripped through the thought, blinking the mind white.

With the leverage of surprise, Rosaline gripped his face tight and pulled him in brutally. Her thumb kept his mouth shut, her fingers clamping his destroyed eyes. His magic was sealed. He felt it beyond the pain in his eyes, behind the silence of his mouth.

Something cold had entered his body and something warm was leaking out.

"Sleep." Her words were hoarse, nothing like a song unburdened of violence. She wasn't clean. He felt her blade leave his heart. Air touched his broken organ, pain left his body and his mind slipped away in favor of death.

***

A loud, shaking breath erupted from Rosaline. Her legs were on fire, her face was in severe pain and every muscle in her body felt like it was ripping itself apart. Her sword clattered to the wet slicked grass below and she fell to her knees. Her mind was too much of a rush to think about the corpse of Esmachus. Dazed, Rosaline looked over the battle on the hill. Maelinn was holding her own, her spiked shield slamming through enemy after enemy, but her troops were fading, similar to Rosaline. Down below, Baldra's forces were still scattered and waning. Esmachus was dead, but the threat was ever alive.

Her chin bobbed to her chest and her eyes glazed at the sight coming up the hill. Smokescreamers, alive and well. She couldn't move to greet them. She hated this. She hated war. She hated battle. She hated killing, and she was sure she'd hate to die. She felt dirty, she felt hopeless. The enemy charged forward, wild and intent on one thing.

A horn blasted.

Surprise jerked Rosaline's head back up and turning, her eyes fell on a red snapping cape in the distance. Breaking from the treeline, an Imperial knight dressed in plate and hauberk with a red cape was riding out on a grey mottled horse. Cheers could be heard from the Imperial lines as they crashed back into the Nachtists with improved morale.

Rosaline knew George's cape, this wasn't it, not at all. Her brow furrowed and the enemies on the hillside slowed for a moment, but not for long. Ignoring the renewed Imperials, the smokescreamers cleared the rest of the way, but before the leader could get closer to Rosaline, a horse whinnied and the edge of a shield snapped outward, slamming into the side of his head. The smokescreamer was sent bouncing across the ground, head cloven.

Reginald's voice rang from the helmet of the mounted knight. "Stay down, Rosaline!" He leaped from his horse, taking strides to get in front of the animal. The Dragonchild grabbed the hilt of his blade and Rosaline froze in place, her strength too gone to do much else.

The smokescreamers on the hill stood still, cautious of the knight-dressed-servant and for a moment, the pocket of battle was frozen. Rosaline stared at Reginald, who stared at the enemy, who stared back. They were all waiting and then, together, the smokescreamers let out a blasting scream and they advanced at shimmering breakneck speeds. As they reformed, they were face to face with Reginald, a lone soldier. Time seemed to slow to a near stop. Reginald's hand erupted into flame and his sword blazed a red hot, metal dripping away from the seal that kept it in its scabbard. Rosaline felt a heat on her cheek and Reginald's sword exploded from its scabbard in a wide arc of flame and molten slag. The hot blade, somehow impossibly sharp, cut through the closest smokescreamer from his stomach to his head and a hurricane of heated pain ended with an explosion of fire.

***

Reginald held his blade in both hands. His enemies' flaming bodies crackling in front of him. A cloak of fire hid the gore of the scene, the smokescreamers mangled and destroyed under the orange and red. Together with Rosaline, he looked down at the battle below. The explosion was large enough for the other smoke-screamers to notice, and the inflated morale of the Imperials and leadership of Baldra on the flanks saw the battle whittling down in the favor of the Jerrovians, the enemy no longer able to put up a unified fight.

"It's done," Reginald heard Rosaline say.

He nodded. "I saw."

Chapter 27
Pacification

East of the Imperial Forest was a quilted land of farms and shallow gullies. While the shadow of the tall forest dominated the Western Horizon, a sobering smoke stained the East and somewhere below its origin laid the Imperial City. George had little room in his mind to think about that, as he sat atop Ai and looked out at the impending battlefield. His eyes threaded over the pastures, cut low by spring grazing and his ears filled with the sounds of singing birds and buzzing insects. The tranquility of the battlefield reminded him of his first battle, except this time he didn't feel anywhere near as confident. He didn't like the idea of going into a headlong battle against a foe he never fought before or even knew too much about, but with the forest garrison and all the survivors it harbored on the line, George knew he needed to create a victory over the mistborn right here and now.

Assuming they would fight at least somewhat like the mist-talkers he and the 11th had fought up north, George put himself in charge of a troop of heavy cavalry to provide flank for a Stromist infantry column lead by Darius. Projectiles were likely to be useless in this coming battle, but just in case, George had some archers positioned to screen the enemy. If at all possible, George wanted them to approach him.

Williams' horse stamped and caught George's attention. The emperor regarded his friend. "Are you ready?"

The knight leaned forward in his saddle. He was on his black horse, wielding a lance with flaretongue on his hip. . "I'm as ready as you are."

George gave a worried look. "Please be more ready than that."

"We won't lose," Williams reassured. He gave George a serious look. "For everyone who has already sacrificed themselves."

That put a serious line on George's face and the emperor gave a shallow nod. "Not a single Jerrovian will die in vain, not now, not then, not ever."

"Well said," Williams agreed. George returned a nod and refocused his gaze.

On the horizon, an ominous cloud of blue mist was rolling in, heralding the sound of marching. Instead of the telltale clank of metal among the marchers, however, there was only a ghastly clink that sounded akin to glass, giving the enemy a sound that George imagined a giant's windchime might sound like. As the hay fields in the distance were parted with enemy soldiers, George finally got a good look at his foe.

Up front, sages were marching, faces blank and eyes glowing blue. They seemed almost lifeless as they marched in their religious gowns. Spearheading them was Father Sage Clement, his face as neutral and pacified as the others. How he escaped his imprisonment only lingered on George's mind for a moment before his eyes adjusted to the enemy behind the sages.

They were tall, and not at all human, or any other creature of Jerrovia. Their bodies were nothing more than condensed mist, contained by shards of crystalline armor and presumably stabilized by an anchor inside, as Freg had mentioned. On their flat crystalline faces they held no expression and as they moved, the wind hissed and was filled with light mist. In the mistborn's hands, they held a whole manner of weapons made of that alien blue crystal.

George's fingers went cold at the sight. They were uncanny and when they moved, it felt like he was staring at the impossible. On his hip, he could feel Sosolam's blade heat up to a warm presence, as if the blade itself was remembering an old enemy. As much as George would have preferred to see what the legendary blade could do against his foe, he remembered Sooslam's words and knew he couldn't release such power until he was prepared to strike down the Dweller.

"Remember our briefing," George said loudly, "a heart-like anchor keeps them bound to this realm, destroy that, and they'll die."

"George Heinrich!" A ghostly voice echoed from Clement. It wasn't his voice, it couldn't be. "The Serene One's army offers peace. Lay down your weapons and accept pacification." The Father Sage's words were mechanical, perfectly spaced and held no personality whatsoever. Even his tone and induction was gone. He sounded like a different man, a hollow. George looked over at Williams.

"Order the archers to hound them."

Williams held up a hand and a horn blasted to the far side of the field. In moments, a flurry of arrows were whirring through the sky. As predicted, the mist caught most of the projectiles, with the sages quickly putting up protective magic around themselves. George let the barrage continue, hoping to find some gaps somewhere; he needed them to approach him. Gritting his teeth, the emperor watched as his arrows fell harmlessly and his enemy stood still and patient. George knew this wasn't a rash enemy, and he knew he had to approach after all.

"Stromist riders!" George called out. His eyes flickered to the flank of the enemy, if only he could break their formation. "On me."

George dug his heels into Ai and the horse spurred forward, erupting into a gallop. Thunderous hooves followed George and his trusted friend flanked his side. Sucking in a long and calm breath, George started to call on the smokeform. His emotions started to boil inside him and wisps of smoke hissed through his hair and teeth. George' skin started to stain red, spreading even onto Ai's mottled coat and just as it was about to reach its pinnacle, George fed it a goal; to defeat the mistborn, to validate Josephine's sacrifice, to see peace return to his land. A great ball of flame burst in his stomach and his hair shocked white. Blood red skin tightened around his engorged muscles and George let out a rocking scream.

Oathkith came shrieking from its scabbard and Ai's hooves pounded so hard that the world blurred and yet despite the chaotic power that surged through him, George could see clearly, his grey eyes like still pools of thought, guiding the stronger waves that torrented inside him.

Not even the mist of the sages could slow George down as he went exploding through their ranks. The ground shook and everyone in Ai's way was sent into the air. Oathkith bit through the neck of a sage before swinging to the other side of Ai and finding another. Williams and the others came trampling through right after, effectively cutting a path to the mistborn.

Ai stampeded over the first one, raging hooves cleaving into the crystalline armor, but before George could cut away and retreat along the flank for another charge, the enemy lines thickened. Ai whinnied and bucked up her front legs. George let out a roar of power, the soundwave forcing the enemy to tighten their grips on their weapons. Williams' lance came darting in soon after, punching into a mistborn's chestplate and biting the core inside. The strange creature dissolved into a cloud of sparkling mist.

The other soldiers came soon after, their lance hitting other mistborn, but that was where their surprise charge lost its momentum. The enemy lines were tightening around them and as their riders in the back came flooding in, the scene turned into a tight brawl. George was forced off his horse, narrowly avoiding a crystalline blade. The enemy hissed and whirred as they fought, and they did so with seasoned expertise and supernatural strength and abilities.

With the initial charge spent, the fighting churned. George's infantry made quick work of the sages, but found themselves stalled at the frontline of the mistborn. The chip George had carved into the enemy forces quickly became the hot point of the battle. Ai had clamored away while George focused his power forward.

A blue axe came swinging towards him but George ducked it, rising to shrug off a sword blow with Rook before bringing Oathkith to bear on a mistborn. His blade screamed through the wind and shrieked as it bit through the crystalline chest armor of the mistborn. Angry sparks escaped the growing wound but the mistborn seemed unbothered, opting to slam its shoulder into George in an attempt to free itself but the mistborn's shoulder met nothing as Goerge released Oathkith to bob to the side, using the momentum of his dodge to bring Rook swinging back around and hammering it against the pommel of Oathkith, nailing the blade in further and snapping through the soft anchor hidden inside. The mistborn started to dissolve and George caught Oathkith from the hissing mess before rushing the next opponent.

George released a puff of steaming purple mist from his nostrils, the red of his skin deepening. His body tightened and then as he kicked off towards the enemy, he brought a clap of wind with him. He slammed into the enemy line, Rook reaching out to bash a mistborn and send them flying into the others. The force of the blow shattered the mistborn's chest entirely, launching the enemy backwards and through several others before crashing to a stop. Dust and dirt plumed.

Before the enemy line could recover, George had already closed the distance. Oathkith slammed through the enemy carapaces as if they were bugs. Anchors were split and crystals were shattered. Behind the emperor, Williams did his best to lead the Stromists of the 11th into the wedge George was creating. Bullets of condensed mist were blasting across the scene, with Williams dodging them and rising and juking to strike where they could and when they could. Some soldiers had brought maces, using it to crush the bodies of the mistborn, while Williams used flaretongue to snake the gaps of their armor. George couldn't focus on them much, as the deeper he cut his way into the mistborn ranks, the tougher and more experienced the mistborn became, until he realized he was fighting elites.

They were taller, had thicker armor, and their weapons seemed almost alien. Pockets of mist started to appear around him, and he knew it was slowing down his allies behind him. Luckily, the smokeform seemed to be the answer to the magical air. He managed to force himself through the thinner clouds, while slipping past the thicker ones. Serrated swords, five pointed spears that seemed to rotate, and horrific bladed weapons all flung past him. George came crashing down from a leap and hooked his shield arm into the crevice of one of the mistborn. With oathkith, he cut the primordial being's gauntlets off, defanging it, before pushing his victim forward. The mass of enemy weapons sparked off the crystal hide of his new living shield.

A whip of mist, with sharp crystalline shrapnel, came cracking by. George released his hostage and kicked off of them, saving himself from the blow while pushing the mistborn into the attack. The crystal-mist whip slashed through the mistborn like butter before snapping back to its owner. It was a mistborn that towered over the others and whose facemask was decorated to look like a snarling human.

"Smoke-pawn," it said in an alien voice. George let his eyes soak on the enemy, he knew he could defeat even a creature such as this while he had the smokeform. A cold feeling tugged at him though, and suddenly he understood that the champion mistborn knew the same. The whip came back as a vortex, snapping over the ranks of mistborn, but instead of heading for George, it unraveled towards where Williams focused on fighting a mistborn. George clenched his jaw and kicked off the ground.

Wind screamed by his ears, his body moving faster than the whip itself. Landing on one foot, he brought Rook upwards. Williams spun to him, shocked and all at once the whip crashed into Rook, pushing George back with incredible force. Golden light screeched across Rook as George's magic kept it intact. He felt a hand on his back and then a shoulder, Williams kept him standing. His sword stabbed, impaling an approaching enemy, covering George's flank.

The whip cracked again and George was leaping to intercept it. Another crack, and George realized there were more than one champion mistborns. Three whips were flinging through the air, going towards his troops, going towards his best friend. It all happened too quickly. George landed, catching one of the whips on Rook, while the ground all around him exploded into plumes as the other whips landed. Dirt and mist curdled the air opaque and screams of blood and pain could be heard on all sides.

"No..." George could feel his heart snap. Wails filled his ears and his eyes frantically looked through the stinging dirt for Williams. He felt his smokeform weaken in his panic and as it did, a creeping chill clung to his body—he couldn't move. A thick cloud of mist had captured him, suspending him above the battleground so his feet couldn't feel the ground. The air was settling, and from his captured state, George's sluggish eyes turned to see Williams guarding the body of a fallen soldier, the screaming man underneath missing their legs and flaretongue doing its best to fend off the mistborn.

All around George, the Imperials were scattering into pockets of resistance. The shouts were muffled and the mistborn surged forward. Dirt and mist, blood and mist, everything was becoming laced with the mist. Scared Imperial eyes looked at George, and he could only look back.

"You see," a voice George had never heard before seeped into his mind and he could feel his body turn even colder, almost inert. "Those who defy uniformity and order bring only conflict. Your struggle causes pain, and causes death. Give in, give in to peace, give in to order. Do not struggle any more, relax, and let yourself become pacified. Every breath spent on defiance is a breath spent in vain. Give in, it shall bring serenity."

George could feel his body relaxing, his lungs were slowing down and his head was turning blank. He knew the words were bullshit. He had heard it all by now and he wasn't about to just let the mist pacify him in the middle of battle; there was too much left to do in this world. The emperor could feel his smokeform somewhere, it just needed a push to get through the mist—just one push.

A pair of amber eyes appeared in George's mind and Opane's voice filled his head, "I'm back."

There was a loud bang and a blast of ice exploded beside George, obliterating the champion mistborn that had captured him and releasing him from the cloud. His smokeform reignited and his hair shocked white. Immediately the oddities of pacification were ripped from his mind, discarded as flimsy falsehoods. George sucked in a large breath of air and turned to see a great force coming in from the west and flanking the mistborn. Giants, Yabban, Kafshe, Ulmi—they were all swarming the mistborn and at their head was the tallest giant George had ever seen, his shoulders draped in a chieftain's cloak. Atop the giant's shoulder stood a man in black with the wide brimmed hat of a farmer. Though his face was scarred, George knew those eyes.

"Fenric?"

Turning still, George could see Opane helping Williams. An Ulmi was stopping the bleeding of the man on the ground while three others assisted Darius in pushing back the mistborn forces. Achians, straight from the mountains, were there, boosting his own infantry. George's brow ruffled in confusion and he drooped his shoulders, all of Jerrovia and beyond were here. The mistborn were being beaten.

George sucked in a breath,he would do his part. He kicked off his back foot and like a clap of thunder, slammed right back into the fray. Another elite appeared in his sights, and before the whip could even snap, George blasted by and landed behind the mistborn. George landed with a bang and the wind snapped by a second later. Bits of blue littered Oathkith and in confusion, the elite burst into pieces. The emperor caved the ground with a kick of his feet and this time, he landed on Ai.

The coat of the beast of war bled perfect red and with wild eyes, George the Smokeform and Ai the Crimson exploded into the enemy. Ai landed each hoof like an anvil and with every gallop the world shook and the ground cratered. George was a god of war, Oathkith slamming through mistborn as if it were a hammer. The emperor's horde followed his lead, bloated with reinforcements. Jerrovia had found her footing and the enemy crumbled.

***

George's army stood victorious alongside Fenric's. Cracked crystal and discarded mistborn weapons were scattered among heaps of the dead. Despite the victory, a lot of soldiers lay still and bloody. Already, auxiliaries were walking shrouds over those that could feasibly be brought back for burial. Those who met a more gruesome end were buried on the spot, or at least what was found of them. It wasn't just the Imperial soldiers, but giants, Ulmi, Acians, Yagan and more laid on the battleground, to say nothing of the now extinct sages whose bodies were long since trampled by the fighting.

It was a macabre scene, flitted with sadness and grief, though hope was beginning to grow. Even still, there wasn't much rush from the victory and as George stood amid the fallen, staring right into Fenric's eyes, the two nemesis shared a somber silence. George was cut up from the battle, his muscles sore and bruised, but Fenric looked a million times worse. His old nemesis was a lot more beat up since he last saw him, with a missing right arm, terribly scarred face, and a dark frown. He was wearing a tattered cloak and a farmers hat, which did its best to hide his features. Distinctly, George noticed there was no sword on his hip and no smoke was slipping from his lips, not even during the battle.

"I thought you were dead," George started.

Fenric's voice was devoid of the arrogance the emperor once knew, "Me too."

"I didn't see any smoke-screaming."

"And you won't," Fenric said, "not anymore."

George looked down at the battle scarred ground. "How did you gather an army?"

"A titan, a lot of promises, and a lot of favors, but mostly," Fenric looked up at George, "mostly, they wanted to help you. I was just a vehicle."

"Me?"

"The Ulmi know about your push to secure their borders, the Giants too. The Kafshe and the Yagan are indebted to you, and the Achians have heard about your exploits and the danger the world is in. It seems their love of you outweighed everyone's hate for me." Fenric fell onto his ass, kicking up dust as he sat on the ground. He looked up at George. "I did my part. I ask you to make my end quick." He turned his head, showing his neck.

George's eyes were wide. This was his nemesis. The man who killed Franklin, who let so many lives die, who aided the

Dweller, who aided Esmachus, who destroyed the North, corrupted the Ulmi, and committed countless sins against the Empire. This was Fenric, the man who was now sitting in the dust, not a glint of nobility in his face. Now he was asking for death, as if George didn't already break Hilda's tear stricken request not to kill her son once. George couldn't help but feel angry. He raised his sword hand.

With a clap, George slapped Fenric across the face, sending the man over onto his back.

"Ow! What the?"

George offered the same hand to Fenric. "Take my hand and get the void up. You may think you've been humbled, but you're arrogant to think you're done with your penance so soon. Hilda is worried sick about you and we have a Dweller to defeat."

Fenric looked at George's hand with hesitation, wincing as if it was causing him pain. "You'd... take me?"

George closed his eyes, not believing his own words. "Yes, just don't grant me any more regret."

Fenric reached up with his left hand and grabbed George's. George could feel Fenric's weight as he hoisted himself up; the man was little more than bones at this point. Now standing, they shared a long look and George couldn't help but think that he was looking at someone else; the Fenric on the tower must have died after all, because this wasn't him.

Chapter 28

Reunion

A silvery dusk chilled the forest garrison. Countless tents were erected around the fort, with people of many different origins and histories intermingling. Commander Maelinn and her troops had made it back safely, as did George. He couldn't help but notice the somber attitude of the camp. A lot of lives were lost, and yet there was also a lining of hope. They were closer to victory than they were yesterday.

As George walked the alleys of the tents, his eyes bounced from group to group. Soldiers were sharpening weapons, hammering out dents in plate, and mending mail. Fletchers were putting the final touches on arrows and medical tents were tending to the survivors. Even in victory, he felt hollow, almost guilty. All these faces and all these souls were counting on him. Before it was just Imperials, but now there was a face for every culture that Jerrovia served.

"Quite the sight, huh?" Rosaline appeared by George's side.

George nodded. "I never even thought to think that I'd see a day where all these people worked together."

"I always hoped for it," Rosaline idled. She turned to the man and with a rare look of nervousness found her face. "Hey, want to go rest somewhere quiet?"

***

"A lot has been weighing on your mind, huh?" It was dusk and Rosaline was sitting in the grassy nook that George had found earlier. There, the sounds of the camp were muffled ever so slightly. George was laying with his head on Rosaline's lap, staring up at her face and the broken sky of warped stars and void beyond. He cracked a smile at her comment.

"Is my head that heavy?"

"No more than usual." She gave his forehead a poke. Rosalione's voice was light, but her eyes still seemed anxious about something.

George probed. "How are you doing?"

Rosaline bobbed her head in thought. "I remember being a pacifist, I remember giving that up to help end a conflict. I don't regret it. I think I'd do this again and again if it meant peace and safety for everyone." Her lips pursed. "But I also hate it. Normally, I'd just spout some Tagist liturgy or lesson to make myself feel better, but that just makes it worse right now." Her jaw tightened. "I'm going to ask Freg about the Iacine church; and I know Cassandra has Clement's book. I think she is at chess with Reginald, but I intend on paying a visit after."

George regarded her from her lap. "You sound determined."

Rosaline looked down at him. "Well, it's important to me, and if it's important to me, I'm sure some others might care to see what the church looked like before it was corrupted."

"I think that's a good idea," George agreed. He watched her face in silence and while her determination bled back behind her eyes, that same nervousness rebounded. George knit his brow and in an attempt at humor he flicked his eyes past her chin to the apocalyptic sky above. A star or two still blinked. "Hey is that the falcon!"

Rosaline's serious face melted into a teasing one "Where!?" She mocked. George rolled his eyes and gave a smug look.

"I guess some of us are just better at constellations than others."

"Oh yeah..." Rosaline shared in his eye rolling. The two fell into a companionable silence, the buzzing of the camp and the rare chirp of crickets taking over.

As George laid there, he couldn't help but think about Rosaline—how she appeared when he needed her the most when he had first met her, and how she was always there since. She never left his side, even when they weren't next to each other, he could feel her; he knew she was there for him. Every desire inside of him echoed that care and compassion, wanting to be the same for her, especially now with the world being flipped upside down.

"George?"

He was pulled from his thoughts. "Hm?" He refocused on her face. She was looking down at him, right into his eyes. If she was nervous before, now she was a near mess. Her cheeks were burned dark and her voice shook a little.

George sat up. "What..." But before he could say "is wrong" Rosaline cut him off.

"Will you marry me?" Immediately her nervousness drained from her face, as if there was no returning from what she had done.

Surprised, George sucked in a breath too quickly and coughed on his own spit. Choking, he sat up. Rosaline slapped her hand against his back. All semblance of unease was gone as she returned to her usual self. "Wow, geez, alright."

"No! No, that's not it," George pushed with a hoarse voice. "I was just surprised."

They now sat face to face, a little bit of tears watering George's face from the coughing fit. Rosaline was giving him a funny look, clearly trying not to laugh at him. "So?" She said, "what do you think? After the war, of course."

"I think, yes," George said. A brilliant smile curved on Rosaline's face. They leaned closer and George placed a kiss on her forehead.

"I don't mean to interrupt." A familiar voice called out from the secret entrance to the little nook. Both George and Rosaline nearly jumped out of their skin and spun backwards to look at the intruder. George's eyes fell on his uncle's face, weathered and tan. Uncle Caleb stood there in a wax cloak and a friendly smile on a serious face. "But I'm in need of the emperor."

***

The entire garrison had exploded into a buzz of rumors and energy, even more than before. George, Rosaline and Caleb were walking quickly through the camps towards the main keep, while a crowd of leaders formed behind them, from Darius to Freg to Catherine to Fenric.

"I can hardly believe it," George remarked, looking up at his cousin Catherine's boat, now somehow impaled on the tallest tower of the keep. Caleb grunted.

"If you can't, imagine being the one who was on the boat when it happened."

Freg's voice boomed into the conversation. "The Sondoper find no barriers when it comes to time and space, I am not surprised if you did indeed meet one, that they would bring you home in such a way, Hinan."

Caleb regarded the Harnian for a moment, at a loss for words before looking at his nephew. "Is that the horned prophet?"

"Yep."

"Void. You've been as busy as me."

Catherine raised her brow at that. "Hard to believe, but, well, let's just say I didn't expect to return home to this—oh no."

George's eyes flickered to where his older cousin was looking to see Isabella marching towards the ensemble. Despite the atmosphere and company, she was still in fine clothes, of which George had no idea where she got them from, and wore a fake smile over a frustrated face.

"Was no one going to tell me my sister was here, let alone Caleb!?" Isabella's smile strained at the group, and her eyes jumped between the attendees. "My my, is it meeting time?"

"Yes," George took initiative. "It's time to set the details of our counterassault." Isabella gave George a surprised look, clearly taken aback by him taking control of the situation. Maybe it was because his uncle was next to him, or maybe it was because she wasn't used to an emperor with a voice. George pushed the thought aside. "Well, come on."

"Very well, your highness," Isabella gave George a nod before sharing an approving glance with Caleb.

The young emperor continued his march, Isabella falling back to bicker with Catherine. Williams sped up to walk next to George, and the two friends shared an acknowledging look. Flaretongue was strapped to Williams' belt, he was ready for his revenge. George put his hand on the pommel of Oathkith, only for it to slide off and land on the pommel of the sword of Sosolam. It was warm, and a gentle pulse rhythmically beat through it, as if it had a heart.

As the group reached the keep, the shadow of the building cast them from the glow of the broken moon and sunk them deeper into the chill of the summer night. George lifted his hand from the sword to reach for the keep doors and with a heavy push, he opened the way for his fellows.

***

The group of leaders and commanders was too big for the storeroom and after some quick orders from General Tamara, the foyer of the keep was evacuated for the meeting. Guards were posted around the doors and windows to keep eavesdroppers as far away as possible, although with the host gathered in the hall, George knew it was an exercise in futility. There were so many names surrounding George, and not all were close friends and some even old enemies. With such a group, George stood in front of a seated mess of chatter and debate, Caleb a step behind him.

"The time has come," George said, his voice loud and above the cacophony below. A hush fell on the host of leaders. "The time has come to plan our retaking of the Imperial Capital, the destruction of the Dweller, and revitalization of our collective lands from the invaders from the void. I know you have all come for different reasons and from different places, but know that we will work together and in unison to complete this goal, for the sake of a united and harmonious Jerrovia. Let this struggle be the birth of a new friendship among the many people who call this land home." The faces that looked at him were steeled and approving, from the towering giants to the large-eyed Yabban. "Now, let us discuss." George took a seat, those not seated doing the same.

"The defeat of the enemy forces lies in the defeat of the Dweller," George continued from his seated position. "And to do that, we need to recapture the Imperial Capital. Following the Dweller's defeat, her invaders will lose cohesion. This emergence war and its end lies solely in the battle for the capital."

The Imperials easily agreed, but a hesitation was on the faces of the others. Opane sat with the Yabban and looked around the room before speaking up. "On my respect as Kafshe, I stand with George. He has proven himself a friend to the Kafshe and the Yabban and I do not see his words as misleading." The Yabban host murmured their agreement.

"We marched this far south for a reason," Fenric said in turn, "we knew we came to seek out the cause of the emergent enemy and to destroy their leader. Don't let history get in the way of victory." The man looked at George and gave him a nod.

"The Titan-Spoken is right," a giant who was tattooed in sacred runes boomed. He wore the necklace of a chieftain. "This is for our homeland and a chance at a new golden age."

Another giant sat up straight. Similar to the giant before, this one wore the necklace of a chieftain but on top of that, his long golden hair was bundled in bands of silver. George couldn't help but see a striking and perhaps scarily similar resemblance to Galmun in isr face. "Beyond this, it is our duty to seek justice for the division and factionalization the mist bringers have brought to our people. If the Imperial Dweller is the leader of those forces, then I say let us bring her down."

"We have to do this," A stone-skinned Achian agreed. "We don't have any choice. It's to work together or be destroyed." Her final words were aimed at the other Achians, who sat stoic and in silence. Their host was small, and they dressed in simple furs and had belts adorned with stone knives and wedges. Their faces were stony, wrinkled, and almost devoid of any emotion beyond unamused. Their breathing was shallow, so their chests barely moved, making them look more like old statues than people, save for their burning amber eyes. Finally, one of them spoke and his voice felt like winter, cold and harsh.

"The people of the peaks will assist in the fight but in return we expect negotiations of a border with the Emperor, once he is coronated."

"We assume the same," an Ulmi king threw in.

Older Imperials looked at George with hesitation. It was no secret that the Empire had always put forth that it had sole authority and regency over all of Jerrovia, from the peaks of the Acians to the snow-covered Arctic, and it was no secret that plenty of Imperials still held fast to this idea, reinforced from the era of Emperor Frederick. George knew this, but he also knew he wasn't his grandfather, and that if there was to be peace, social reforms were not only required but the right thing to do. He gave a heavy nod. "As Emperor of the Jerrovian empire, I agree to these talks."

"Great," General Tamara said almost dismissively, "now that the fun part is all said and done, let's actually construct our strategy."

Asharah spoke first. "Has there been any contact with the Stenlings of Alconia?"

"Sadly no," George answered, "contact with the eastern provinces has been severed by the capture of the Imperial Capital."

"Might I request we attempt to send messengers there? If we could coordinate our assault with their own from the East, it could prove to be key to victory."

"I don't disagree," Commander Darius said, "but I'm not sure it would be wise to divert resources to trying, not with the way blocked by enemy encampment. Any messengers would be captured as soon as they tried to cross through the Imperial Province."

"What if they skirted the province by going through the foothills of the Achian mountains?" Commander Maelinn sat up. She then looked at the Achians present.

The Achian who spoke earlier gave Maelinn a long and tired look. "Even for the people of the mountain, traversing the slopes is a dangerous undertaking and must be approached with deep respect and care."

Hector raised a hand and all eyes shifted to him. "With due respect, it might be worth attempting. If the messengers should succeed, we would potentially have a great boon to aid us in the fight. But please, you and your people are the best suited for such a task."

"Very well," the Achian sat back.

"Thank you." George looked at Tamara. "Though we can't put all our hopes on one variable. We have to plan as if no help from the East will come."

Caleb nodded along. "I agree. What do we know about their battle capabilities on the sea? Using the docks and shore as a way into the city might prove useful if combined with a ground invasion. The Imperial Province utilized an active navy to fight piracy, and the city hadn't been a target of aggression in hundreds of years, the sea way is relatively undefended."

"You'd think," Hector scoffed, "but the enemy has these great organ beasts that spew fireballs. They nearly sank our escape boats."

"Other than that?" Caleb pushed.

The room was silent. Hector spoke again. "That's all we saw as we left the city, no real notice of a marine force."

It was starting to sink into George exactly what city they were discussing invading: his home. He closed his eyes, picturing it, but all he could see was how it was when he left. In peace, intact, his father waiting for him. The palace stood tall on its hill overlooking the city, the winding road, the decorated walls, the gatehouse, and how it never closed, with the lifeblood of the roads—the merchants—always flooding through. George's memories churned and he focused on the gatehouses; there were two to the west and two to the east, but none of the four were close to the docks as there wasn't much point in having a gatehouse near a place traversed by water. If he were the enemy, he would put the fireball creating organ beasts behind that wall to guard the waterways and even rain destruction over the walls, meaning to get to them to open up an amphibious assault would require taking a gatehouse and fighting through the city in the opposite direction of the palace just to assault the organ beasts... unless.

George opened his eyes and adjusted his ears to the chatter of the room. "If we can destroy the organ beasts, do you believe we could land boats?"

"I think so," Hector answered.

Nodding, George continued, "then we have to break through the Imperial wall. Attempting to capture a gatehouse is asking to be destroyed by targeted fire, those structures were made to hold the capital at all costs."

Commander Darius seemed to pull himself from a thought. "Why don't we send a false assault to a gatehouse, then another assault to the wall. The enemy has to meet both assaults even if they know we are feigning the first attack—because if they don't, and leave a token force in their defense we could apply pressure and potentially take the gate. We only need enough people to threaten that possibility."

"Even if they hold reserves." Commander Maelinn was looking up, as if watching Darius's plan play out. "We would at least be spreading their forces out along the wall, opening the way for an amphibious attack from their flank."

"Not to be the sourpuss of the group, dears," Isabella piped up from the comfiest seat in the hall. "But that's assuming we *can* break the wall."

"We can," it was Caleb's turn to speak. With a small flourish he produced a leatherbound book from his cloak. It was wrinkled and old. "Mondaral of the Sondoper has gifted us this book. Inside it are the secrets of IAO, including his wallkneel technique." The Imperial's eyes drifted over to Hector. "I believe the Stromist Marshal should be able to replicate these forms and bring down the walls."

Swallowing, and clearly unsure, Hector gave a curt nod. He reached for the book and after Caleb showed him the appropriate pages, he nodded again. "Give me enough time to meditate and I can try, but I'd prefer it if we have back up ideas."

"What about you?" Catherine pointed to Freg, "You're big, why don't you help out?"

Freg snorted, as if amused. "This is a battle that I cannot help you with, Hinan. I cannot take this experience away from you, if not for you all now, than for the consequences of the far future."

With a frown, Catherine answered, "Fine," before looking back at George.

The emperor's eyes went out to the rest of the crowd. Fenric stirred before sitting up. His voice was low, as if not confident in his own words, "If Hector can't find a way through the wall, why not use the height of the giants to get us over it? They can carry ladders fit for humans and Kafshe in a fraction of the time."

The chieftain who reminded George of Galmun chortled. "Easily."

Fenric sank back into his seat, and let his hat shadow his face. "And don't forget that some of your better Stromists can probably make quick work of scaling the wall face."

"Those are good contingency plans," Caleb agreed, "and likely what we should plan for. I don't know exactly what you expect Hector to do by himself, though I also know better than to underestimate a Stromist Marshal."

"I'll be more than happy to help with the amphibious assault," Catherine said. She gave a crooked smile. "But, um, I'm going to go out on a limb here and guess a forest garrison doesn't have any boats."

General Tamara looked at the Yabban and then at Catherine. "It has... trees."

The Yabban shaman from Lor Kabblest's village started to speak in kafshe and Lor translated. "We will mark the trees by the Yakarrin river to the south suitable for ships. The current and depth of the water should be sufficient to move the boats to the sea. We only ask that the felling does not leave that area."

"I'll send some Auxiliaries to aid in the marking," General Tamara insisted. "This is no time to be reserved."

Dame Honora finally spoke up, "if that's the case, I'll make the necessary arrangements. Might I also suggest that Commander Baldra oversee the security of the operation with an escort? We do not know if any covert enemies lurk around us."

Baldra nodded. "I think that's a good idea."

"It sounds like we have a plan, then," Honora continued, "everything else to discuss would be logistical."

"Indeed." General Tamara looked to George, who nodded in return.

"This operation will require our utmost cohesiveness. I sincerely thank each and every one of you in advance and pray to whatever forces truly look after our cosmic health that when it comes to an end, I get the chance to thank every one of you again and again." George turned to his Uncle. The two shared a look and at that moment George could see that Caleb was no longer looking at him with the coddling eyes of an older family member, but with a bright respect, and a glimmer of pride. They nodded at each other and Caleb gave a reassuring grin.

Chapter 29
Beginning of the End

Finding a quiet spot anywhere near the forest garrison and its city of tents was next to impossible, yet with the invasion creeping ever closer, George had to find a place to rest his racing mind. Amid the canopies just outside the limit of the camps, George found a glade of emerald leaves, mossy beds and shafts of golden light. A babbling brook gurgled through, hidden by ground brush and harmonizing with the song of summer birds. It was there George knew Hector had decided to undertake his weeks-long meditation and so George assumed it was there he could find peace in his own meditation.

The Stromist marshal was deep in a trance below one of the mighty oak trees, legs folded together and hands tucked into his lap. His head was bowed towards the hidden brook in front of him and his body was completely still. Sensitive to the flow of the smoke and the mist surging through life itself as well as the altars of creation that littered the world, George could feel Hector's here. It was massive and completely still, with each would-be wave of smoke and each tide of mist stilled to complete balance. George could feel the power Hector was storing up for his task.

Finding a suitable mat of moss for himself to sit on, George did his best to get comfortable in silence so as to not disturb his friend. He wriggled into place and folded his legs only to have Oathkith snag the ground and prod his rib, the Sword of Prax and the Shard following suit. He rolled his eyes and undid his sword belt, laying the weapons across his lap. The dagger stole his attention.

George looked down at the weapon that had sacrificed his sister and ultimately his father. Perhaps he didn't need to keep such a thing on his belt. The emperor let out a long sigh and decided that after his meditation, he would lock it away in the garrison until after the battle. Looking at the shard, though, only reminded George why his mind was so furiously racing. His own time on Jerrovia was coming to an end.

His head thumped against a tree trunk behind him, and George stared blankly up at the canopies. His own life would have to be sacrificed for the people of Jerrovia; the Achians won't have an emperor to talk to, nor the Ulmi. A hot tear streaked down his cheek, Rosaline won't get her wedding, her husband, at least not from him. She had said they would find another way, but as it stood, George knew he had to be ready to make the ultimate sacrifice and yet he couldn't help but curse his fate at that moment.

Since the beginning, his fate had been that of a tool. To be used and then discarded. The errant boy to the pawn of war, to an ingredient of a greater ritual. Through the machinations of others beyond his own hands, he lost his mother, his childhood, his dreams, his peace, his friends. George's hand reached up to trace the bumpy scar on his cheek. He lost his ability to relax, his sister, and his father and he was still expected to give. Another hot tear ran down his face.

George closed his eyes, feeling the chaotic smoke in his chest. He also gained a lot from his journey, he couldn't deny that. A cool rain to quell the fires of pain. He had gained friends from every corner of the world, found an everlasting love, delved deep into the cosmos of his existence and pulled back the ability to make sure no one would have to suffer as he did. He gained the ability to make sure others could be safe. He found his name, and in his painful journey, he found his life. So many faces, so many hearts, so many laughs and so many grins even in the middle of the storms. His fingers clenched as his altar was balanced, no matter what had happened in the past, it was up to him to step forward out of the dusk and into the dawn. George opened his eyes, even if this dawn might be his last.

A hot breath tousled George's hair, snapping the man back to reality. Looking to his left, George was face to face with Ai. The old mare gave his face a hearty sniff. A smile broke across George's face before he quickly looked over to Hector, the marshal seemingly undisturbed. The Emperor put a happy hand on Ai's muzzle. "Did you come to check up on me?" he whispered.

"She did," Williams whispered back, making George jump. His best friend was hiding behind a set of trees. The knight revealed himself. George gave him a look that Williams answered, "I was watching over Josephine when I saw Ai through the window, she seemed troubled, as if she knew you were crying."

George let out a single chuckle and rubbed his forearm against the tear stains on his face. "Yeah, well, you try not to cry after all of this."

Williams shook his head. "I've been crying too." The knight looked over at Hector. "Let's leave Hector be."

George nodded and stood up. "Sure, hey, where is Rosaline?"

Putting a hand on George's shoulder and starting his walk out of the glade with Ai in tow, Williams shrugged. "She went to go check up on the boats with Baldra."

***

The distant call of seabirds mixed with the perfume of the forest, creating a concoction that pleased both the love of the ocean and appreciation of the gentle forest. Rosaline let the scents fill her nostrils as she walked along the river bed with Baldra, the hammering of boats and the sawing of wood putting a third mask over the scene. There was something that Rosaline enjoyed about the smell of cut wood, but there was nothing she was enjoying at the moment. Her brow was furrowed with worry, matching the stress on the face of the Yabban and Imperial workers as well as the concern on Baldra's face. The only difference was that Rosaline wasn't thinking about the boats.

"You're quiet," Baldra said, forcing Rosaline to look her way. She gave her old friend a short apologetic smile.

"I'm sorry, a lot's on my mind."

Baldra waved a hand as they passed a group of black tunics sanding down freshly cut planks and boiling pitch. "I get it, but I have faith in our plan. We will take back the capital."

Rosaline looked down at the smooth stones of the bank and frowned. "I agree."

"Then why so glum?"

She looked up at Baldra. "If I tell you, you have to keep it a secret." The soldier considered her words for a moment. Rosaline bunched her brow. "Forget it, that might be too much to ask."

"No, no!" Baldra resigned. "I'll keep it a secret."

"Swear to it?"

"I swear to it."

"Do you think it's weird we are fighting the Dweller, or even the Graces?"

Baldra looked her over. "How is that a secret?"

"Please just answer," Rosaline said defeated.

"Well, yeah, but it's clear that this *is* what we are doing. We can't deny the supernatural elements and as whiplash as it is to fight the Graces on top of the Dweller, I guess it's true I always found the Sages to be dodgy."

Rosaline looked up at Baldra and stopped walking. "So you have no doubts about this?"

"George said it," Baldra answered, "he knows what he is talking about."

A pale crept over Rosaline's face. "I know, and I agree... which is why I'm worried."

"Is this the secret?"

A silent couple of nods.

Baldra tucked a frown into her cheek. "Well, I'm here to listen."

"I asked George to marry me after the war."

"That's great!" Baldra's grin did not match the mood.

"It is..." Rosaline admitted, "and don't get me wrong, he agreed... but I'm worried."

"Hm?"

"I'm worried that he..." Her tongue snagged on her words. She frowned. "I'm worried he won't come back from the fight. I guess I asked him to marry me because a piece of me felt like it was a promise not even fate could break, but—"

"Wait." Baldra shook her head. "Fate? Not coming back? What's this all about?"

They shared a glance and Rosaline sighed. She didn't want to say it, as if saying it outloud made it more true than it already was. "George told me that in order to save Jerrovia, after defeating the

Dweller, he will have to sacrifice himself to end the invasion and bring Jerrovia to its rightful place in Ampexida."

"Ampexida..." Baldra thought to herself. "I was debriefed on the stories... and I guess I've always been a believer in the strange, and on top of it I have no reason not to believe George—" Baldra froze, staring silently at Rosaline. A heat was behind Rosaline's eyes that she didn't notice until Baldra called attention to it. The heroine squeezed her eyes shut.

"I'm okay Baldra, it's just hard to hear someone else talk about all of this crazy stuff. It makes it seem less crazy and the sacrifice more real. I just don't want to lose him."

Rosaline opened her eyes to watch Baldra's face grow soft and sad. She nodded. "Trust me, I know what it's like to lose someone and I wouldn't want to see you go through that. I live with a certain regret in my heart... so I'll do everything I can to make sure George sticks around, even if it's not much. I'd take his place as a sacrifice, even. Void, I'll already be by his side as the regulars' commander during the seige, I'll be right there for him!"

"You're a good friend." Rosaline put her hand on Baldra's arm. "But neither me or George would ever ask you to do that."

Baldra gave an acknowledging nod and continued her walk along the bank with Rosaline, the two sinking back into the ambience of woodworking and hammering. Obviously the worry wasn't suddenly gone from Rosaline's mind, she recognized that, but she also didn't know what else to say about it. It was terrible to think about and it left a sore in her heart. Even if it hadn't been so long, she couldn't imagine her life without George, the veritable goof. Rosaline found her smile.

"I struggle to follow a lot of this," Baldra said suddenly.

"I did too," Rosaline agreed. "But to be honest with you, it's sort of given me a purpose, even after the war."

"A purpose?"

"Yeah." Rosaline was resolute. "I'm going to reform the Tagist church." She said it so easily, she said it like she was even an authority on it. Baldra stared at her with wide eyes, but instead of judging her, Baldra found a soft grin.

"It's about damn time someone tried. The thing was unrecognizable as a church even before this mess. I suppose every organization is doomed to corruption."

Rosaline replied, "it doesn't help that in this particular case, it was a corrupted form of the Iacine Church."

"Iacine? What's that?" Baldra gave a quizzical look, but before Rosaline could answer, a shout came from behind them. They spun around, minds tossed back into the moment. A humanoid twisted with the taint and covered in black metallic sores and oozing boils of smoke had appeared from the tree-line. They held a jagged sword of alien metal, now shoved roughly through the back of a gasping auxiliary and by time the scene registered, a small ambush of the tainted creatures came barreling out of the woods.

"How'd they get this far unnoticed!?" Baldra barked, his sword ripping free from its scabbard. Rosaline mirrored the action, wielding her sword, Peacemaker. She stared down the tip of her blade, right at a charging enemy. It was uncanny, the human-like face and the open mouth, as if it were screaming and yet only a harsh hissing sound could be heard. One, two — Rosaline slapped the enemy weapon away and flicked Peacemaker across their neck, splitting it wide open and felling the enemy. More were coming, and the auxiliaries were now fighting back with whatever they had on hand, be it hammer or chisel. Shouts of 'Yabbadai!' cleared the birds from the trees as the Yabban joined the fray, utilizing a fierce and wild style against the creatures of chaos. Rosaline's attention was brought back to bear.

One, two, three; Rosaline counted her motions as the enemy closed in. One, a parry, propping the sword up. Two, a thrust from Peacemaker through the rib and into the heart. Three, a juke to the side away from another enemy's swing and a short, cutting riposte to the neck.

Another enemy came running in, swinging a brutal war cleaver. Rosaline's eyes bounced over their form. Four, sweep the legs with a cut. Five, a sturdy knee to the face as they go down. Six, coup de grace.

Rosaline yanked her black stained blade from the corpse and spun around, meeting Baldra's eyes for a moment. Baldra gave her a nod before diving back into the fray, but no sooner than she engaged the enemy, two jumped Baldra from the side. A jagged sword punched into Baldra's side and pain flashed over her face. Rosaline's eyes widened, and her adrenaline pushed her towards her friend.

Fighting through the pain, Baldra drove her sword into the enemy in front of him and threw her free arm back to elbow the stabbing assailant off of him. Rosaline cut in, sending Peacemaker down in a deadly arc and severing the arm of the assailant, leaving the sword firmly and now freely stuck in Baldra.

"Leave it!" Rosaline commanded before slashing at the final assailant. The enemy parried their blade, but Rosaline was quick and she grabbed the sharp edge of her sword as it bounced back and in one fluid motion, flipped the sword around and sent the crossguard into the temple of the enemy with a loud crack. The tainted creature hit the ground just as the rest of the ambush was being cleared.

Rosaline whipped back around to Baldra, sweat dripping off her brow. The ex-medic's keen eyes focused on Baldra's wound and she let a breath snake through her teeth, the rage of battle escaping her blood. Another breath and she nodded at Baldra, sheathing Peacemaker. "I don't think you're going to any sieges anytime soon."

Baldra looked up and groaned through the pain. She lifted his hand from the wound, showing a stain of red. "It's not that deep, the maille is keeping the sword up." Rosaline gave her a look and leaned in to observe her wound.

"How are you standing?" She chastised. "Your rib is broken. Come on, let me close you up and get you back to camp for proper setting."

"Rib?" Baldra croaked, "But the siege."

Rosaline had her hand pressed against the wound as she thought. Without looking up from the laceration, she said, "Don't worry about it, I'll be there for George."

***

"They did it, they killed the graces," A soldier said with wide eyes. He wore the filigree of the 10th and sat wounded on a bench outside the keep. Maelinn sat next to him with her hands folded and Tagist prayer beads between her fingers. Her eyes were as much in disbelief as the soldiers.

"We did," she said.

"Philosophy before a siege? Save that for the aftermath," A haughty voice trilled. Maelinn and the soldier looked to their right in sync. Isabella was standing against the chaotic sky, an impossibly clean dress clinging to her form and a fan in her fingers. She looked less perturbed by the apocalypse than any sane person should be.

Maelinn sputtered for a moment. "Duchess Heinrich."

Isabella cocked a brow and gave the commander a sidelong glance before fanning herself. The three of them remained in an uncomfortable silence long enough for Isabella to comment on something completely different. "Seems the sun doesn't mind the broken sky." Her eyes were towards the bruised sunset.

"We killed the gods of Jerrovia," Maelinn finally said, "Duchess, we... we... killed order."

"Pah," Isabella dismissed. "We *defeated* the Graces, who were simply masquerading as gods. I know he is rather droll, but listen to my cousin a little closer next time." Her fan snapped, not a concern on Isabella's face. "And don't cloud your mind before the big day. Your empire needs you."

"But—"

Isabella's glare came blazing down at the two, shutting them up. "Perhaps I need to remind you that your beloved traitors destroyed Jerrovian lives? No order was lost when we bit back, it was gained." She turned her nose up and gave a dramatic twirl from the conversation, declaring it over. "I'll see you at the palace, dears."

***

Dusk cast its veil over the forest garrison and the final night before mobilization was upon the denizens of the refuge. The camp was noisy, but somehow quieter than the last few nights with a hush of anticipation in every action. Between the anxiety of the impending battle and a rush of thoughts, not everyone was asleep when they should have been. Tomko was no exception, except it wasn't the battle that kept him awake.

Tomko walked the wooden passageways of the keep, his breath shallow and his stride quiet and sneaky. His vision was unique. It was sharper and more clear than the average humans' even in the dark of the night, an absolute epitome of vision engineering first pioneered by Stenmur so long ago. Even more impressive was Tomko's ability to see a small glinting path floating in the air. He had spent so many centuries with the shard of Prax, that the path it took was now as easy to pick apart as footprints in the sand. He followed the path until he came to a closed door.

The door was nothing special, with a rudimentary lock keeping it closed. Tomko gave it a single glance, mapping out every weakness in the design, right down to the composition of the metal. He gave it a sturdy tap and the mechanism opened with a click. Giving the door a gentle push, Tomko slipped into the dark room.

Another click and the door was closed behind him. Even with his eyes, the room was too dark to see, with not a window or a light to provide any relief. Despite that, Tomko knew where the shard was, the glittering path floating over a trunk. Tomko kneeled by the vessel and gripped the lip of the trunk, only to hear rattling chains. Letting a soft swear exit his lips, Tomko rubbed his fingers over the chains, finding their locks and latches. By human standards, the locks he found were quite expensive and elaborate, but to a Precursor; click.

Lifting the lid of the trunk, a soft shimmer bled through a simple cloth that bundled the shard of Prax. Without hesitating, Tomko grabbed the tool and stuffed it under his shirt. Not wanting to spend any more time in this room than he had, the Precursor put everything back as it was and jumped back to his feet to beeline for the door. With a fluid motion, he slipped back into the hall.

"Hello." The voice caused Tomko to jump. He stood in the dimly lit hall, eye to eye with the grim face of Fenric. A scar rode down Fenric's right cheek and a thick fur cloak draped over his shoulders, hiding his missing arm. There was a darkness in this man's eyes, a darkness that put a chill down Tomko's spine.

"Hello..." Tomko went to move past the man, but Fenric stepped in his way.

The Gavarian simply stared at Tomko, not a smile or a frown. "I wanted to talk to you, Precursor."

Tomko swallowed and let loose a steadying breath. Taking a stance that would minimize suspicion of holding something under his shirt, he nodded. "Fine, what is it?"

"You're a villain, did you know that?"

A sharp strike entered Tomko's gut and he felt a spurt of anger. "A villain? I've done nothing wrong!" Ignoring his currency thievery.

"Neither have I, really, but that in itself is the source of my evil," Fenric cracked a sinister grin. "I didn't stop my father's murder, I didn't stop the Dweller's plans, I certainly didn't aid the Imperials at Kors. I didn't do anything... not much of a defense, though, is it?" Fenric took a step closer, putting forth an oppressive wave of judgment. "You didn't do anything, either, did you? You ran away, created this environment, which in turn created me, and created this war. Nothing, that's our crime, isn't it?"

Tomko took a step back. "You're a human; a composite creation of the Dreamers and Disharmonic Precursors. Your kind were mere babies during the Cacophony—"

"And yet," Fenric cut the Precursor off, "here I am lecturing you. I'm not just a human, I'm a dredge of a human, a dirty rag of a man." Fenric stepped forward again. "And yet I seem to know something you don't know... or maybe you do." Fenric reached out with his left hand and placed a heavy poke into Tomko's stomach, pressing the shard against his skin. Fenric never broke his stare and his grin faded into a serious frown. "It's time for you to do something for once. We're both villains, and only a villain can set right their own wrongs." Fenric's hand pushed hard, knocking Tomko back a step and out of his way. With little else, Fenric floated past the Precursor, the wind off his cloak slapping Tomko in the face. Tomko stood there stunned, watching the broken man disappear back into the shadows of the halls.

Chapter 30

The Capital City

The day of battle had finally come. The garrison and its connected armies emptied the fort before the sun even rose and began their trek across the farmland of the Imperial Province. The march was eerie if not uneventful. The once bustling farmlands and villages that dotted the exterior of the province were ghost towns, with a haze of smoke collecting along the ground. It was clear the misttalkers had lost the province to the Dweller and her tainted beings, leaving George and the remnants of the Imperial forces as the sole antagonist of her whims. There still was no word from the Achians and if they ever got into contact with Alconia, let alone any word from the Caldoran Duke in Gavaria, but by Fenric's account, the northern provinces already had their hands full.

Regardless of the empty atmosphere, no enemies appeared to stop them. The march was secure and quiet, which was not unexpected with the enemy likely taking a defensive position. The Dweller knew well that she had the advantage of the walls and when those walls came into view over the horizon, with the central hill and palace towering over even those, the Imperials and their allies knew that the final battle was imminent. A dark halo of smoke swirled over the palace, and plumes of black piped from behind the walls, betraying the position of the mighty organ beasts. To the south, a sea breeze filtered northwards, reminding George and his soldiers that reinforcements were waiting patiently on the water. A roster of Jerrovia's most powerful heroes strengthened the ranks of the resistance army, putting a spark of hope in the chests of all who stared forward at the Imperial City.

***

War drums reverberated through the thick, smokey air. The steady beats matched Opane's own heart. Adrenaline rattled in her chest as she stared forward at the lingering wall of the Imperial City. She was detached with Hector and an army of Giants as well as some Kafshe and the Yabban. To the north, the assault on the gatehouse was already underway with General Tamara and George overseeing the battle alongside the majority of the regular troops. This strategy kept most of the enemy pinned to the defense of the gates. Down here, in spite of that, fresh and intimidating faces still peered at Opane and her allies from over the battlements of the wall. The stare down only started a few heartbeats ago, but the seasoned Kafshe knew all too well that true war was about to be let loose. Plumes of black smoke billowed from behind the walls and the groan of organ beasts matched the war drums.

Opane and her army marched towards the walls, stopping just outside of the range of any wall-mounted defenders. The air was thick between her and the walls, as if a shroud of knowing fear kept her and the giants at bay. Instincts were strong and they all knew that soon there would be no turning back. Beyond the groaning of organ beasts on the other side of the wall and the clatter of idle giants and battle-dressed Yabban, the sound of a wagon rumbled to the front of the line.

The wooden vehicle was walled and roofed with pounded sheets of metal. Instead of animals, a rather strong looking trio of giant pulled it over the scorched ground and loose stones. Opane walked beside the wagon and by throwing out her altar of creation, she could feel a great power inside. So many years of training had led Hector to his current mastery of his altar and now he sat shrouded, pulsing with gathered magic. She in turn looked to her left, towards Tennil, a large giant who Opane could only assume was somehow related to Galmun. Looking up at the red-painted face of the giant, Opane said, "Once Hector is ready, we'll begin the ladder rush. We have to do this quickly." Opane looked forward again, eyes squinting at the wisping smoke. "The enemy won't give us a lot of room to do this once let alone twice."

Tennil simply gave a nod of his head with a grim look of seriousness carved across his visage. He held a mighty sword in his hand, a legacy weapon of giant chieftains and looking along its impressive length, Opane saw the notch taken out of the metal, courtesy of Oathkith. The brutality of the weapon gave Opane a strange hope as she focused back on the wagon. This time the blade was not aimed at her and her allies.

The shift in energy was tangible and Opane's eyes widened with surprise as Hector pulled back the canvas of the wagon and hopped to the ground. As if someone dropped an anvil of lead, the ground shook with Hector's landing, his body impossibly heavy. The soldier's eyes were glowing gold and his dark skin was gilded with equally golden ribbons. He looked celestial in his armor, he looked powerful. A strict concentration was on his face, and Opane knew he was holding onto an immense amount of power. Opane didn't dare call out, no one did, as if they could break his inner focus. Tennil gave the Kafshe a look. "Ready?"

"Hold on..." Opane was studying Hector. "Wait for him to charge."

Inaudible, Hector mouthed something to himself, perhaps a prayer. Opane turned from the man and held up a hand, which in turn caused Yabban spread across the ranks to hold up flags. Opane held her breath and as the flags dropped, the front lines surged forward and Hector burst into a heavy run. Tennil gave a shout and Opane followed suit — the battle had begun.

The enemy didn't give them a second of silence as soon as they began their march. Blasts drowned out the drums of the march and pierced Opane's ears. Rumbles from behind the wall produced sickly flashes of light and the sky stained orange. Streaks of fire and smoke carved upwards into the black clouds and as the sky started to glow yellow and heat kissed Opane's cheeks, the composure of the march was lost. The drums were abandoned and the front lines started to run towards the walls rather than march, jagged and unorderly with ladders and javelins in hand.

They hadn't gotten a few steps before the fireballs started to rain back down to the ground. Explosions dotted the land between the reserves and the wall. Opane herself was running now, Tennil on her flank. Dirt and shards of rock erupted in plumes as the fiery assault shook the world around her. Sulfur and brimstone sucked into Opane's nostrils and if not for her affinity with the ice spirits, she wagered her lungs would be burning. Tennil didn't seem to fare well, and the giants holding the ladders slowed. With each burst, a scream, and uncounted injuries flew through the air and painted the scene red and wretched.

Atop the walls, a black metal machine of malice was grinding. Opane could see the creatures of the Dweller loading it with large javelins. Her eyes followed where it pointed and she caught her breath. Through the clouds and gore, a golden streak charged towards the walls. With each pounding step, Hector carved the way as a beacon. The machine fired and the bolt barely missed, slamming behind the hero and obliterating a line of Yabban warriors.

As Opane ran, she watched them start to reload and gritted her teeth. Without thinking about it further, she knew that if they lost Hector, they lost everything. "Tennil!" Opane shouted over the cry of battle. The huffing giant barely responded as his arm was readying a javelin. Opane shouted again. "Tennil! Throw me!"

Tennil didn't ask questions, she simply dropped her javelin and grabbed Opane with one hand, much like a doll. Opane pointed to the machine on the walls. "There!"

Tennil ran forward with all his strength, a fact that Opane could feel traveling through his grip and then with a shaking stomp and a powerful swing of Tennel's Stromism coated arm, Opane was hurled into the air, eyes dried against the rushing wind and the horror of battle below. Fireballs rained all around her and with a tug of her own magic, she summoned a great storm from within.

***

Wind and ash burned at Hector's eyes as he sprinted forward. His legs felt weightless, swollen with the golden feel of magic. All around him, dirt kicked and flames licked. Shockwaves from the explosions rippled through his chest and his vision was stained with negatives from the flashes. A great thunderous bang sounded as a black bolt slammed behind him. Hector gritted his teeth, doing his best to maintain concentration on the hum of Stromism. Even so, mentally he was counting down the time he had before another bolt would be launched.

As the numbers dwindled down in his mind and his legs pumped against the rocky ground, a ball of blue magic caught his attention. Instead of raining down on him and his allies, this one was rocketing upwards towards the walls. Hector's eyes widened, was that? He could make out Opane's frame as she passed overhead, enveloped in near white light, the air crackling around her. Her image only lasted a second before ramming into the wall and sending out a backwave of jagged frost. Blues and whites consumed the top of the wall and an intense freeze sliced through the heat and hit Hector's face. Not having enough time to see if Opane was alright, Hector continued his sprint, knowing there would be no more interruptions from the wall.

Even with the machines on the wall silenced, the organ beasts continued to send down their fury. Hector ran with a kafshe stranger to his side, the pair dodging rocks and debris being thrown into the air by the endless barrage of fireballs. Some of the rocks came close, too close to dodge. Angry blue light pulsed from the kafshe unknown whenever a rock came too close to the pair and a blast of lightning would knock it off course. All around Hector and his sprint, he watched the yellow of the fireballs fight with the blue of kafshe magic. He could hear the ground groaning as it broke, the growl of organ beasts and the screams of his unlucky comrades. Each sound imprinted on his heart beat and rang in his ears until his eyes finally zeroed in on the flat of the Imperial wall, so close, almost there.

The power Hector was nursing inside him burst forward and ran down his limbs. A golden glow entered the marshal's eyes and as he met the wall, he spoke a grinding word, "kneel."

A great crack of sound drowned out the explosions on the field and a shockwave stole the air from any lingering flames. Stone snapped. A sharp pain entered Hector's body and just when he felt his power dwindle, the world colored white. The ground shook as the walls crumbled around Hector, the marshal now on the other side of a craterous hole he had run through the structure. In front of him was an array of organ beasts and the blackened carcass that once was the docks of the Imperial City. A rush entered Hector's head and he fell to his knees, he felt his mind fading to black—he was passing out. Enemy soldiers were quickly threading between the mighty elephantine beasts, heading his way.

A missile of ice shot from behind Hector, followed by ten more and impaling some of the approaching enemy. Hector's vision fuzzed again. His head was bobbing to the ground, and only when Opane kneeled in front of him, looking over his face while the backs of his own troops rushed ahead of him, surging to fight the enemy, did Hector grin. He did his job. Opane was speaking to him, but her words were gurgled by his exhaustion. He did his job.

***

Rough waves bobbed Caleb's warship up and down. His eyes were steeled ahead while his troops waited by their oars. Sails were raised and anchors were set. The city was close enough to watch but far enough to be safe from enemy assault. Maelinn and the 10th were spread out across several more boats, making up the marine assault team. The Commander herself stood next to Caleb, with Catherine on the other side. Asharah was on another boat, helping to keep the small fleet in sync.

This far out from the city, the sea air had mixed with the oppressive smoke coming from the capital, giving the air a haunting fog that while merely a thin veil, made the less sea-worthy troops uncomfortable. The wind was quiet, leaving the empty atmosphere with muffled echoes from the battle on land. Pangs of distant explosions rippled by now and then, while sudden shouts or screams filled the interim. That was, until a great clapping shockwave sped across the ocean surface and pressed into Caleb's chest. His eyes widened as he witnessed a portion of the western wall burst inward and the fighting spill over. Slowly, the artillery of the organ beasts began to slow and understanding his cue, Caleb gave Maelinn a nod.

"Alright, soldiers!" Maelinn shouted to the onlooking faces, "We have an opening, but make it quick, the enemy will send reinforcements to the breach!"

"Ho-ah!" The anchors were raised and with a few mellow trumpet sounds, the fleet was moving forward as one, and at a water ripping speed. Golden ribbons spun around the rower's arms, pushing the boat faster than normal. Caleb stole a glance at Maelinn who looked back with a proud gleam, but a twitch in her eyes spoke that she knew as well as Caleb that they could only keep this pace up for so long, they needed to land, and then fight.

"With the wind blowing back to sea, and away from the city," Catherine said, as if reading their minds, "this is the best we can do without sails." She was chewing on her lip. "And void be damned if one of those fireballs makes it our way."

Caleb cracked a grin at that, causing Catherine to furrow her brow. "What?"

"You must be nervous," Caleb replied over the waves, "let's put some trust in our troops on the shore." He turned from his cousin to face forward and quietly removed his blade from its scabbard. Sword in hand, he watched the coast creep closer and closer, the screams of battle growing louder. Caleb knew what he said to Catherine, but he was just hiding his own anxiety.

The docks of the city were close enough in detail now. The rowers strained to keep the pace, and Caleb had to keep reminding himself to unclench his teeth. Along the docks and in between the rubbled buildings of the city, Caleb could make out the great organ beasts, a few marked by their ability to still fire. Great projectiles of flame erupted from their smoking pipes, only for the fire to splash down somewhere near the wall. Hector and the Giants seemed too pinned to get any further into the city from their breach. This marine assault was essential. Caleb's eyes started to dart around, as if calculating the avenues to entrap the enemy forces between his own and Hector's. If they could remove the organ beasts and fight further north enough to capture one of the wall towers, they could begin their takeover of the wall and open the city up to General Tamara's troops for the final assault.

"Prince Regent!" Maelinn suddenly called out and her gauntleted hands shoved Caleb forward. He was so trapped inside his own mind, he didn't notice the orange glow spreading across the sky. Maelinn tackled him to the deck of the ship with a rough thud, only for all the pain from such a fall to be overshadowed by an ear shattering explosion and sizzling heat. The boat sundered into flames and splinters of woods ricocheted everywhere, only to be swallowed by hissing sea water.

Chapter 31

Maelinn's Run

Salt. Salt and blood. The taste overwhelmed Caleb's mouth. His lungs were on fire yet he was cold. Caleb's eyes shot open and he rolled on his side. The world was a barrage of sounds as Caleb laid on an ash covered pier. As soon as he rolled over, he felt his stomach flip and he threw up sea water. His eyes burned from the pressure and he gasped for air in between the retches. His right hand still gripped his sword and after his fit was over, he brought himself to his feet. A piece of wooden shrapnel was hanging in his chainmail, having broken a link but gone no further. His nose and mouth hurt, and he had bitten into his tongue, but otherwise, he was alive, and he was in the city.

Two boats of Caleb's had docked and were surging to his location. Fire was still being flung overhead, and soldiers who survived the impact were crawling out of the ocean. A quick look and Caleb knew they weren't at their strongest and only fate knew what happened to the other boat that didn't make it. Taking a big breath through his nose, Caleb could taste the cinders in the air. He swirled the blood, sea and ash in his mouth for a moment, making sure to get all of it before spitting it out and tapping the pommel of his blade against his helmet.

"Thank goodness," Maelinn called out from behind him and when Caleb turned to meet the gaze of the seaweed littered warrior, she quickly changed her tone. "I mean, welcome back Regent. Catherine and Asharah are organizing the survivors, but I'm sure the enemy saw our landing."

"It's a matter of seconds not minutes," Caleb agreed, looking over his weakened force. "Form a column on me, we need to push towards Hector."

"Yes, sir."

"And Maelinn," Caleb caught her attention. "Thank you."

She gave him a hearty bow of her head before sprinting off to where Catherine was standing. She was waving her sword around and barking orders while Asharah was leaning over some less than well off survivors of the blast. Some were laying on their backs, shivering with charred tabards and red scars against their skin. Caleb swallowed his worries and looked ahead. The buildings that once thrived with seaside restaurants and warehouses, the winding spider web of roads that were routinely packed with people of every type, all of it was empty and hollow. Organ beasts and tainted creatures were the only residents now. Caleb didn't want to even think of what happened to those who never escaped—not that he had the time.

His troops shuffled into position around him, the better simply caked in salt, the worst with superficial wounds. In all, Caleb clearly noticed he was missing nearly a quarter of his forces. The only stroke of luck was that the enemy only just arrived. Weaving through the maze of buildings and warehouses, Caleb could see the blackened soldiers of the Dweller approaching. He would need to push them back towards Hector and ultimately pinch them between the two forces. Caleb raised his sword arm, pointing Oathkith's twin, his sword, Whitethorn, at the enemy. "Shields forward, march together, we push forward!"

With that command, Caleb fell into the ranks with himself at the front and center. Together they closed the gap to the streets, doing their best to fill out the width of the road to avoid being flanked by the larger enemy. Almost immediately the tainted creatures came sprinting full force down the cobblestones. Their strange black metal armor clanked loudly and among the twisted monstrosities were Nachtists or perhaps victims of the smoke, minds gone and bodies pocked with metallic rashes. Uniquely, both the monsters and the Nachtists' eyes were stained a misty blue as if marked by their allegiance to the Dweller.

Without concern, the enemy slammed into the shields of the Imperials, immediately opening them into the fray. Golden ribbons glistened among the Stromists of the 10th and the attempt to keep formation against the onslaught began. Caleb stabbed from behind his shield, his blow reaching out and cutting down one of the creatures. The weight of the enemy forces retaliated and in moments a wall of tainted beings were pushing against the shield wall, stopping the Imperials in their tracks.

Arms strained and muscles flexed with magic, keeping the shaky line from collapsing. Caleb swore through his teeth, they needed to break through this, they needed to reach Hector. Letting his shield pull back slightly, Caleb's shoulder and arm coiled and flexed, a deep golden shimmer weaving around it. A hot breath steamed out of Caleb's mouth and with a shout he slammed his shield forward with an airborne crack. His form shimmered and an ethereal echo of himself repeated the shove, and with the second crack, the enemy was violently blown backwards.

Body's slammed into the buildings and bones smacked across the cobble, a pocket of freedom being forced into the enemy and opening up the path beyond them. Capitalizing, Caleb surged forward, Maelinn and her troops wedging behind him to keep the enemy from reforming. Now with a clear way ahead, Caleb could see the organ beast batteries beyond the scrambling enemy units and destroyed city. The great elephantine lumps were towering over crumbled buildings as well as their dangerous looking keepers, all the while a thick soot was swirling by their heads. The sky was as dark as the black stained chimneys that rose from the organ beast's backs. Every so often, a great blast would erupt from them, sending fire into the sky. With the backdrop of fire-ripped-darkness and clamoring minions of smoke, Caleb looked to Maelinn and Catherine.

"We need to get through there—" Caleb ducked a sudden arrow before throwing up his shield to slap another one away. The 10th moved forward past the regent, shields raised and swords meeting the irregular charges of the enemy. Caleb kept his gaze on his companions. "Listen, we need to have Hector's group withdraw from their northern flank and focus their energy on their southern so we can pincer the enemy between us and link up for our northern assault. We are short too many soldiers to do it alone."

Catherine gave Caleb a nod. "Hector is probably thinking the same thing, no?"

Caleb shook his head. "There is no guarantee, and we need a guarantee."

"Then I'll tell them," Maelinn spoke up. "You seem to have things handled over here with the 10th." She kept her shield forward.

The prince regent gave Commander Maelinn a pointed look. "I won't fight you on this Commander, but neither will I order you to do it."

Maelinn gave a respectful dip of her head. "For Jerrovia."

Caleb returned the gesture. "For Jerrovia..." he continued, "you won't have much time. I doubt the enemy will let us linger here and the street can only cover our flanks for so long."

"I understand." Maelinn gave another nod.

Catherine was looking at the sky. "I'm just thankful the fireballs aren't heading towards us."

Maelinn gave them both a worried look. "Let's get on with it before they reconsider their policy on blowing up their own soldiers."

"Agreed." Caleb turned back to the frontlines. "Get into position."

***

Maelinn stood behind Caleb and Catherine, a nervous shake in her sword hand. A lot was riding on this, her life included. She looked past Caleb and to the soot covered battleground of ruins that she was about to sprint through. She couldn't even see Hector's forces clearly from here, just hear their clash past the battery of organ beasts. How was she even going to get through them? Maelinn's eyes wandered over to the half standing buildings that littered the place and a gentle hum started in her throat. Regardless of what she had to do, first she needed to remain centered, she was a Stromist first and foremost.

Her hand stopped shaking and just in time. Caleb slammed his shield into the amassing enemy, throwing them back once again and as soon as he did, Maelinn's legs erupted with golden ribbons. The wind hit her eyes and Maelinn was bounding through the opening. Her spiked shield was held in front, the deadly point threatening all in her way, but she was too quick.

With boots slamming against the broken street, Maelinn took a sharp right to avoid running right into the rest of the enemy units, instead opting to sprint into an alley between a standing building and one that had seen better days. Her eyes quickly snapped to a pile of stone that had collapsed from one of the homes. She jumped on it and with a push of her legs, spun around right into the standing building's wall, kicking off it and up to the roof. Her armor clanked as only her upper half made it above the lip of the wall but with a quick scramble, Maelinn managed to roll onto the roof and back to her feet, sword and shield still in hand.

From her new vantage point, Maelinn could make out her pathway. Behind her, the column of 10th Vanguard soldiers were holding steady from a consistent flow of enemy units. Ahead, the clearing with the organ beast battery, and beyond that, the back lines of the enemies fighting Hector's group. Fireballs were still being sent to the sky and arcing over the walls. Time was important on all sides. An arrow zipped by, glancing off Maelinn's cheek plate and sending adrenaline into her heart. Realizing she wasn't yet dead, Maelinn pushed off into a sprint; she would use the roofs as far as she could.

Even with the vigor of her sprinting, the crashing sounds of the organ beasts drowned out Maelinn's footsteps and even her huffing breath, making it all the more horrifying whenever a segment of charred roof felt as if it was going to give away, as if she was in a city of brittle paper. Maelinn leaped from the end of one roof to the beginning of the next, each time with a prayer on her lips. Sometimes she would feel a crack rise up her leg, but she kept the Stromist sprint going.

Arrows zipped by and Maelinn was quickly running out of roof. She leapt to the final building before the clearing. Her foot connected with the tiles but punched through it. In a snap second, her body crashed through the roof, but Maelinn landed in a roll and kept her momentum as she burst out of the dilapidated building and into the clearing. Here the sounds were overwhelming to the point she couldn't feel her heartbeat any longer. Adrenaline was burning through her body and a lace of magic burned along with it.

What once was a man came barreling towards her, a wicked axe of black metal raised. Maelinn shoved her shield forward, the spike punching into the creature's body. The enemy was launched backwards, black ooze spilling from its wound. Maelinn continued her run, ducking a thrown spear. She was now in the most dangerous part of the clearing, and the closer she got to the organ beasts, the larger she realized they were. Her teeth clenched. Enemy soldiers were rounding to the side of the beasts, the keepers eager to trap her. It seemed the large size of the organ beasts was suddenly a boon, one that Maelinn still hated. With ears ringing and face hot with energy, Maelinn ran right for the organ beasts.

The first beast Maelinn darted towards was something horrifying and curious at the same time. Nothing in nature could have made such a thing, its body was grey and lifeless, and yet it moved willingly. The legs were more like tree trunks and the pores and pipes that rose from it seemed impossible. No eyes, no mouth—this was a creature made for war and war alone. Such a fact was one that Maelinn realized the truth of when the beast turned to her and raised its legs with devious intent.

Time slowed as survival took over Maelinn's brain. Two rearing legs with metal bottomed feet were blotting the sun. The organ beast had weight, the organ beast had power, and the legs were coming down hard. Maelinn snapped to the left and time sped up. Metallic ringing exploded to her right as the beast smashed through the street. Maelinn spun and reached out with her blade, engulfed in magic. The sword sank into the beast's back leg, though it didn't seem to react to any pain and soon Maelinne realized the mistake she made. Her sword was stuck.

Even with her magic, the blade managed halfway through the dense flesh and bone before the tremendous weight clamped down on and froze her sword in place. Time. Time was of the essence. Maelinn wrenched her fingers from her blade, hating every second of the thought and pushed away from the beast. She nearly fell as the rubble under her feet shifted, but Maelinn found her balance and continued her run.

Bellows from the organ beasts deafened her ears as she cut through the battery. A pair of legs slammed into the ground next to her, but she dodged it, only to leap away from another thunderous bang. The ground was shaking with retaliation and just as Maelinn thought she was clear, one of the keepers jumped in front of her.

Putting all her magic in her legs, she tried to leap away but it was too late. Her face slammed into the chest of the being, giving her a noseful of a sooty, death-ridden smell. The two were flung to the ground. It was a rough landing punctuated by the scraping of metal. Maelinn rolled off her assailant, but the smoke-filled being quickly pinned her, holding her to the ground and freeing a jagged dagger from its scabbard.

The magic was still in Maelinn's legs and after giving the tainted creature a defiant growl, she planted her knee into the creature with a golden bag, launching it into the air. Maelinn quickly grabbed her shield from the ground, point up and as the creature came wriggling back down, its weight slammed against the shield, impaling it. Maelinn let go and scrambled back to her feet, swordless and shieldless. The enemy was pooling behind her. Looking forward to her goal, she only had one way to go.

Behind was the haze of the organ beasts, in front was a field of debris and rubble, and beyond that was a line of buildings with the enemy backs filling the gaps. There was no time to waste, nothing to hold back. Maelinn was running at full speed, using every ounce that remained of her magic. The wind was whipping her eyes teary, and her soot filled lungs were on fire. She had lost feeling in her feet and her ears were ringing sharp. Enemy backs, buildings, there was only one thing left to do.

All her magic screamed and as the final burst of golden Stromism erupted across her legs, Maelinn kicked off the ground. She sprung upwards, the carcass of the city block below. Something bit into her thigh and she winced, but kept her eyes on the pocket of giants and Yabban fighting by a breach in the wall. She was coming back down, and she wasn't sure she had any magic left to land. Her eyes turned blurry as the ground came rushing towards her, but before she could hit the grey surface, a stony skinned Kafshe rushed in her way.

***

Opane held out her arms, just in time to get hit with the full weight of Maelinn, sending both of them to the ground. Maelinn had an arrow in her leg and a delirious look in her eye, and all Opane could wonder was what she was doing here falling out of the sky itself.

Maelinn looked up at her savior and rose to her knees. The two of them were inside a shell of fighting, as safe as one could be during such a battle. "Regent Caleb is to the south past a battery," Maelinn managed, "withdraw from the north and attack it in conjunction, then we can consolidate." The Commander was holding her head, clearly in pain, but this wasn't the place. Opane hooked her hands under Maelinn's arms and hoisted her to her wobbly feet.

"Understoond. Take this." Opane shoved a simple dagger with bone totems hanging from its handle into Maelinn's hand. "And get to the back line with Hector."

"Thanks," Maelinn took the blade readily and fell back to the quiet of the rear flank. Opane waited only one extra moment to ensure her safety before running off.

It was quick to find Tennil and with one bellow and blast of a horn later, the giants and Yabban turned their attention south. Opane fell shoulder to shoulder with fierce Yabban warriors. sharp witted Kafshe and powerful giants. Looking south, they could see the shimmering Stromists starting their advance northwards through the battery of organ beasts. Opane could see it now, this part of the city would soon be retaken and then, the walls.

Chapter 32
The Return of the Emperor

Outside of the city gates, George Heinrich sat on his horse, Ai. The ground was crumbled with craters and the walls were blasted with soot. Over the shouts of medical auxiliaries and captains, the shriek of the gates were rocking George's heart. Above, unseen, Imperial soldiers cranked the gate open, leaving George to watch as his home was finally revealed. Plum and wine flags were being thrown over the walls to the south, and the walls to the north still clamored with residual fighting. Williams sat on his horse to George's right and Rosaline to his left. The trio sat ahead of the remnants of the 1st vanguard, Rosaline's regulars, as well as the 11th and Commander Darius. According to reports, the Eastern gate was currently being besieged by forces from Alconia, the Stenlings having finally arrived.

With a slam, the gates locked into place, open. Beyond the iron maw, George witnessed the desolate Imperial wastes. So much pain and death lingered in the air, so much so that George couldn't help but wonder out loud, remembering the Dweller's goals, "what peace?"

Rosaline looked over to him then looked back at her group of elite regulars. She steeled herself and caught George's eye. "I'm ready to go find it, if you are."

"I couldn't have said it better myself," Darius added from behind.

George gave Williams a glance, looking for some final sentiment from his closest and oldest friend. The blonde haired knight offered a grim smile, with more emotion in his eyes than typical. The emperor pursed his lips and unsheathed Oathkith, grazing his thumb over the Blood of Prax to quell his anxiety. "Time to go home..." He whispered to himself and then gave Ai a gentle kick.

Together with his troops, George funneled through the gates. On the other side, Uncle Caleb and troops from the wall break to the south were lingering. Auxiliaries were treating the worst of the soldiers while the healthy patrolled and secured the captured area. Active fighting had ceased when the enemy retreated to the Imperial palace on the top of the city hill.

"Reports from our Achian allies," Caleb called out to George. "Across Jerrovia the enemy is mobilizing, if we are going to strike, we have to strike now and end it now. This lull won't last."

George nudged Ai to a stand still. He thought for a moment. He knew what he had to do to end this war, but the weight of it was impossible. George shifted, and this time the Blood of Prax felt more like his own murder weapon than the key to victory. "If you keep the city secure, I'll do my best up there."

"I know you will," Caleb answered before looking over at one of his lieutenants. "I won't keep you. Next time we chat, let's do it in the tower, yeah?"

"Yeah," George felt the same guilt he once felt years ago, knowing that he was making promises he couldn't keep, not while his life was the only key for peace. He pushed Ai back into a trot, eager to leave before his Uncle could read his face.

Together with his troops, the Emperor made his way to the city's main road: a wide artery of cobblestone that followed the slope of the capital all the way up to the palace gates. Down here, though, all George saw was the ruins of the city, and the impending battle that loomed ahead. "Stromists to the front." The column shifted, George and his generals in the middle.

With little else, the army started its march towards the palace, desolation to the right, and destruction to the left. Ahead, a dark cloud hid the spires of the palace, and the alabaster walls were dusted in black ash. The cathedral of the Tagists lay in complete ruins, still crackling from a fire. There was no love between the Mistborn and the Dweller, their relationship long since divorced from cooperation. Thinking of it put the cosmic battle on George's mind. He was on his way to fight a being older than time to save his people who live in a land cut from reality. It was bizarre and truth be told even after all of this and all he's witnessed, if not for the current state of his beloved sister, he wouldn't believe as much as he did. But here he was, about to face destiny, about to finally complete his purpose. He was going to lead them safely through.

The iron gate of the palace was in view, and behind it was the enemy horde. They were armed with bows and sat at every angle in the courtyard. As soon as the two forces locked eyes, the arrows started to fly. Dark points came darting towards the Imperials, but their shields rose high, protecting the front line and keeping George and his mount safe. "Advance!' George hollered and his troops obediently listened. The Stromist front walked as one, a wall of shields, towards the gate, eager to plug the slots with the flat of their shields.

As they did, George reached inside himself. He focused, visualizing the altar of harmony that undulated inside him. He saw his goals, he saw what he had to do, and he saw the power he needed to do it. His heart hurt as he summoned the power from within and his nerve ends burned as energy started to rupture across his body. A hiss to challenge the whistle of arrows sounded as smoke steamed into his skin, staining it red. His hair shocked white, and as he felt the pulse of Ai under him, he saw the creature turn just as bloody red as him. George didn't feel himself slip or his mind go, but felt every second of the transformation, his eyes a bright glowing grey. This was for Josephine, this was for his father, this was for Jerrovia.

Ai stamped her hoof and snorted. George gritted his teeth and clenched Oathkith tight. "Clear!" His voice bellowed, shaking the ground. At his command, the troops at the gate created an alley and Ai reared. The great war horse exploded into a gallop, cracking the ground and ripping stone into the air. Steam was hissing through her teeth, and George's red cape snapped behind him. A hot wave preceded the horse, thick with pure magic, and as the duo rocketed into the gate, the iron doors were blown back, tearing off their hinges and flying into the crowd behind.

Ai and George didn't stop, their charge continuing. The enemy let out a surprised sound, the first cry of anguish George heard from these creatures, as the emperor and his steed cleaved through. Oathkith came arcing down, tainted blood spraying back. The Imperials came rushing in to fill the path created by George and soon the courtyard was split in two by the army. Darius and Rosaline took either side while Williams and George met up by the palace door. Already George's smokeform was fading, not willing to push it too long for the sake of his lucidity.

Looking back, George watched as the regular elites and the Stromists pushed the divided enemy back. Rosaline was a dance of blades and Darius was a rook of Imperial might. With the courtyard secure, George and Williams shared a nod, hopped off their mounts and pushed the palace doors open.

A hollow breeze met the pair as they spilled into the carcass of George's home. Decorations littered the ground and the bodies of the long dead were still strewn about from the original siege upon the palace. A thick stink filled the air, matched only by the burn of sulfur and brimstone. Otherwise, the halls were empty, not an enemy to be seen. Stromists from the first vanguard were quick to enter behind the emperor and his knight, fanning out to check the halls. George and Williams, however, headed straight towards the large doors of the throne room. It stood to reason that's where their enemy will be. Together they shoved the door open.

The bang reverberated throughout the room and as they stepped into it, Flaretongue and Oathkith ready, a laugh greeted them. Instead of the Dweller, a familiar face looked at them with a white smile. Gennisberg stood in front of the dias, sword out, and a darkness in his eyes. What once was a usual and unassuming face, was now cracked with black metal. George felt his hand tighten around his sword and the smokeform asked to be released. Williams shook next to George and the rattle of his armor and Flaretongue caught the emperor's attention.

"Keep moving," Williams said, low and serious. "The Dweller isn't here."

"Are you sure?" George pointed his sword at Gennisberg. "I won't let you fight alone."

"George," Williams started, "you only have so much time, who knows when the Dweller will grow impatient. You need to be there to stop her."

George swallowed hard. Williams was right, but he couldn't let Williams do this alone, could he?

"George."

The emperor sucked in a breath and lowered Oathkith. "I'm going to the red door. Destroy this traitor and come find me as quickly as you can."

"I'll be there, friend," Williams replied as George backed away.

***

Williams looked straight ahead, lost in Gennisberg's taunting grin. Flaretongue rotated in his hand. The knight dropped his shield to the floor below. Gennisberg stepped down into the common area of the throne room. "You seem to have dropped something, Williams."

The knight didn't reply. A dark anger stuck in his chest and his new training fresh on his mind. Without breaking his gaze, he untied his scabbard, letting it fall to the ground as well before taking up his sword in both hands.

"No scabbard?" Gennisberg knitted his brow at the strange sight.

"I have somewhere else I can put Josephine's sword," Williams growled. Gennisberg curled his smile.

"We know how this went last time."

Williams dashed forward and Gennisberg matched the speed, hissing smoke from his mouth. At the center of the room, they met with a clash of swords and their blades shrieked down each other in a spray of sparks. In moments Gennisberg was shrouded in smoke, moving at an unnatural pace. Williams kept his mouth shut, teeth tight as he attempted to keep up with his foe. Sweat broke on his brow and Flaretongue shot out just in time for Gennisberg's blade to shred off of it instead of his neck. Gennisberg twisted his blade, locking the two and shooting out with his elbow. Williams ducked, freed Josephine's sword, and punched Gennisberg with the pommel, knocking the man back.

Gennisberg let out a scream of smoke and dove back in, but this time Williams held his blade back in an offensive guard. Gennisbeg's body was a blur, faster than ever as he moved to strike, but Williams didn't even attempt to block. Before the blow hit, Williams twisted ever so slightly.

With a squelch, blood sprayed onto the floor, but it wasn't Williams'. The two were staring at each other, the knight' eyes emotionless while Gennisberg looked on with hollow surprise. Flaretongue was in his heart and poking out of his back. In just a few swipes, Williams had tricked him. The knight let go of his sword and watched Gennisberg fall to the floor, lifeless. Tarry black blood pooled around the defeated villain.

Tears blurred Williams' vision and he could have sworn he felt a familiar embrace touch his shoulder. He fell to his knee, his body spent, and his anxiety pushed through his adrenaline. He did it. A weight left his chest and the heat of his tears sobbed down his cheeks. Clenching his teeth through the pain, he cried, tears pattering on the bloody floor. His voice reverberated through the empty room, "Wake up, please. I did it. Please wake up."

⚜ ⚜ ⚜

While George ran through the halls and Rosaline wrapped William's wound, Fenric lurked in the shadows of the elm tree. The old nemesis of George was staring up at the balcony of the room behind the red door. Next to him stood Tomko, a nervous look on his

400

cowardly face. The Precursor opened his mouth, but before he could speak, Fenric answered his question, turning to the man and giving him a deadly stare.

"He will arrive, he knows where she will be, and when he does, you know what to do."

Tomko hesitated and looked down at the shard of Prax he had cradled in his hands. "I do."

Chapter 33
The Graceful One

Oathkith was drawn, Rook was ready, and George stood alone in front of the forbidden red door. Only once before had George entered this room, and only through the actions of Josephine. Now here he stood, without her. No he had her, he had her in his heart. His knuckles burned white and with a hefty kick of his boot, he knocked the red door clear off its hinges.

The wood splintered and smacked against the stairs behind it before scattering all over the floor. George didn't pay it any mind as he walked up the steps, his foot falls echoing one after the other and his tattered red cape catching an invisible breeze. It smelt of flowers, it smelt of home. He mounted the final step and took his first on the wooden ground of the training room.

"George..." Her voice was silk, motherly and familiar. The emperor looked ahead and his eyes traced the Graceful One's outline against the light of the balcony. Shards of crystal mist scabbed her foggy skin and smoke flowed gently from her nostrils. Her appearance was between an alien mistborn, the tainted creatures below, and that of a regular hurting human. Ethereal fabric seemed to cling to her body, floating on unknown currents. The reports of a faceless crystal seemed to be false as George found her with a feminine visage, but more striking, her eyes weren't blue as he knew them from the dreams, but held the same stormy grey as his own. "I see you opened the red door."

Steeling his gaze, George pointed Oathkith forward. "Stand for your crimes. Give up now, and allow me to vanquish you and end this once and for all." He didn't know why he was asking, and not just fighting.

"As I tried to vanquish you and end it once and for all?" The Dweller answered softly. "You can see how that turned out. After all I tried, yet here you are, alive and standing against me."

"You killed my father, you killed my mother, you killed my sister, you killed so many people..." George felt his sword shake. "What ever gave you the right?"

She answered, "I was stuck for so long. From my humble beginnings as an automaton of the mist, I was fed pain, the pain of being human, and I couldn't bear it. I looked down and saw that Jerrovia couldn't bear it either, and so I came to save us all from it. Those who died did so I could push this goal forward." The Dweller held out a hand. Her form bent fluidly, a flicker of smoke before resetting into a strange foggy flesh. "I'll be your mother, George, I'll take all the pain for you and the others."

"You're not my mother..."

"Maybe," the Dweller answered, "but in a way, I might just be. You have my altar, after all, conceived from me. Your mother had already died before I sent your father to kill her. It was only myself that kept her moving, and in that time, you were born as a piece of me. I only wanted to take that piece back before it could..." A sigh.

"Before it could stand here?" George straightened Oathkith. "Before I could stand here."

"My curse, my beloved son, my curse," the Dweller's eyes shimmered. "Let me take away the pain of it all."

"No." George sucked in a deep breath. "Allow me to be the one to end it."

The Dweller lifted her hand and a blue blade formed in her grasp. "I care for you and I love you, but I won't let your selfishness cost the rest their peace."

"I know," George said simply and pulled at his smokeform. His hair stained white and his skin grew red, but his eyes stayed their stormy grey, staring into the Dweller's own. She stood there, the two unmoving. George knew that once one of them even flinched, the fight would begin. Even in his smokeform, George could feel his heart bristle with anxiety. There was so much riding on this fight, and even if he won there was still... His eyes narrowed, chest heavy.

Oathkith started to shake, but before George lost himself, he remembered who he was doing this for. His father's smile played in his mind, Josephine's grin, stories of his true mother. George's eyes fell to the back of Rook—Franklin. Oathkith stabbed forward and with a shout ripping from George's throat, he lunged forward.

The Dweller parried his sword with a shriek of metal and the two collided. She grabbed George's shield with her free hand and used his momentum to spin him right through the glass of the balcony. Glass exploded and George's back slammed into the railing of the balcony; the Imperial Gardens shimmered below him in the open air. George's body glimmered with magic and he threw Rook between him and the charging Dweller, catching her swing and parrying it away. He stabbed Oathkith forward, but she grabbed his wrist with lightning reflexes. The two struggled for a moment, until the Dweller bucked out with her forehead, smashing George's helmet right off his head. Stunned, George couldn't resist when the Dweller used her unfathomable strength to launch him into the air.

Wind rushed by George's ears and the garden shrunk underneath him, only to quickly snap back up. With a bang, George landed on the hard ground. Ribbons of magic kept his bones from shattering but before he could do much else, the Dweller pounced from the balcony above as a smokey, blue blur. George put Rook in between them and she slammed into it, the Dweller's blade thrusting right through the wood. Her sword's cutting edge glanced off George's gauntlet, but the weight of her blow blasted his arm against his torso with a gross snap. The emperor used his working shoulder to pull his shield closer, dragging the Dweller forward. George slammed Oathkith's crossguard into her face, once, twice. The Dweller wrenched a leg between them and shoved off with otherworldly strength.

The garden soils plumed as George slammed back into its surface, only to bounce to his feet with pain evident on his sweaty face. Rook clattered away from George and his shield arm dangled useless. The Dweller quickly regained her stance, a pool of wispy mist seeping from her facial wounds. George held Oathkith between them. A stray wind from their battle caught the garden flowers. Pedals fluttered around them and with a kick of their back feet, they rushed each other again. A bang and their swords collided, they pulled back, struck out again and caught each other's swords with another bang. The Dweller twisted her grip and with immense speed she slipped by George's guard. The pommel of her blade pounded against his forehead. George's vision flickered black for a moment and a wet heat started to trickle from his head.

The Dweller went for another strike, but George flexed his magic and pushed her off; Oathkith bit the air in some attempt to keep a recovering distance. The tip of his blade ripped into her side and she hissed in pain. The emperor's nose was whistling and blood was trickling from his forehead, his right arm was useless, and his magic was waning under the pressure. The Graceful one stared back at him, her chest expanding heavily, each breath putting out a puff of mist and smoke. Oathkith cut her deeper than he expected, but as he stared, he saw her healing right before his eyes, flesh knitting back together.

George's teeth clenched together, his skin crawled and the smoke of his altar pushed his mist into a pressure. Red ribbons screamed across his body, and heat seeped from his lips. The Dweller seemed to notice, putting her blade in a ready ward. The emperor let out a roar and rushed to his enemy. Pedals whipped by the pair and Oathkith came slashing forward. A clash with the Dweller's blade, another clash, another, and another. George's roar came back double, and he kicked forward with his boot, cleanly connecting with the Dweller and sending her back. With a crack, the Dweller slammed into the alabaster walls of the palace. George's fingers fell off of Oathkith and the blade hit the grass below. The Graceful One's eyes widened and the Emperor ripped the Sword of Prax from its sheath. The golden blade let out a metallic hum as it was freed and enchanted the area with a blast of sun. George glew, his body and face suddenly replaced with the cream colored armor of Sosolam. His eyes were two raging stars behind a visor.

"No!" The Dweller screamed with absolute fear. Two heavenly wings exploded from George's back and as a shimmer of light, Sosolam appeared before the Dweller at neck breaking speeds. Wind peeled the garden plants to the ground and forced a croak in the stones of the palace. An explosion of power broke sound and the Sword of Prax snapped through her chest and cleanly through her anchor.

"Harmony will reign!" Sosolam boomed. As the words passed through his lips, a cough of blood followed and the light started to fade from George's eyes, turning grey once again, and in a fraction of a second, Sosolom's form was gone as quickly as it appeared. George was left standing in the gardens with blood dribbling off his chin and the Sword of Prax in his hand. The end of the blade was still inside the Dweller and the pitiful creature looked up at him with fading eyes.

She gaped. "George..."

The emperor was barely able to stay on his feet, and a terrible pain rippled back and forth through his whole body. The smokeform was long gone and his mortal form was frail and exhausted. George's heart felt like it was about to pop. He could barely hold the blade still. "You..." was all he could muster. "Lie in peace..."

"No," The Graceful One whispered, panicked, and a crystalline tear fell from her eyes. "Not yet... I have to... Everyone" A wheezing breath. Her eyes were frantic. "Hurting... No... One last wish..." The Dweller's body pulsed with power for a moment. "One more pain... I can take... away... my son...I can give her..." Her words fell silent and her face froze in a picture of anxiety. Her flesh sizzled, slowly unraveling into a crystalline mist that then faded into the garden air until nothing was left. George fell to his knees, the Blood of Prax falling out of his hands and his one good palm slapping the ground to keep him from falling face first into the bloody grass. His vision was shimmering and drops of red were falling down the tip of his nose. He could hear the sounds of the garden, as if a battle hadn't been fought, as if he never left. The swooshing of the old elm tree was behind him, reminding him of the final task. His final task.

A blade was unsheathed behind him with a rasp. George's ears perked and then the unmistakable sound of a knife cutting into flesh rang through the garden. George froze. He fell to his side, too weak to move in any other direction. From his place on the ground, he looked onward towards the elm tree. Under its ancient boughs, Tomko stared at him, his hands on the shard of Sol with the pommel sticking out of his stomach. He stood backed up against the tree, Fenric next to him. Blood was trickling down the tree. "But..." George managed.

"He stole the dagger to try and escape again, to cut out another paradise," Fenric accused the dying Precursor. The Gavarian looked over the wound. "I guess in a way he is escaping."

"I wanted..." Tomko sputtered, his hands tight on the dagger in his stomach. "I wanted to end what I started..."

"But you need the blood of," George started, but Tomko's dying breath cut him off.

"The blood of a... Jerrovian who entered by the Elm..." A weak smile. "Elmborn or... maybe someone whose first steps in Jerrovia were by the Elm they created." A pause. "Am I still a coward?" His question hung in the air, and his body slumped. No words would ever reach him now, no answer for his ears, not in this realm. George continued to stare. Tomko was dead, dead in George's place, or perhaps that was never his role.

Fenric remained silent, stepping between them both. The sky overhead was closing, slowly regaining its azure glory. Something was different and the air was sweeter. In the distance, George could hear Williams and Rosaline shouting, cheers reverberating throughout the city. Fenric knelt in front of George, blocking his view. George's old nemesis gave him a crooked mix of a grin and a frown. "The gloried son, having his cake and eating it too. Just don't forget the people who baked it."

George gave a red stained smile and closed his eyes. "Never."

***

The sky was healing, but George's eyes were fixed on a sight he never expected to see again. He stood on wobbly legs inside a battle tent set up outside the city limits. Williams and Rosaline stood next him, all three of them out of breath, having moved as quickly as they could despite their injuries. George was looking down at a bed, and looking back up at him were two sapphire eyes set on his sister's face. She was breathing, pale, but breathing and looking up at him with the faintest smile. Tears were rolling down everyone's cheeks as George croaked, "how?"

"The weight pressing me down," Josephine's voice came drifting up. "It left." Williams fell to his knees and planted his face on her bedside. Her hand came down on the back of his head as he cried.

Rosaline was speechless, gaping, and George furrowed his brow. "Josephine," he started, "where were you?"

His sister laid her head back on the bed. "A valley. A valley of cottages and trees and brooks—but I didn't have a home there, not yet." A wetness grew on her eyes. "I saw mom."

George kneeled next to the bed. "You did?"

"She told me you did it, it's over," Josephine gave a warm smile.

"It is."

Josephine let out a relieved breath before looking deep into George's eyes. "Hey George?"

"Yeah?"

"Remember when you ran away and left me to be regent?"

George was struck by the randomness of the question and sat straight. "Yes?"

"I think it's my turn. I have a knight I want to see and I think you have an Empire that needs you more than it needs me." Williams looked up at that and Josephine glanced down at his face. They shared a smile. She looked at George. "I know it's a lot to ask, but I can't think of a better person to guide Jerrovia."

George let out a small puff of breath, finding a smile. "I'll do it."

"You're the best brother," Josephine leaned back in her bed and smiled a curled grin. Those words and that smile put a heat in George's heart. He looked over at Rosaline, who looked back at him with an exhausted yet relieved smile of her own. George was happy, himself, and he knew why. The worst was finally over, and it was time to heal.

Chapter 34
Aftermath

With the Dweller destroyed and the elm tree seal broken, the smoke tainted enemies were driven into chaotic madness, ripe for a counterattack by the Imperials. George wasn't able to wield the blade of Sosolam any longer, nor was he able to contact the strange ethereal champion as his body was presumably destroyed by the smoke king's assault. Regardless, the reunited provinces were able to solidify enough power to sweep the lands and root out the remaining soldiers of the Dweller. Even months upon months later, though, there remained some pockets hidden in the darkest corners, but that was not enough to dampen the celebration of Jerrovia's victory. The skies were blue once again and Jerrovia now lived in its rightful spot in Ampexida. To the west and across the sea, a continent known as Yzaille was discovered when their diplomats arrived on the Caldoran shores. They claimed heritage from nations called Charlin, Lynnfaire, and a distant desert known as Ashishia. From the far east, representatives from a continent called Befur arrived. Unlike the human Yzaillians, they were bestial. Harnian, centaur, nightchildren, and many mixes in between.

George hosted many of these diplomats, eager to hear about the new lands Jerrovia now neighbored and the lands beyond. Quickly, Caleb's study was stuffed with maps of continents and peoples never heard of, from the lizard men of Verdokia to the bird scholars of the Jexian cloud cities. But the stories didn't all extend from outside the borders of the Empire, much changed inside it as well.

George sat in his grandfather's old study with Rosaline. He sat with his forehead cradled in his fingers, and stress on his face. A scar marked his forehead, a memory of the Dweller and his tattered red cape was as beaten as ever, contrasting the rich clothes of an emperor. A lot was on his mind as he stared ahead at the desk under his nose. Papers littered it, the light of the garden seeping in from the window. Rosaline idled, sat deep into a book on the Iacine Church's doctrines.

"I just don't want to be accused of favoritism..." George said under his breath, catching Rosaline's attention.

"He's not just your favorite," Rosaline said. "He's a hero, and he is more than qualified. He's clever and smart, and loyal, and..." Rosaline listed off on her fingers. George cracked a smile and looked up at his wife. She sat with the regality of an empress, his mother's old crown adorning her head and a new silver necklace around her neck.

"I know..." George admitted. "Williams is perfect to chair the assembly. I don't think the nobles will like it, though, and I'm not sure being married to Josephine is going to help his case."

Rosaline rolled her eyes. "The nobles don't like the assembly, period."

"All the more reason to have it," George laughed to himself, shaking his anxiety. "Not like we can give it back to the Tagists. Besides, I think it makes the most sense to have a commoners assembly mirror the noble assembly."

His wife held up her hand. "Save the speech for the throne room, you know I already understand and back your decision."

"It is truly amazing," Fenric's voice seeped in from behind the pair. They turned to look at the man. He was dressed in dark clothes, his face shadowed and discreet. "That an emperor can be so loved and yet so controversial at the same time. The treaties with the other peoples of Jerrovia alone..."

"Fenric." George turned to his old rival. "What's the news?"

"My time with the giants was fruitful. Many of the chieftains are agreeing to the border assignment and the Duke of Gavaria has already ratified their side of the agreement." Fenric's face fell into a frown. "But George."

"Hm?"

"The giants want their Titanspoke, so I'm afraid this might be the last time we talk for a long while."

George mirrored the frown, he never thought he'd miss Fenric of all people, but George could swallow his pride and admit to himself that Fenric had been nothing but useful since he swore his allegiance. The silence between them didn't last long as had Reginald poked his head in. His presence put a smile on George and Rosaline's face—especially considering what he was holding.

Fenric's eyes widened at the baby in Reginald's arms. It was a newborn girl, no more than a few weeks old with dark curls on her head and tired grey eyes. The old rival caught himself staring and sputtered. "The princess Sophia?"

"Sophie," George corrected, and held out his arms. Reginald gently placed the baby on George's chest and the sleepy infant nuzzled into his shoulder. Rosaline placed a hand on Sophie's back and Fenric took a step towards the door, a rare grin on his face as he looked back at the family.

"Until next time, then."

George looked up from his daughter to Fenric. "Of course. Farewell, Fenric."

"Farewell, George. Rosaline." Fenric gave Reginald a nod and then took one last look at Sophie. "And you too, Sophie."

***

Caleb sat alone by a gravestone. It was white and set in front of the old Elm Tree. Underneath was his older brother, or at least the last place he was ever seen alive. Caleb didn't have time when he returned to Jerrovia to be hit with the shock of his brother's death, but now that peace was spreading, all he could feel was grief. Esmachus, Wilhelm, Sophia, he was the last of the original group left alive.

The birds of the garden were loud, loud enough to cover the gentle steps of Cassandra as she appeared behind Caleb. The man looked up over his shoulder and gave a weak grin of a greeting. Cassandra returned it and sat next to him. Caleb watched as she pulled her knees up to her chest and looked over at him. Caleb held her gaze before looking back at the tombstone. The prince's eyes read the name of his brother over and over again but then a foreign pressure formed against his side and a gasp of surprise caught his throat—Cassandra was leaning against him. Caleb cast his eyes down, falling from the tombstone and let his body lean against her in return.

"I know he wouldn't want me to sulk like this," Caleb said, "Especially with so many new things to learn, but I started learning because of him, to help him, and now, I guess I don't have to do that anymore."

He looked over at Cassandra and she signed. "So what do you want to do?"

"I guess I found a love for it despite it all, so I guess I'll just keep doing what I do." Caleb looked up at the blue sky. "I could always travel. I'm sure Catherine would like to sail around and get the first rights on trading agreements with all these new nations." He looked back down at his friend.

Cassandra signed. "Can I come?"

Caleb smiled, genuinely. "Sure. I think Reginald has this place locked down right without us."

Cassandra smiled and gave a nod.

"What about me?" Asharah called out from behind the two. Caleb turned to smile at his stenling friend, Asharah returning it warmly.

"I wouldn't have it any other way." Caleb looked back at his brother's tomb and gave it a final nod of respect before rising to his feet. Even if the past was heavy, Caleb knew he had to look forward.

***

Turmgarten used to be one of the most famous Tagist cathedrals in the entire Mortal Empire, until the War of the Emergence, and now it lay abandoned. Some Tagists survived the war, some avoided the pacification, and of course there were endless Jerrovians who still held onto the Tagist ways either through confusion or stubbornness. Rosaline, who stood in the carcass of the cathedral was dressed in her purple and crown, but she wasn't here as the empress. Father Sage Clement's old book was under her arm as was her notes on the Iacine church, corroborated through study.

"What are your final thoughts?" Freg's voice came snaking through the stone pillars.

Rosaline kept her eyes on a defaced mural. "Long ago the Tagists took the Iacine away from us and twisted it to meet their political machinations. I think we should give the people a chance to accept it back."

"Does the teachings of Iac sit well with you?" Freg asked.

Rosaline cracked a smile. "Very much so, but even if it didn't, what sort of person would I be if I let this remain buried?" Her brow furrowed. "I was faithful my whole life. I kept the word of the Graces and prayed every meal and every night. I fought for peace and compassion." Her eyes shimmered and for a moment she could see the face of her younger self, the medic who swore to never cause pain. "I've killed, but now I want to create life. Iac speaks of life and compassion, of hope and harmony. Those teachings teach acceptance of the kaleidoscope that is our world and others, as well as the truth deep within us. It counters violence or vengeance and practices humility."

The empress turned to Freg. "I hear that the other continents of Ampexida have Iacists themselves."

"They do," Freg tipped his head. "A mysterious God, Iac." A pause. "But you'll find Iac's words repeated in so many ideas around every land, as it was in Tagism. I must ask, though, are you sure the people will accept the Iacine Church? After they had been so betrayed by religion?"

A puff of air left Rosaline at that. It wasn't a laugh, but it wasn't a sigh. "I'm not so sure it was religion that betrayed us. Good words need to be said, so let them be said. I'll learn more of this God, and then I'll make my final decision for myself of my own path, but I won't let my findings live in the shadows. The faithful like me need to know about the mask the Tagist put over our teachings. We need to correct what they twisted." Rosaline smiled at the bullman.

Freg tipped his head. "If you give me your notes, I'll see them spread to the churches that still live, to the hearts that still hope, and to the minds that still think beyond the mundane."

A rustle of paper, and Rosaline's work was in Freg's hands. "Thank you."

***

"Thank you for inviting me," Opane said with a bright smile. She sat in a country cottage stealthily decorated with objects both rustic and expensive. From the window, a great orchard could be seen, with the blue Achians dominating the horizon. The door to the abode was held open by a white stone, letting in a warm wind. Josephine sat on a rocking chair by an empty fireplace while Williams sat on a chair nearby, polishing a wooden handle.

Josephine offered a crooked grin. "It's the least I could do after all the worry I put on you."

"Hello!" George called from the doorway. The emperor walked in holding a basket of apples. He was wearing his cape, as always, but underneath he wore a simple olive tunic. Opane turned her smile to the Emperor.

"And thank you for all your work in the courts!"

"Of course," George walked past the group and plopped into a seat by his sister and friend. "You know, between that and you leading the talks, the Achian and Yabban treaties are coming along really well."

Rosaline popped her head in from the kitchen. Her black hair was frazzled and her eyes energetic. "George! Did you get the apples!?"

"Oh void, yes," George shot back up with the basket, and rushed over. Rosaline all but ripped the basket from his hands with a quick thanks before disappearing again and the emperor followed suit.

"Announcing," Reginald called as he walked into the cottage, "Princess Sophie." He wore the scabbard of the dragonchild on his hip, but otherwise the clothes of the head steward. In his arms, the baby Sophie was giggling happily and her great Uncle Caleb was a step behind with Cassandra, Asharah, Darius and Catherine. Josephine immediately stood up to rush to her niece, eyes wide with maternal care.

"Williams, look!" Josephine babbled over the baby and the knight looked up with a softer smile. Catherine gave a snake's grin.

"Watch your step, knight, I think Josephine is thinking about giving Sophie a cousin."

Josephine snapped her eyes to Catherine and rolled them. "Not a single person alive can look at this baby and not swoon."

Cassandra frantically signed, "It's true!"

"I'll say," Hector piped in as he strolled into the cottage. "Is it almost ready? Keeping Ai from following George inside is turning into a full time job" A whinny called from somewhere outside. Josephine chewed her cheek and looked back at the door where Rosaline and her husband had disappeared into.

"Any moment now I think."

"You can handle busting a wall but you can't handle a single horse, is that what I'm hearing, Marshal?" Commander Darius chided.

"A-ha!" George called as he came bursting back into the cottage room with Rosaline hidden behind his cape. She stepped to the side to reveal a large cake on a silver platter. Atop the dessert were sliced apples neatly arranged and drizzled in honey with a single white candle stuck in the center. Everyone's smile faded to a somber grin and the pair brought the treat to the center of the room.

Placing the platter on a small table by the chairs, Rosaline took a few steps back and folded her hands in front of her in quiet prayer. Everyone was silent. A weight fell upon the group as they all stared at the candle, until finally George said, "Happy birthday, Dad."

Epilogue
The Prophecy of Silver and Gold

The swamps of Beyonder were a chorus of croaks and crickets. Dense tree canopies kept the moonlight from laying on the muddy waters and twisted roots below. Twinkling fireflies provided some light, but otherwise, it was a night of loud darkness and quiet destiny. The Aquatid, Master Frugi, sat at the base of a gnarled stump with his staff laid across his lap and his face looking upwards at Mondaral. Her breathing was more haggard than before as her mysterious illness clearly had worsened from her use of magic to aid Caleb. Their meeting was lonely, with just the two amid the night sounds.

"Frugi," Mondaral started, "it is time I tell you of the second prophecy. The prophecy of silver and gold."

Frugi said nothing, but bowed his head in obedience. Mondaral sucked in a shaking breath and closed her eyes. "Before the time of the Cacophony, before the treachery of Stenmur, there was a juvenile race that was freshly born. They were born from a Sondoper obsessed with life and death, and were called the Dreamers. Prolific they were then, and they spread to different continents. Two such Dreamers were born as twins somewhere in a land that would eventually split and become Yzaille. Their names are lost to history and to my memory, but they were of a certain nobility, loved by the creations of harmony. Two ribbons were tied in their hair, marks of their strange lineage and almost otherworldly nobility. One bore a ribbon of gold, another of silver and together they were the gold and silver children. Their exploits as youths were many, from their daring deals with dragons, to them losing their ribbons to their own generosity. They bested strange caves and deep hidden areas. They inspired those around them."

A loud cough sounded from Mondaral and Frugi nearly jumped to his flippered feet. The Sondoper held up a hand and swallowed hard. "When the cacophony came, the children were men and they took up arms to defend the harmony of the land. When the cacophony left, they were no mere gold and silver children anymore, but the gold and silver king. The peoples of Ampexida looked to them for guidance and they led them into an age of peace and prosperity. The Gold King took the south and ruled with wisdom and mental clarity. He introduced philosophy and higher thinking. The Silver King ruled the north and taught strength, balance of mind and body, health and community. Together, they ushered in a peace not seen since before the cacophony. You see, they combated a new enemy as chaos and pacification had entered Ampexida and mortality had infected the people. A new duty was brought forth, to restore harmony, and so the two kings did such a thing, but not forever.

"In time, age whittled them down, and the chaos bled into the minds of the newer generations while pacification stalled the old. Together the kings eventually passed back into the Valley of Unifax, as all souls do, and were entombed together as the world unraveled into factions and ideologies. Together they were laid and on their tomb was written a simple prayer: *We hope, as they did, that perhaps we can find balance once more. Wish harmony, that they rise to finish their task before we forget.*"

Frugi tugged at his wispy beard. "So they will be resurrected?"

"No," Mondaral answered, "two people will arise in the coming decades who will take over their tasks, but not because of peace. A second Cacophony is coming, and here are its conditions: first, Jerrovia will return to Ampexida... which it has. The Tainted One and the Serene One will be reformed in their primordial realms... which I fear may be almost complete. Next, the artifacts of Unifax will resurface in Yzaille. Then, the return of the Generals of the Tainted One will occur. After that, the veil will be ripped asunder, and the second Cacophony will blaze across the realms of existence."

"What should we do?" Frugi's hands were tight on his staff.

"You must go into the world, Frugi, and find the remnants of the Praxian Storm Guard in the country of Garthil. In twenty years time, a defeated champion will rise from there, they will be the first step to creating a victory against the primordial powers. After you find them, look for the artifacts of Unifax, and then the rest will become clear. The new Gold and Silver King will return, Sosolam will be recreated by the blood of a warrior queen, an army unseen will rise in defense of Ampexida, and two brothers bound in slavery will break their chains and defeat the generals of the smoke and the mist."

Mondaral closed her eyes and folded her legs under her. She slumped forward, breathing slowly. "That is the prophecy of silver and gold."

Frugi slowly stood and planted his staff in a puddle of water. "I know my task."

"Then I wish you well, brave frog," Mondaral smiled, chin against her chest. "Until I see you all again."

The End.

A special thanks to everyone who read this tale. I feel it is also my duty to let you know I had to cut out a scene where Reginald and Cassandra finally decide who the best chess player in the palace is. The stakes were a best of three and the challenge raged all the way to a tie breaker game. So who won, you might wonder? If you really want to know, the answer is on the next page, or you can live in wonder, putting forth your favorite champion as the winner.

Either way! I appreciate your patronage and indulgence of my story about Jerrovia and hope to see you in my many other stories (with quite a few about this little world of Iac).

The answer is on the other side of this page.

It was Cassandra.